My Little Pony™
Friendship is Magic

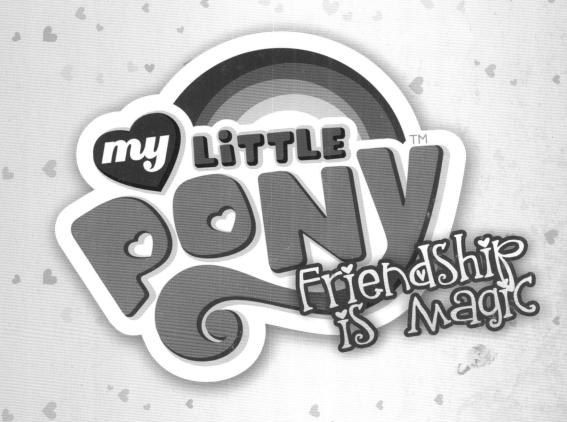

APR 1 4 2014

3 9082 12649 6069

MY LITTLE PONY ™

Friendship is Magic

WRITTEN BY

Katie Cook

ART BY

Andy Price

COLORS BY

Heather Breckel

LETTERS BY

Neil Uyetake

EDITED BY

Bobby Curnow

COVER BY

Andy Price

COLLECTION EDITS BY

Justin Eisinger & Alonzo Simon

COLLECTION DESIGN BY

Neil Uyetake

Special thanks to Erin Comella, Robert Fewkes, Heather Hopkins, Pat Jarret, Ed Lane, Brian Lenard, Marissa Mansolillo, Donna Tobin, Michael Vogel, and Michael Kelly for their invaluable assistance.

IDW founded by Ted Adams, Alex Garner, Kris Oprisko, and Robbie Robbins |

ISBN: 978-1-61377-854-8

17 16 15 14   1 2 3 4

Ted Adams, CEO & Publisher
Greg Goldstein, President & COO
Robbie Robbins, EVP/Sr. Graphic Artist
Chris Ryall, Chief Creative Officer/Editor-in-Chief
Matthew Ruzicka, CPA, Chief Financial Officer
Alan Payne, VP of Sales
Dirk Wood, VP of Marketing
Lorelei Bunjes, VP of Digital Services

Become our fan on Facebook facebook.com/idwpublishing
Follow us on Twitter @idwpublishing
Check us out on YouTube youtube.com/idwpublishing
www.IDWPUBLISHING.com

Originally published as MY LITTLE PONY: FRIENDSHIP IS MAGIC issues #9–12.

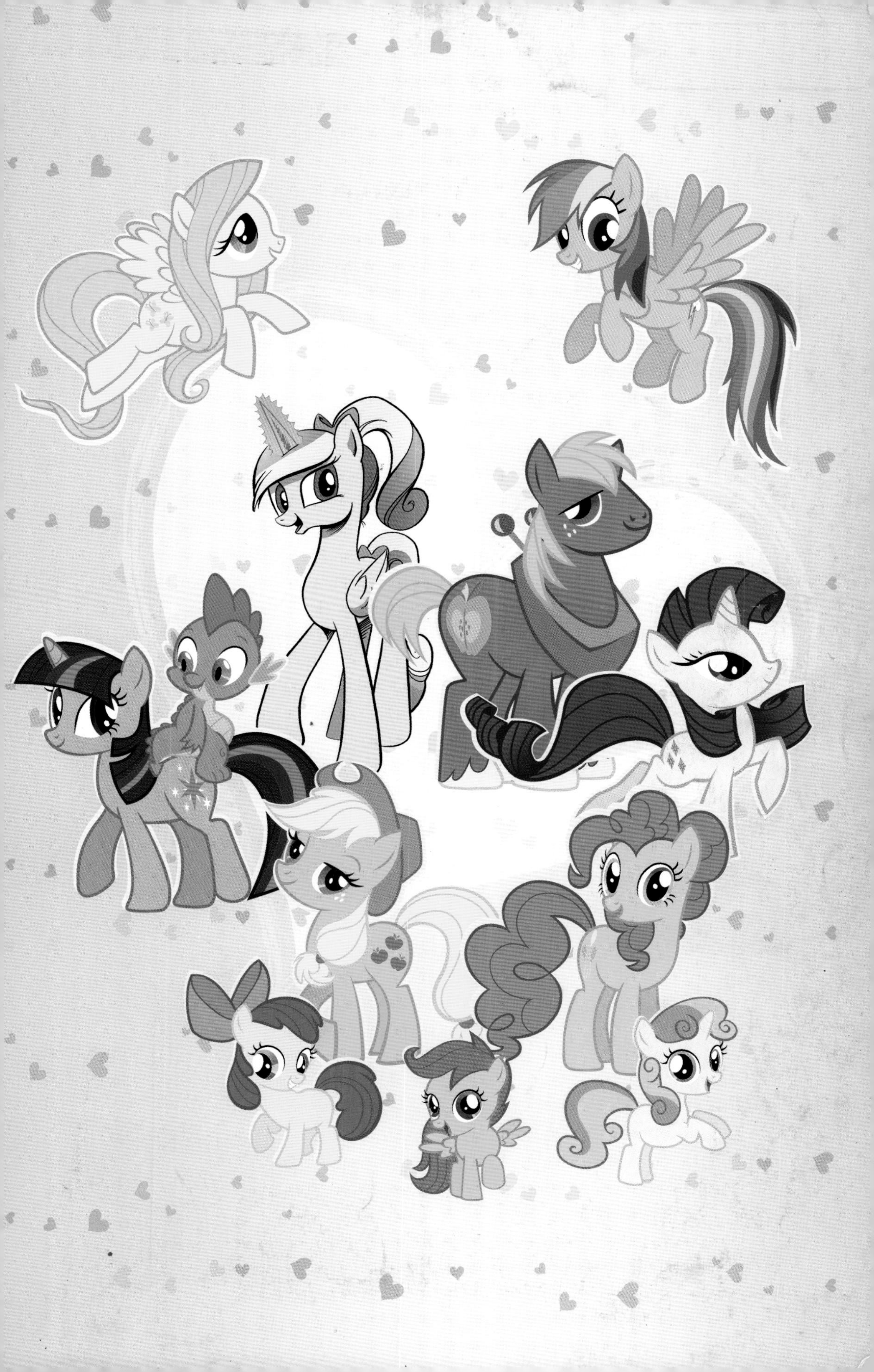

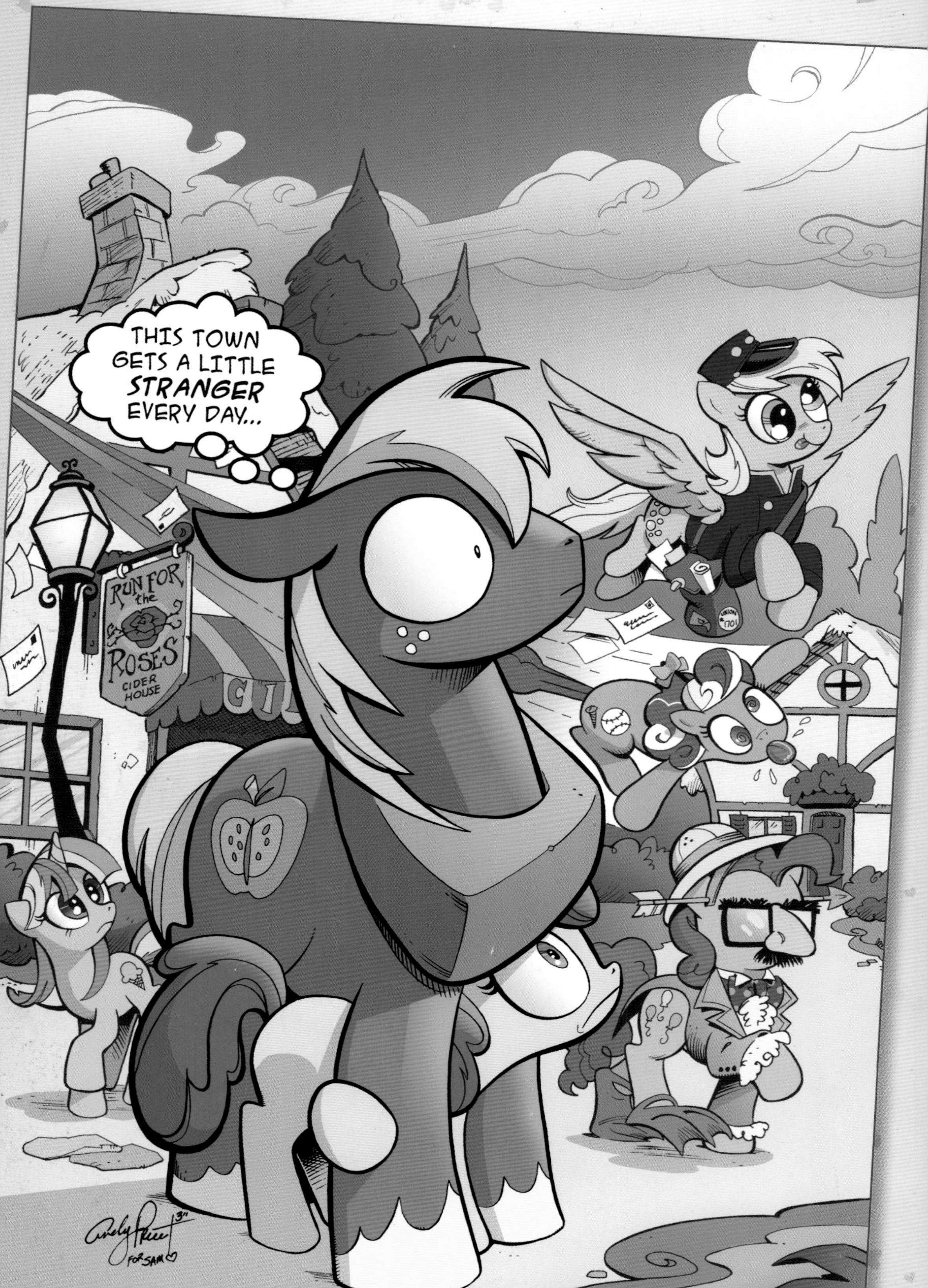
THIS TOWN GETS A LITTLE STRANGER EVERY DAY...
RUN FOR the ROSES CIDER HOUSE

art BY Andy Price

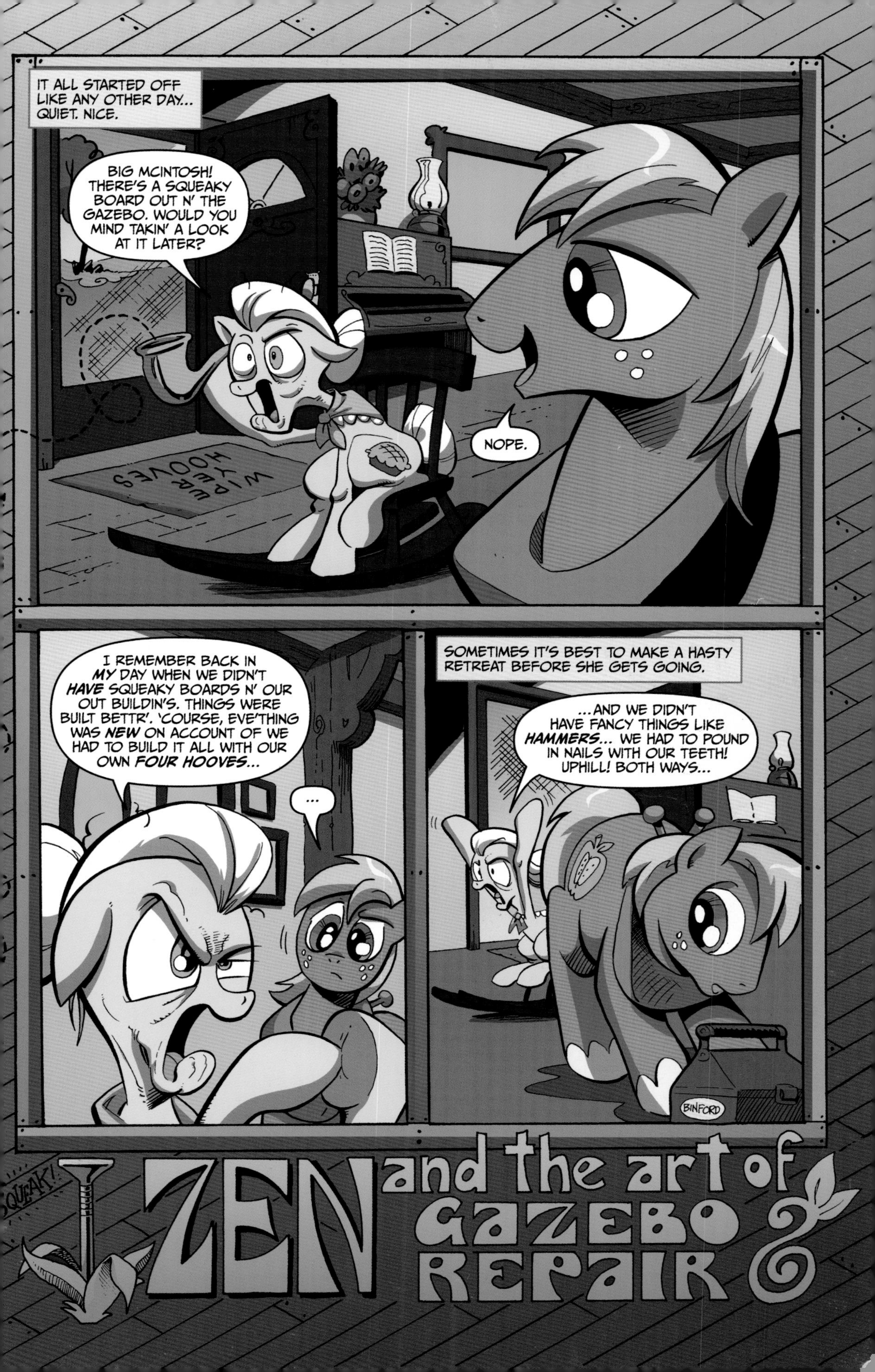
IT ALL STARTED OFF LIKE ANY OTHER DAY... QUIET. NICE.
BIG MCINTOSH! THERE'S A SQUEAKY BOARD OUT N' THE GAZEBO. WOULD YOU MIND TAKIN' A LOOK AT IT LATER?
WIPE YER HOOVES
NOPE.
I REMEMBER BACK IN MY DAY WHEN WE DIDN'T HAVE SQUEAKY BOARDS N' OUR OUT BUILDIN'S. THINGS WERE BUILT BETTR'. 'COURSE, EVE'THING WAS NEW ON ACCOUNT OF WE HAD TO BUILD IT ALL WITH OUR OWN FOUR HOOVES...
...
SOMETIMES IT'S BEST TO MAKE A HASTY RETREAT BEFORE SHE GETS GOING.
...AND WE DIDN'T HAVE FANCY THINGS LIKE HAMMERS... WE HAD TO POUND IN NAILS WITH OUR TEETH! UPHILL! BOTH WAYS...
BINFORD
SQUEAK!
ZEN and the art of GAZEBO REPAIR

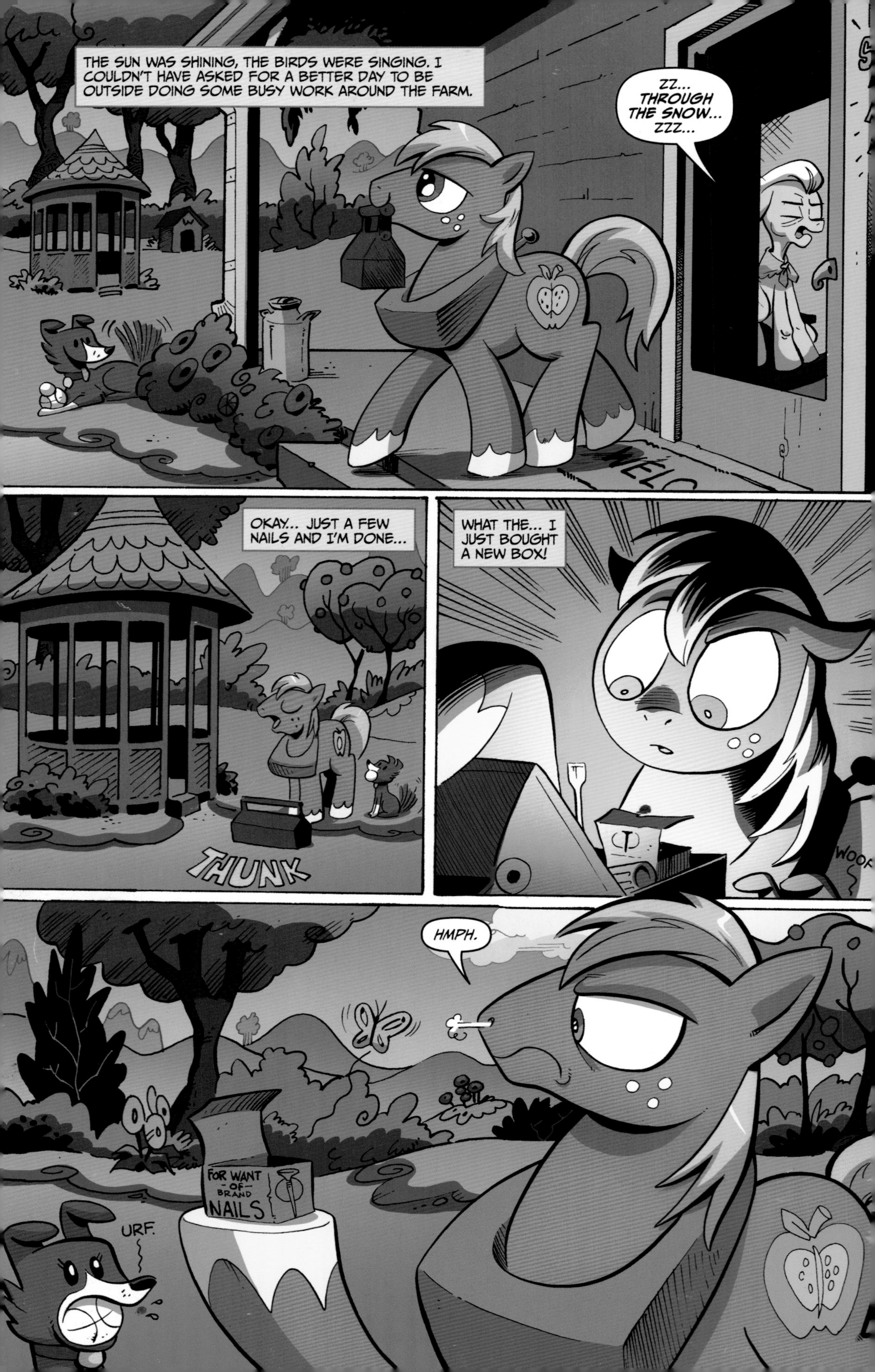
THE SUN WAS SHINING, THE BIRDS WERE SINGING. I COULDN'T HAVE ASKED FOR A BETTER DAY TO BE OUTSIDE DOING SOME BUSY WORK AROUND THE FARM.
ZZ... THROUGH THE SNOW... ZZZ...
OKAY... JUST A FEW NAILS AND I'M DONE...
THUNK
WHAT THE... I JUST BOUGHT A NEW BOX!
WOOF
HMPH.
FOR WANT -OF- BRAND NAILS
URF.

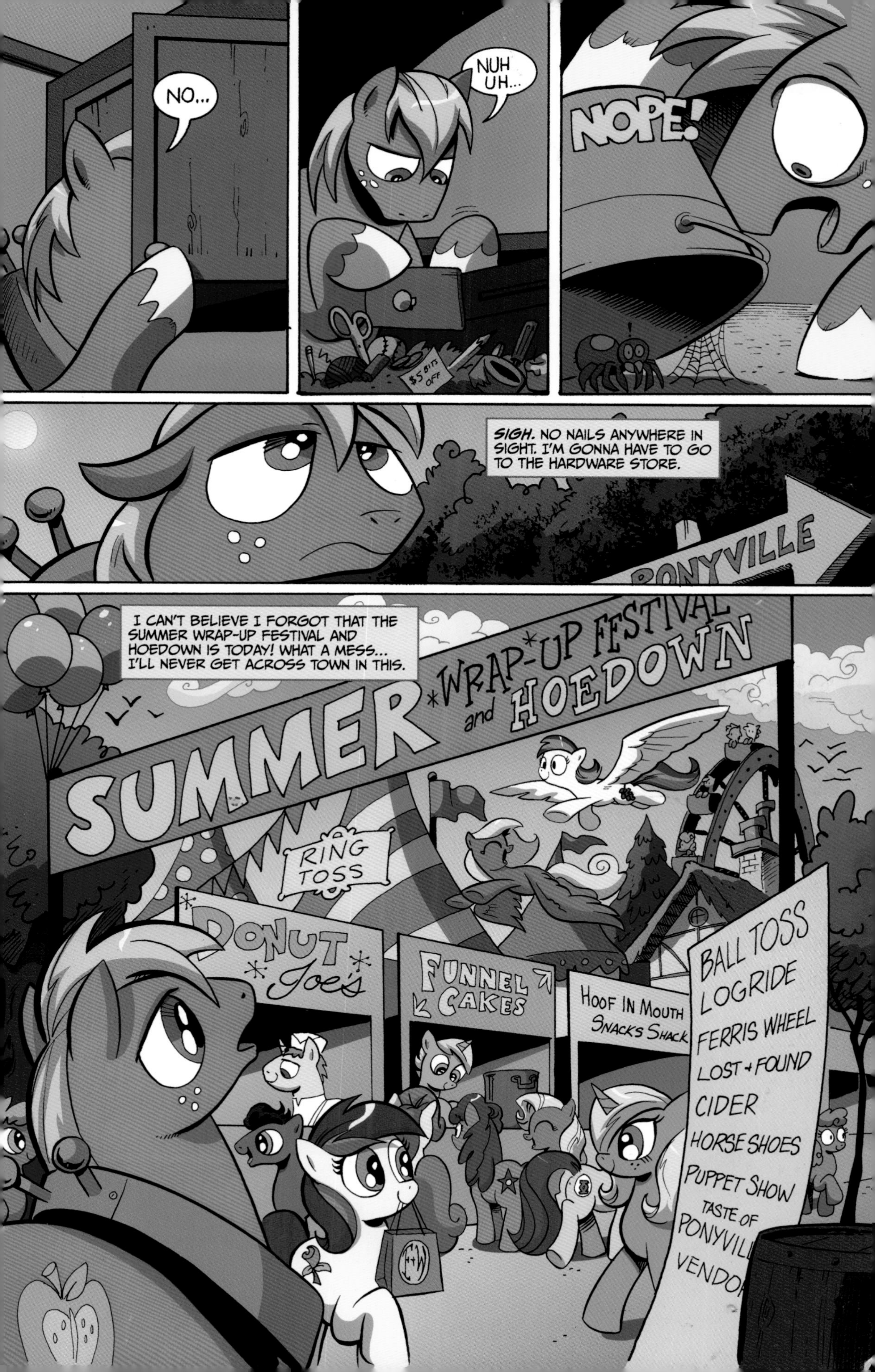
NO...
NUH UH...
NOPE!
$5 BITS OFF
SIGH. NO NAILS ANYWHERE IN SIGHT. I'M GONNA HAVE TO GO TO THE HARDWARE STORE.
PONYVILLE
I CAN'T BELIEVE I FORGOT THAT THE SUMMER WRAP-UP FESTIVAL AND HOEDOWN IS TODAY! WHAT A MESS... I'LL NEVER GET ACROSS TOWN IN THIS.
SUMMER WRAP-UP FESTIVAL and HOEDOWN
RING TOSS
DONUT Joe's
FUNNEL CAKES
HOOF IN MOUTH SNACKS SHACK
BALL TOSS
LOGRIDE
FERRIS WHEEL
LOST + FOUND
CIDER
HORSE SHOES
PUPPET SHOW
TASTE OF PONYVILL
VENDO

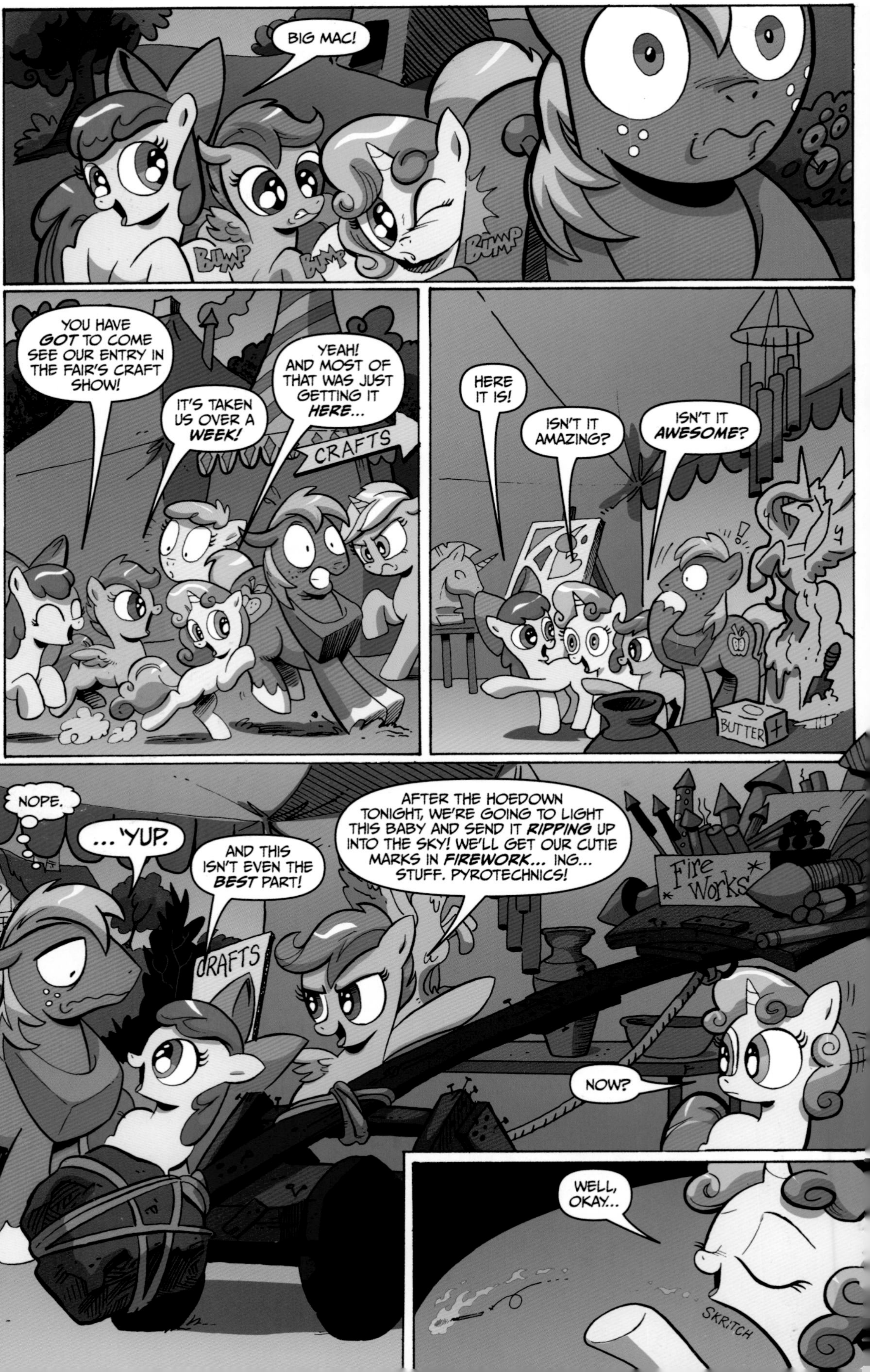
BIG MAC!
BUMP
BUMP
BUMP
YOU HAVE GOT TO COME SEE OUR ENTRY IN THE FAIR'S CRAFT SHOW!
IT'S TAKEN US OVER A WEEK!
YEAH! AND MOST OF THAT WAS JUST GETTING IT HERE...
CRAFTS
HERE IT IS!
ISN'T IT AMAZING?
ISN'T IT AWESOME?
BUTTER
NOPE.
...'YUP.
AND THIS ISN'T EVEN THE BEST PART!
AFTER THE HOEDOWN TONIGHT, WE'RE GOING TO LIGHT THIS BABY AND SEND IT RIPPING UP INTO THE SKY! WE'LL GET OUR CUTIE MARKS IN FIREWORK... ING... STUFF. PYROTECHNICS!
Fire Works
CRAFTS
NOW?
WELL, OKAY...
SKRITCH

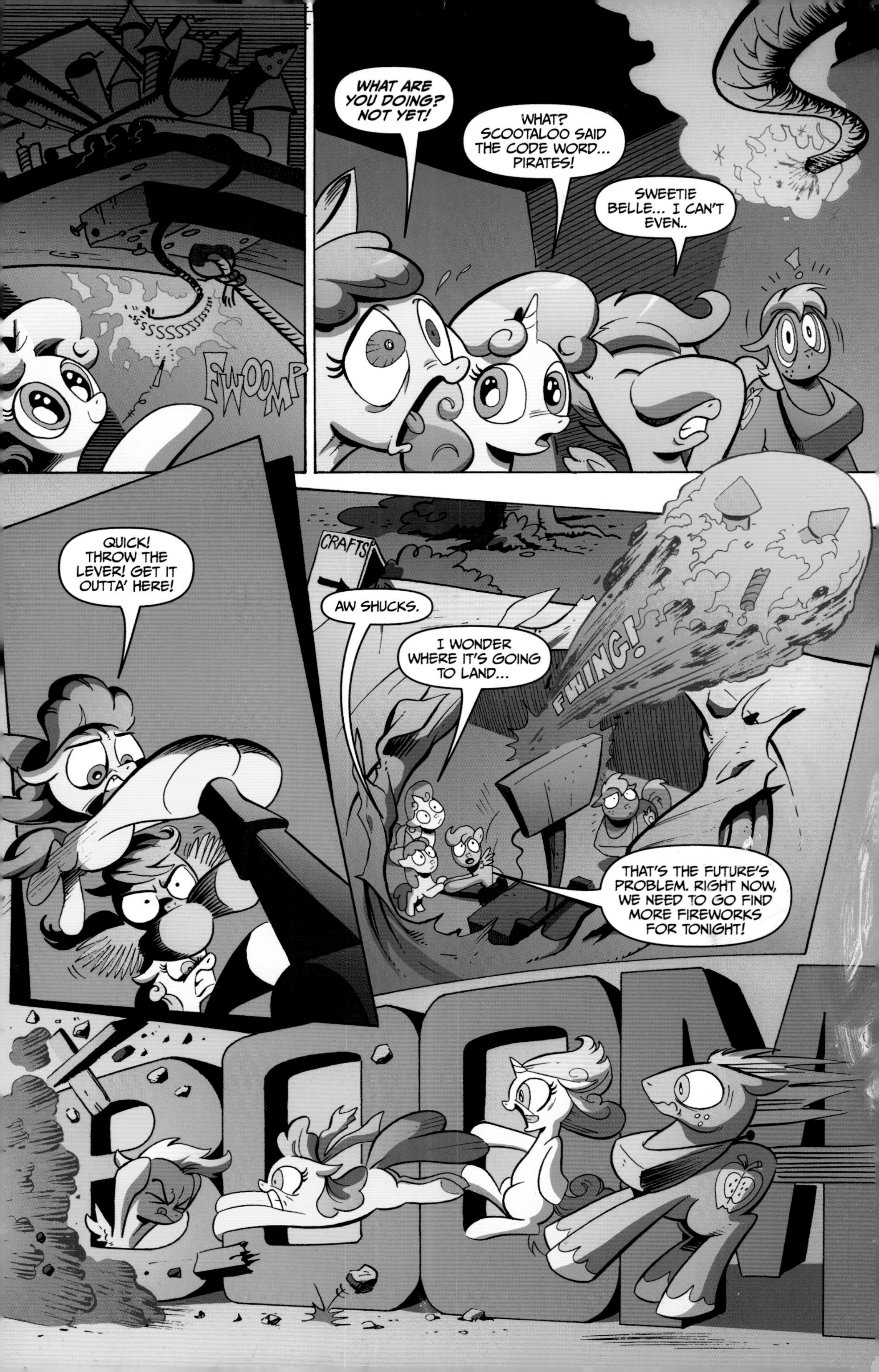
SSSSSSSSSSSS
FWOOMP
WHAT ARE YOU DOING? NOT YET!
WHAT? SCOOTALOO SAID THE CODE WORD... PIRATES!
SWEETIE BELLE... I CAN'T EVEN..
QUICK! THROW THE LEVER! GET IT OUTTA' HERE!
CRAFTS
AW SHUCKS.
I WONDER WHERE IT'S GOING TO LAND...
FWING!
THAT'S THE FUTURE'S PROBLEM. RIGHT NOW, WE NEED TO GO FIND MORE FIREWORKS FOR TONIGHT!

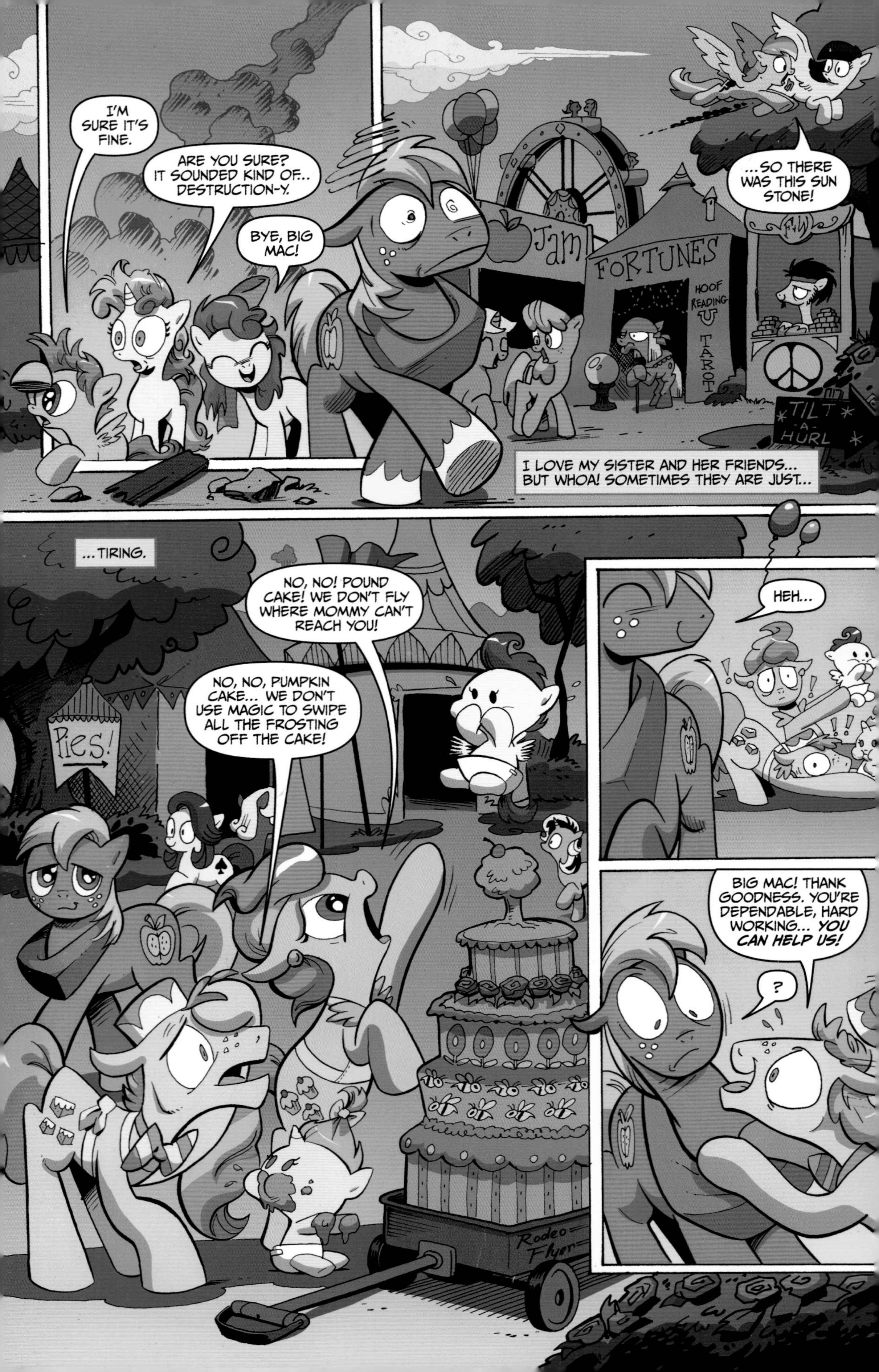
I'M SURE IT'S FINE.
ARE YOU SURE? IT SOUNDED KIND OF... DESTRUCTION-Y.
BYE, BIG MAC!
...SO THERE WAS THIS SUN STONE!
Jam
FORTUNES
HOOF READING
TAROT
TILT A HURL
I LOVE MY SISTER AND HER FRIENDS... BUT WHOA! SOMETIMES THEY ARE JUST...
...TIRING.
NO, NO! POUND CAKE! WE DON'T FLY WHERE MOMMY CAN'T REACH YOU!
NO, NO, PUMPKIN CAKE... WE DON'T USE MAGIC TO SWIPE ALL THE FROSTING OFF THE CAKE!
Pies!
Rodeo Flyer
HEH...
BIG MAC! THANK GOODNESS. YOU'RE DEPENDABLE, HARD WORKING... *YOU CAN HELP US!*
?

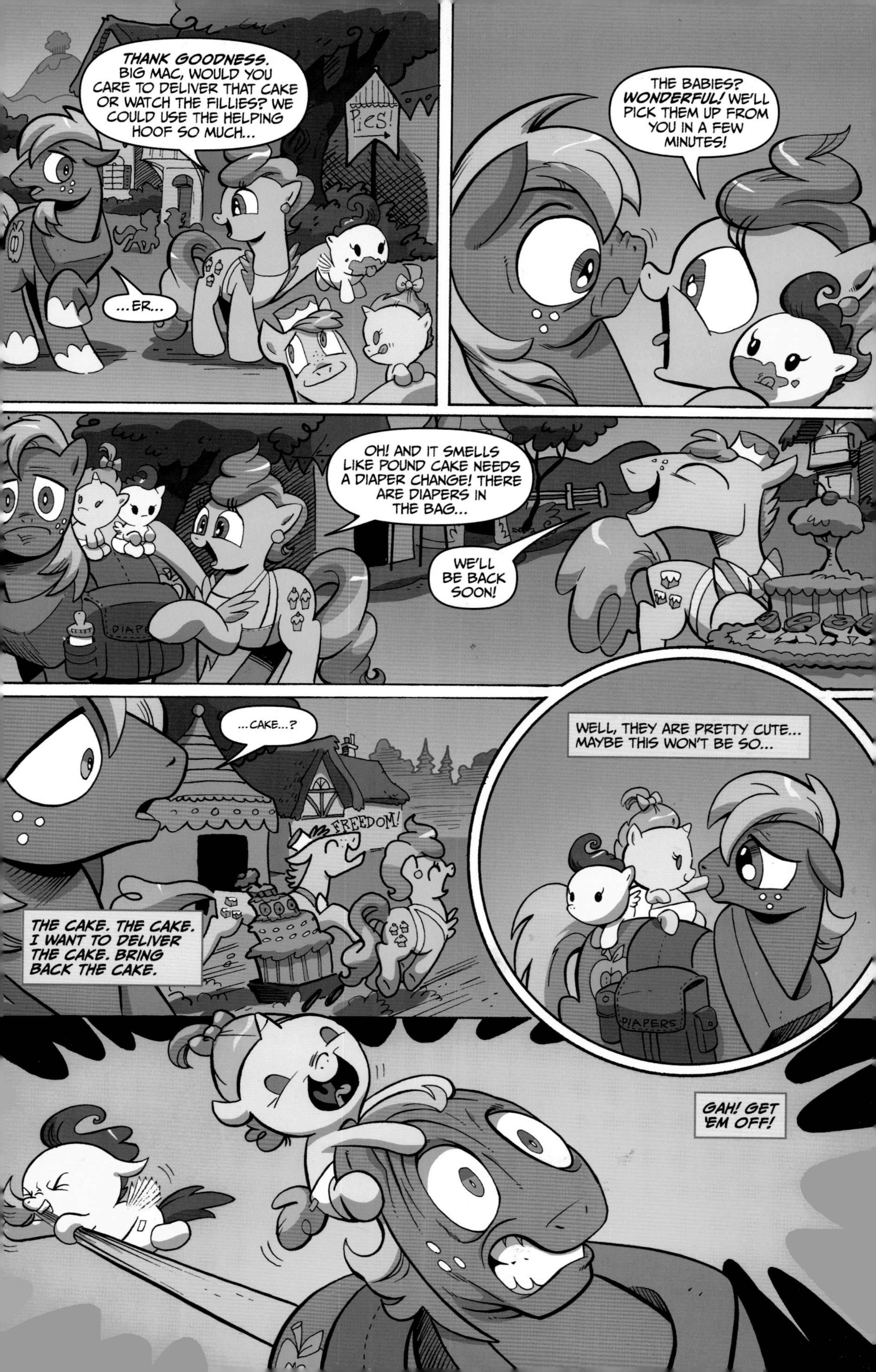
THANK GOODNESS. BIG MAC, WOULD YOU CARE TO DELIVER THAT CAKE OR WATCH THE FILLIES? WE COULD USE THE HELPING HOOF SO MUCH...
PICS!
...ER...
THE BABIES? WONDERFUL! WE'LL PICK THEM UP FROM YOU IN A FEW MINUTES!
OH! AND IT SMELLS LIKE POUND CAKE NEEDS A DIAPER CHANGE! THERE ARE DIAPERS IN THE BAG...
WE'LL BE BACK SOON!
...CAKE...?
FREEDOM!
THE CAKE. THE CAKE. I WANT TO DELIVER THE CAKE. BRING BACK THE CAKE.
WELL, THEY ARE PRETTY CUTE... MAYBE THIS WON'T BE SO...
DIAPERS
GAH! GET 'EM OFF!

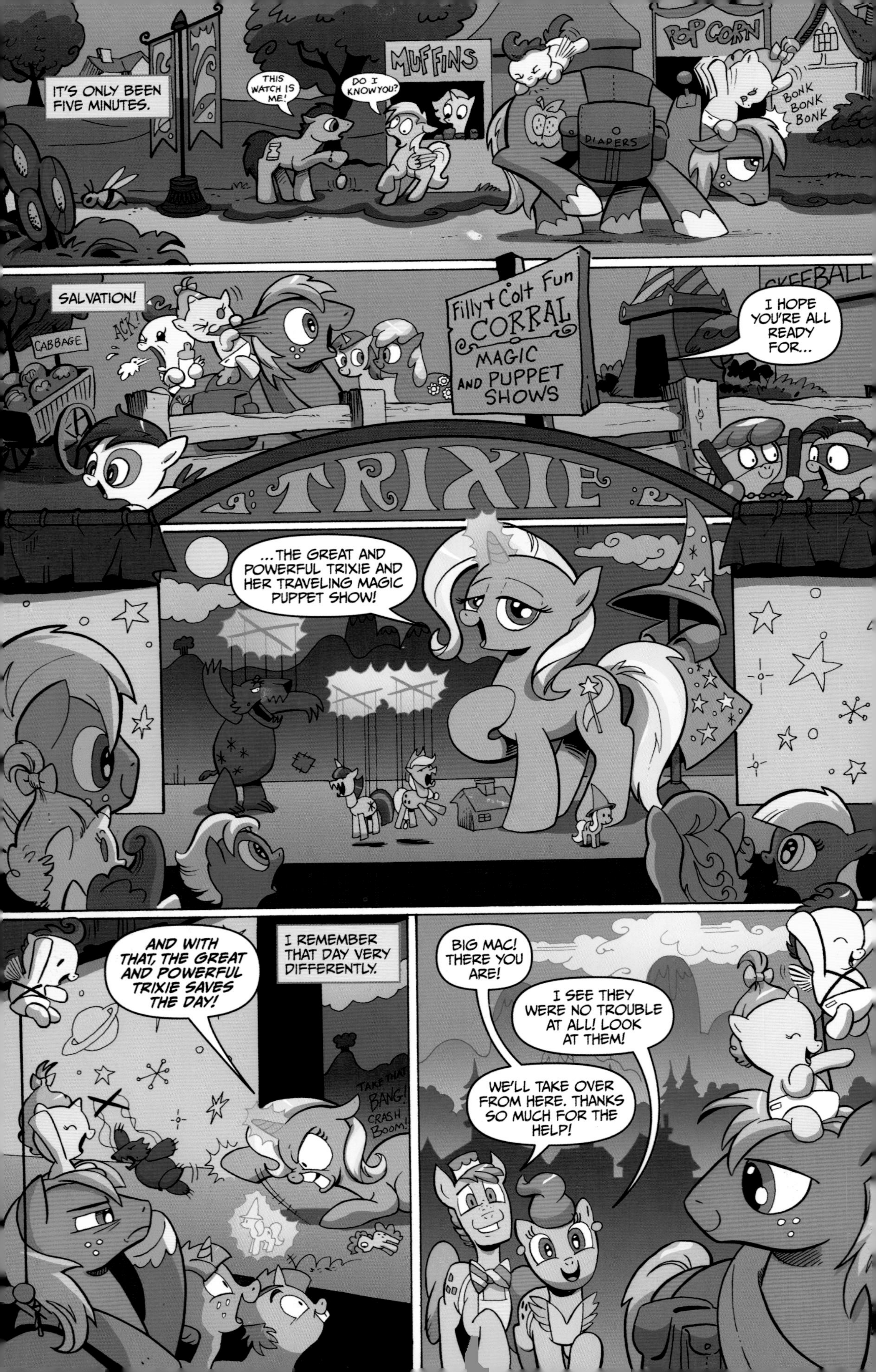
IT'S ONLY BEEN FIVE MINUTES.
MUFFINS
THIS WATCH IS ME!
DO I KNOW YOU?
POP CORN
DIAPERS
BONK BONK BONK
SALVATION!
CABBAGE
ACK!
Filly + Colt Fun CORRAL MAGIC AND PUPPET SHOWS
I HOPE YOU'RE ALL READY FOR...
TRIXIE
...THE GREAT AND POWERFUL TRIXIE AND HER TRAVELING MAGIC PUPPET SHOW!
AND WITH THAT, THE GREAT AND POWERFUL TRIXIE SAVES THE DAY!
I REMEMBER THAT DAY VERY DIFFERENTLY.
TAKE THAT! BANG! CRASH BOOM!
BIG MAC! THERE YOU ARE!
I SEE THEY WERE NO TROUBLE AT ALL! LOOK AT THEM!
WE'LL TAKE OVER FROM HERE. THANKS SO MUCH FOR THE HELP!

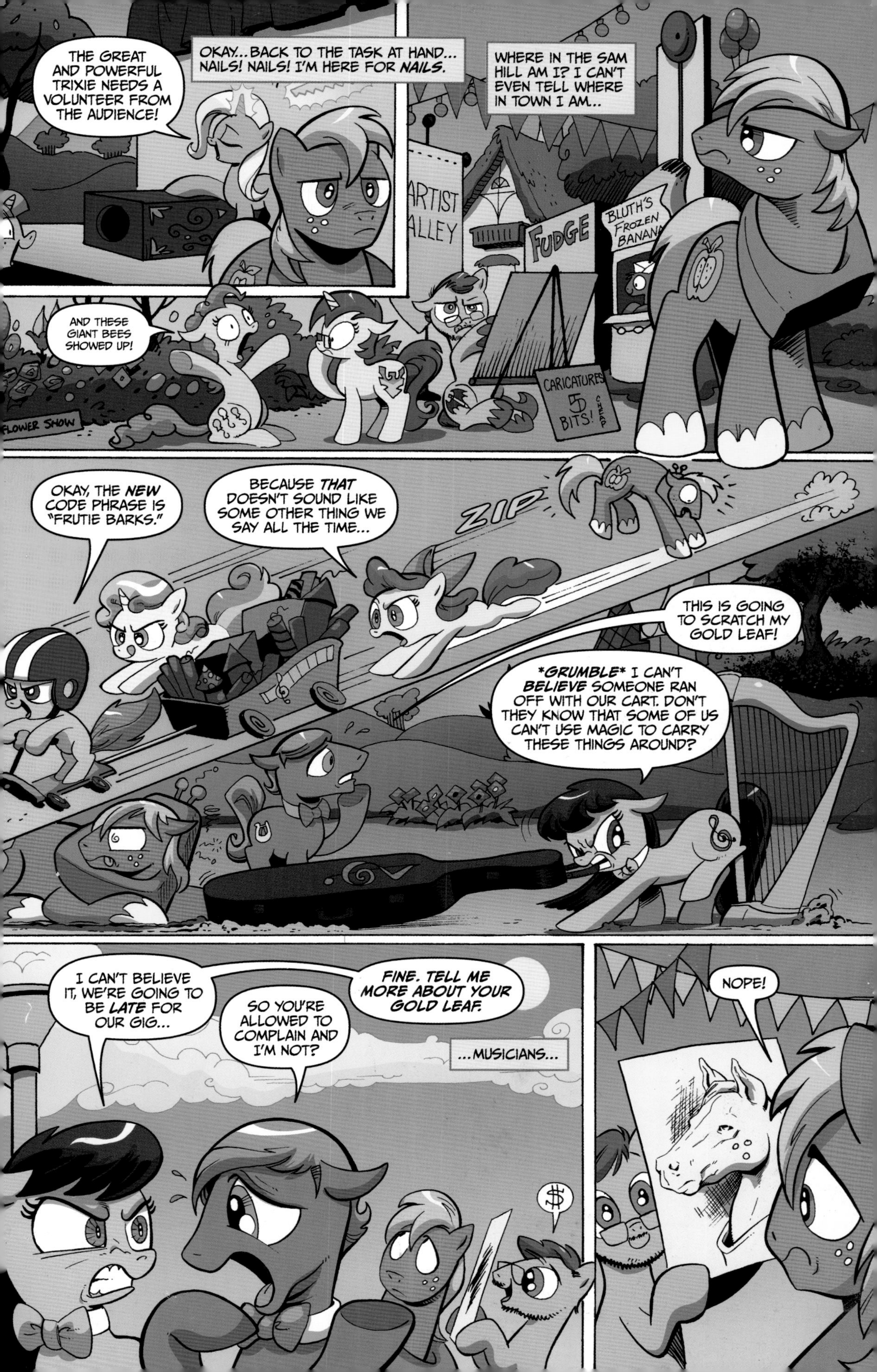
THE GREAT AND POWERFUL TRIXIE NEEDS A VOLUNTEER FROM THE AUDIENCE!
OKAY... BACK TO THE TASK AT HAND... NAILS! NAILS! I'M HERE FOR NAILS.
WHERE IN THE SAM HILL AM I? I CAN'T EVEN TELL WHERE IN TOWN I AM...
ARTIST ALLEY
FUDGE
BLUTH'S Frozen BANANA
AND THESE GIANT BEES SHOWED UP!
FLOWER SHOW
CARICATURES 5 BITS! CHEAP
OKAY, THE NEW CODE PHRASE IS "FRUTIE BARKS."
BECAUSE THAT DOESN'T SOUND LIKE SOME OTHER THING WE SAY ALL THE TIME...
ZIP
THIS IS GOING TO SCRATCH MY GOLD LEAF!
GRUMBLE I CAN'T BELIEVE SOMEONE RAN OFF WITH OUR CART. DON'T THEY KNOW THAT SOME OF US CAN'T USE MAGIC TO CARRY THESE THINGS AROUND?
I CAN'T BELIEVE IT, WE'RE GOING TO BE LATE FOR OUR GIG...
SO YOU'RE ALLOWED TO COMPLAIN AND I'M NOT?
FINE. TELL ME MORE ABOUT YOUR GOLD LEAF.
...MUSICIANS...
$
NOPE!

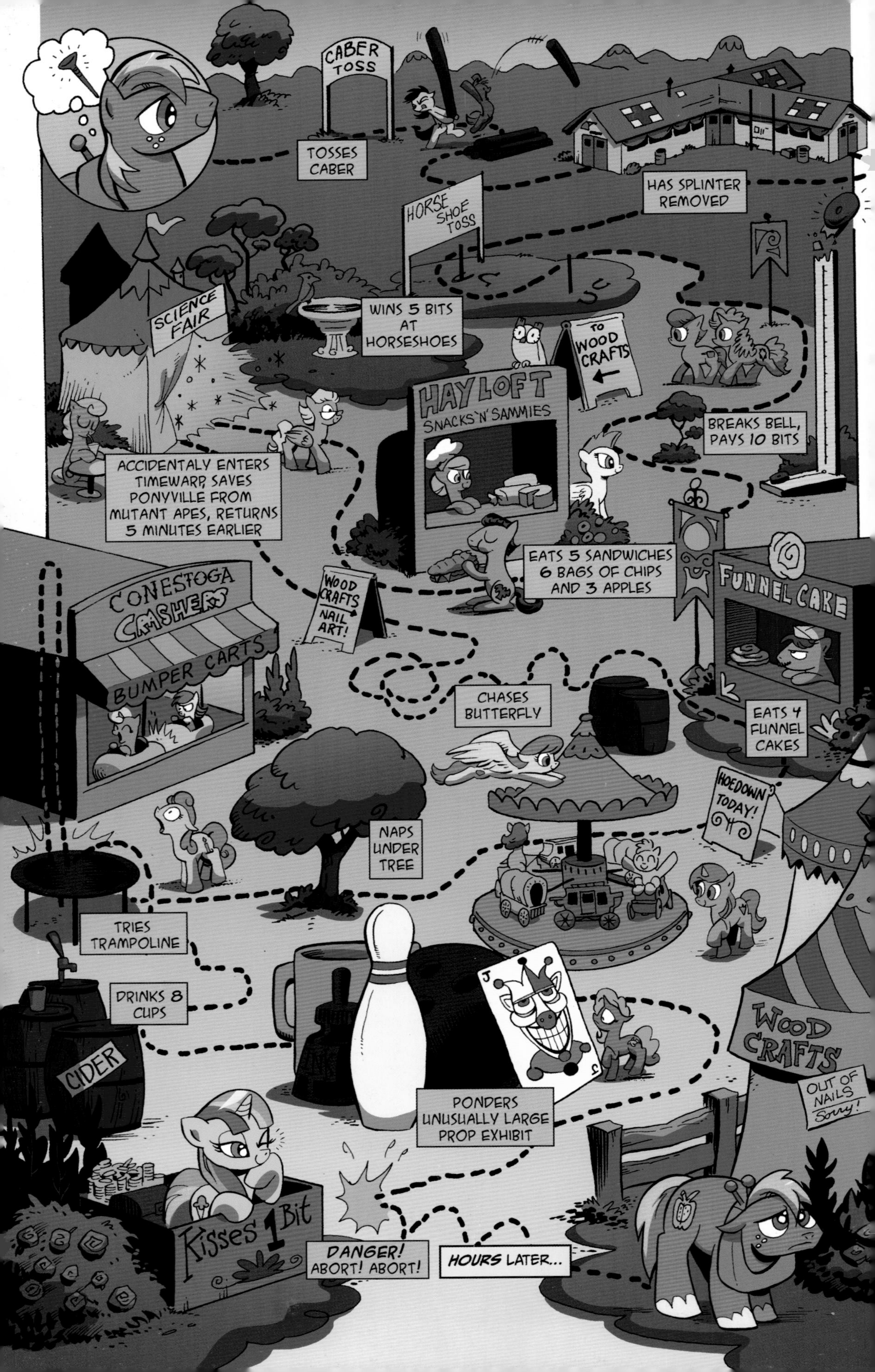

CABER TOSS
TOSSES CABER
HAS SPLINTER REMOVED
HORSE SHOE TOSS
SCIENCE FAIR
WINS 5 BITS AT HORSESHOES
TO WOOD CRAFTS
HAYLOFT SNACKS 'N' SAMMIES
BREAKS BELL, PAYS 10 BITS
ACCIDENTALY ENTERS TIMEWARP, SAVES PONYVILLE FROM MUTANT APES, RETURNS 5 MINUTES EARLIER
EATS 5 SANDWICHES 6 BAGS OF CHIPS AND 3 APPLES
CONESTOGA CRASHERS
BUMPER CARTS
WOOD CRAFTS NAIL ART!
FUNNEL CAKE
CHASES BUTTERFLY
EATS 4 FUNNEL CAKES
HOEDOWN TODAY!
NAPS UNDER TREE
TRIES TRAMPOLINE
DRINKS 8 CUPS
CIDER
WOOD CRAFTS
OUT OF NAILS Sorry!
PONDERS UNUSUALLY LARGE PROP EXHIBIT
Kisses 1 Bit
DANGER! ABORT! ABORT!
HOURS LATER...

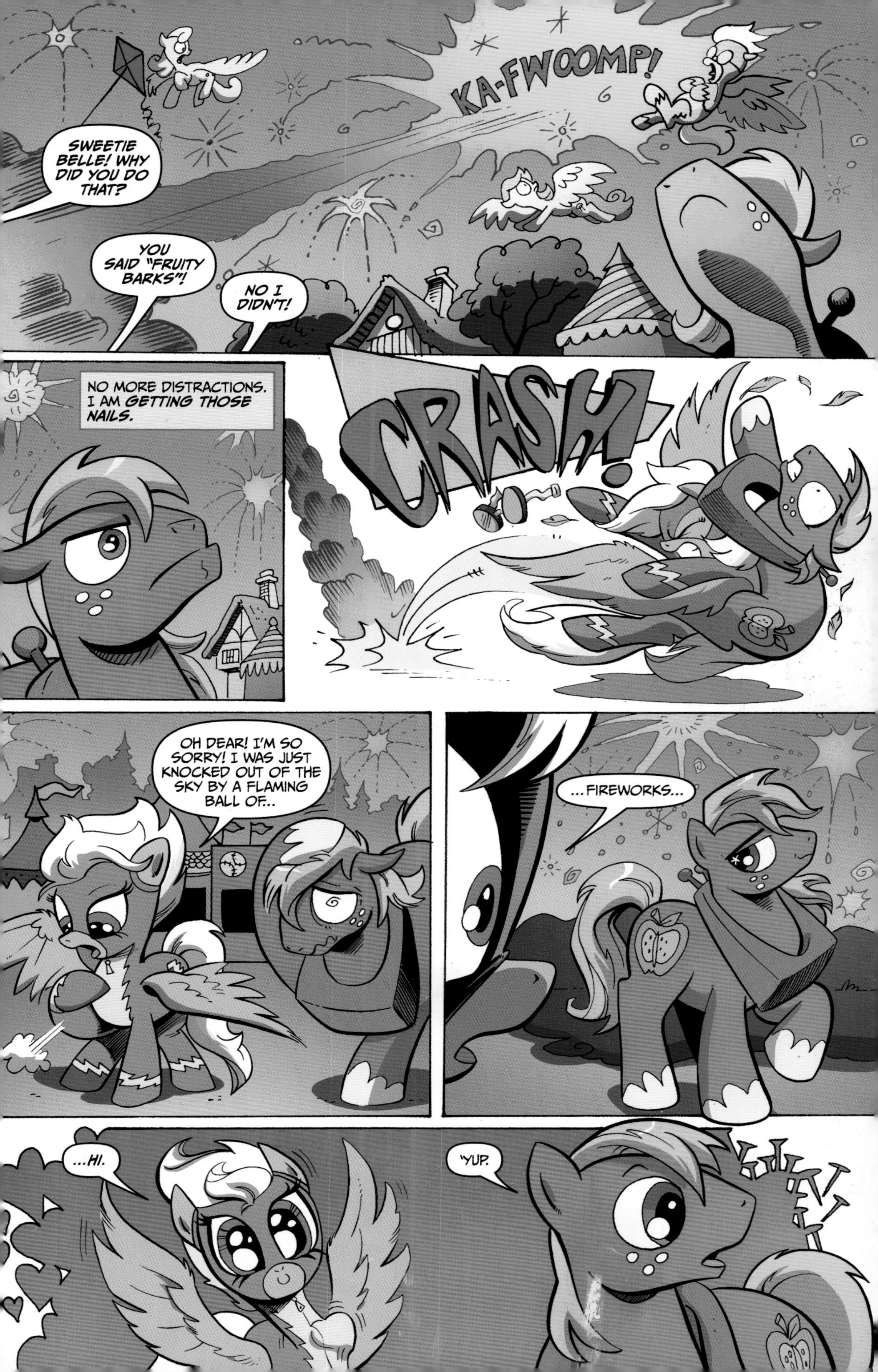
KA-FWOOMP!
SWEETIE BELLE! WHY DID YOU DO THAT?
YOU SAID "FRUITY BARKS"!
NO I DIDN'T!
NO MORE DISTRACTIONS. I AM GETTING THOSE NAILS.
CRASH!
OH DEAR! I'M SO SORRY! I WAS JUST KNOCKED OUT OF THE SKY BY A FLAMING BALL OF...
...FIREWORKS...
...HI.
'YUP.

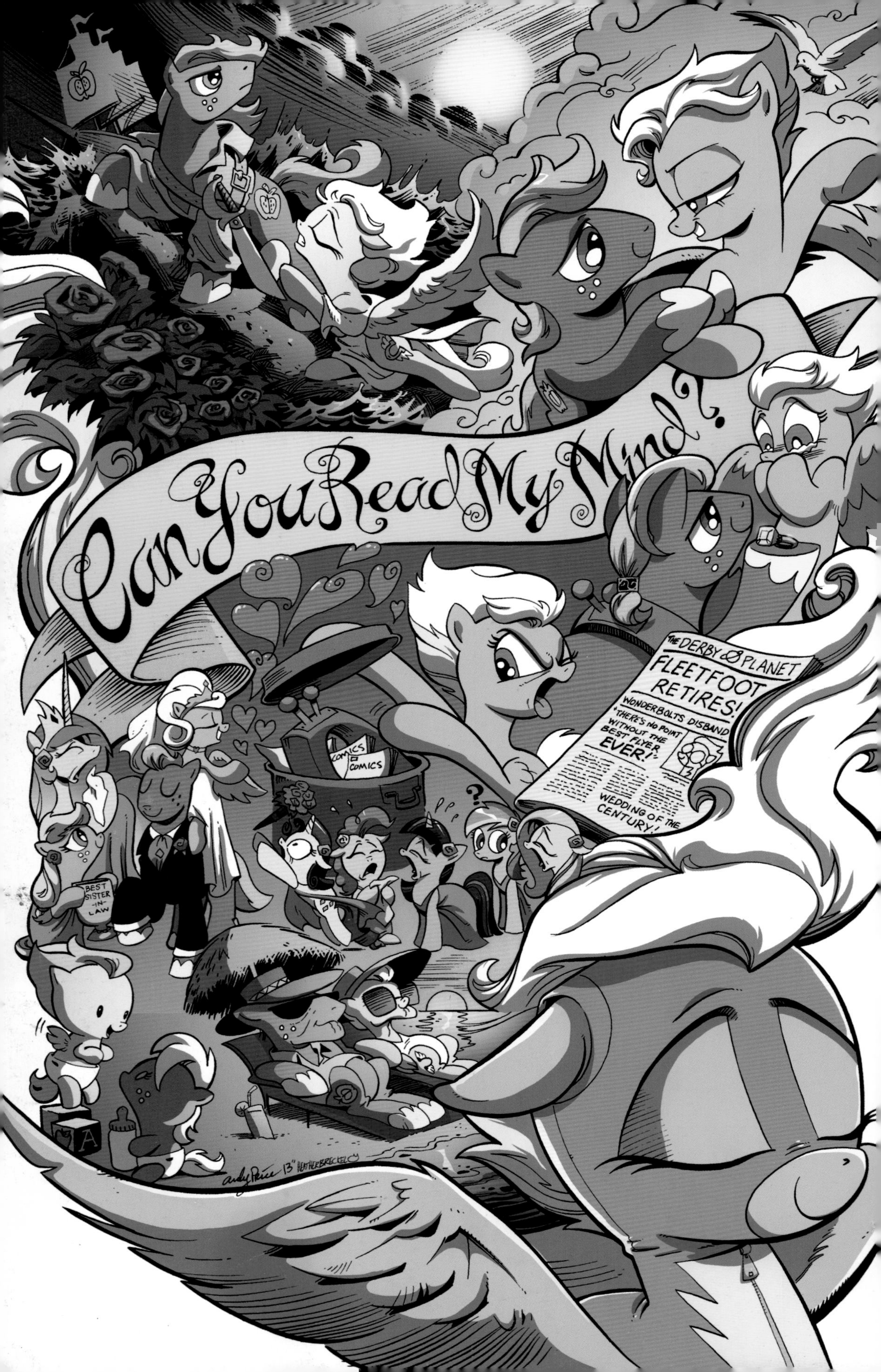
Can You Read My Mind?
THE DERBY PLANET
FLEETFOOT RETIRES!
WONDERBOLTS DISBAND
"THERE'S NO POINT WITHOUT THE BEST FLYER EVER!"
WEDDING OF THE CENTURY!
COMICS
COMICS
?
BEST SISTER -IN- LAW
A
Andy Price '13
HEATHERBRECKEL

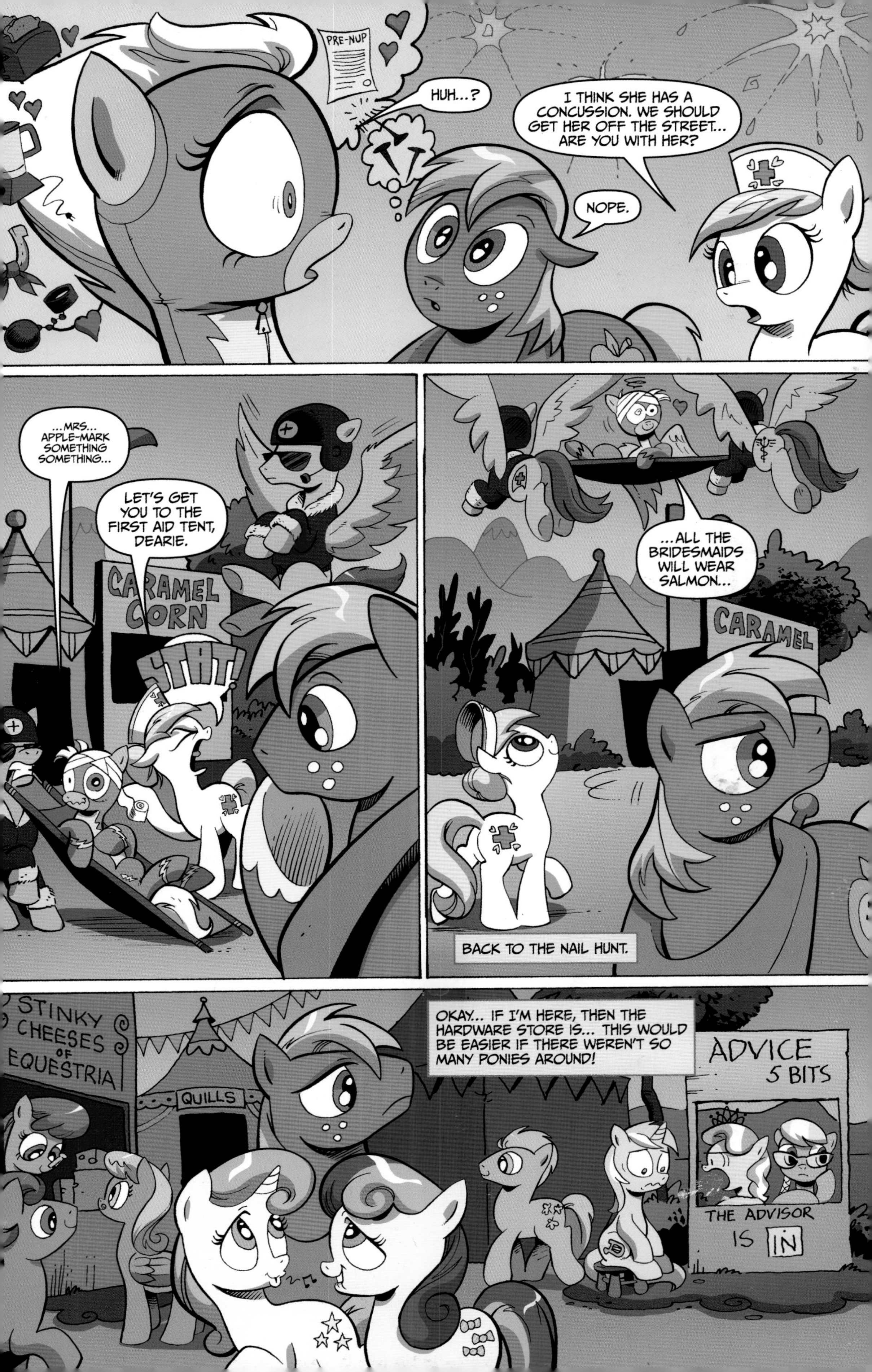
PRE-NUP
HUH...?
I THINK SHE HAS A CONCUSSION. WE SHOULD GET HER OFF THE STREET... ARE YOU WITH HER?
NOPE.
...MRS... APPLE-MARK SOMETHING SOMETHING...
LET'S GET YOU TO THE FIRST AID TENT, DEARIE.
CARAMEL CORN
STAT!
...ALL THE BRIDESMAIDS WILL WEAR SALMON...
CARAMEL
BACK TO THE NAIL HUNT.
STINKY CHEESES OF EQUESTRIA
QUILLS
OKAY... IF I'M HERE, THEN THE HARDWARE STORE IS... THIS WOULD BE EASIER IF THERE WEREN'T SO MANY PONIES AROUND!
ADVICE 5 BITS
THE ADVISOR IS IN

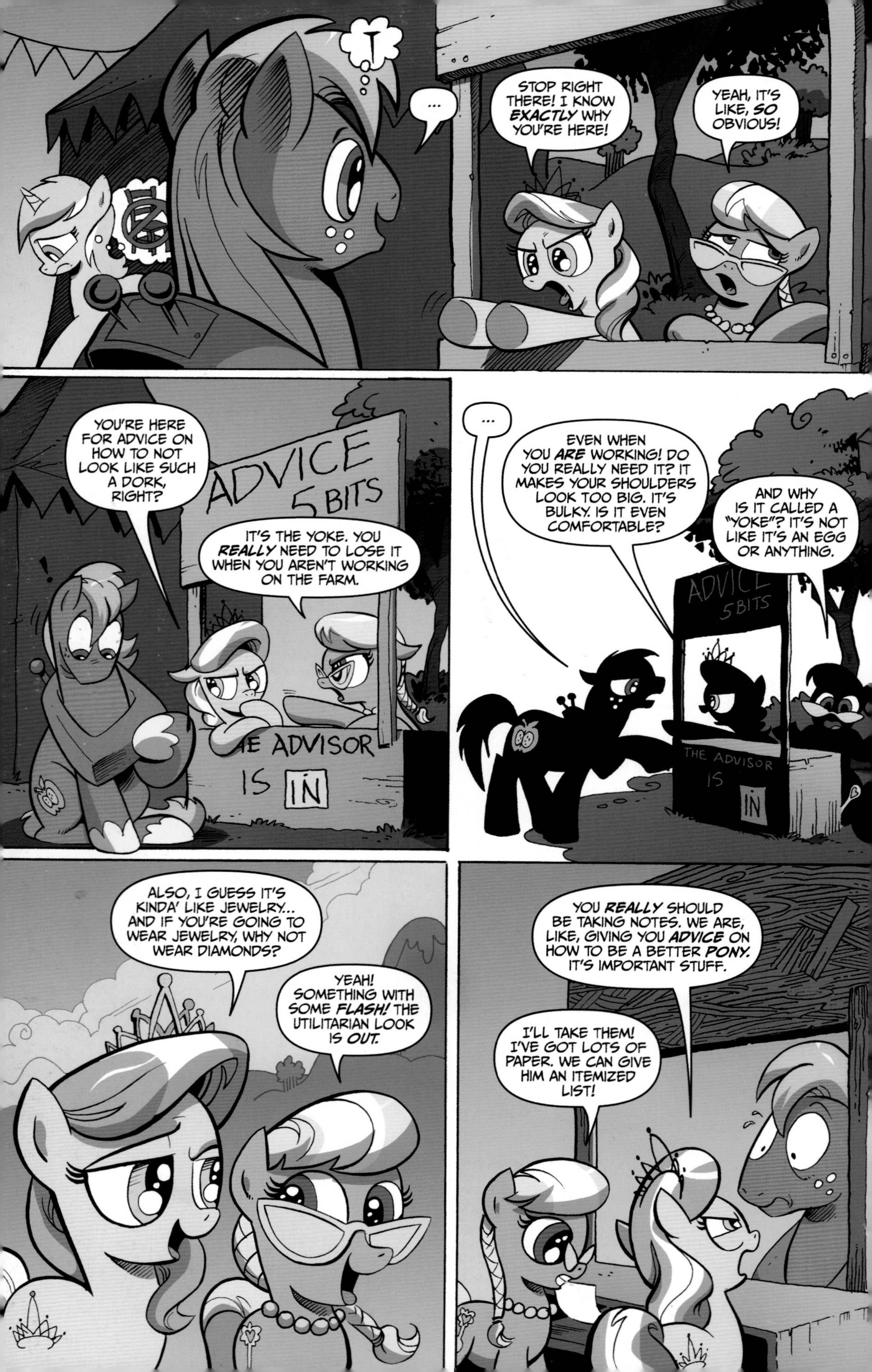

!
...
STOP RIGHT THERE! I KNOW *EXACTLY* WHY YOU'RE HERE!
YEAH, IT'S LIKE, *SO* OBVIOUS!
YOU'RE HERE FOR ADVICE ON HOW TO NOT LOOK LIKE SUCH A DORK, RIGHT?
ADVICE 5 BITS
IT'S THE YOKE. YOU *REALLY* NEED TO LOSE IT WHEN YOU AREN'T WORKING ON THE FARM.
!
THE ADVISOR IS IN
...
EVEN WHEN YOU *ARE* WORKING! DO YOU REALLY NEED IT? IT MAKES YOUR SHOULDERS LOOK TOO BIG. IT'S BULKY. IS IT EVEN COMFORTABLE?
AND WHY IS IT CALLED A "YOKE"? IT'S NOT LIKE IT'S AN EGG OR ANYTHING.
ADVICE 5 BITS
THE ADVISOR IS IN
ALSO, I GUESS IT'S KINDA' LIKE JEWELRY... AND IF YOU'RE GOING TO WEAR JEWELRY, WHY NOT WEAR DIAMONDS?
YEAH! SOMETHING WITH SOME *FLASH!* THE UTILITARIAN LOOK IS *OUT.*
YOU *REALLY* SHOULD BE TAKING NOTES. WE ARE, LIKE, GIVING YOU *ADVICE* ON HOW TO BE A BETTER *PONY.* IT'S IMPORTANT STUFF.
I'LL TAKE THEM! I'VE GOT LOTS OF PAPER. WE CAN GIVE HIM AN ITEMIZED LIST!

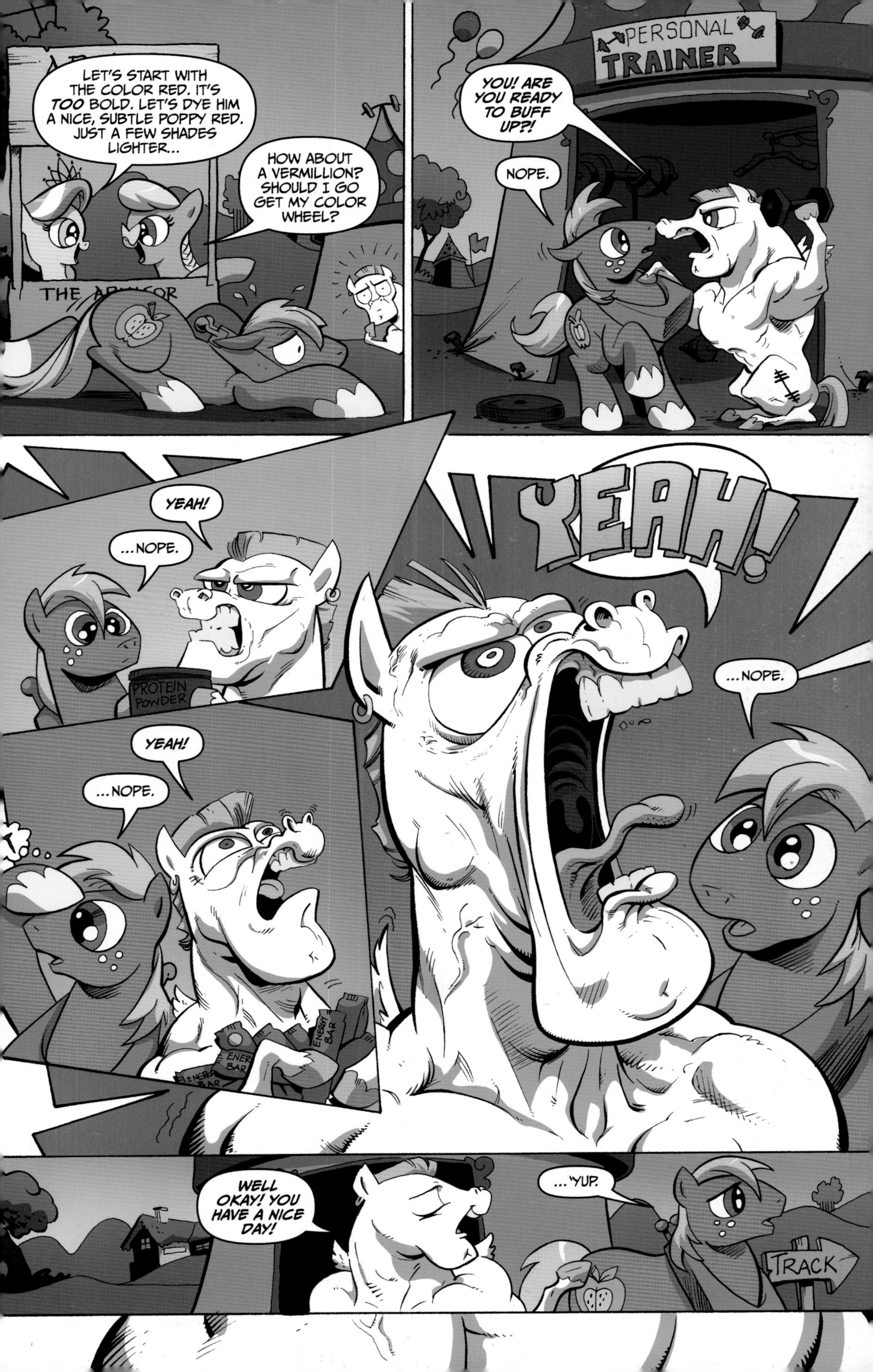
LET'S START WITH THE COLOR RED. IT'S TOO BOLD. LET'S DYE HIM A NICE, SUBTLE POPPY RED. JUST A FEW SHADES LIGHTER...
HOW ABOUT A VERMILLION? SHOULD I GO GET MY COLOR WHEEL?
PERSONAL TRAINER
YOU! ARE YOU READY TO BUFF UP?!
NOPE.
YEAH!
...NOPE.
PROTEIN POWDER
YEAH!
...NOPE.
ENERGY BAR
YEAH!
...NOPE.
WELL OKAY! YOU HAVE A NICE DAY!
...'YUP.
TRACK

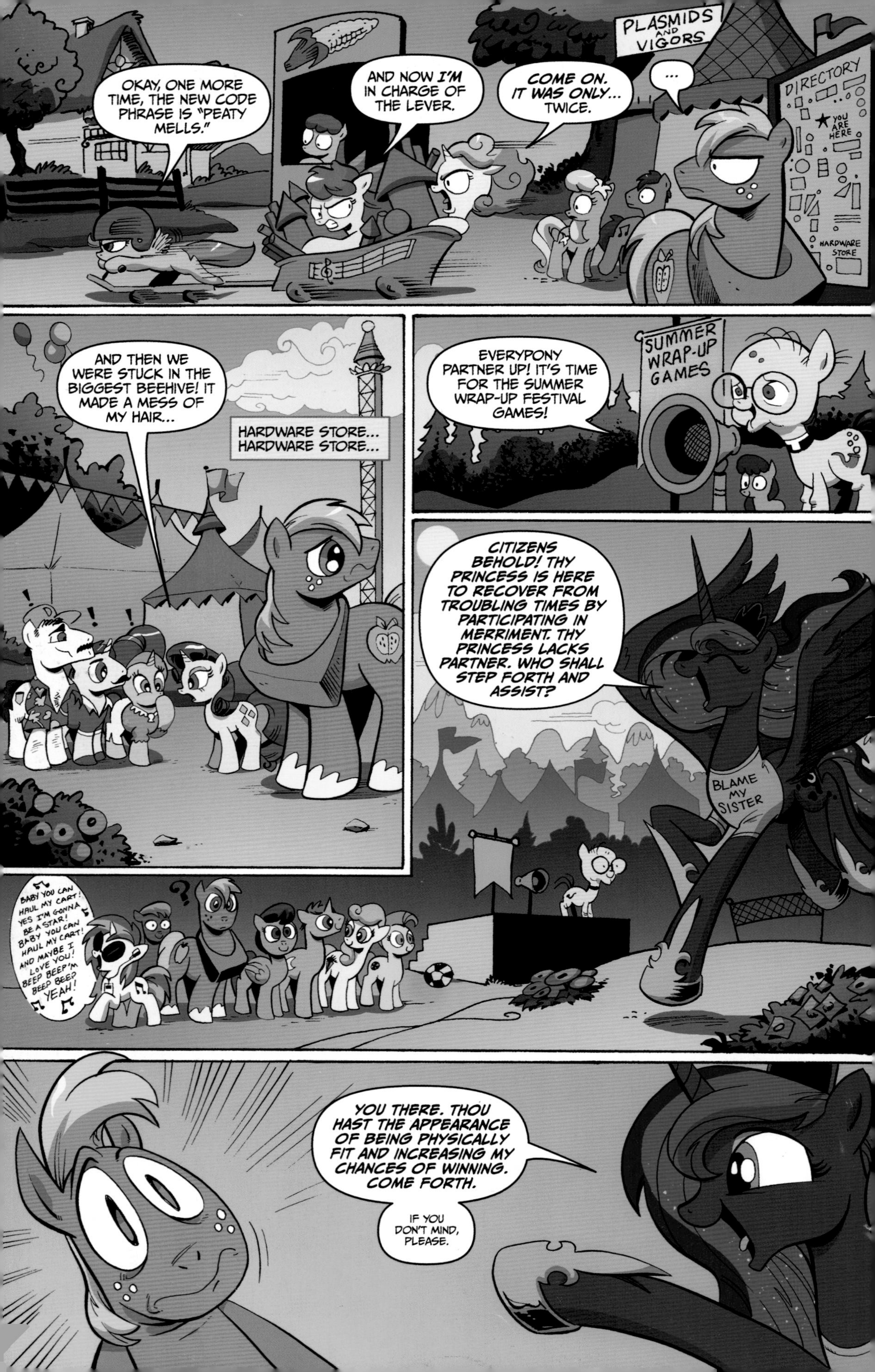
PLASMIDS AND VIGORS
DIRECTORY
YOU ARE HERE
HARDWARE STORE
OKAY, ONE MORE TIME, THE NEW CODE PHRASE IS "PEATY MELLS."
AND NOW I'M IN CHARGE OF THE LEVER.
COME ON. IT WAS ONLY... TWICE.
...
AND THEN WE WERE STUCK IN THE BIGGEST BEEHIVE! IT MADE A MESS OF MY HAIR...
HARDWARE STORE... HARDWARE STORE...
SUMMER WRAP-UP GAMES
EVERYPONY PARTNER UP! IT'S TIME FOR THE SUMMER WRAP-UP FESTIVAL GAMES!
CITIZENS BEHOLD! THY PRINCESS IS HERE TO RECOVER FROM TROUBLING TIMES BY PARTICIPATING IN MERRIMENT. THY PRINCESS LACKS PARTNER. WHO SHALL STEP FORTH AND ASSIST?
BLAME MY SISTER
BABY YOU CAN HAUL MY CART! YES I'M GONNA BE A STAR! BABY YOU CAN HAUL MY CART! AND MAYBE I LOVE YOU! BEEP BEEP'M BEEP BEEP YEAH!
YOU THERE. THOU HAST THE APPEARANCE OF BEING PHYSICALLY FIT AND INCREASING MY CHANCES OF WINNING. COME FORTH.
IF YOU DON'T MIND, PLEASE.

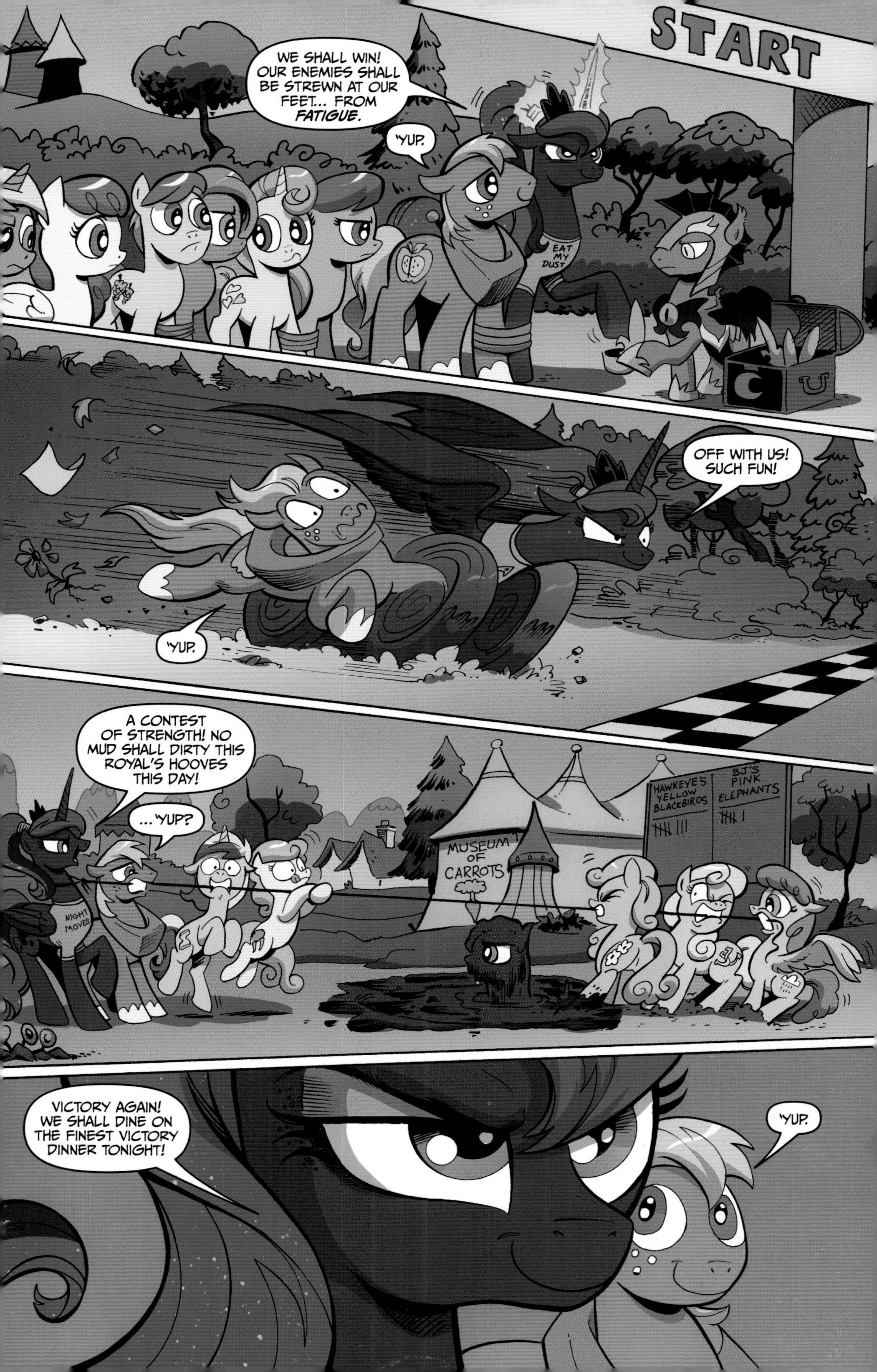
START
WE SHALL WIN! OUR ENEMIES SHALL BE STREWN AT OUR FEET... FROM *FATIGUE*.
'YUP.
EAT MY DUST
OFF WITH US! SUCH FUN!
'YUP.
A CONTEST OF STRENGTH! NO MUD SHALL DIRTY THIS ROYAL'S HOOVES THIS DAY!
...'YUP?
HAWKEYE'S YELLOW BLACKBIRDS
BJ'S PINK ELEPHANTS
MUSEUM OF CARROTS
NIGHT MOVES
VICTORY AGAIN! WE SHALL DINE ON THE FINEST VICTORY DINNER TONIGHT!
'YUP.

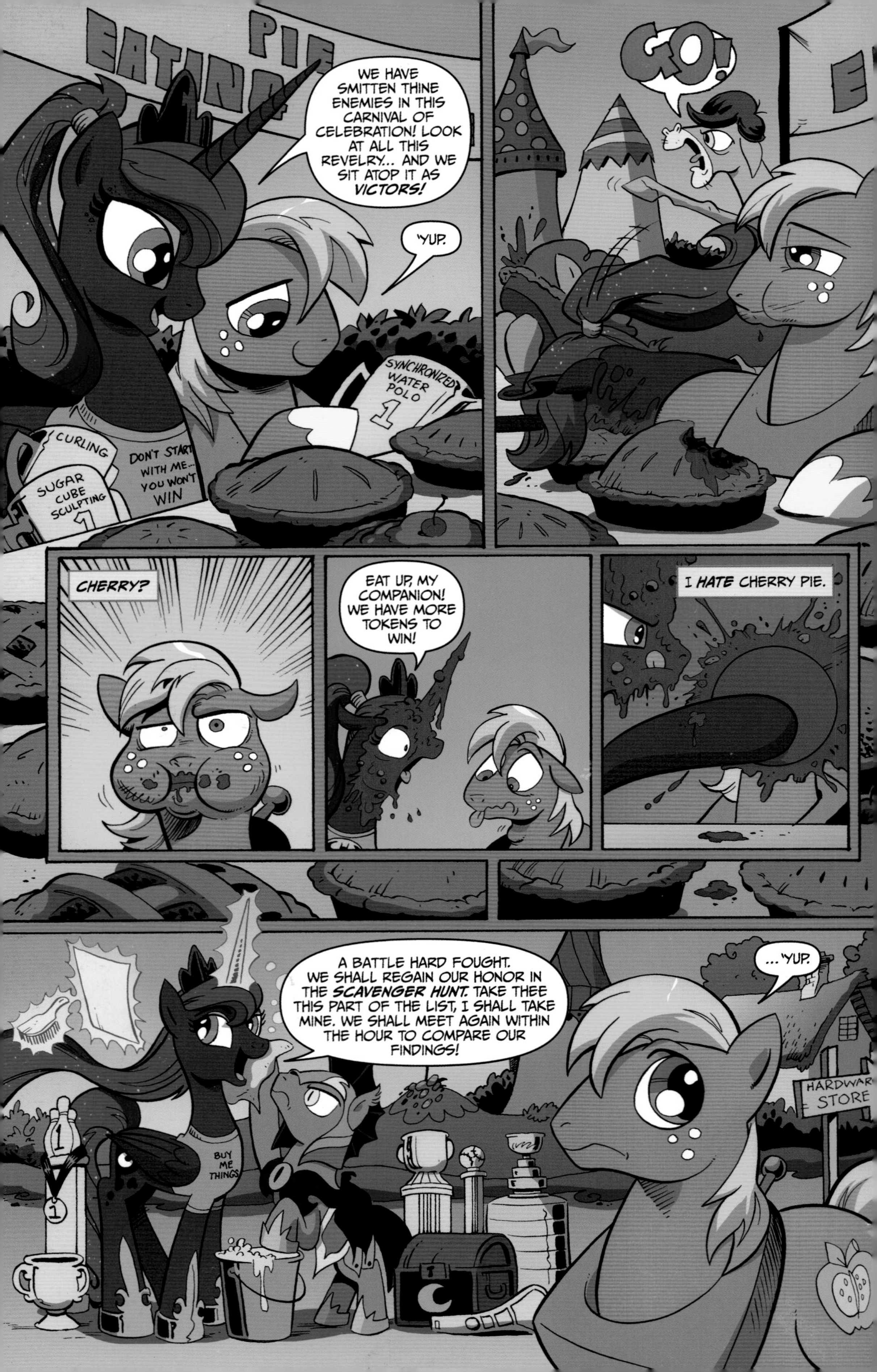
PIE EATING
WE HAVE SMITTEN THINE ENEMIES IN THIS CARNIVAL OF CELEBRATION! LOOK AT ALL THIS REVELRY... AND WE SIT ATOP IT AS *VICTORS!*
'YUP.
SYNCHRONIZED WATER POLO 1
CURLING
SUGAR CUBE SCULPTING 1
DON'T START WITH ME... YOU WON'T WIN
GO!
CHERRY?
EAT UP, MY COMPANION! WE HAVE MORE TOKENS TO WIN!
I *HATE* CHERRY PIE.
A BATTLE HARD FOUGHT. WE SHALL REGAIN OUR HONOR IN THE *SCAVENGER HUNT.* TAKE THEE THIS PART OF THE LIST, I SHALL TAKE MINE. WE SHALL MEET AGAIN WITHIN THE HOUR TO COMPARE OUR FINDINGS!
...'YUP.
BUY ME THINGS
HARDWAR STORE

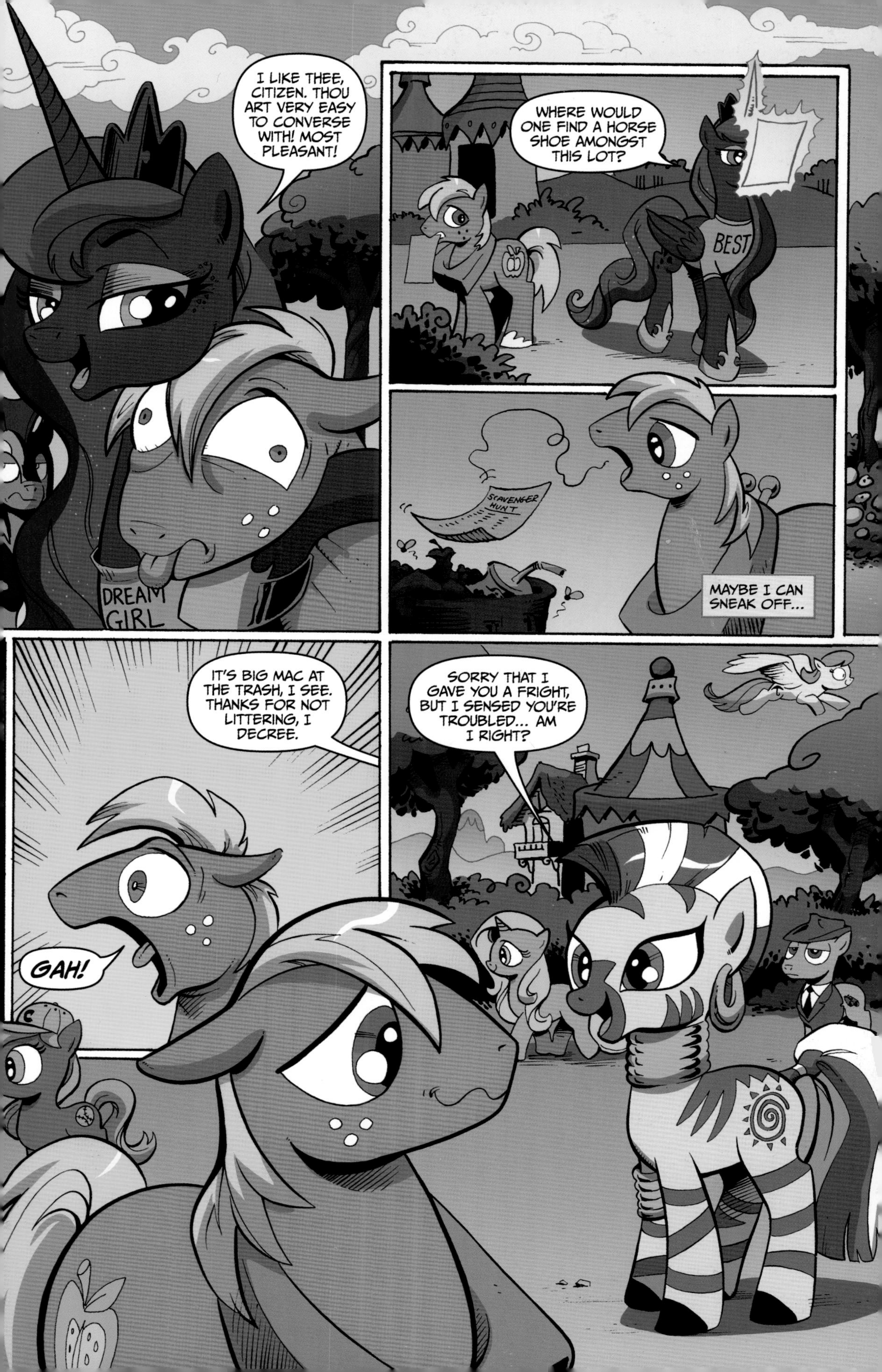
I LIKE THEE, CITIZEN. THOU ART VERY EASY TO CONVERSE WITH! MOST PLEASANT!
DREAM GIRL
WHERE WOULD ONE FIND A HORSE SHOE AMONGST THIS LOT?
BEST
SCAVENGER HUNT
MAYBE I CAN SNEAK OFF...
IT'S BIG MAC AT THE TRASH, I SEE. THANKS FOR NOT LITTERING, I DECREE.
GAH!
SORRY THAT I GAVE YOU A FRIGHT, BUT I SENSED YOU'RE TROUBLED... AM I RIGHT?

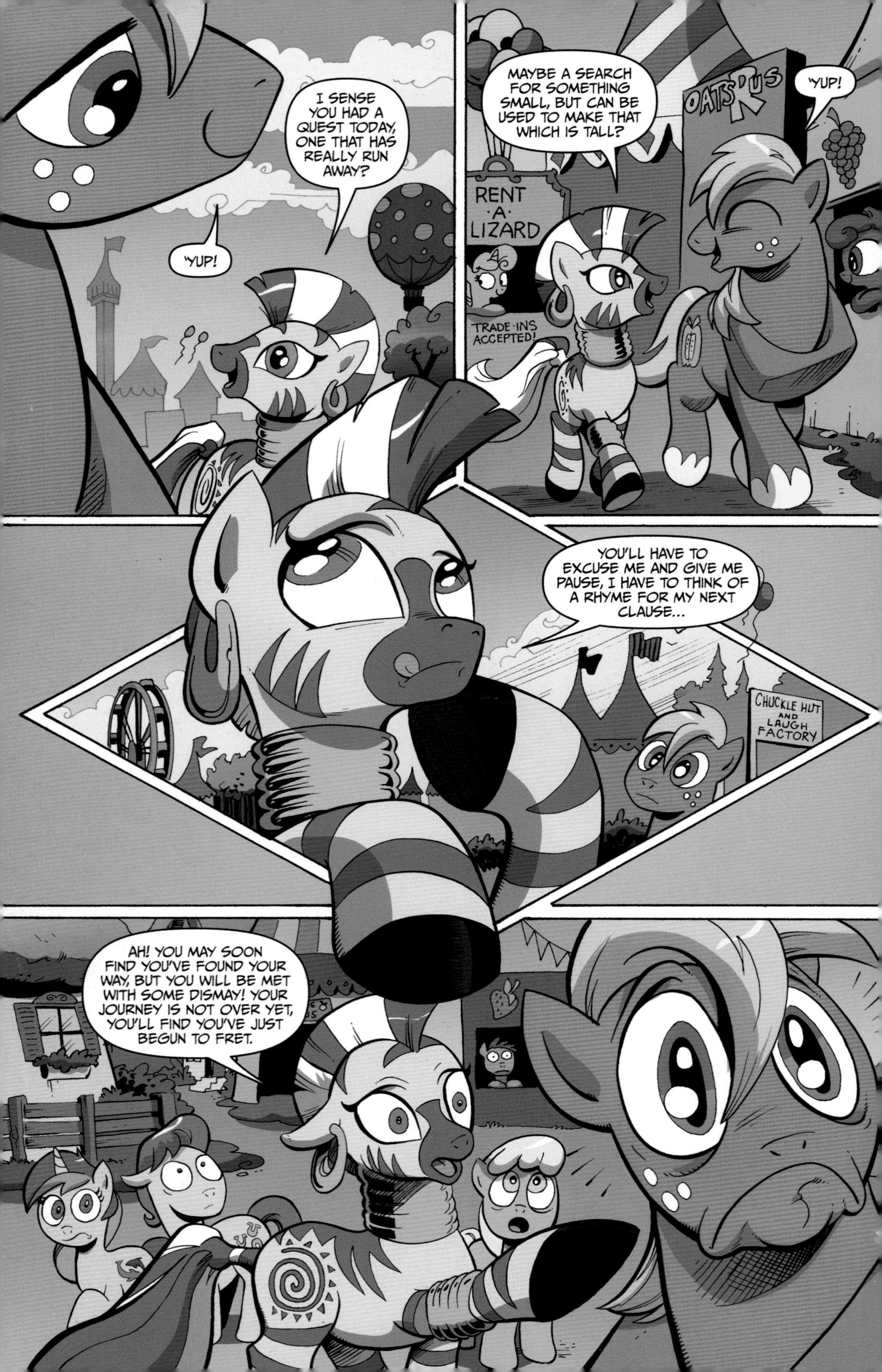
I SENSE YOU HAD A QUEST TODAY, ONE THAT HAS REALLY RUN AWAY?
'YUP!
MAYBE A SEARCH FOR SOMETHING SMALL, BUT CAN BE USED TO MAKE THAT WHICH IS TALL?
'YUP!
OATS R US
RENT A LIZARD
TRADE-INS ACCEPTED!
YOU'LL HAVE TO EXCUSE ME AND GIVE ME PAUSE, I HAVE TO THINK OF A RHYME FOR MY NEXT CLAUSE...
CHUCKLE HUT AND LAUGH FACTORY
AH! YOU MAY SOON FIND YOU'VE FOUND YOUR WAY, BUT YOU WILL BE MET WITH SOME DISMAY! YOUR JOURNEY IS NOT OVER YET, YOU'LL FIND YOU'VE JUST BEGUN TO FRET.

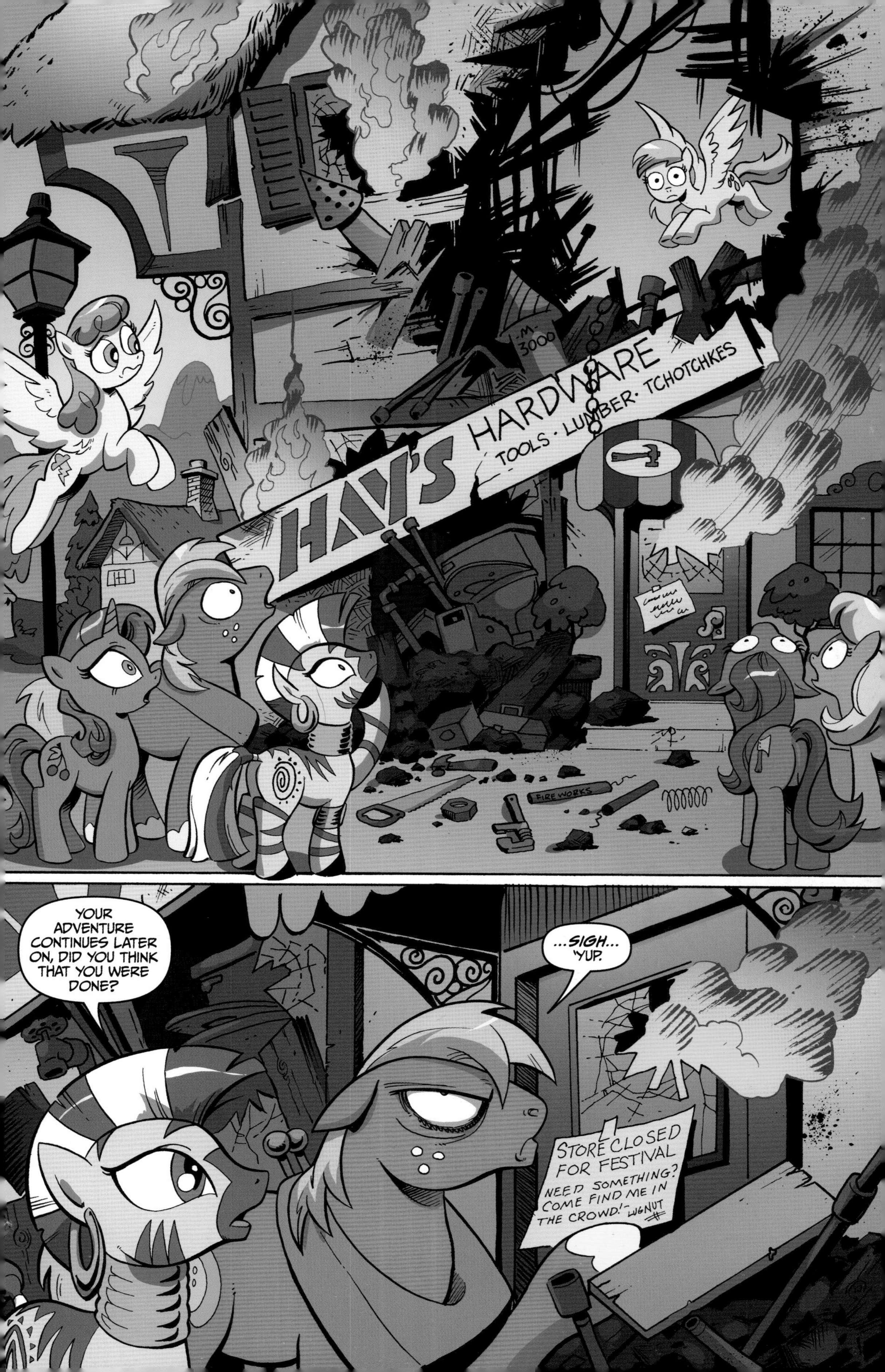
-M-
3000
HAY'S HARDWARE
TOOLS · LUMBER · TCHOTCHKES
FIREWORKS
YOUR ADVENTURE CONTINUES LATER ON, DID YOU THINK THAT YOU WERE DONE?
...SIGH... 'YUP.
STORE CLOSED FOR FESTIVAL
NEED SOMETHING? COME FIND ME IN THE CROWD! - LUGNUT

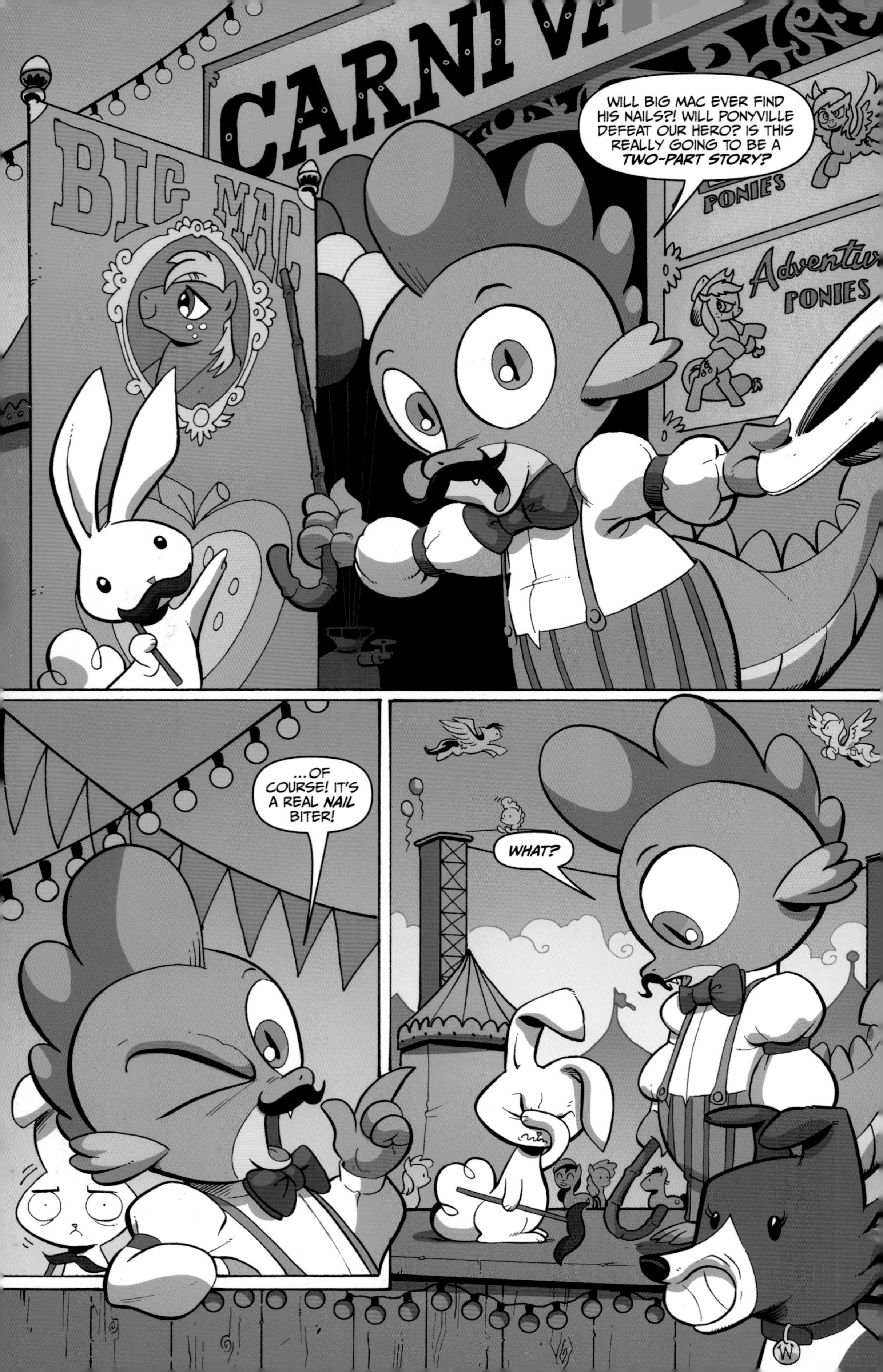
BIG MAC
WILL BIG MAC EVER FIND HIS NAILS?! WILL PONYVILLE DEFEAT OUR HERO? IS THIS REALLY GOING TO BE A *TWO-PART STORY?*
PONIES
PONIES
...OF COURSE! IT'S A REAL *NAIL* BITER!
WHAT?

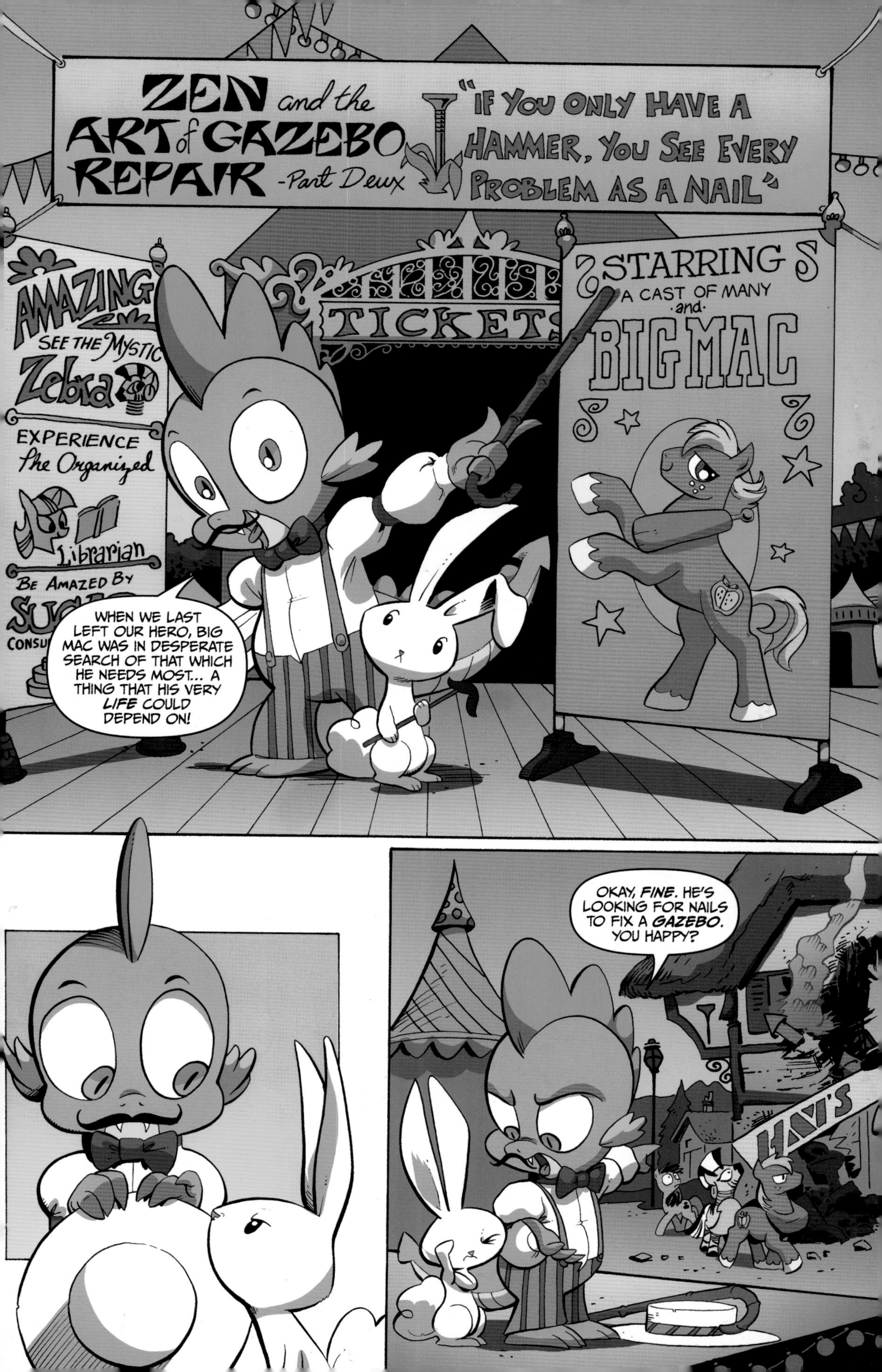
ZEN and the ART of GAZEBO REPAIR -Part Deux
"IF YOU ONLY HAVE A HAMMER, YOU SEE EVERY PROBLEM AS A NAIL"
AMAZING
SEE THE MYSTIC Zebra
EXPERIENCE The Organized Librarian
BE AMAZED BY
TICKETS
STARRING A CAST OF MANY and BIG MAC
WHEN WE LAST LEFT OUR HERO, BIG MAC WAS IN DESPERATE SEARCH OF THAT WHICH HE NEEDS MOST... A THING THAT HIS VERY *LIFE* COULD DEPEND ON!
OKAY, *FINE*. HE'S LOOKING FOR NAILS TO FIX A *GAZEBO*. YOU HAPPY?

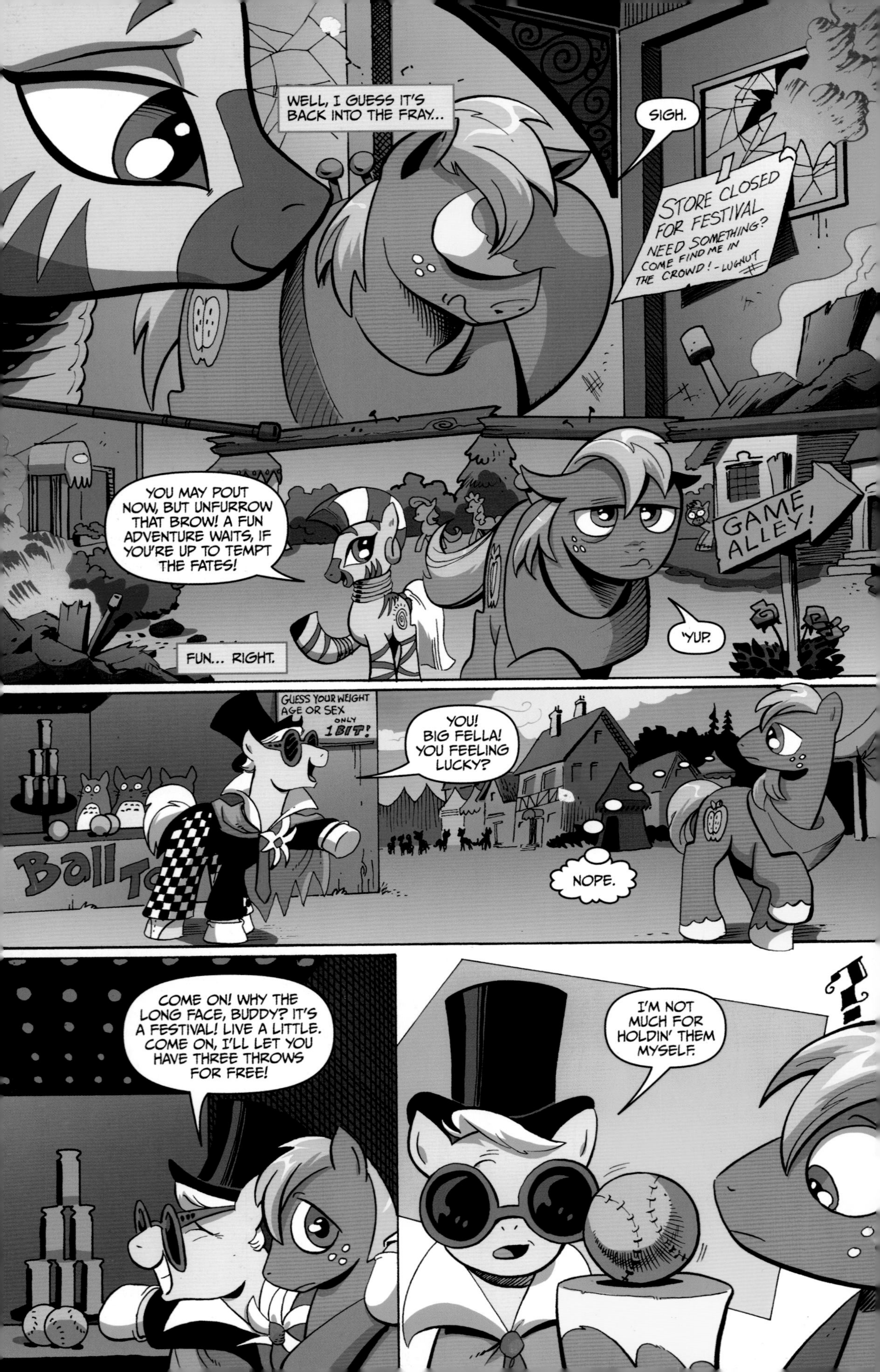
WELL, I GUESS IT'S BACK INTO THE FRAY...
SIGH.
STORE CLOSED FOR FESTIVAL
NEED SOMETHING? COME FIND ME IN THE CROWD! -LUGNUT
YOU MAY POUT NOW, BUT UNFURROW THAT BROW! A FUN ADVENTURE WAITS, IF YOU'RE UP TO TEMPT THE FATES!
GAME ALLEY!
FUN... RIGHT.
'YUP.
GUESS YOUR WEIGHT AGE OR SEX ONLY 1 BIT!
YOU! BIG FELLA! YOU FEELING LUCKY?
NOPE.
Ball To
COME ON! WHY THE LONG FACE, BUDDY? IT'S A FESTIVAL! LIVE A LITTLE. COME ON, I'LL LET YOU HAVE THREE THROWS FOR FREE!
I'M NOT MUCH FOR HOLDIN' THEM MYSELF.

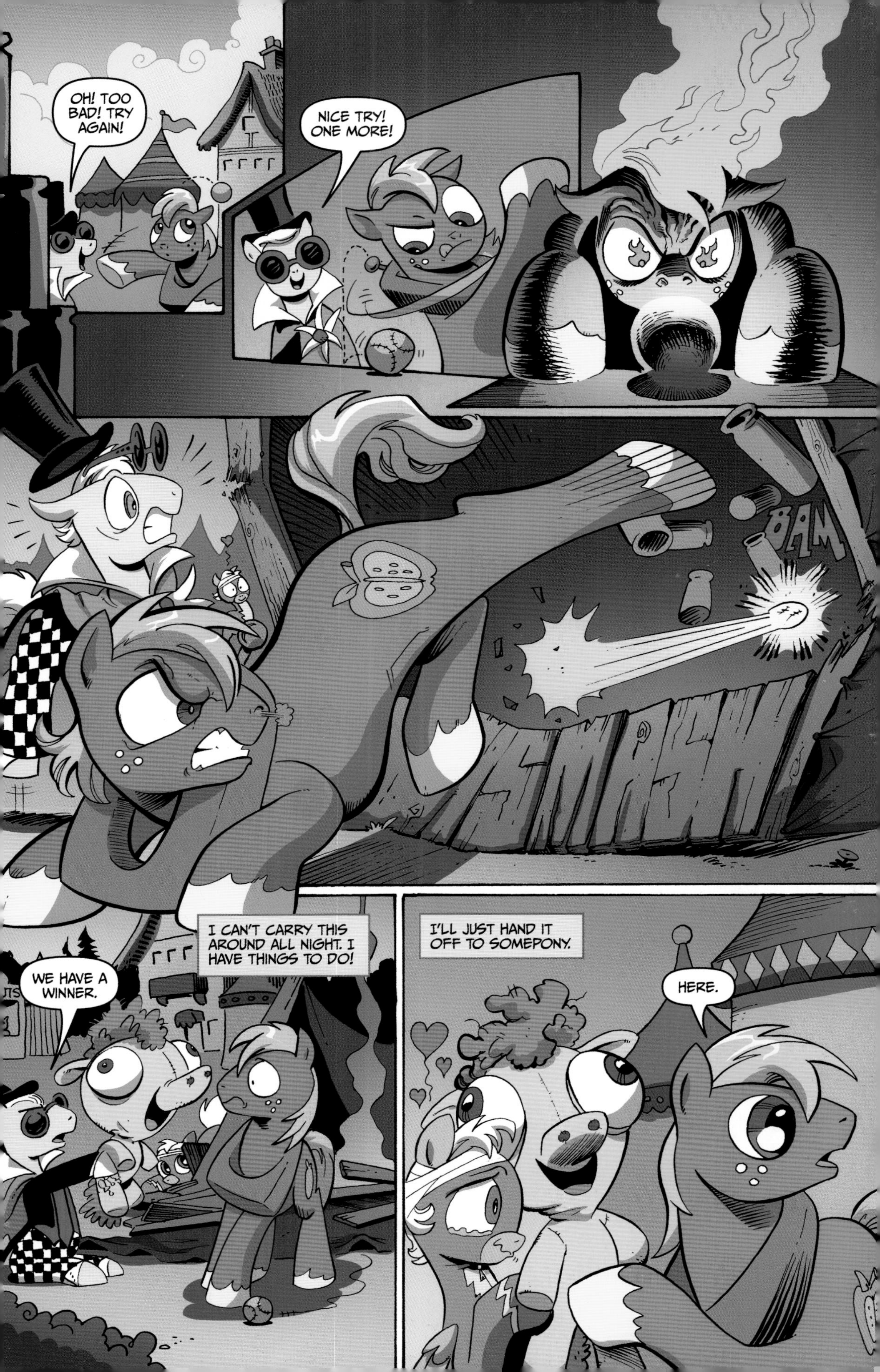
OH! TOO BAD! TRY AGAIN!
NICE TRY! ONE MORE!
BAM
SMASH
I CAN'T CARRY THIS AROUND ALL NIGHT. I HAVE THINGS TO DO!
WE HAVE A WINNER.
I'LL JUST HAND IT OFF TO SOMEPONY.
HERE.

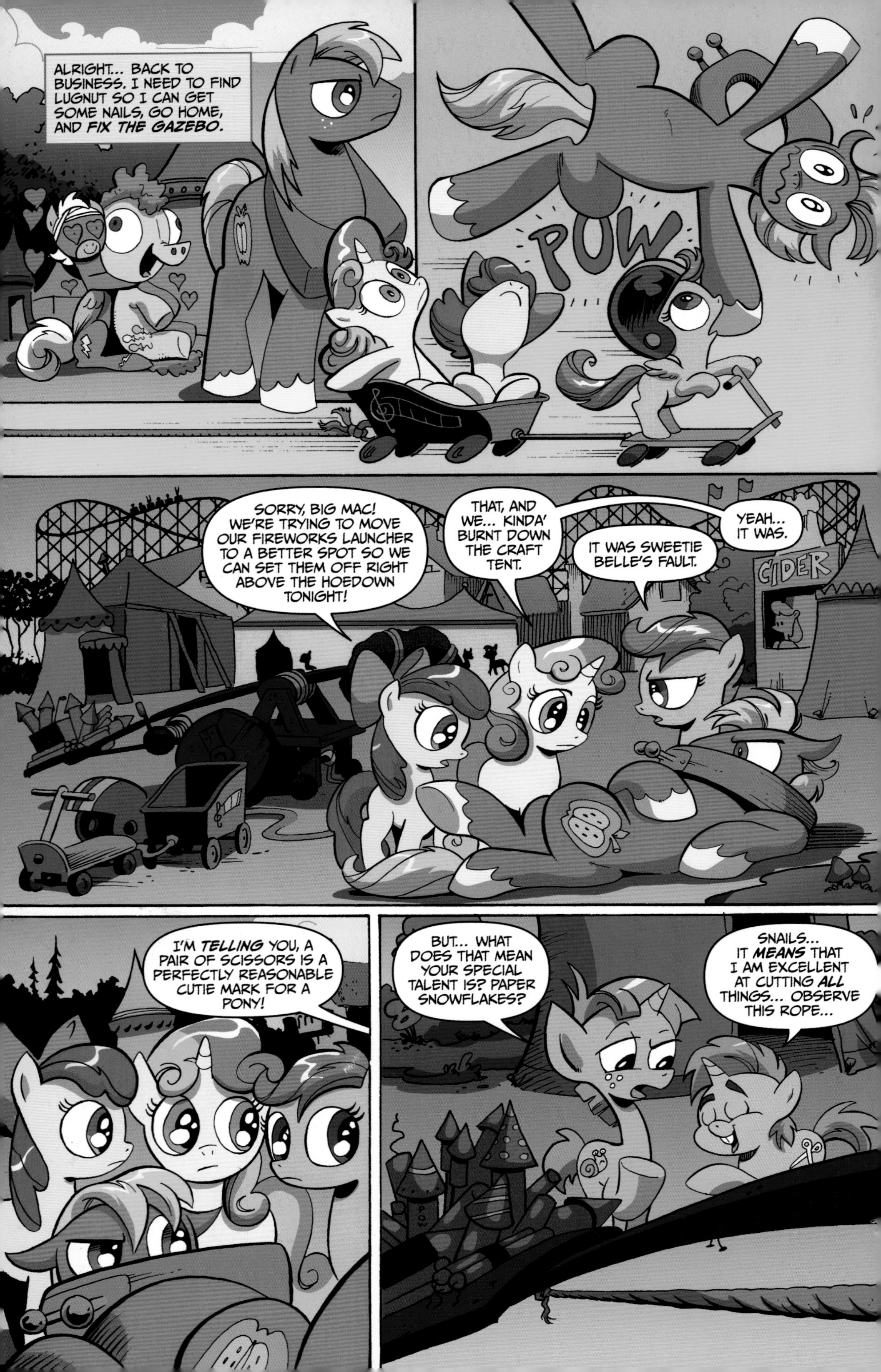
ALRIGHT... BACK TO BUSINESS. I NEED TO FIND LUGNUT SO I CAN GET SOME NAILS, GO HOME, AND *FIX THE GAZEBO.*
POW
SORRY, BIG MAC! WE'RE TRYING TO MOVE OUR FIREWORKS LAUNCHER TO A BETTER SPOT SO WE CAN SET THEM OFF RIGHT ABOVE THE HOEDOWN TONIGHT!
THAT, AND WE... KINDA' BURNT DOWN THE CRAFT TENT.
IT WAS SWEETIE BELLE'S FAULT.
YEAH... IT WAS.
CIDER
I'M *TELLING* YOU, A PAIR OF SCISSORS IS A PERFECTLY REASONABLE CUTIE MARK FOR A PONY!
BUT... WHAT DOES THAT MEAN YOUR SPECIAL TALENT IS? PAPER SNOWFLAKES?
SNAILS... IT *MEANS* THAT I AM EXCELLENT AT CUTTING *ALL* THINGS... OBSERVE THIS ROPE...

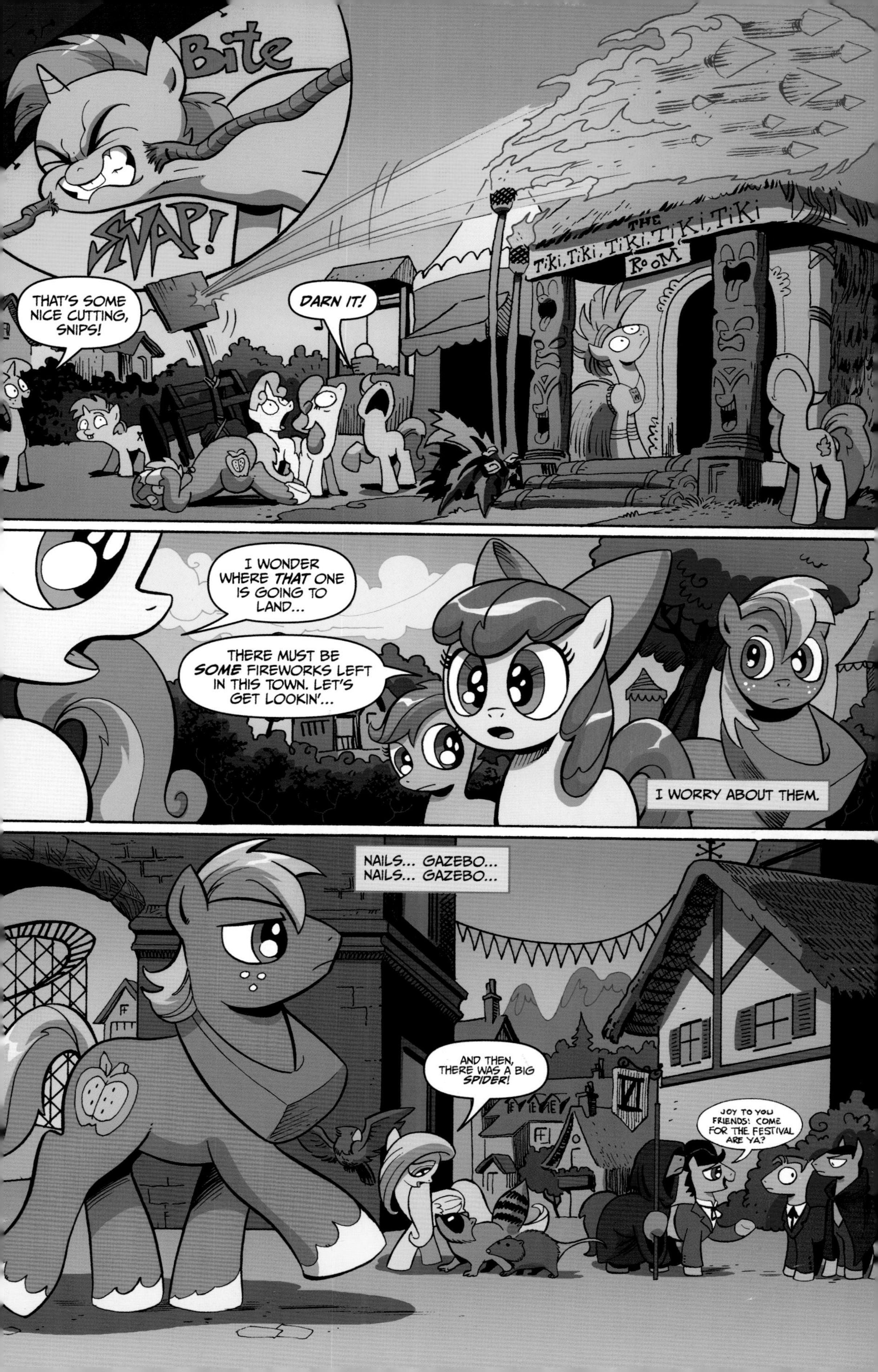
Bite
SNAP!
THE TIKI, TIKI, TIKI, TIKI, TIKI ROOM
THAT'S SOME NICE CUTTING, SNIPS!
DARN IT!
I WONDER WHERE *THAT* ONE IS GOING TO LAND...
THERE MUST BE *SOME* FIREWORKS LEFT IN THIS TOWN. LET'S GET LOOKIN'...
I WORRY ABOUT THEM.
NAILS... GAZEBO... NAILS... GAZEBO...
AND THEN, THERE WAS A BIG *SPIDER*!
JOY TO YOU FRIENDS: COME FOR THE FESTIVAL ARE YA?

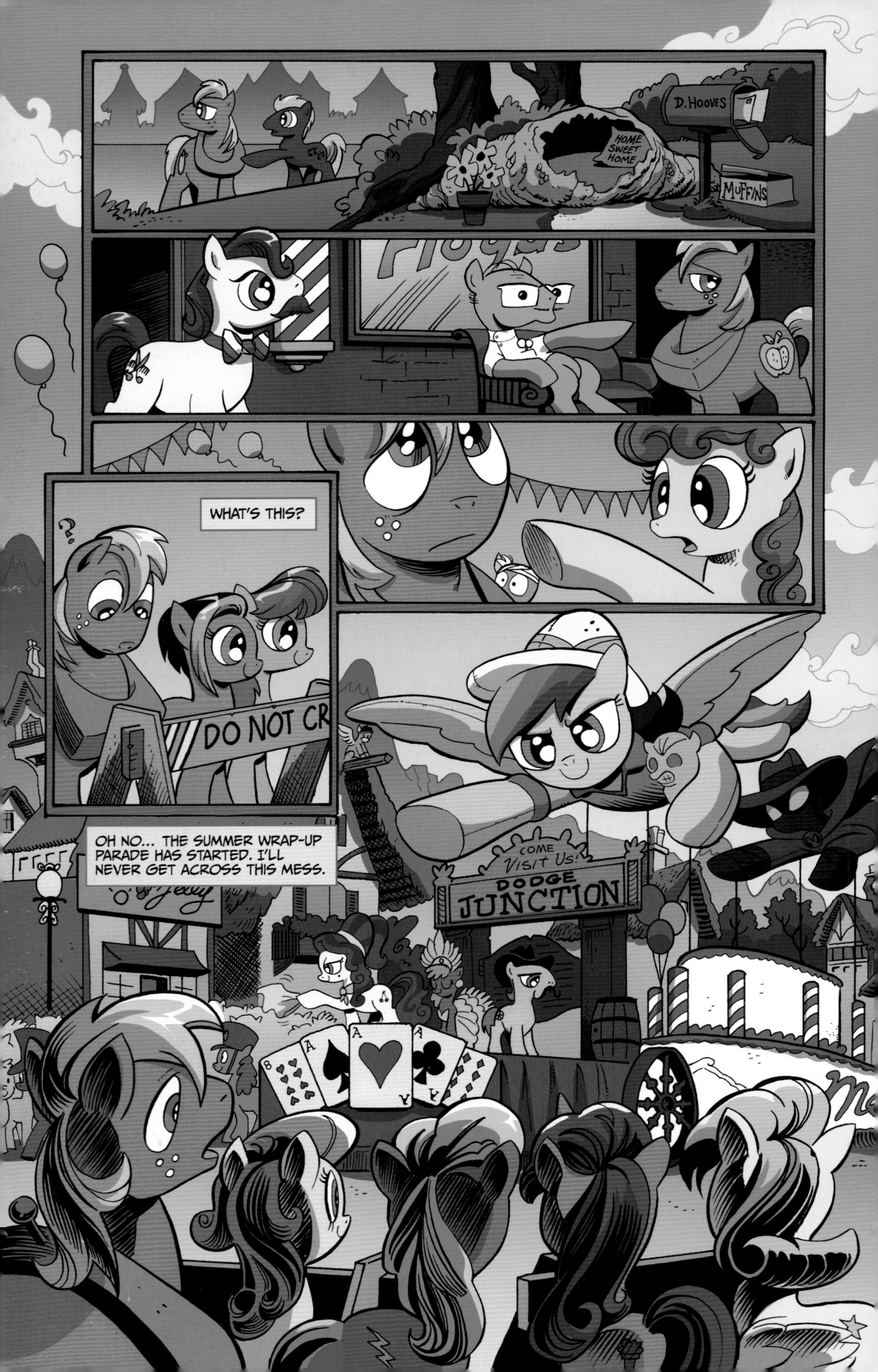

D. HOOVES
HOME SWEET HOME
MUFFINS
WHAT'S THIS?
DO NOT CR
OH NO... THE SUMMER WRAP-UP PARADE HAS STARTED. I'LL NEVER GET ACROSS THIS MESS.
COME Visit Us!
DODGE JUNCTION

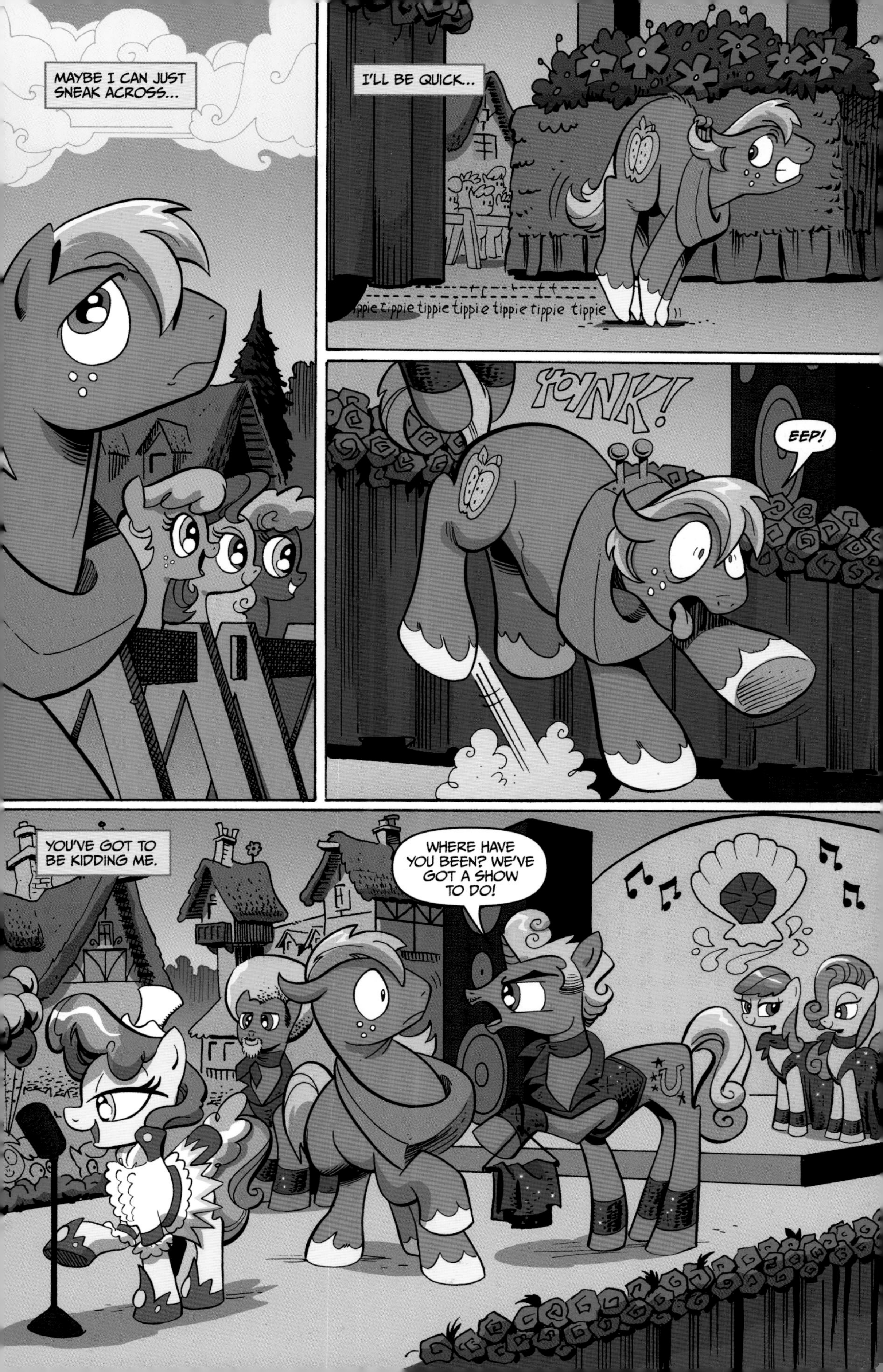
MAYBE I CAN JUST SNEAK ACROSS...
I'LL BE QUICK...
tippie tippie tippie tippie tippie tippie tippie
YOINK!
EEP!
YOU'VE GOT TO BE KIDDING ME.
WHERE HAVE YOU BEEN? WE'VE GOT A SHOW TO DO!

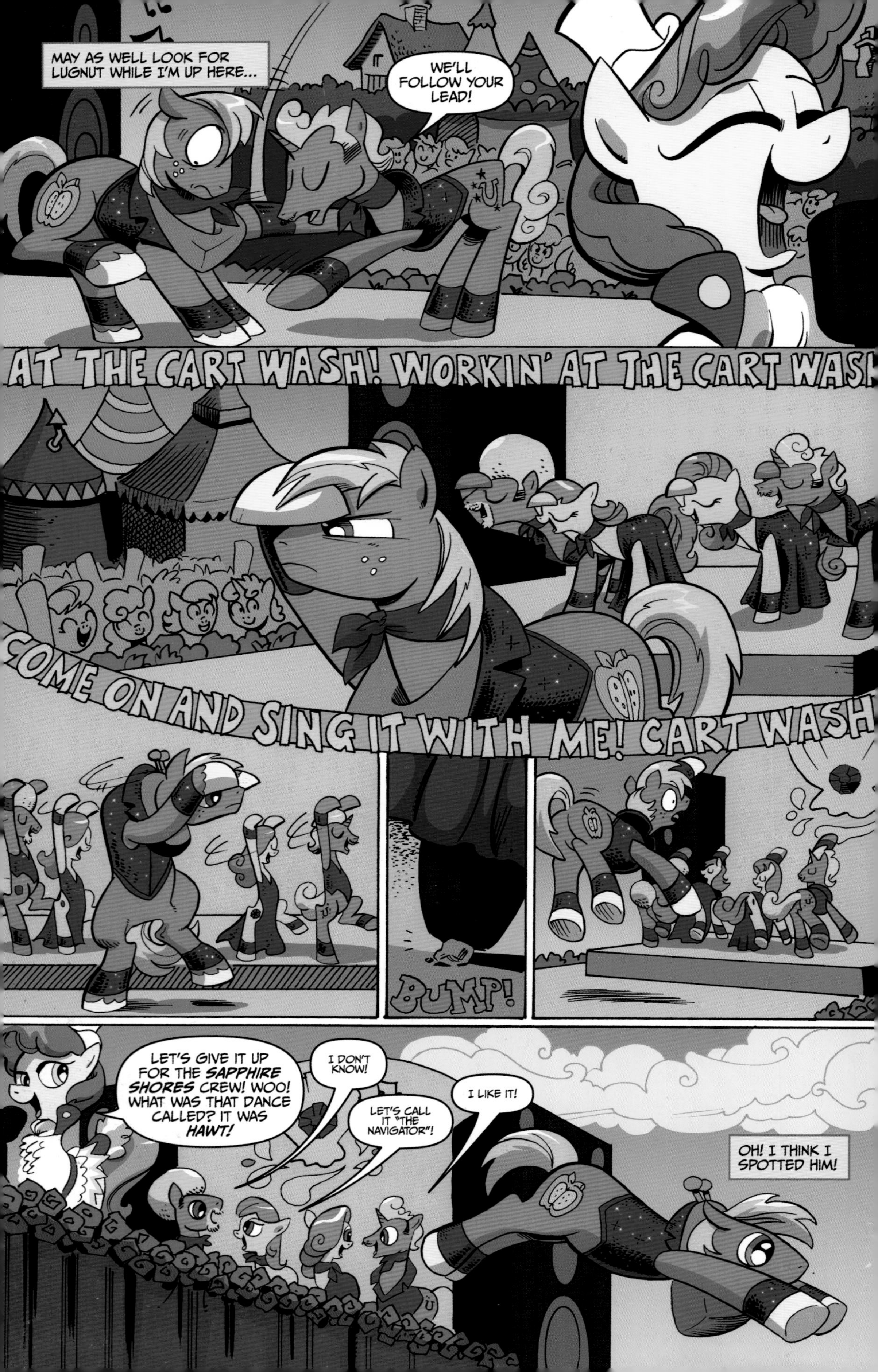

MAY AS WELL LOOK FOR LUGNUT WHILE I'M UP HERE...
WE'LL FOLLOW YOUR LEAD!
AT THE CART WASH! WORKIN' AT THE CART WASH
COME ON AND SING IT WITH ME! CART WASH
BUMP!
LET'S GIVE IT UP FOR THE SAPPHIRE SHORES CREW! WOO! WHAT WAS THAT DANCE CALLED? IT WAS HAWT!
I DON'T KNOW!
LET'S CALL IT "THE NAVIGATOR"!
I LIKE IT!
OH! I THINK I SPOTTED HIM!

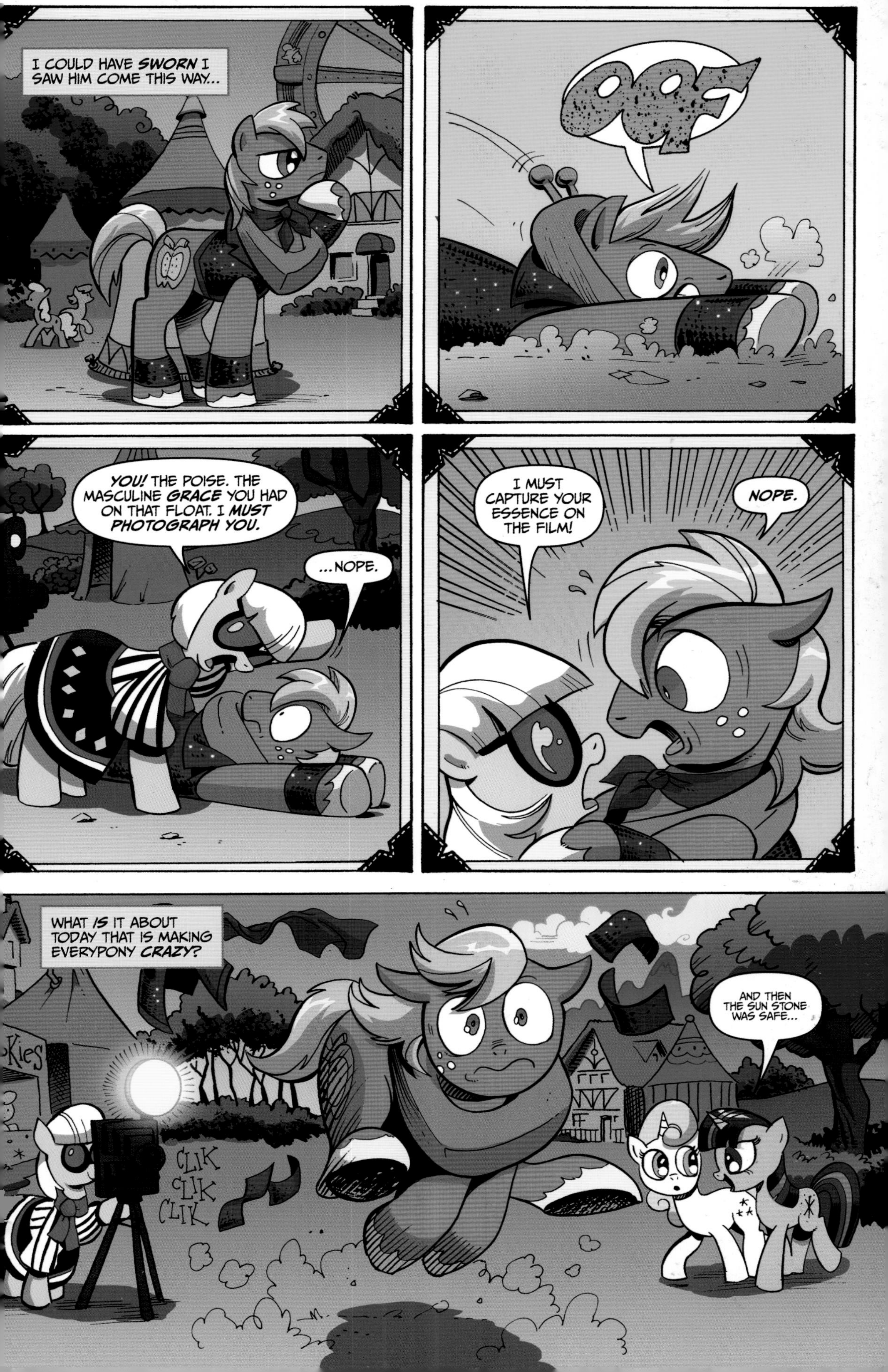
I COULD HAVE *SWORN* I SAW HIM COME THIS WAY...
OOF
YOU! THE POISE. THE MASCULINE *GRACE* YOU HAD ON THAT FLOAT. I *MUST PHOTOGRAPH YOU.*
...NOPE.
I MUST CAPTURE YOUR ESSENCE ON THE FILM!
NOPE.
WHAT *IS* IT ABOUT TODAY THAT IS MAKING EVERYPONY *CRAZY?*
AND THEN THE SUN STONE WAS SAFE...
CLIK CLIK CLIK

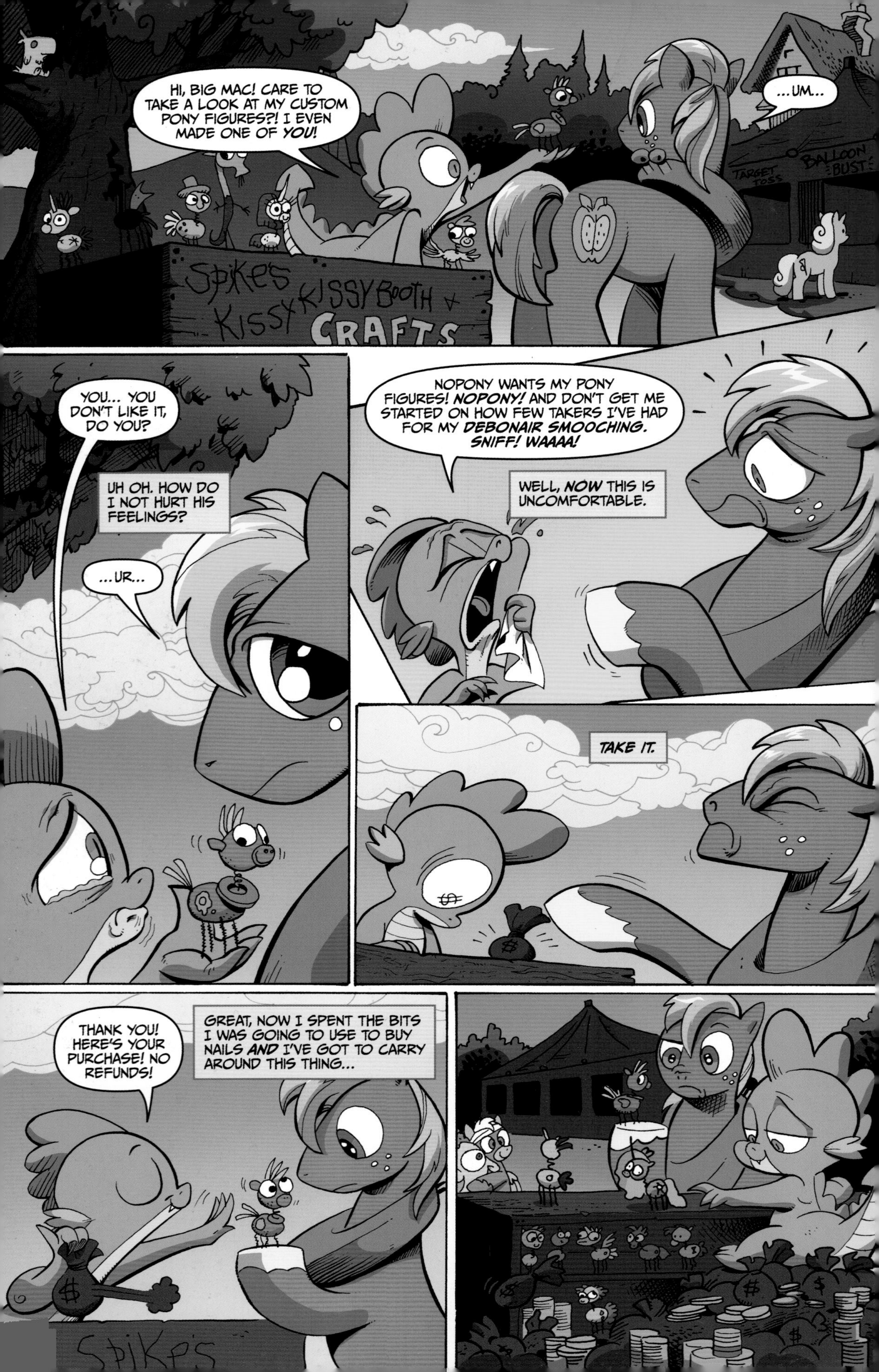
HI, BIG MAC! CARE TO TAKE A LOOK AT MY CUSTOM PONY FIGURES?! I EVEN MADE ONE OF *YOU*!
...UM...
SPIKE'S KISSY KISSY BOOTH + CRAFTS
TARGET TOSS
BALLOON BUST
YOU... YOU DON'T LIKE IT, DO YOU?
UH OH. HOW DO I NOT HURT HIS FEELINGS?
...UR...
NOPONY WANTS MY PONY FIGURES! *NOPONY!* AND DON'T GET ME STARTED ON HOW FEW TAKERS I'VE HAD FOR MY *DEBONAIR SMOOCHING. SNIFF! WAAAA!*
WELL, *NOW* THIS IS UNCOMFORTABLE.
TAKE IT.
THANK YOU! HERE'S YOUR PURCHASE! NO REFUNDS!
GREAT, NOW I SPENT THE BITS I WAS GOING TO USE TO BUY NAILS *AND* I'VE GOT TO CARRY AROUND THIS THING...
SPIKE'S

HERE.

WELL, *THAT* GOT RID OF *THAT*.

SPRING... WEDDING...

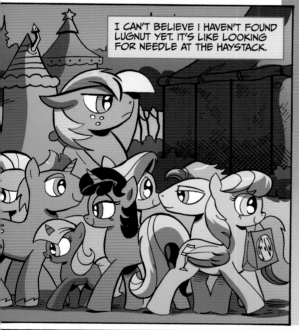

I CAN'T BELIEVE I HAVEN'T FOUND LUGNUT YET. IT'S LIKE LOOKING FOR NEEDLE AT THE HAYSTACK.

AND BY THAT, I MEAN IT'S HARD TO FIND GREAT UNCLE NEEDLE AT THE HAYSTACK APPLE FESTIVAL. THAT PLACE IS A MADHOUSE.

STICK AROUND EVERYONE! WE'VE GOT A *MUSICAL NUMBER* COMING UP ABOUT THIS GREAT PRODUCT!

THE BROTHERS FLIM & FLAM
PARASPRITE Away

STAY FOR THE WHOLE SONG AND YOU'LL GET 5 BOTTLES FOR THE PRICE OF 7!

RELIABLE! CITRUS SCENT

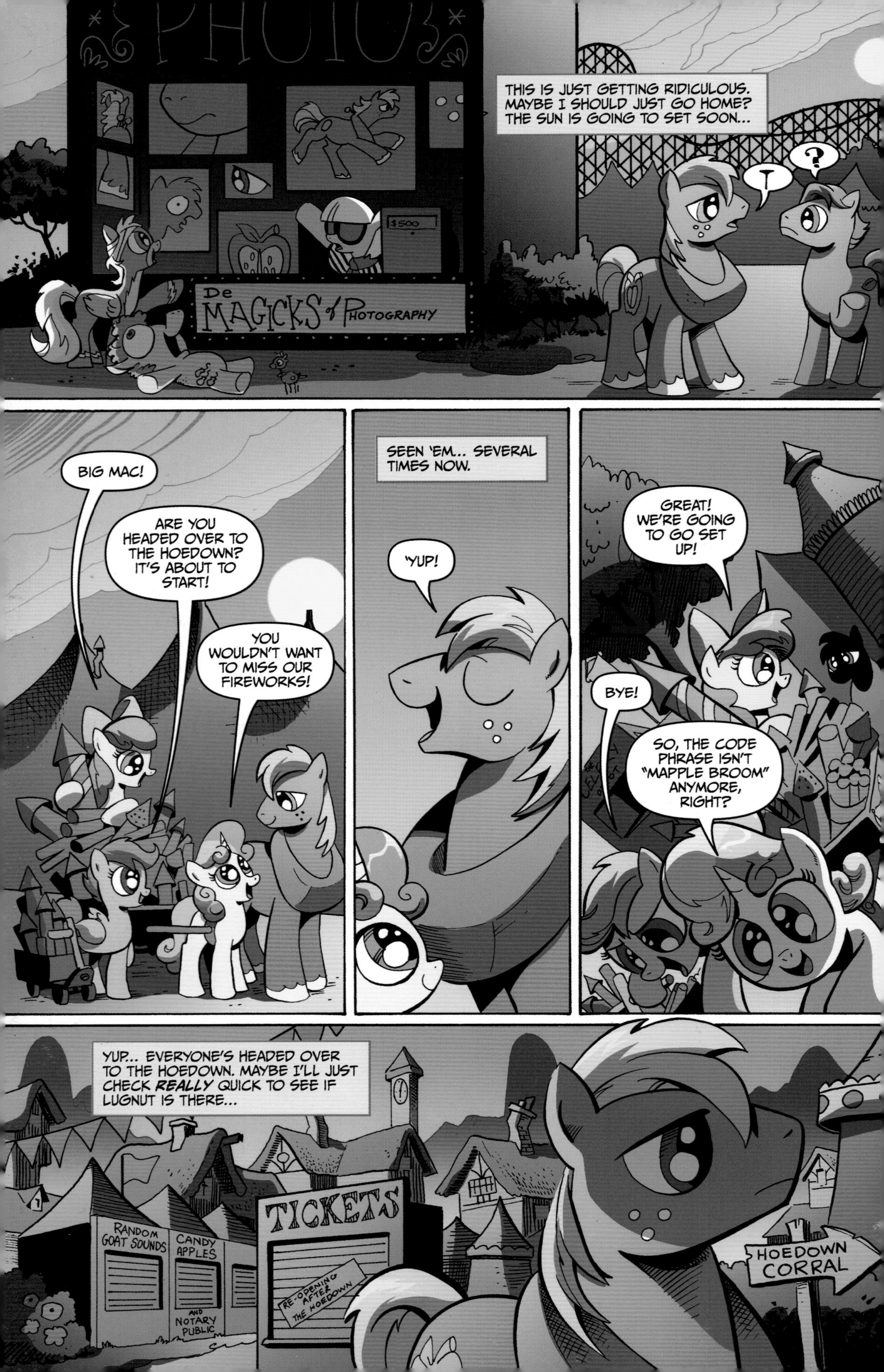
PHOTO
$500
De MAGICKS of PHOTOGRAPHY
THIS IS JUST GETTING RIDICULOUS. MAYBE I SHOULD JUST GO HOME? THE SUN IS GOING TO SET SOON...
?
BIG MAC!
ARE YOU HEADED OVER TO THE HOEDOWN? IT'S ABOUT TO START!
YOU WOULDN'T WANT TO MISS OUR FIREWORKS!
SEEN 'EM... SEVERAL TIMES NOW.
'YUP!
GREAT! WE'RE GOING TO GO SET UP!
BYE!
SO, THE CODE PHRASE ISN'T "MAPPLE BROOM" ANYMORE, RIGHT?
YUP... EVERYONE'S HEADED OVER TO THE HOEDOWN. MAYBE I'LL JUST CHECK *REALLY* QUICK TO SEE IF LUGNUT IS THERE...
RANDOM GOAT SOUNDS
CANDY APPLES
AND NOTARY PUBLIC
TICKETS
RE-OPENING AFTER THE HOEDOWN
HOEDOWN CORRAL

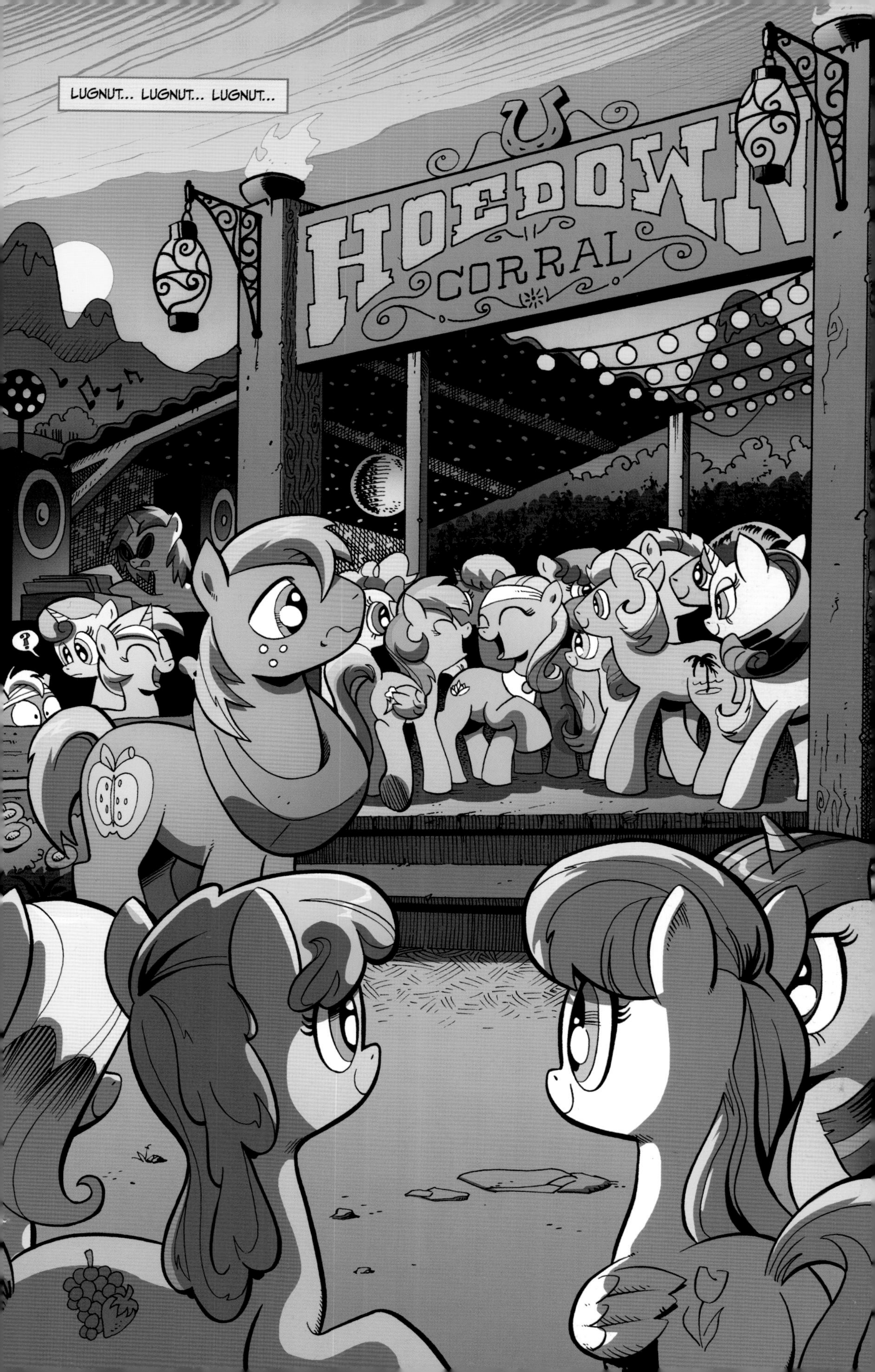
LUGNUT... LUGNUT... LUGNUT...
HOEDOWN
CORRAL
?

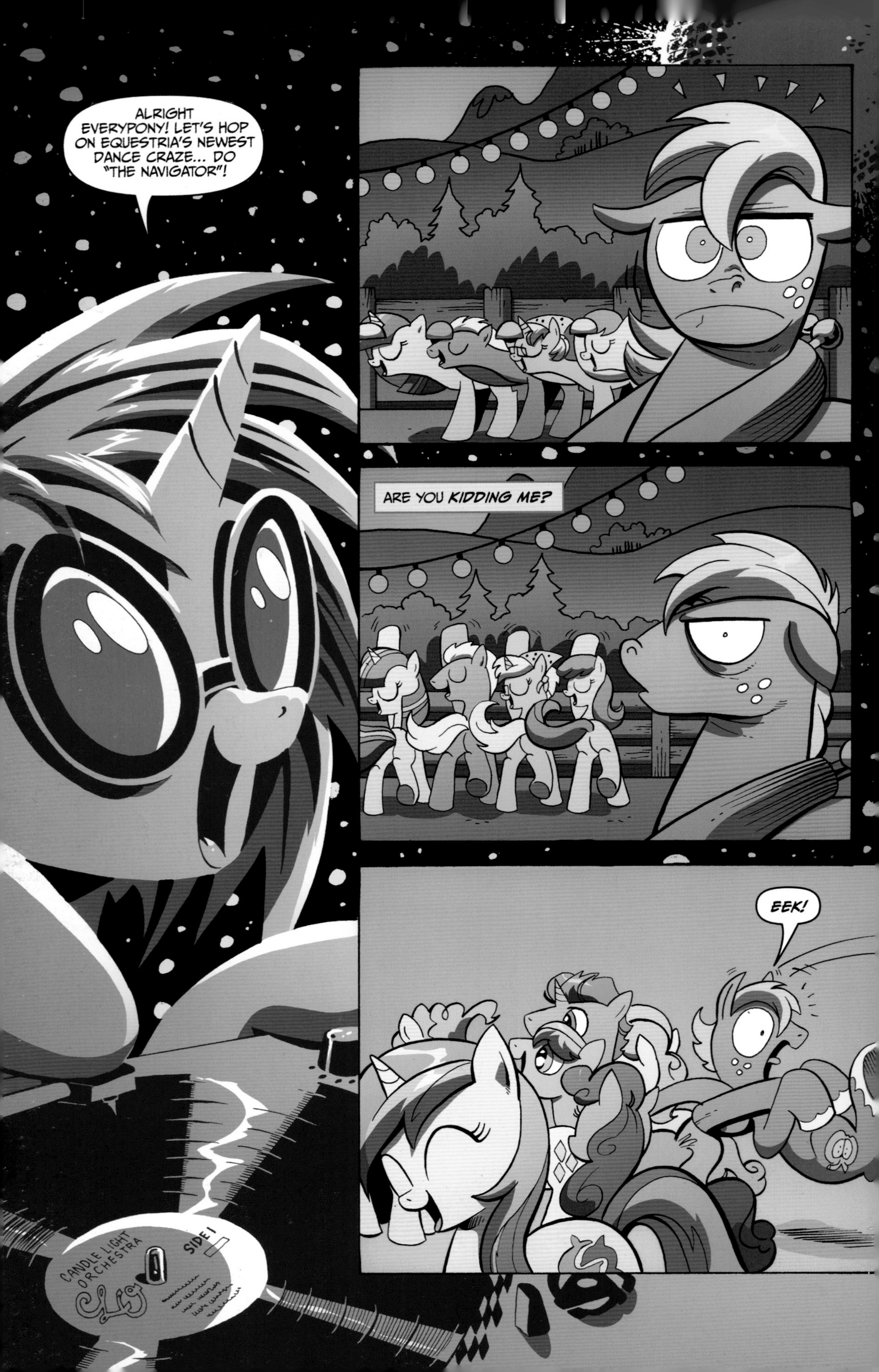
ALRIGHT EVERYPONY! LET'S HOP ON EQUESTRIA'S NEWEST DANCE CRAZE... DO "THE NAVIGATOR"!
ARE YOU *KIDDING ME?*
EEK!
CANDLE LIGHT ORCHESTRA
SIDE I

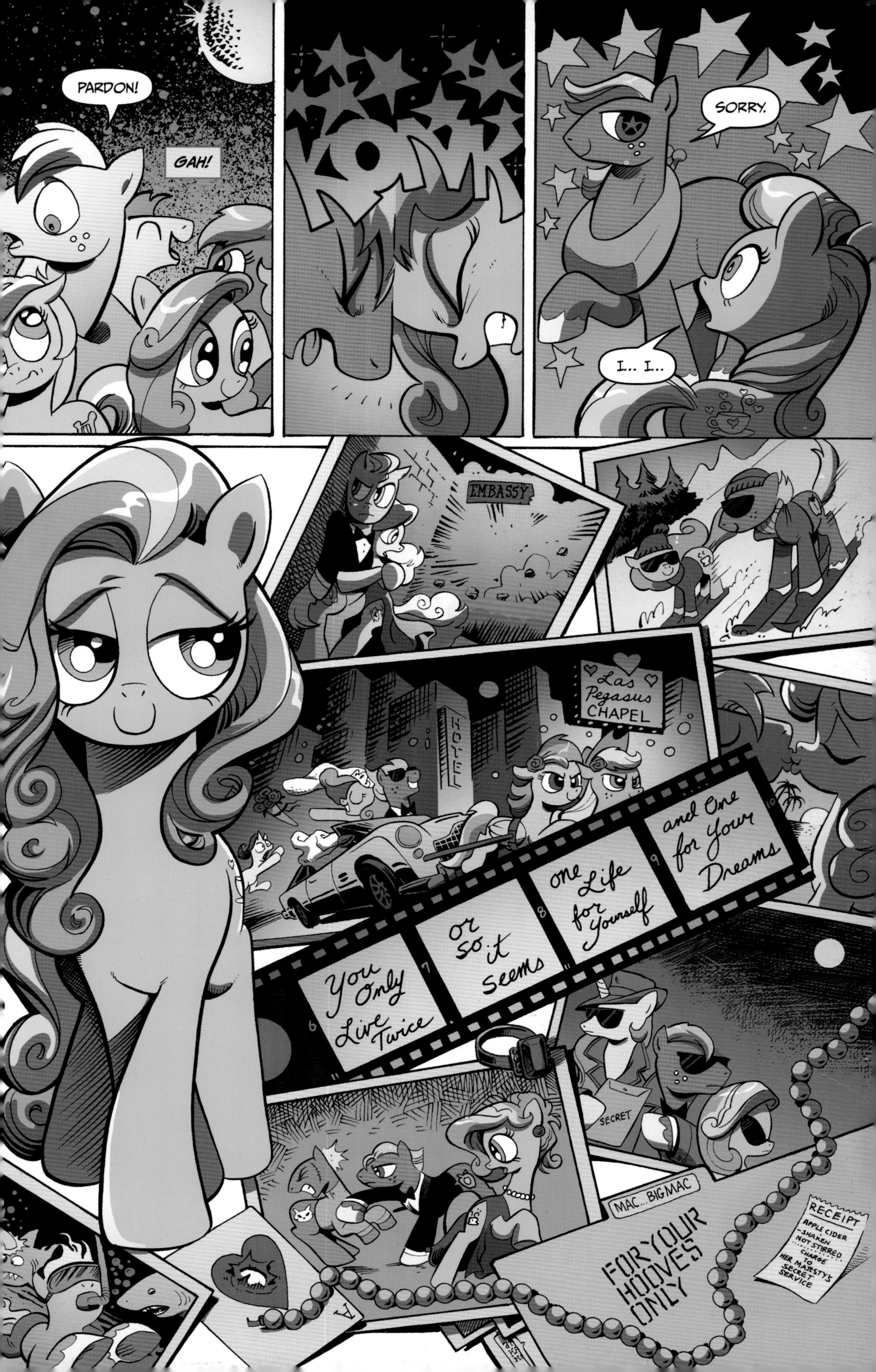
PARDON!
GAH!
KONK
SORRY.
I... I...
EMBASSY
Las Pegasus CHAPEL
HOTEL
You Only Live Twice
or so it seems
one Life for yourself
and One for Your Dreams
SECRET
MAC... BIG MAC
FOR YOUR HOOVES ONLY
RECEIPT
APPLE CIDER
-SHAKEN
NOT STIRRED
CHARGE TO
HER MAJESTY'S SECRET SERVICE

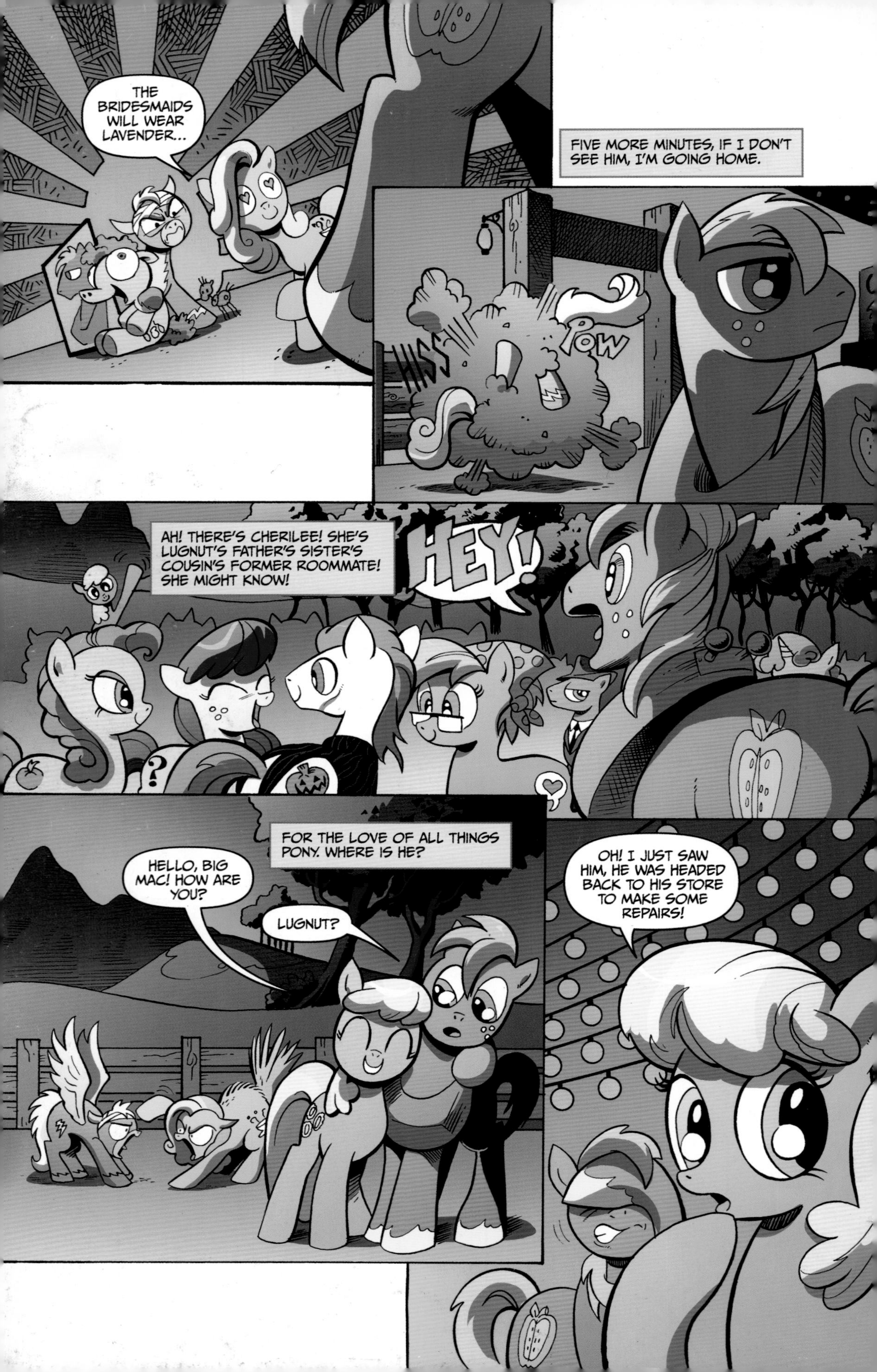
THE BRIDESMAIDS WILL WEAR LAVENDER...
FIVE MORE MINUTES, IF I DON'T SEE HIM, I'M GOING HOME.
HISS
POW
AH! THERE'S CHERILEE! SHE'S LUGNUT'S FATHER'S SISTER'S COUSIN'S FORMER ROOMMATE! SHE MIGHT KNOW!
HEY!
FOR THE LOVE OF ALL THINGS PONY. WHERE IS HE?
HELLO, BIG MAC! HOW ARE YOU?
LUGNUT?
OH! I JUST SAW HIM, HE WAS HEADED BACK TO HIS STORE TO MAKE SOME REPAIRS!

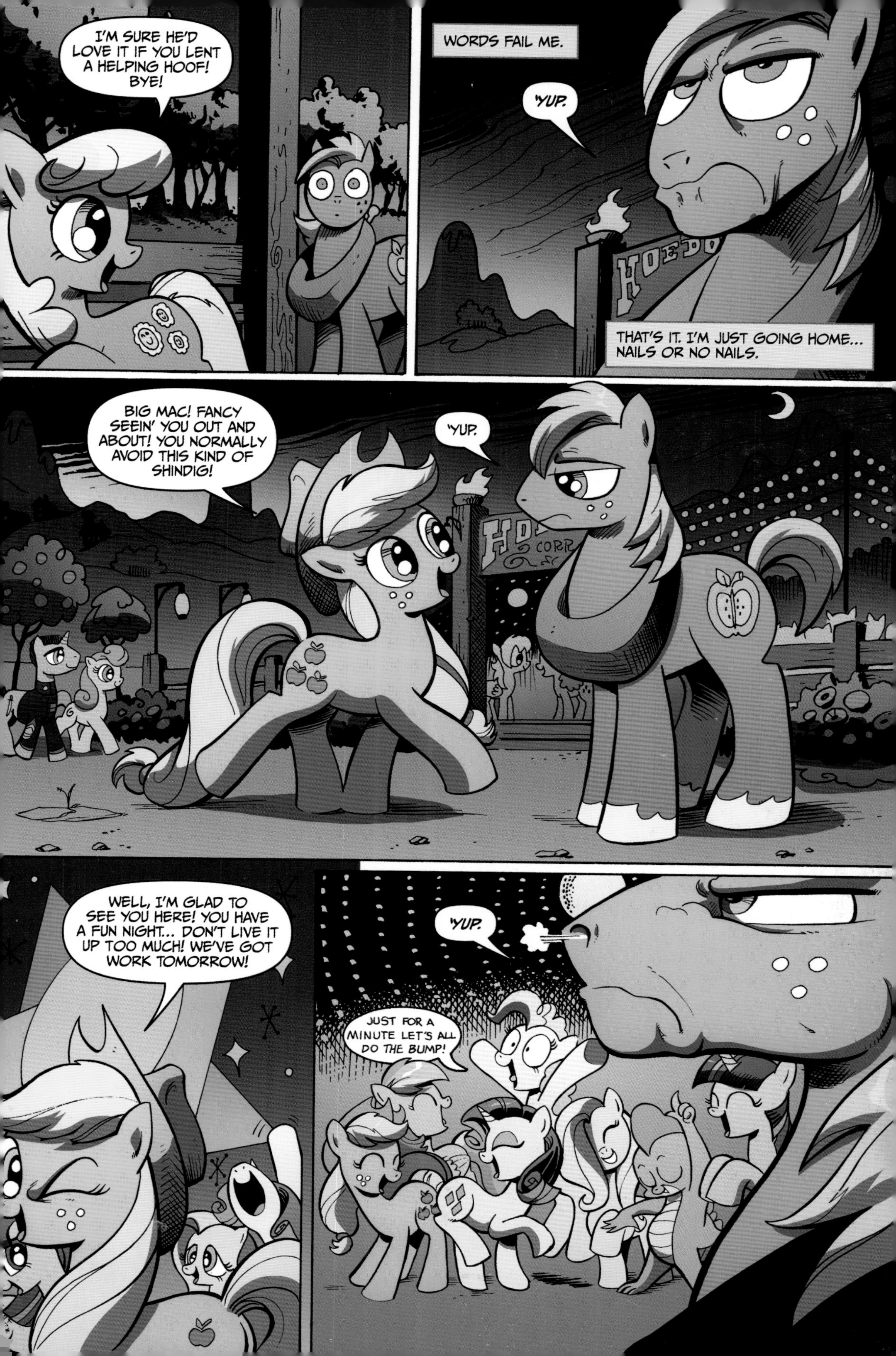
I'M SURE HE'D LOVE IT IF YOU LENT A HELPING HOOF! BYE!
WORDS FAIL ME.
'YUP.
THAT'S IT. I'M JUST GOING HOME... NAILS OR NO NAILS.
BIG MAC! FANCY SEEIN' YOU OUT AND ABOUT! YOU NORMALLY AVOID THIS KIND OF SHINDIG!
'YUP.
WELL, I'M GLAD TO SEE YOU HERE! YOU HAVE A FUN NIGHT... DON'T LIVE IT UP TOO MUCH! WE'VE GOT WORK TOMORROW!
'YUP.
JUST FOR A MINUTE LET'S ALL DO THE BUMP!

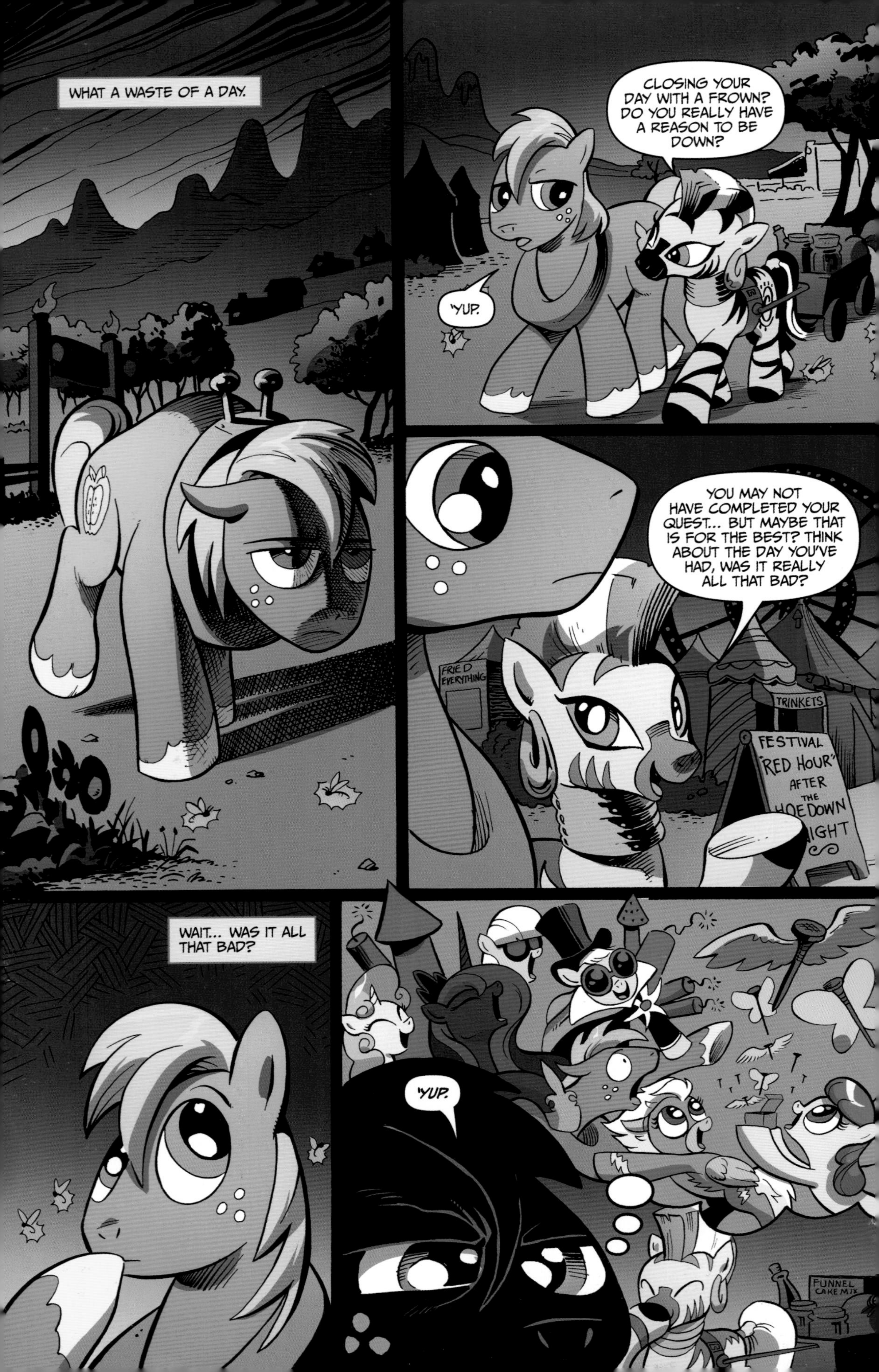
WHAT A WASTE OF A DAY.
CLOSING YOUR DAY WITH A FROWN? DO YOU REALLY HAVE A REASON TO BE DOWN?
'YUP.
YOU MAY NOT HAVE COMPLETED YOUR QUEST... BUT MAYBE THAT IS FOR THE BEST? THINK ABOUT THE DAY YOU'VE HAD, WAS IT REALLY ALL THAT BAD?
FRIED EVERYTHING
TRINKETS
FESTIVAL "RED HOUR" AFTER THE HOEDOWN
IGHT
WAIT... WAS IT ALL THAT BAD?
'YUP.
FUNNEL CAKE MIX

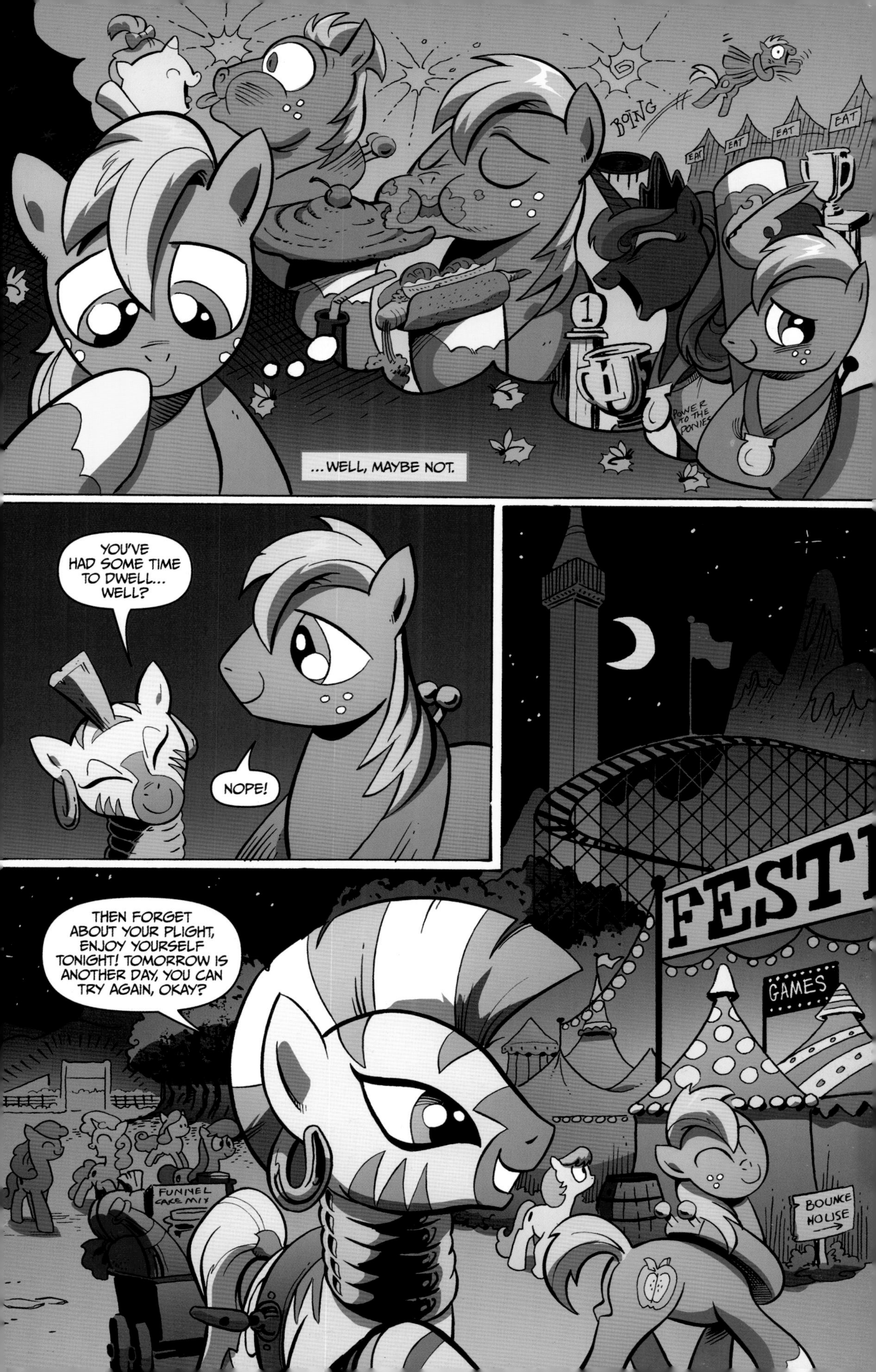
BOING
EAT
EAT
EAT
EAT
1
POWER TO THE PONIES
...WELL, MAYBE NOT.
YOU'VE HAD SOME TIME TO DWELL... WELL?
NOPE!
FEST
GAMES
THEN FORGET ABOUT YOUR PLIGHT, ENJOY YOURSELF TONIGHT! TOMORROW IS ANOTHER DAY, YOU CAN TRY AGAIN, OKAY?
FUNNEL CAKE MIX
BOUNCE HOUSE

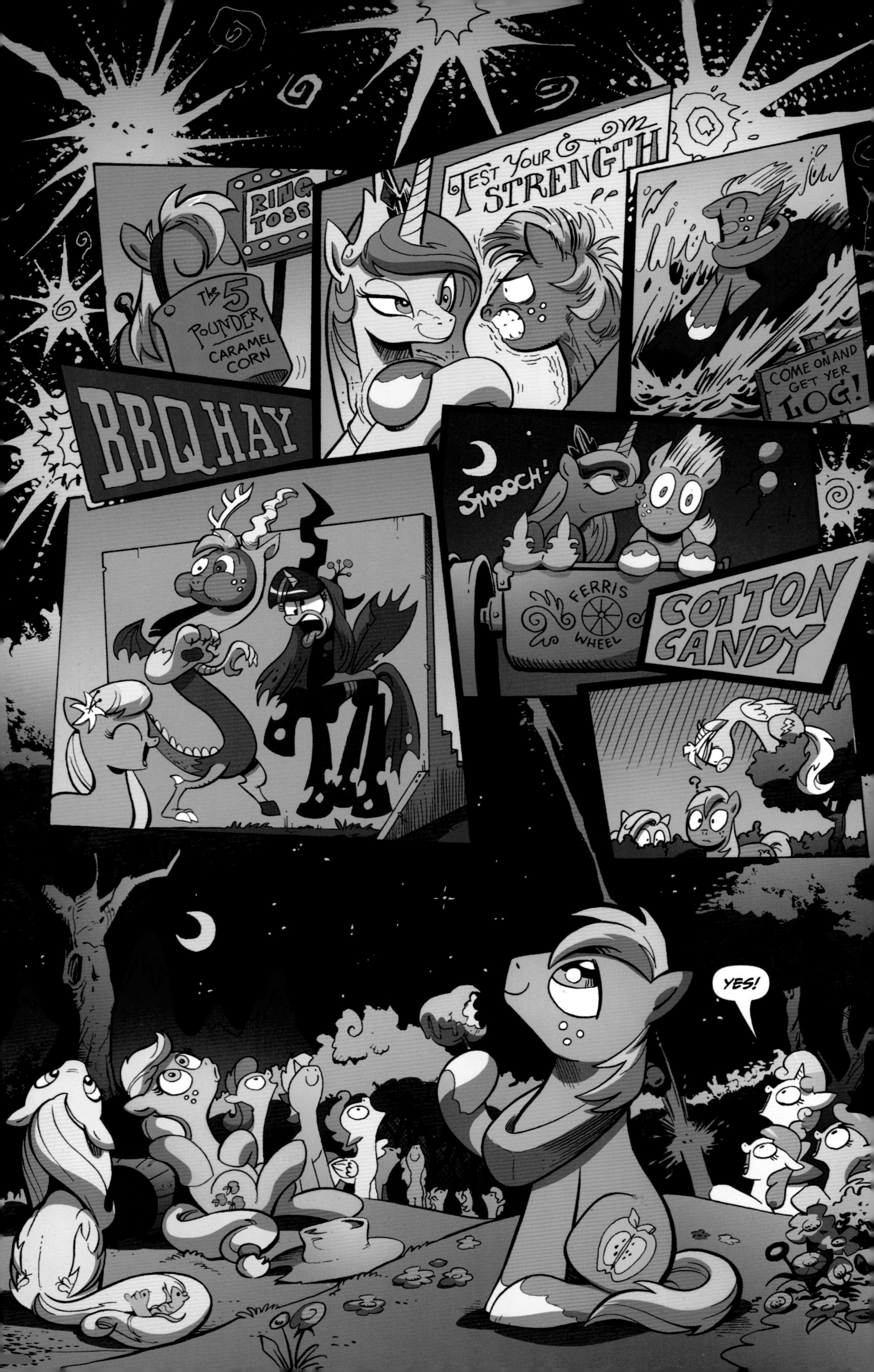

RING TOSS
The 5 POUNDER CARAMEL CORN
TEST YOUR STRENGTH
COME ON AND GET YER LOG!
BBQ HAY
SMOOCH!
FERRIS WHEEL
COTTON CANDY
YES!

WHATA' NIGHT... SO TIRED...

HAY'S HARDWARE

HARDWARE

RECEIVING

BIG MAC! THERE YOU ARE! I WAS LOOKING FOR YOU!

?

ROASTED CARROTS

I NEEDED SOME NAILS TO DO SOME REPAIRS... ALL MINE MELTED IN THE BLAST! SO I WENT AND BORROWED SOME FROM THE FARM, IS THAT OKAY?

FARM... HAD... NAILS?

WHAT?

HAY'S HARDWARE STORE 15 GANDOLFINI LANE

YEP! YOUR LITTLE SISTER HAD THEM ALL OUT AT HER CLUBHOUSE! BETWEEN HER STASH AND TAKING APART *THAT* THING, I'M GOOD!

...'YUP.

APPLE BLOOM IS MUCKING OUT EVERY PIG STALL TOMORROW. EVERY ONE OF THEM.

SHORT NAILS   BLACK NAILS   LONG NAILS   SILVER NAILS   TINY NAILS

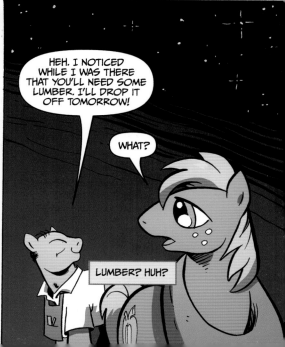

HEH. I NOTICED WHILE I WAS THERE THAT YOU'LL NEED SOME LUMBER. I'LL DROP IT OFF TOMORROW!

WHAT?

LUMBER? HUH?

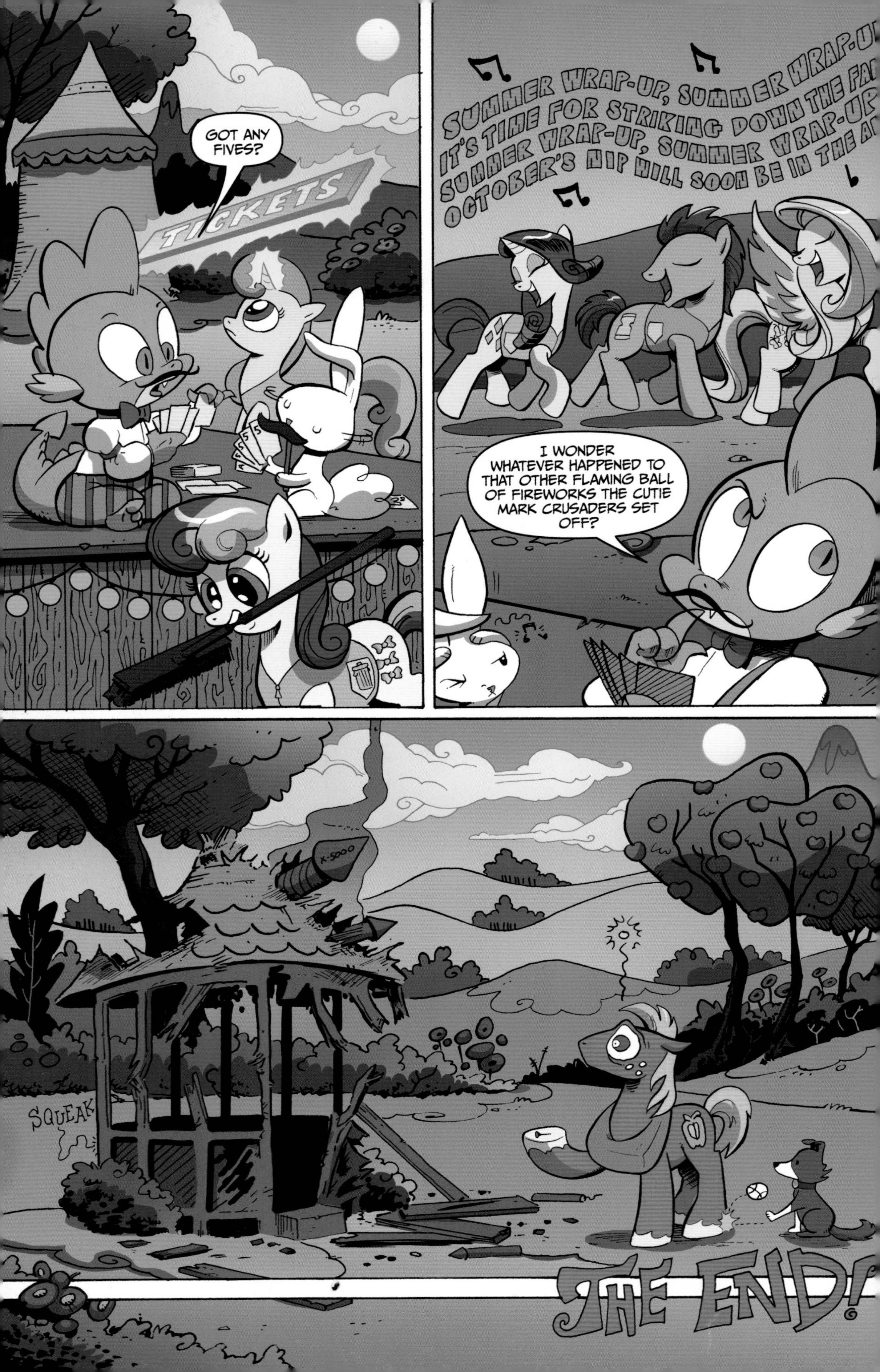
GOT ANY FIVES?
TICKETS
SUMMER WRAP-UP, SUMMER WRAP-U
IT'S TIME FOR STRIKING DOWN THE FA
SUMMER WRAP-UP, SUMMER WRAP-UP
OCTOBER'S NIP WILL SOON BE IN THE A
I WONDER WHATEVER HAPPENED TO THAT OTHER FLAMING BALL OF FIREWORKS THE CUTIE MARK CRUSADERS SET OFF?
X-5000
SQUEAK
THE END!

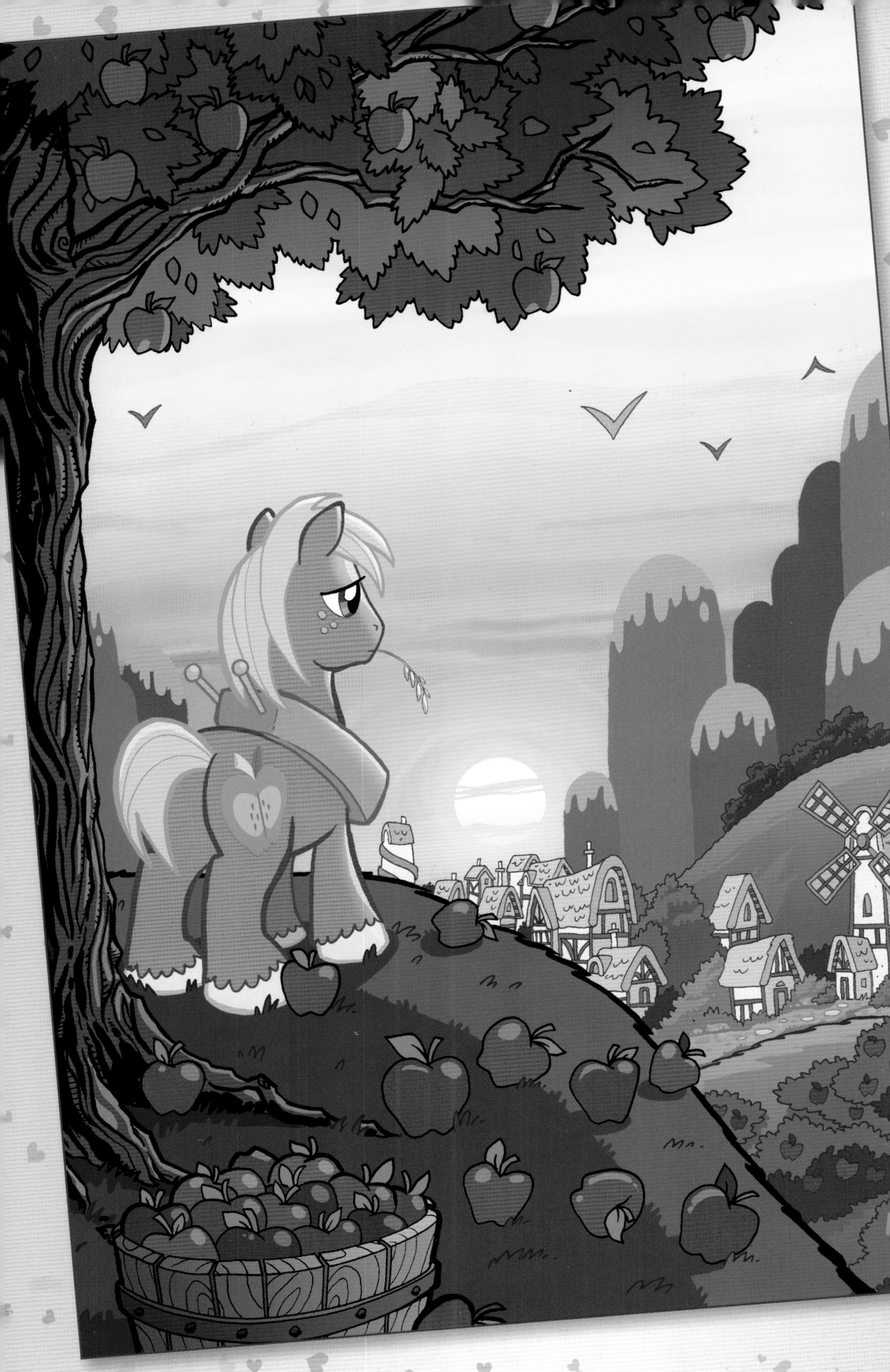
AMF! '13

art BY Tony Fleecs

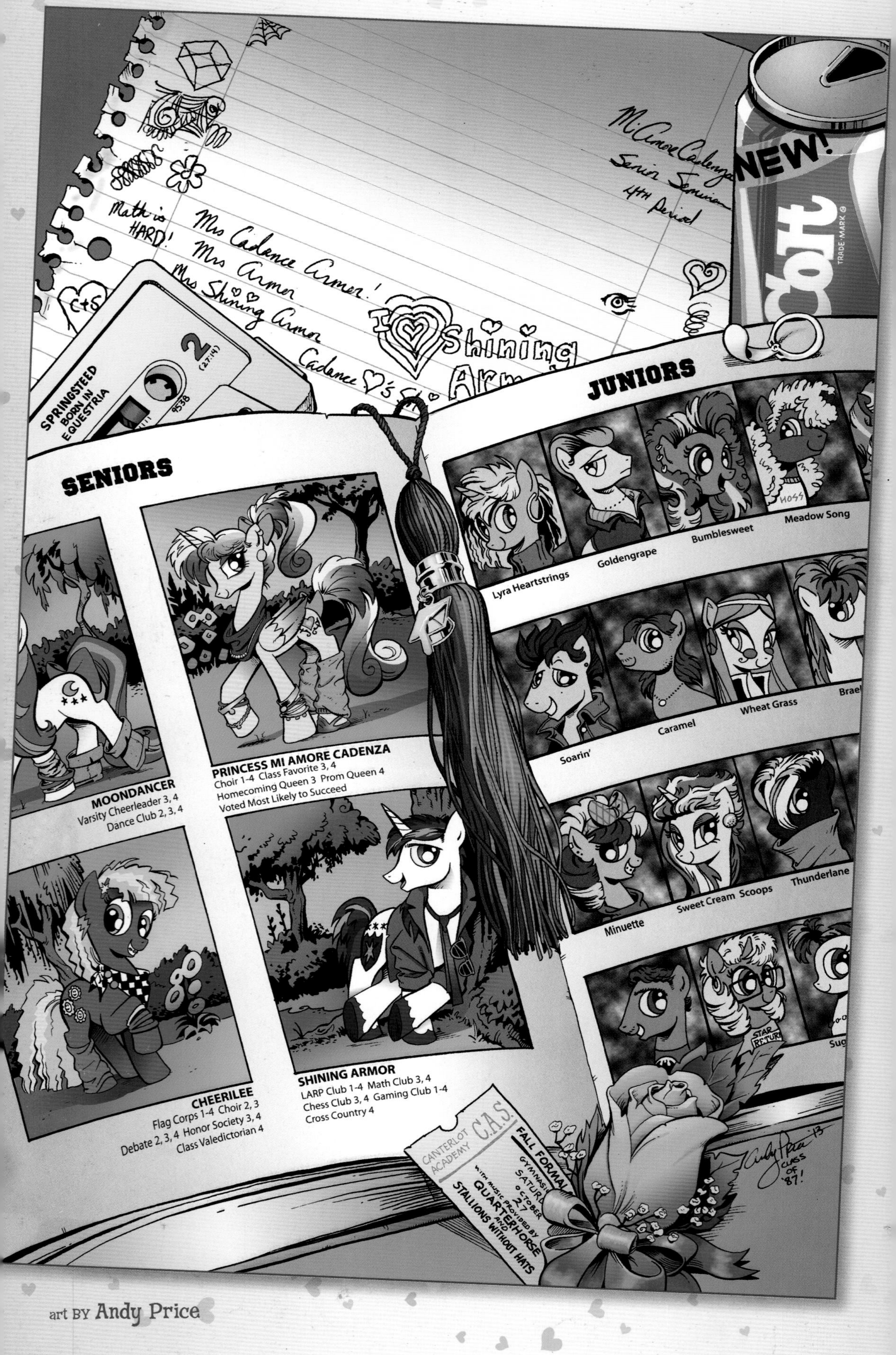
Mi Amore Cadenza
Senior Seminar
4th Period
Math is HARD!
Mrs Cadance Armor!
Mrs Armor
Mrs Shining Armor
Cadance ♡'s
I ♡ Shining Armor
NEW!
TRADE-MARK
SPRINGSTEED
BORN IN EQUESTRIA
2
(27:14)
4538
SENIORS
MOONDANCER
Varsity Cheerleader 3, 4
Dance Club 2, 3, 4
PRINCESS MI AMORE CADENZA
Choir 1-4 Class Favorite 3, 4
Homecoming Queen 3 Prom Queen 4
Voted Most Likely to Succeed
CHEERILEE
Flag Corps 1-4 Choir 2, 3
Debate 2, 3, 4 Honor Society 3, 4
Class Valedictorian 4
SHINING ARMOR
LARP Club 1-4 Math Club 3, 4
Chess Club 3, 4 Gaming Club 1-4
Cross Country 4
JUNIORS
Lyra Heartstrings
Goldengrape
Bumblesweet
Meadow Song
Soarin'
Caramel
Wheat Grass
Minuette
Sweet Cream Scoops
Thunderlane
CANTERLOT ACADEMY C.A.S.
FALL FORMAL
GYMNASIUM
SATURDAY
OCTOBER 27
WITH MUSIC PROVIDED BY
QUARTERHORSE
AND
STALLIONS WITHOUT HATS
Andy Price '13
CLASS OF '87!

art BY Andy Price

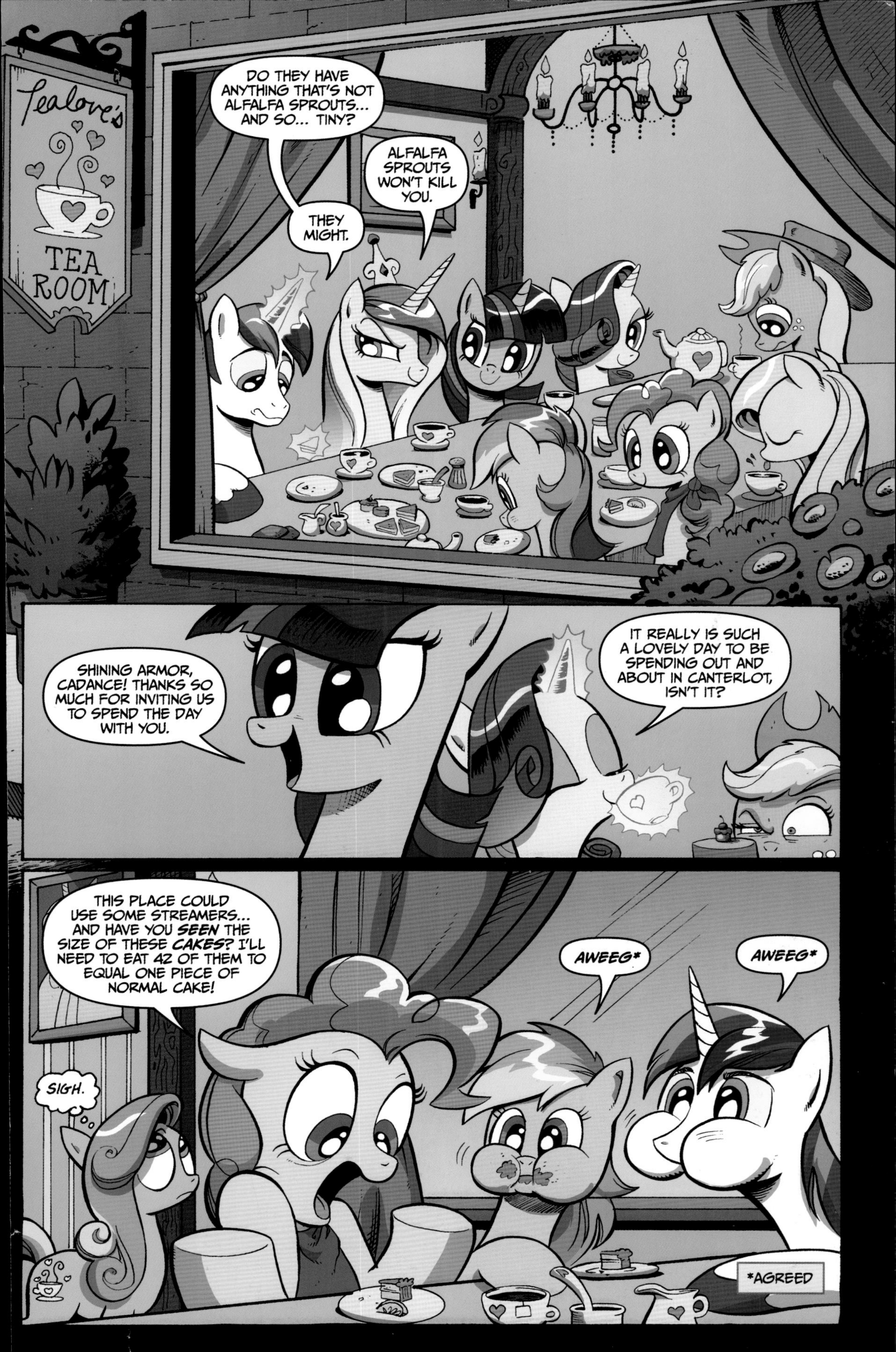
Tealove's
TEA ROOM
DO THEY HAVE ANYTHING THAT'S NOT ALFALFA SPROUTS... AND SO... TINY?
ALFALFA SPROUTS WON'T KILL YOU.
THEY MIGHT.
SHINING ARMOR, CADANCE! THANKS SO MUCH FOR INVITING US TO SPEND THE DAY WITH YOU.
IT REALLY IS SUCH A LOVELY DAY TO BE SPENDING OUT AND ABOUT IN CANTERLOT, ISN'T IT?
THIS PLACE COULD USE SOME STREAMERS... AND HAVE YOU SEEN THE SIZE OF THESE CAKES? I'LL NEED TO EAT 42 OF THEM TO EQUAL ONE PIECE OF NORMAL CAKE!
AWEEG*
AWEEG*
SIGH.
*AGREED

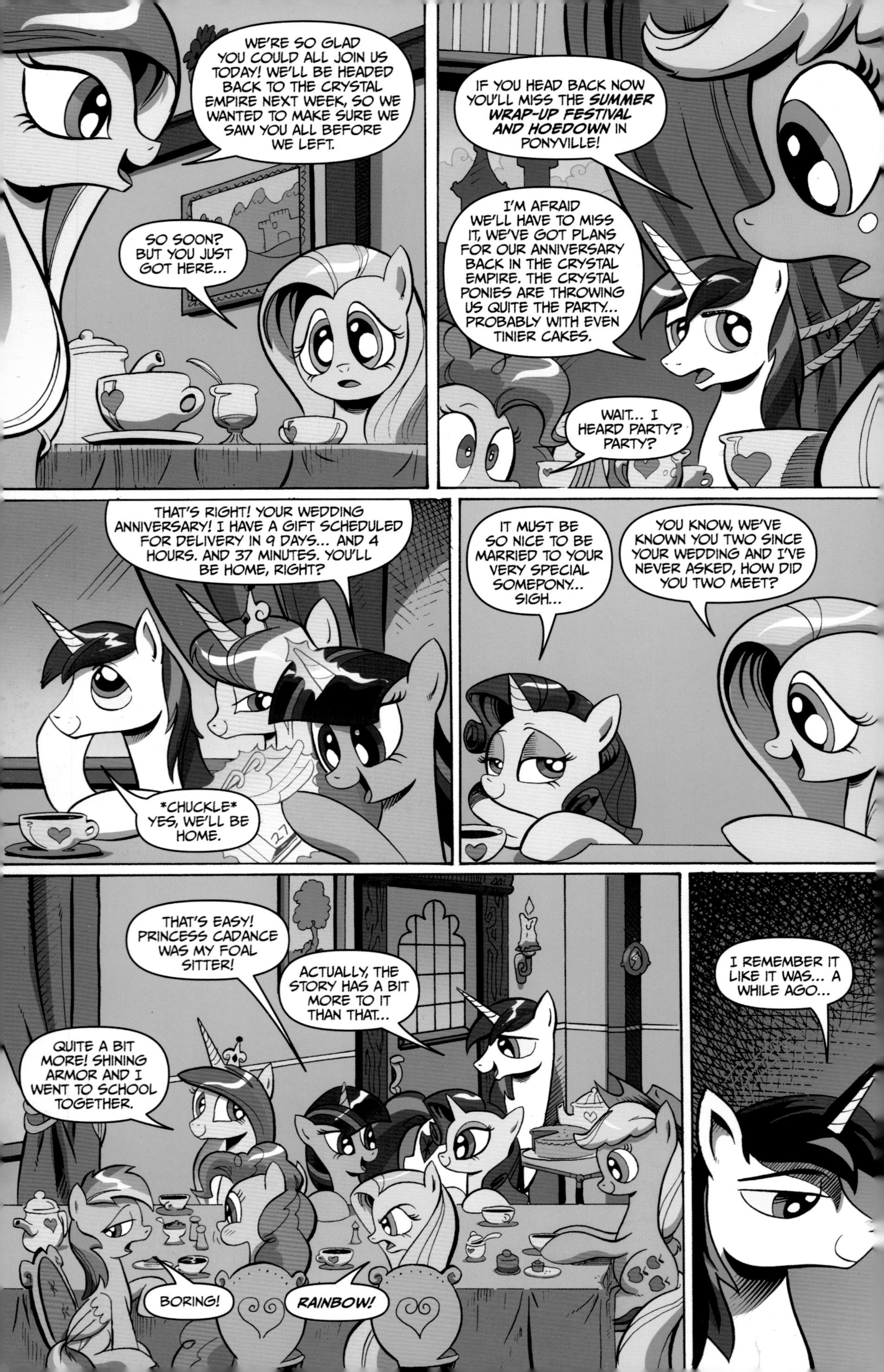
WE'RE SO GLAD YOU COULD ALL JOIN US TODAY! WE'LL BE HEADED BACK TO THE CRYSTAL EMPIRE NEXT WEEK, SO WE WANTED TO MAKE SURE WE SAW YOU ALL BEFORE WE LEFT.
SO SOON? BUT YOU JUST GOT HERE...
IF YOU HEAD BACK NOW YOU'LL MISS THE SUMMER WRAP-UP FESTIVAL AND HOEDOWN IN PONYVILLE!
I'M AFRAID WE'LL HAVE TO MISS IT, WE'VE GOT PLANS FOR OUR ANNIVERSARY BACK IN THE CRYSTAL EMPIRE. THE CRYSTAL PONIES ARE THROWING US QUITE THE PARTY... PROBABLY WITH EVEN TINIER CAKES.
WAIT... I HEARD PARTY? PARTY?
THAT'S RIGHT! YOUR WEDDING ANNIVERSARY! I HAVE A GIFT SCHEDULED FOR DELIVERY IN 9 DAYS... AND 4 HOURS. AND 37 MINUTES. YOU'LL BE HOME, RIGHT?
CHUCKLE YES, WE'LL BE HOME.
27
IT MUST BE SO NICE TO BE MARRIED TO YOUR VERY SPECIAL SOMEPONY... SIGH...
YOU KNOW, WE'VE KNOWN YOU TWO SINCE YOUR WEDDING AND I'VE NEVER ASKED, HOW DID YOU TWO MEET?
THAT'S EASY! PRINCESS CADANCE WAS MY FOAL SITTER!
ACTUALLY, THE STORY HAS A BIT MORE TO IT THAN THAT...
QUITE A BIT MORE! SHINING ARMOR AND I WENT TO SCHOOL TOGETHER.
BORING!
RAINBOW!
I REMEMBER IT LIKE IT WAS... A WHILE AGO...

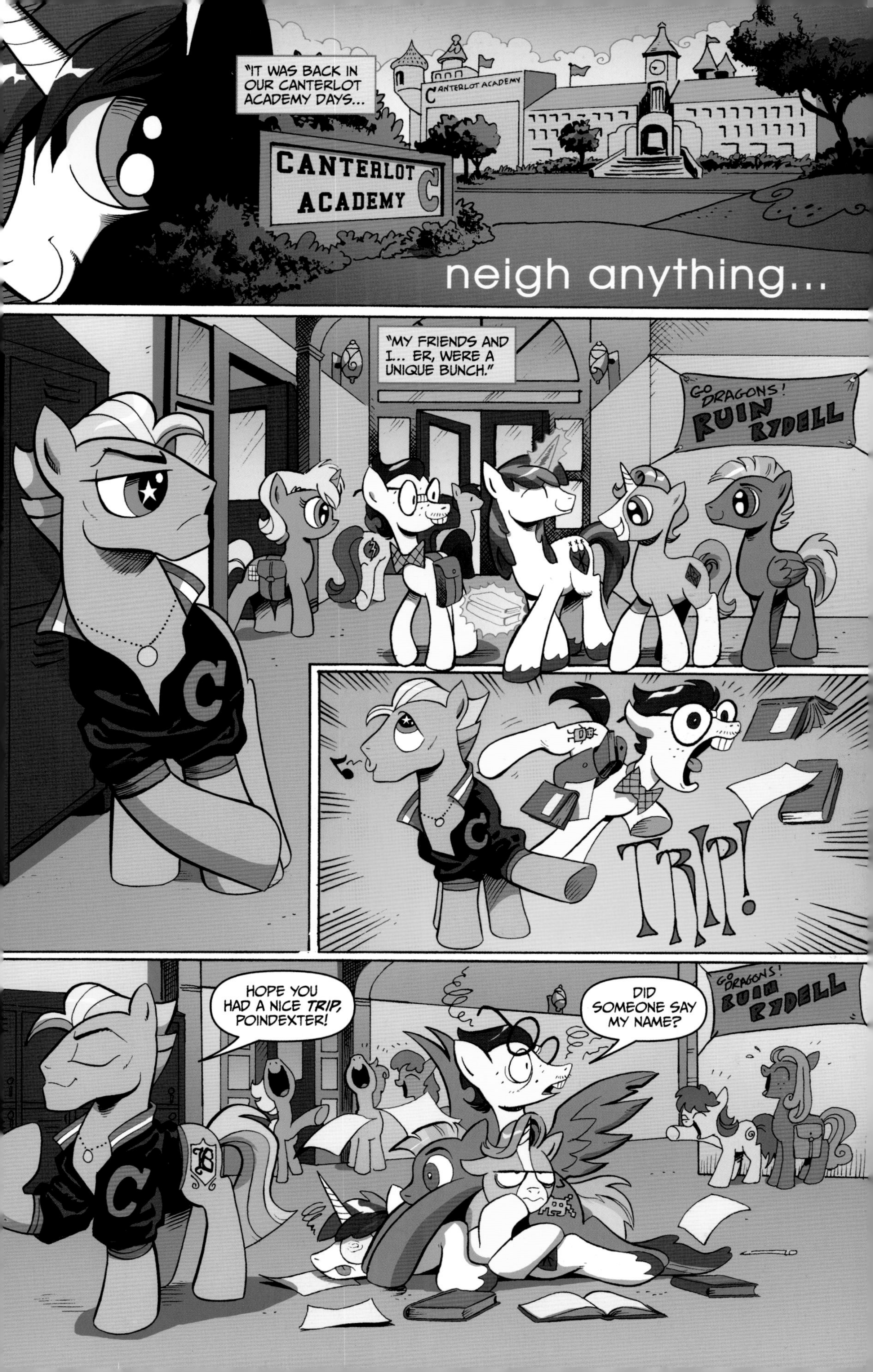

"IT WAS BACK IN OUR CANTERLOT ACADEMY DAYS...
CANTERLOT ACADEMY
CANTERLOT ACADEMY
neigh anything...
"MY FRIENDS AND I... ER, WERE A UNIQUE BUNCH."
GO DRAGONS! RUIN RYDELL
TRIP!
HOPE YOU HAD A NICE *TRIP*, POINDEXTER!
DID SOMEONE SAY MY NAME?
GO DRAGONS! RUIN RYDELL

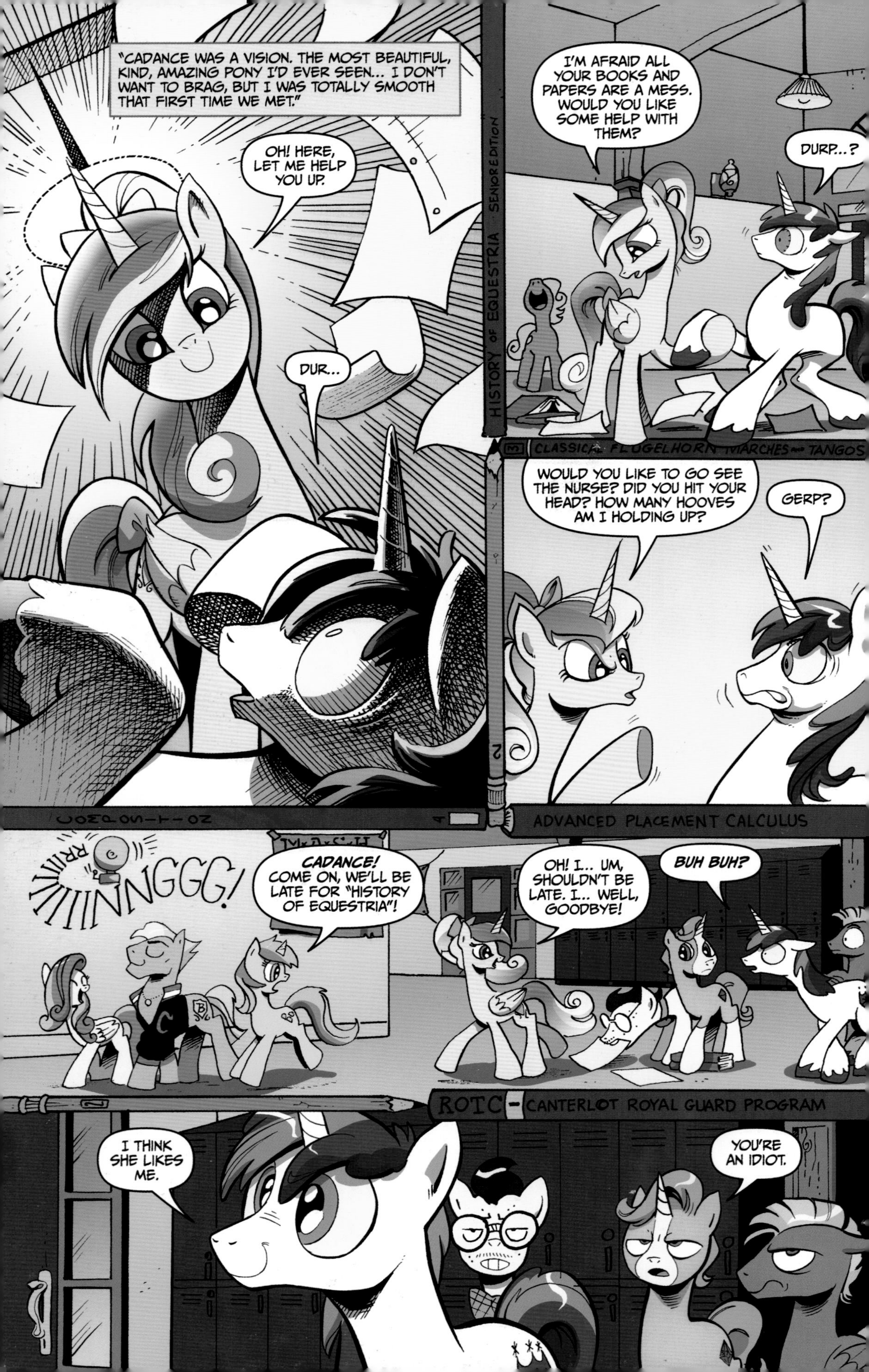
"CADANCE WAS A VISION. THE MOST BEAUTIFUL, KIND, AMAZING PONY I'D EVER SEEN... I DON'T WANT TO BRAG, BUT I WAS TOTALLY SMOOTH THAT FIRST TIME WE MET."
OH! HERE, LET ME HELP YOU UP.
DUR...
HISTORY of EQUESTRIA SENIOR EDITION
I'M AFRAID ALL YOUR BOOKS AND PAPERS ARE A MESS. WOULD YOU LIKE SOME HELP WITH THEM?
DURP...?
CLASSICAL FLUGELHORN MARCHES and TANGOS
WOULD YOU LIKE TO GO SEE THE NURSE? DID YOU HIT YOUR HEAD? HOW MANY HOOVES AM I HOLDING UP?
GERP?
ADVANCED PLACEMENT CALCULUS
RRIIIIIINNGGG!
CADANCE! COME ON, WE'LL BE LATE FOR "HISTORY OF EQUESTRIA"!
OH! I... UM, SHOULDN'T BE LATE. I... WELL, GOODBYE!
BUH BUH?
ROTC - CANTERLOT ROYAL GUARD PROGRAM
I THINK SHE LIKES ME.
YOU'RE AN IDIOT.

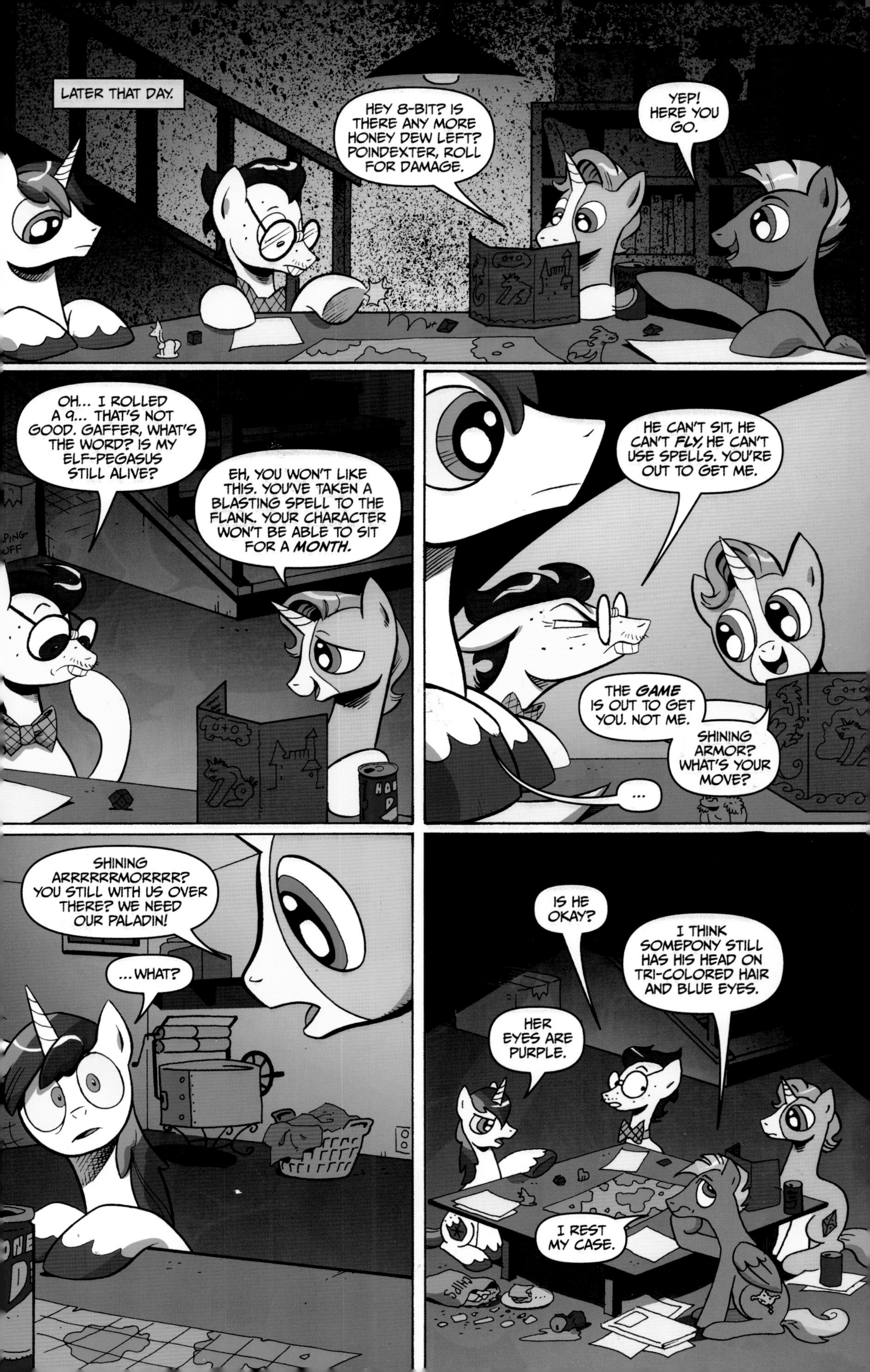

LATER THAT DAY.
HEY 8-BIT? IS THERE ANY MORE HONEY DEW LEFT? POINDEXTER, ROLL FOR DAMAGE.
YEP! HERE YOU GO.
OH... I ROLLED A 9... THAT'S NOT GOOD. GAFFER, WHAT'S THE WORD? IS MY ELF-PEGASUS STILL ALIVE?
EH, YOU WON'T LIKE THIS. YOU'VE TAKEN A BLASTING SPELL TO THE FLANK. YOUR CHARACTER WON'T BE ABLE TO SIT FOR A MONTH.
HE CAN'T SIT, HE CAN'T FLY, HE CAN'T USE SPELLS. YOU'RE OUT TO GET ME.
THE GAME IS OUT TO GET YOU. NOT ME.
SHINING ARMOR? WHAT'S YOUR MOVE?
...
SHINING ARRRRRRMORRRR? YOU STILL WITH US OVER THERE? WE NEED OUR PALADIN!
...WHAT?
IS HE OKAY?
I THINK SOMEPONY STILL HAS HIS HEAD ON TRI-COLORED HAIR AND BLUE EYES.
HER EYES ARE PURPLE.
I REST MY CASE.

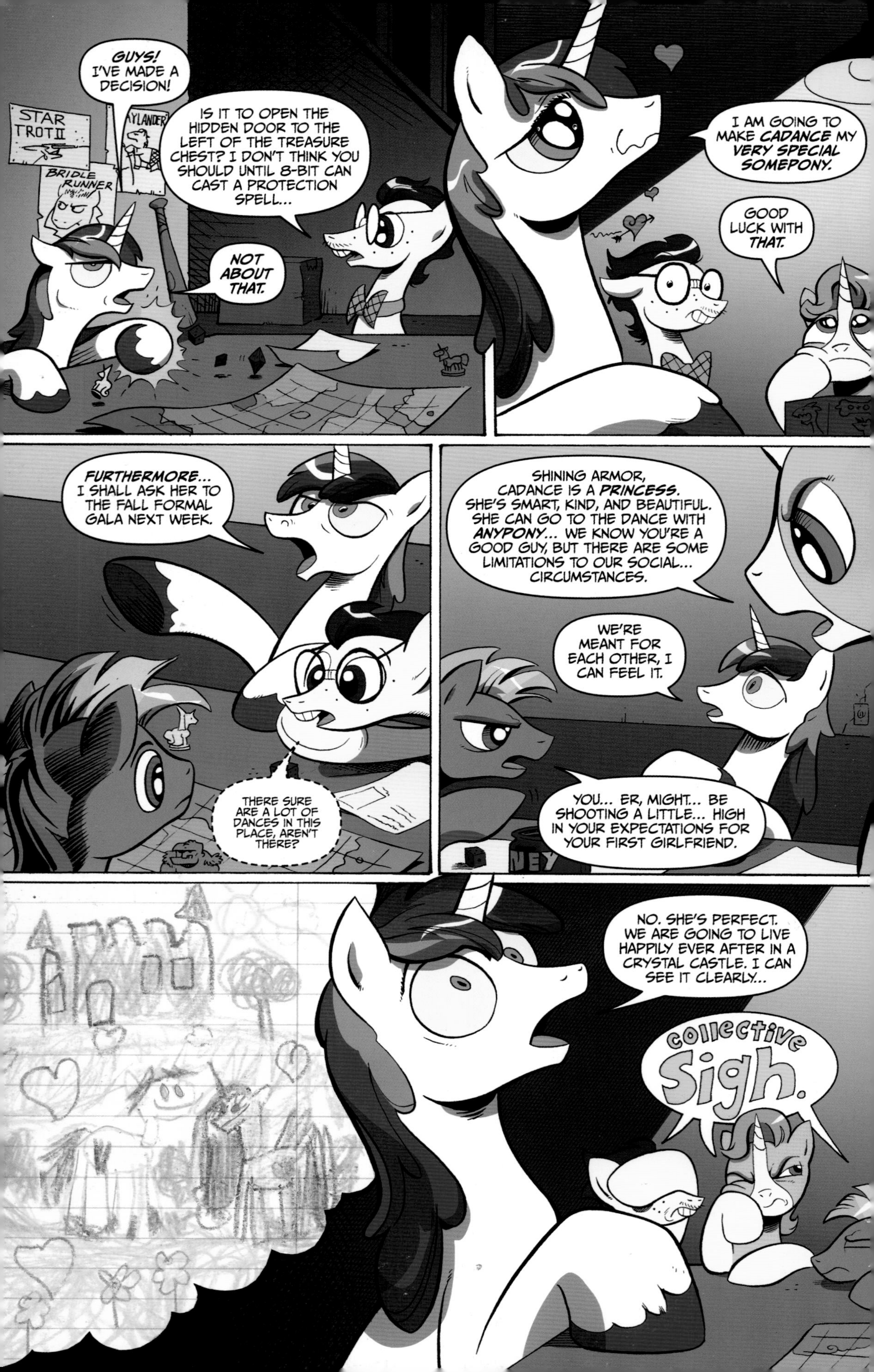
GUYS! I'VE MADE A DECISION!
STAR TROT II
BRIDLE RUNNER
IS IT TO OPEN THE HIDDEN DOOR TO THE LEFT OF THE TREASURE CHEST? I DON'T THINK YOU SHOULD UNTIL 8-BIT CAN CAST A PROTECTION SPELL...
NOT ABOUT THAT.
I AM GOING TO MAKE CADANCE MY VERY SPECIAL SOMEPONY.
GOOD LUCK WITH THAT.
FURTHERMORE... I SHALL ASK HER TO THE FALL FORMAL GALA NEXT WEEK.
THERE SURE ARE A LOT OF DANCES IN THIS PLACE, AREN'T THERE?
SHINING ARMOR, CADANCE IS A PRINCESS. SHE'S SMART, KIND, AND BEAUTIFUL. SHE CAN GO TO THE DANCE WITH ANYPONY... WE KNOW YOU'RE A GOOD GUY, BUT THERE ARE SOME LIMITATIONS TO OUR SOCIAL... CIRCUMSTANCES.
WE'RE MEANT FOR EACH OTHER, I CAN FEEL IT.
YOU... ER, MIGHT... BE SHOOTING A LITTLE... HIGH IN YOUR EXPECTATIONS FOR YOUR FIRST GIRLFRIEND.
NO. SHE'S PERFECT. WE ARE GOING TO LIVE HAPPILY EVER AFTER IN A CRYSTAL CASTLE. I CAN SEE IT CLEARLY...
collective Sigh.

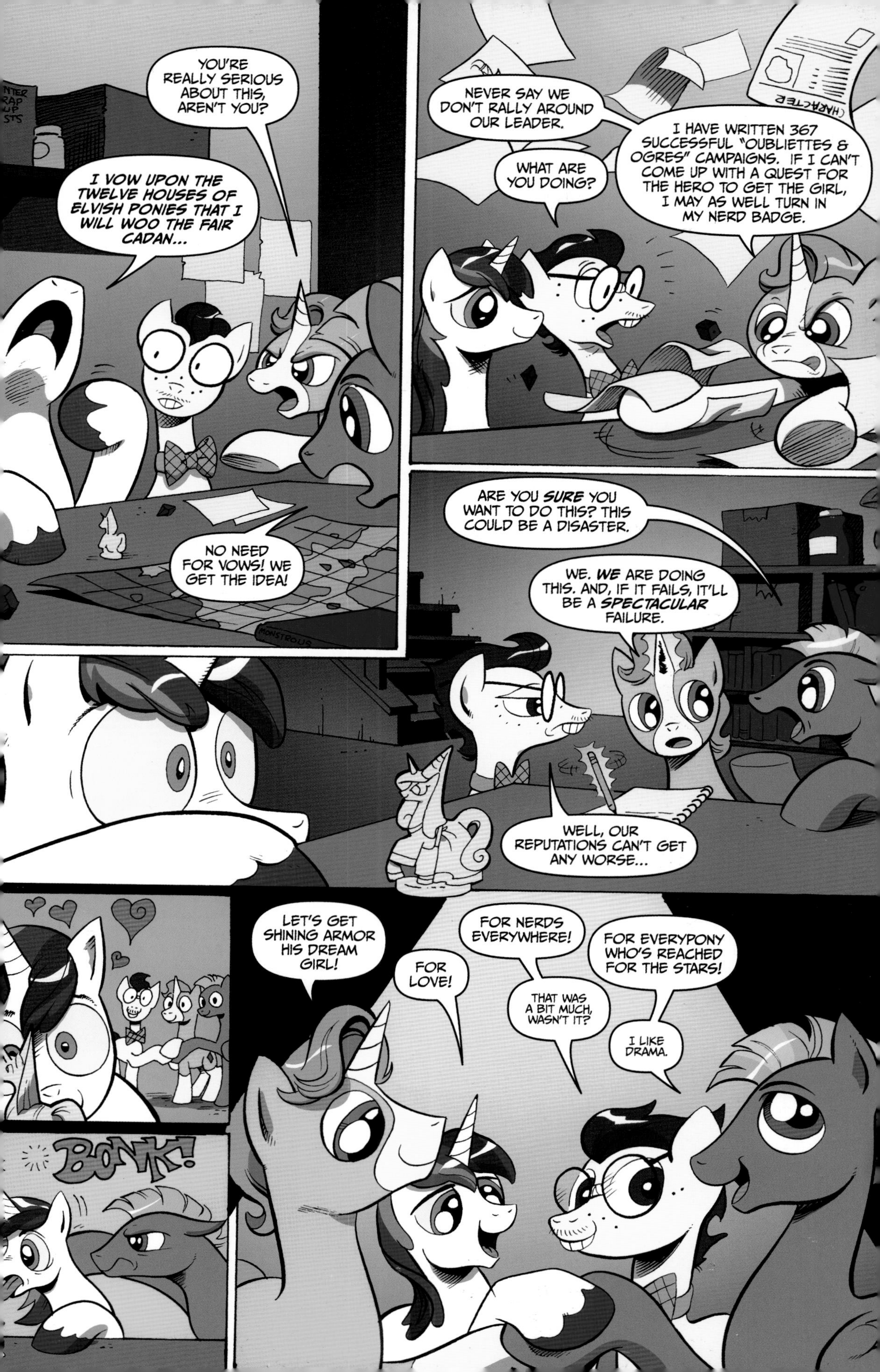

YOU'RE REALLY SERIOUS ABOUT THIS, AREN'T YOU?
I VOW UPON THE TWELVE HOUSES OF ELVISH PONIES THAT I WILL WOO THE FAIR CADAN...
NO NEED FOR VOWS! WE GET THE IDEA!
MONSTROUS
NEVER SAY WE DON'T RALLY AROUND OUR LEADER.
WHAT ARE YOU DOING?
I HAVE WRITTEN 367 SUCCESSFUL "OUBLIETTES & OGRES" CAMPAIGNS. IF I CAN'T COME UP WITH A QUEST FOR THE HERO TO GET THE GIRL, I MAY AS WELL TURN IN MY NERD BADGE.
ARE YOU SURE YOU WANT TO DO THIS? THIS COULD BE A DISASTER.
WE. WE ARE DOING THIS. AND, IF IT FAILS, IT'LL BE A SPECTACULAR FAILURE.
WELL, OUR REPUTATIONS CAN'T GET ANY WORSE...
BONK!
LET'S GET SHINING ARMOR HIS DREAM GIRL!
FOR LOVE!
FOR NERDS EVERYWHERE!
THAT WAS A BIT MUCH, WASN'T IT?
FOR EVERYPONY WHO'S REACHED FOR THE STARS!
I LIKE DRAMA.

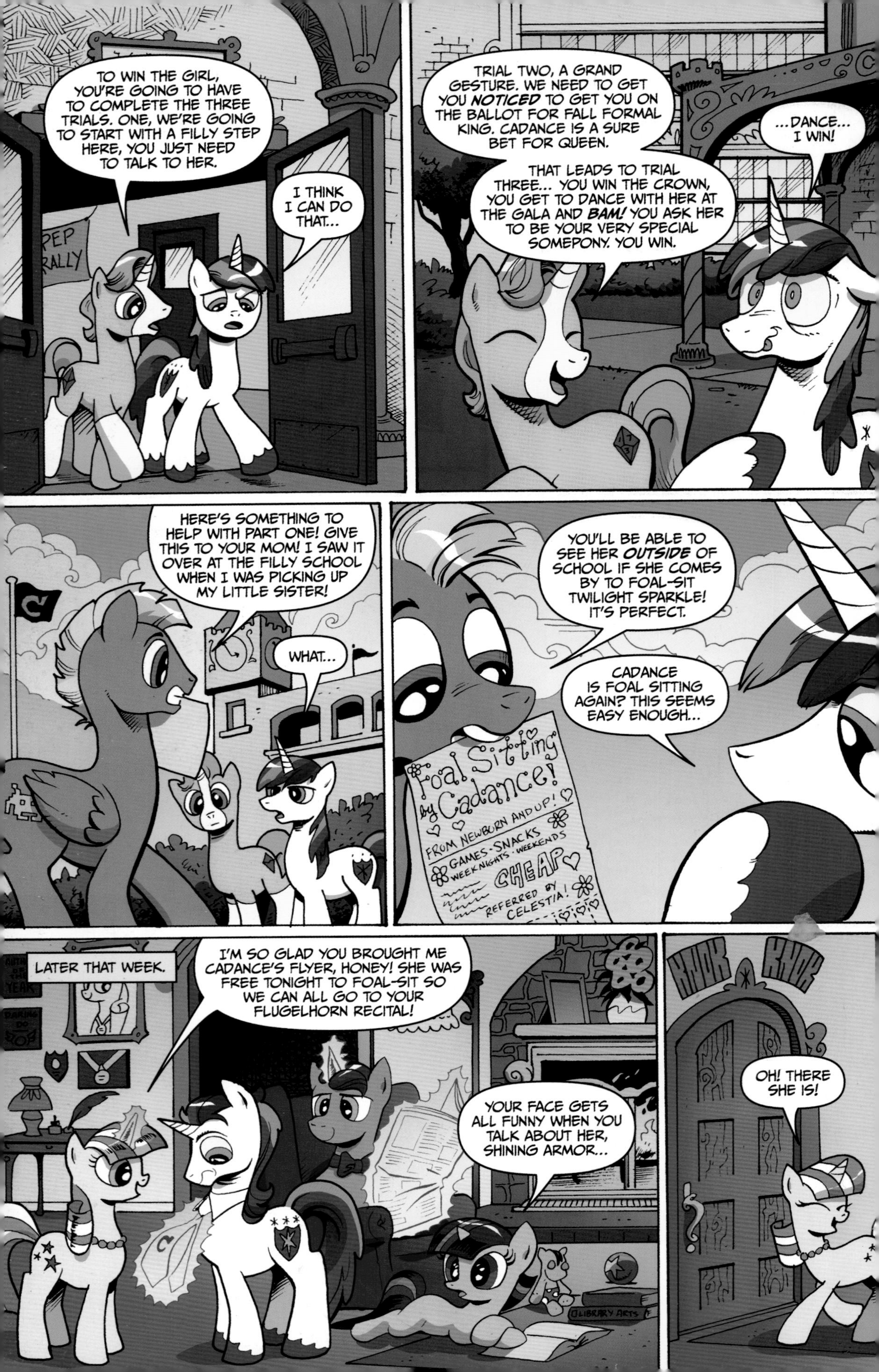
TO WIN THE GIRL, YOU'RE GOING TO HAVE TO COMPLETE THE THREE TRIALS. ONE, WE'RE GOING TO START WITH A FILLY STEP HERE, YOU JUST NEED TO TALK TO HER.
PEP RALLY
I THINK I CAN DO THAT...
TRIAL TWO, A GRAND GESTURE. WE NEED TO GET YOU **NOTICED** TO GET YOU ON THE BALLOT FOR FALL FORMAL KING. CADANCE IS A SURE BET FOR QUEEN.
THAT LEADS TO TRIAL THREE... YOU WIN THE CROWN, YOU GET TO DANCE WITH HER AT THE GALA AND **BAM!** YOU ASK HER TO BE YOUR VERY SPECIAL SOMEPONY. YOU WIN.
...DANCE... I WIN!
HERE'S SOMETHING TO HELP WITH PART ONE! GIVE THIS TO YOUR MOM! I SAW IT OVER AT THE FILLY SCHOOL WHEN I WAS PICKING UP MY LITTLE SISTER!
WHAT...
YOU'LL BE ABLE TO SEE HER **OUTSIDE** OF SCHOOL IF SHE COMES BY TO FOAL-SIT TWILIGHT SPARKLE! IT'S PERFECT.
CADANCE IS FOAL SITTING AGAIN? THIS SEEMS EASY ENOUGH...
Foal Sitting by Cadance!
FROM NEWBORN AND UP!
GAMES - SNACKS
WEEKNIGHTS - WEEKENDS
CHEAP
REFERRED BY CELESTIA!
LATER THAT WEEK.
I'M SO GLAD YOU BROUGHT ME CADANCE'S FLYER, HONEY! SHE WAS FREE TONIGHT TO FOAL-SIT SO WE CAN ALL GO TO YOUR FLUGELHORN RECITAL!
DARING DO
YOUR FACE GETS ALL FUNNY WHEN YOU TALK ABOUT HER, SHINING ARMOR...
LIBRARY ARTS
KNOK KNOK
OH! THERE SHE IS!

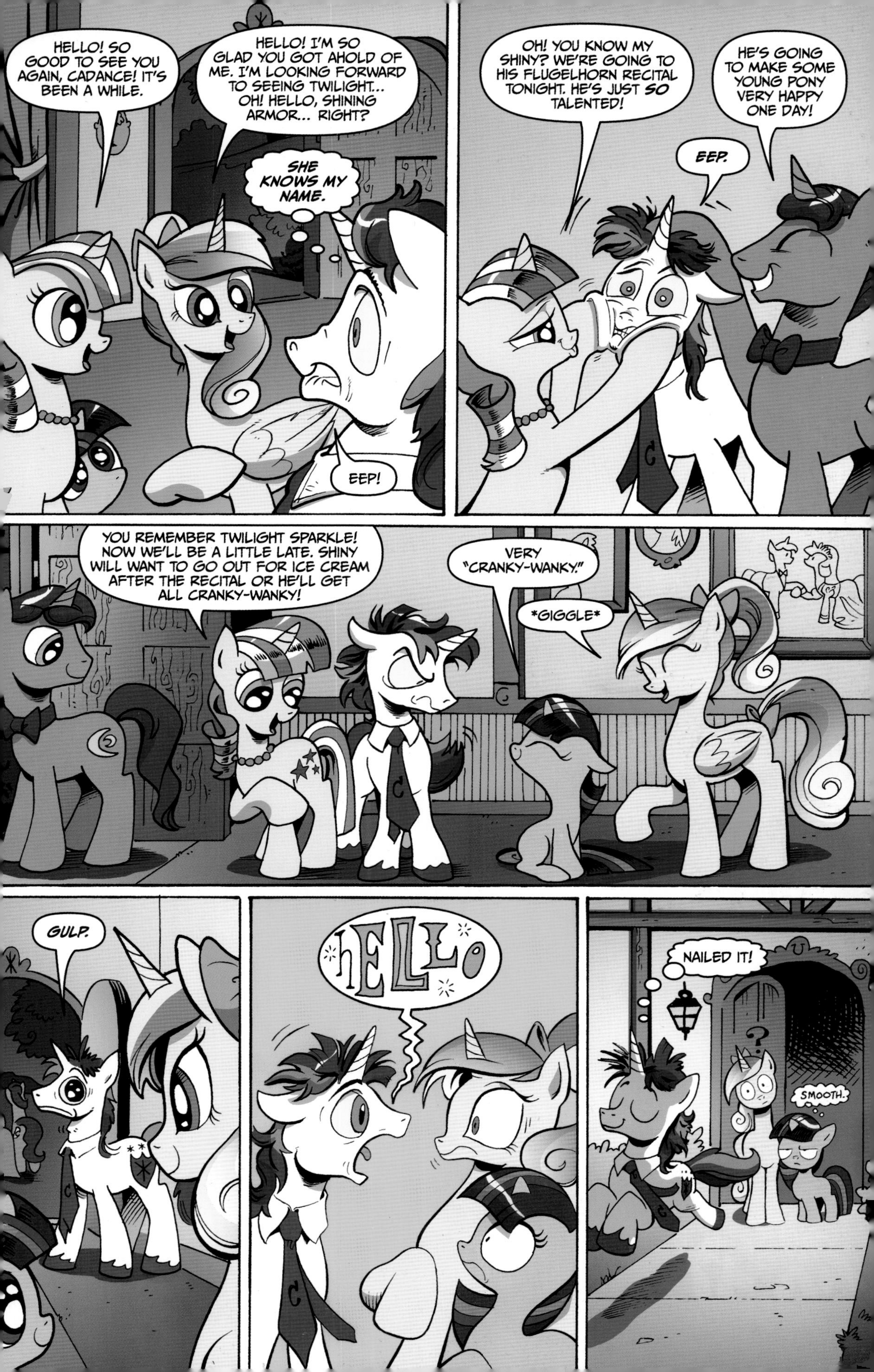
HELLO! SO GOOD TO SEE YOU AGAIN, CADANCE! IT'S BEEN A WHILE.
HELLO! I'M SO GLAD YOU GOT AHOLD OF ME. I'M LOOKING FORWARD TO SEEING TWILIGHT... OH! HELLO, SHINING ARMOR... RIGHT?
SHE KNOWS MY NAME.
EEP!
OH! YOU KNOW MY SHINY? WE'RE GOING TO HIS FLUGELHORN RECITAL TONIGHT. HE'S JUST SO TALENTED!
HE'S GOING TO MAKE SOME YOUNG PONY VERY HAPPY ONE DAY!
EEP.
YOU REMEMBER TWILIGHT SPARKLE! NOW WE'LL BE A LITTLE LATE. SHINY WILL WANT TO GO OUT FOR ICE CREAM AFTER THE RECITAL OR HE'LL GET ALL CRANKY-WANKY!
VERY "CRANKY-WANKY."
GIGGLE
GULP.
HELLO
NAILED IT!
SMOOTH.

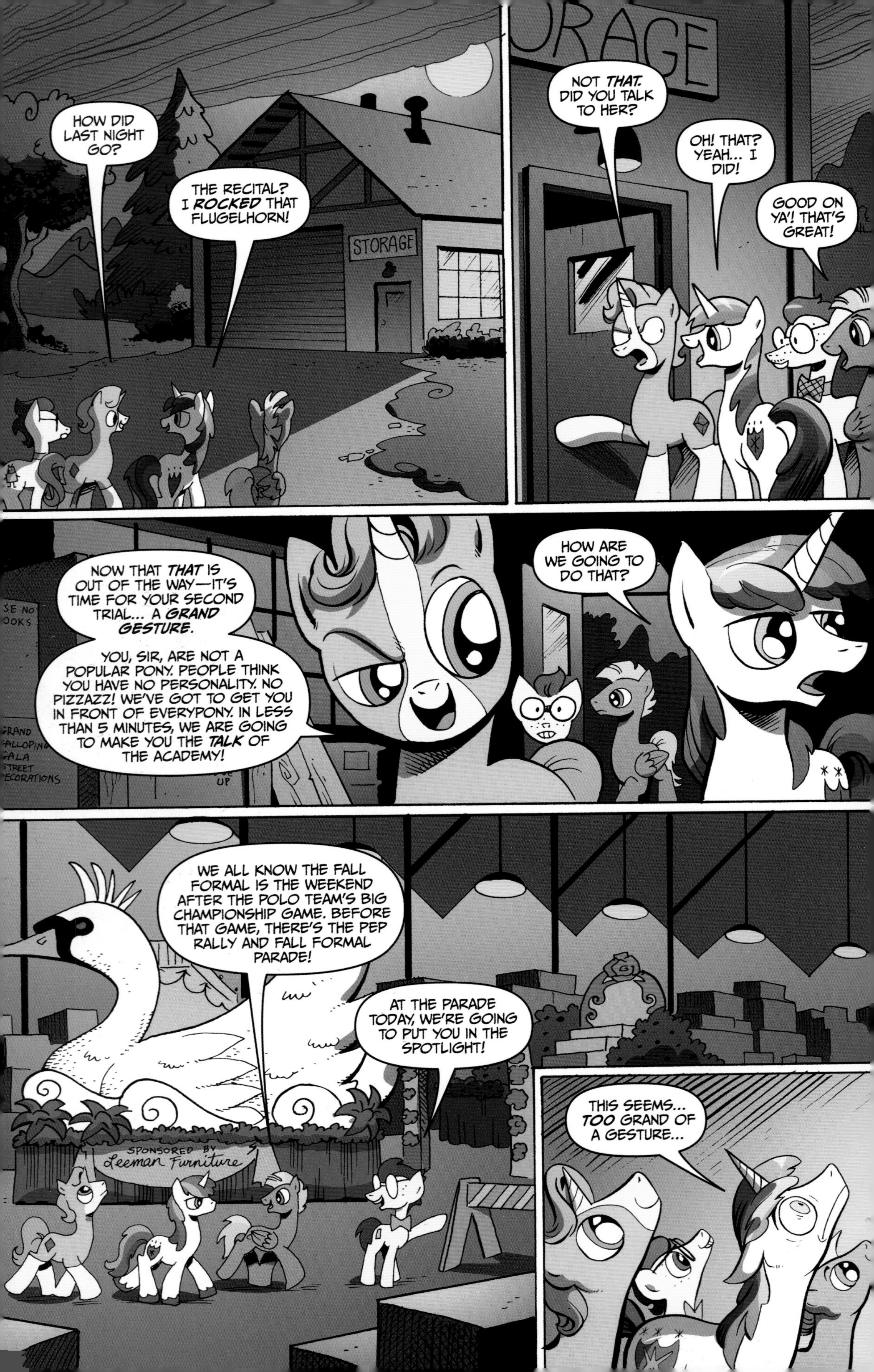
STORAGE
HOW DID LAST NIGHT GO?
THE RECITAL? I *ROCKED* THAT FLUGELHORN!
ORAGE
NOT *THAT.* DID YOU TALK TO HER?
OH! THAT? YEAH... I DID!
GOOD ON YA'! THAT'S GREAT!
NOW THAT *THAT* IS OUT OF THE WAY—IT'S TIME FOR YOUR SECOND TRIAL... A *GRAND GESTURE.*
YOU, SIR, ARE NOT A POPULAR PONY. PEOPLE THINK YOU HAVE NO PERSONALITY. NO PIZZAZZ! WE'VE GOT TO GET YOU IN FRONT OF EVERYPONY. IN LESS THAN 5 MINUTES, WE ARE GOING TO MAKE YOU THE *TALK* OF THE ACADEMY!
HOW ARE WE GOING TO DO THAT?
GRAND GALLOPING GALA STREET DECORATIONS
WE ALL KNOW THE FALL FORMAL IS THE WEEKEND AFTER THE POLO TEAM'S BIG CHAMPIONSHIP GAME. BEFORE THAT GAME, THERE'S THE PEP RALLY AND FALL FORMAL PARADE!
AT THE PARADE TODAY, WE'RE GOING TO PUT YOU IN THE SPOTLIGHT!
SPONSORED BY Leeman Furniture
THIS SEEMS... *TOO* GRAND OF A GESTURE...

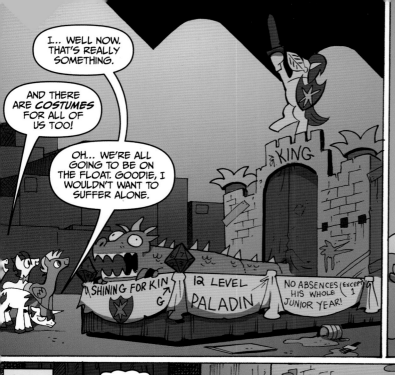

I... WELL NOW. THAT'S REALLY SOMETHING.

AND THERE ARE *COSTUMES* FOR ALL OF US TOO!

OH... WE'RE ALL GOING TO BE ON THE FLOAT. GOODIE, I WOULDN'T WANT TO SUFFER ALONE.

KING

SHINING FOR KING

12 LEVEL PALADIN

NO ABSENCES (EXCEPT 1) HIS WHOLE JUNIOR YEAR!

COME ON, WE NEED TO PRACTICE THE MUSICAL NUMBER!

I WROTE IT MYSELF!

SOON...

THIS IS A TERRIBLE IDEA.

THIS IS A *GREAT IDEA!*

GATE 3

HAS HIS CART LICENSE!

ZACHERLE STADIUM PEP RALLY ENTRANCE

GO DRAGONS

EXIT

GO TEAM! RAH-RAH

THERE SHE IS! AW MAN, SHE'S SITTING WITH BUCK WITHERS, THE CAPTAIN OF THE POLO TEAM?! I HATE THAT GUY...

YOU SHOULD... I HEARD HE WAS PLANNING ON ASKING CADANCE TO THE DANCE AFTER HIS POLO GAME TODAY.

SHINING ARMOR! IT JUST BECAME *IMPERATIVE* THAT WE DO THIS AND GET YOU ON CADANCE'S RADAR *RIGHT NOW. ARE YOU READY?*

I'M READY.

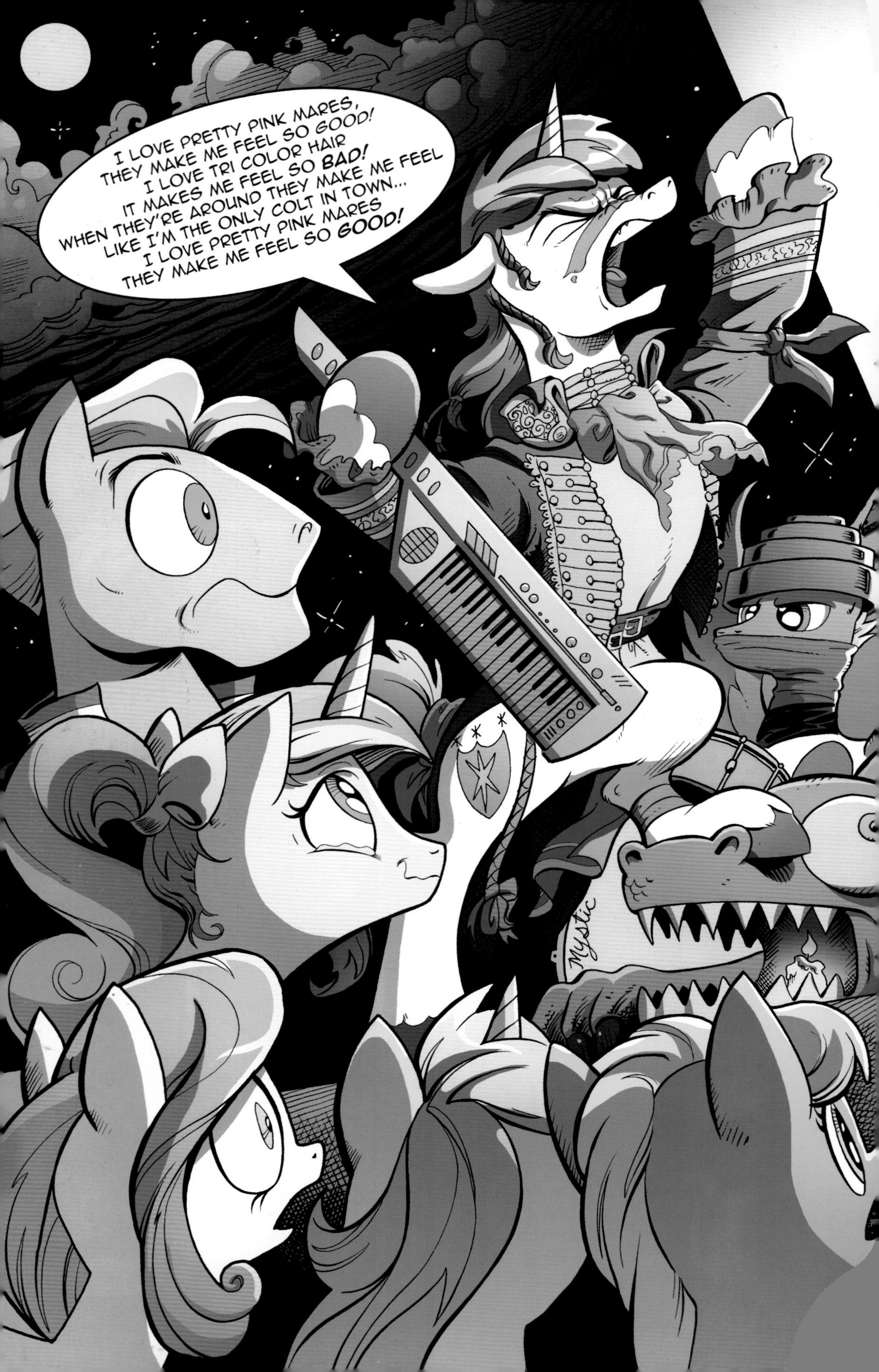
I LOVE PRETTY PINK MARES, THEY MAKE ME FEEL SO GOOD! I LOVE TRI COLOR HAIR IT MAKES ME FEEL SO BAD! WHEN THEY'RE AROUND THEY MAKE ME FEEL LIKE I'M THE ONLY COLT IN TOWN... I LOVE PRETTY PINK MARES THEY MAKE ME FEEL SO GOOD!
Mystic

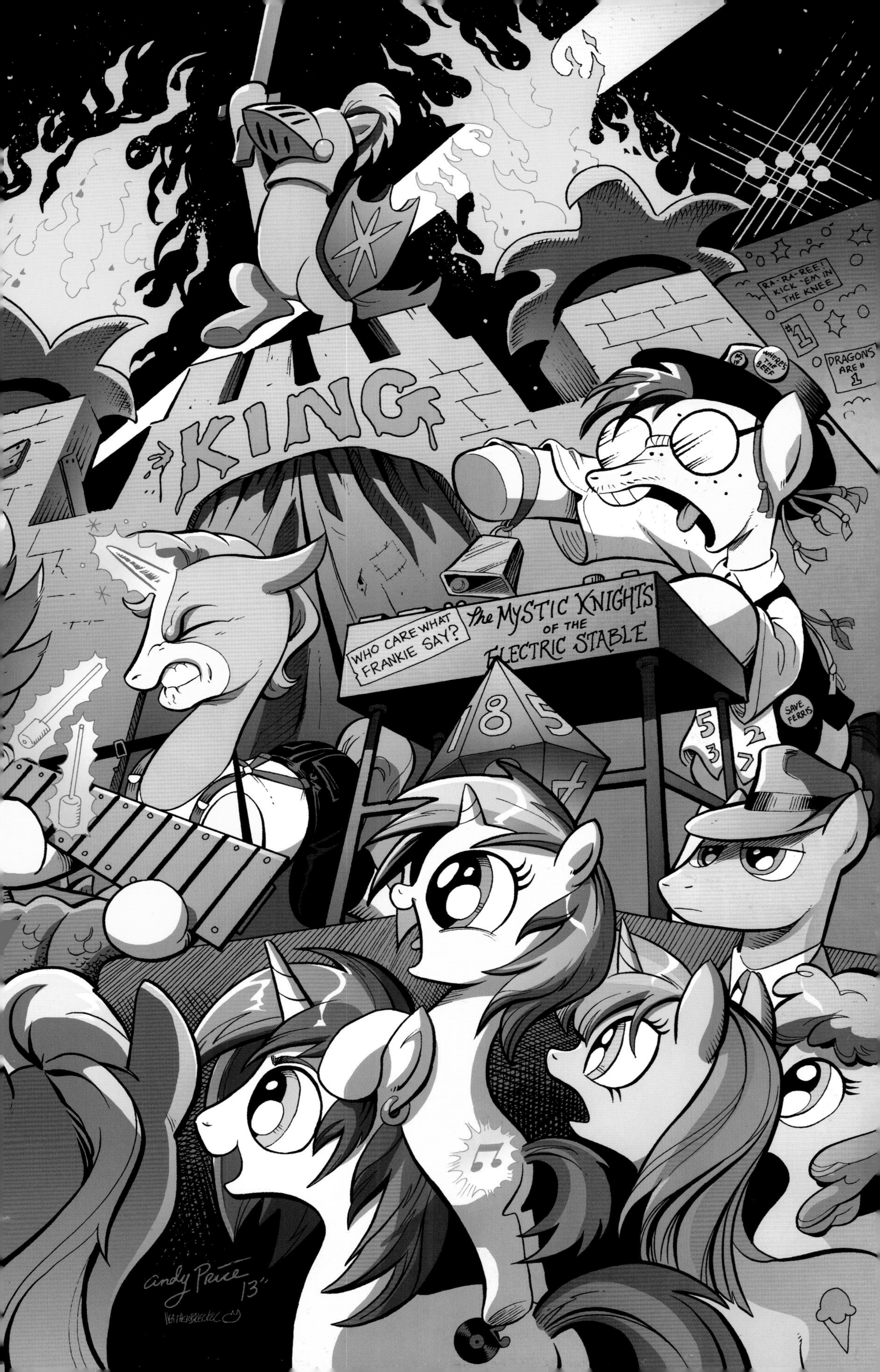

RA-RA-REE! KICK 'EM IN THE KNEE
#1
DRAGONS ARE #1
WHERE'S THE BEEF
KING
WHO CARE WHAT FRANKIE SAY?
The MYSTIC KNIGHTS OF THE ELECTRIC STABLE
SAVE FERRIS
andy Price 13

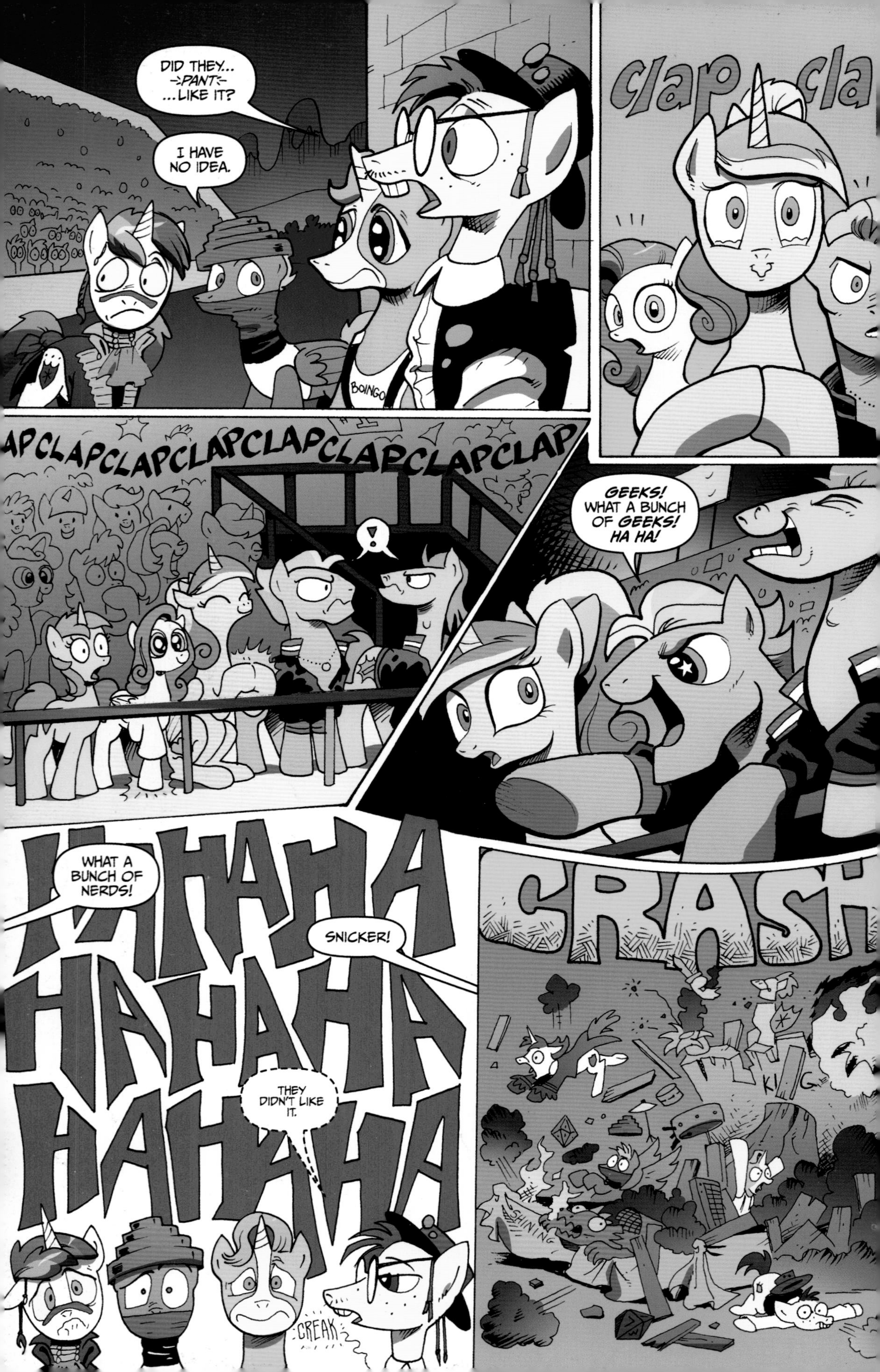

DID THEY... -PANT- ...LIKE IT?
I HAVE NO IDEA.
BOINGO
clap clap
CLAPCLAPCLAPCLAPCLAPCLAPCLAPCLAP
!
GEEKS! WHAT A BUNCH OF GEEKS! HA HA!
HAHAHA HAHAHA HAHAHA
WHAT A BUNCH OF NERDS!
SNICKER!
THEY DIDN'T LIKE IT.
CREAK
CRASH

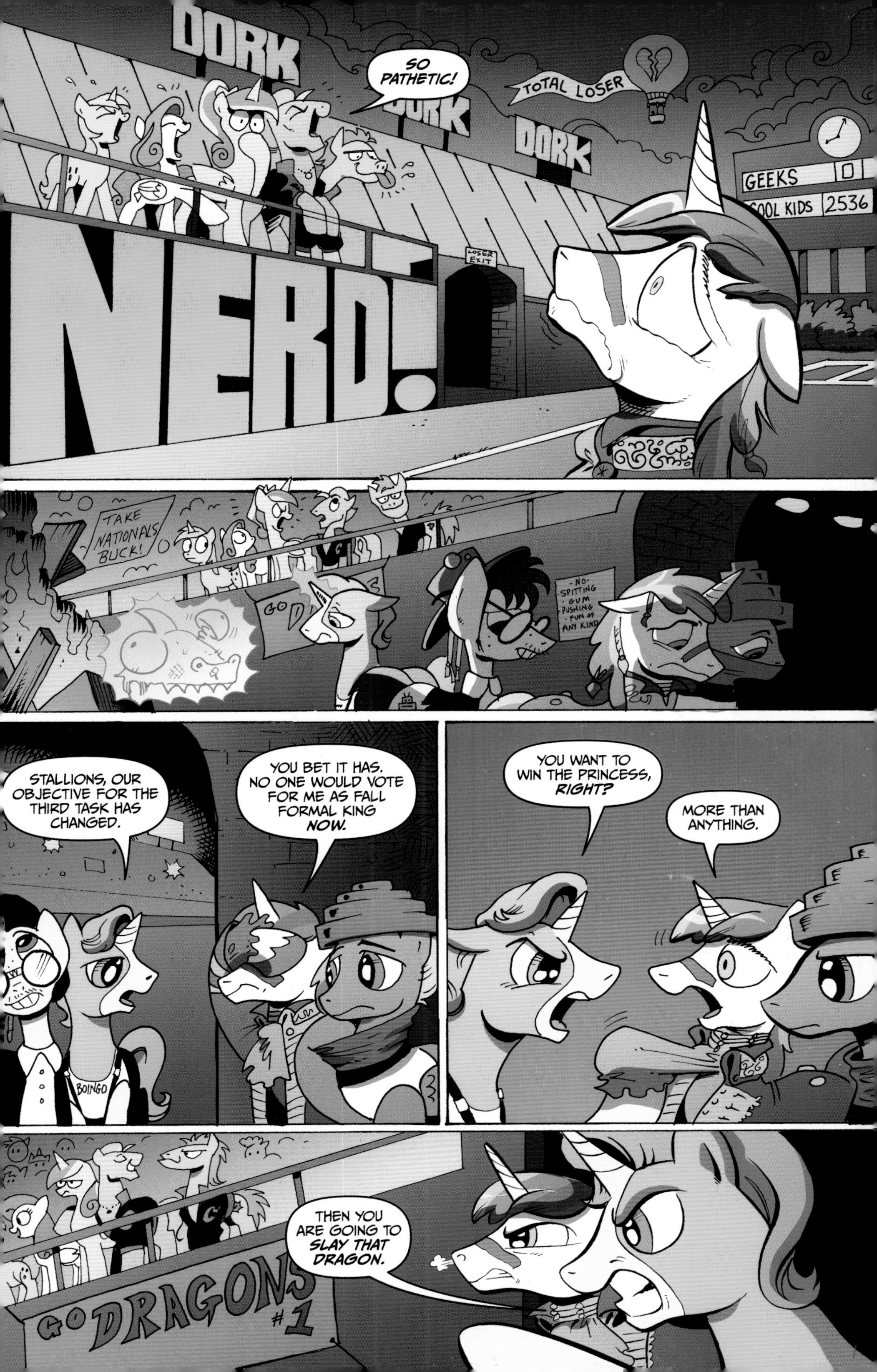
DORK
SO PATHETIC!
DORK
DORK
TOTAL LOSER
GEEKS 0
COOL KIDS 2536
LOSER EXIT
NERD!
TAKE NATIONALS BUCK!
GO D
-NO- SPITTING GUM PUSHING FUN OF ANY KIND
STALLIONS, OUR OBJECTIVE FOR THE THIRD TASK HAS CHANGED.
YOU BET IT HAS. NO ONE WOULD VOTE FOR ME AS FALL FORMAL KING *NOW.*
BOINGO
YOU WANT TO WIN THE PRINCESS, *RIGHT?*
MORE THAN ANYTHING.
THEN YOU ARE GOING TO *SLAY THAT DRAGON.*
GO DRAGONS #1

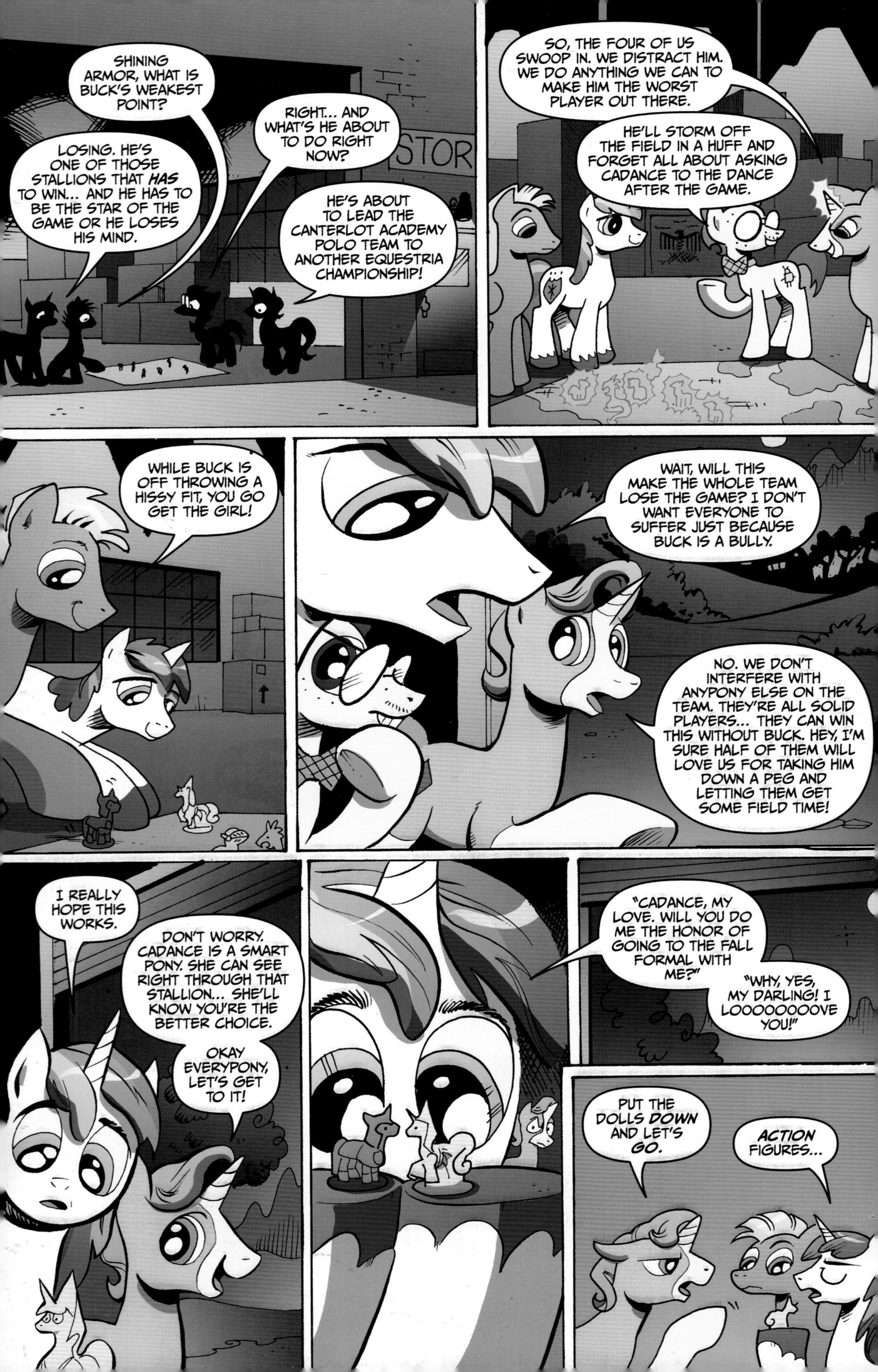
SHINING ARMOR, WHAT IS BUCK'S WEAKEST POINT?
LOSING. HE'S ONE OF THOSE STALLIONS THAT HAS TO WIN... AND HE HAS TO BE THE STAR OF THE GAME OR HE LOSES HIS MIND.
RIGHT... AND WHAT'S HE ABOUT TO DO RIGHT NOW?
STOR
HE'S ABOUT TO LEAD THE CANTERLOT ACADEMY POLO TEAM TO ANOTHER EQUESTRIA CHAMPIONSHIP!
SO, THE FOUR OF US SWOOP IN. WE DISTRACT HIM. WE DO ANYTHING WE CAN TO MAKE HIM THE WORST PLAYER OUT THERE.
HE'LL STORM OFF THE FIELD IN A HUFF AND FORGET ALL ABOUT ASKING CADANCE TO THE DANCE AFTER THE GAME.
WHILE BUCK IS OFF THROWING A HISSY FIT, YOU GO GET THE GIRL!
WAIT, WILL THIS MAKE THE WHOLE TEAM LOSE THE GAME? I DON'T WANT EVERYONE TO SUFFER JUST BECAUSE BUCK IS A BULLY.
NO. WE DON'T INTERFERE WITH ANYPONY ELSE ON THE TEAM. THEY'RE ALL SOLID PLAYERS... THEY CAN WIN THIS WITHOUT BUCK. HEY, I'M SURE HALF OF THEM WILL LOVE US FOR TAKING HIM DOWN A PEG AND LETTING THEM GET SOME FIELD TIME!
I REALLY HOPE THIS WORKS.
DON'T WORRY. CADANCE IS A SMART PONY. SHE CAN SEE RIGHT THROUGH THAT STALLION... SHE'LL KNOW YOU'RE THE BETTER CHOICE.
OKAY EVERYPONY, LET'S GET TO IT!
"CADANCE, MY LOVE. WILL YOU DO ME THE HONOR OF GOING TO THE FALL FORMAL WITH ME?"
"WHY, YES, MY DARLING! I LOOOOOOOOVE YOU!"
PUT THE DOLLS DOWN AND LET'S GO.
ACTION FIGURES...

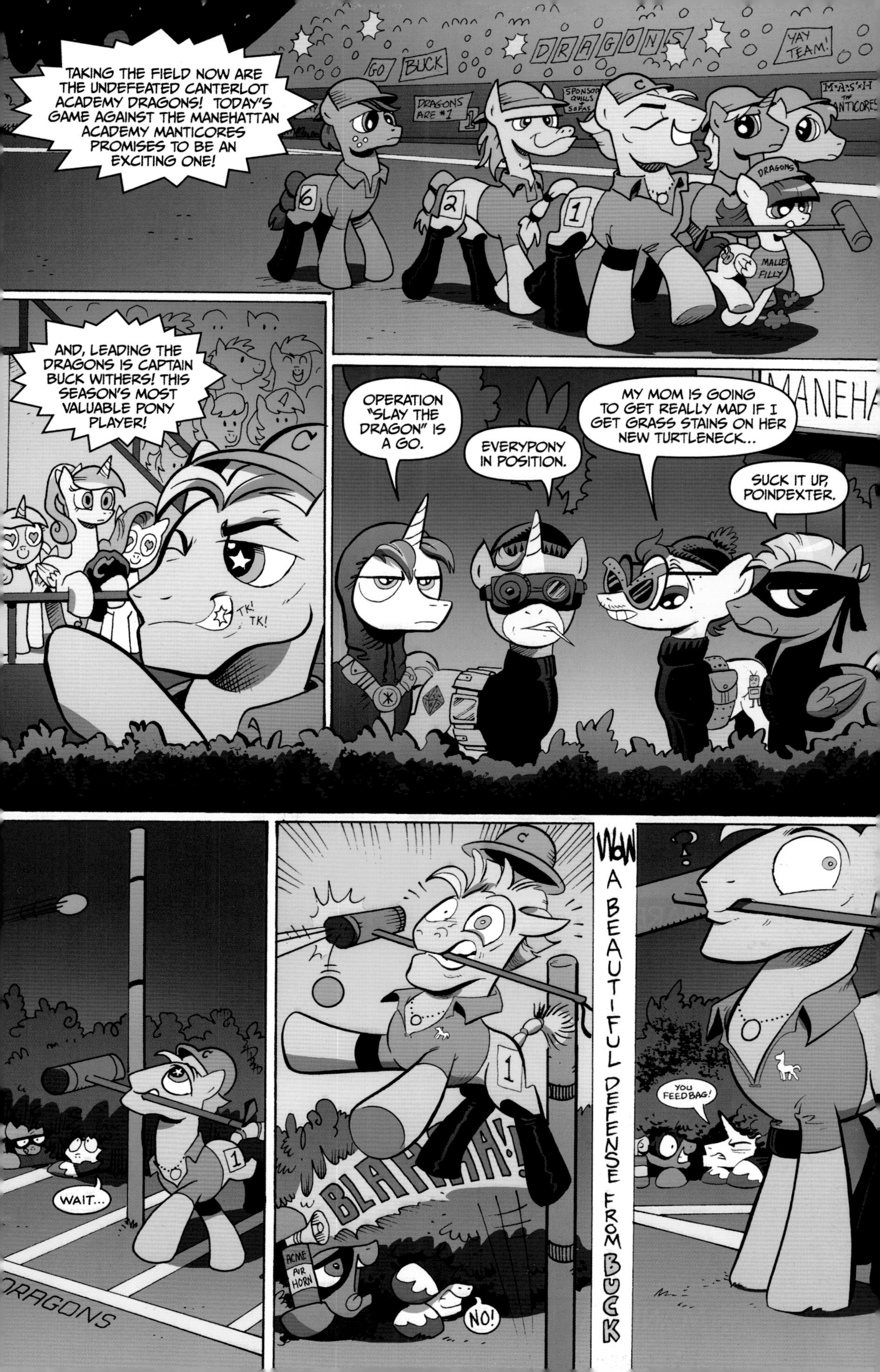

GO
BUCK
DRAGONS!
YAY TEAM!
DRAGONS ARE #1
M*A*S*H THE MANTICORES
TAKING THE FIELD NOW ARE THE UNDEFEATED CANTERLOT ACADEMY DRAGONS! TODAY'S GAME AGAINST THE MANEHATTAN ACADEMY MANTICORES PROMISES TO BE AN EXCITING ONE!
DRAGONS
MALLET FILLY
AND, LEADING THE DRAGONS IS CAPTAIN BUCK WITHERS! THIS SEASON'S MOST VALUABLE PONY PLAYER!
TK! TK!
MANEHA
OPERATION "SLAY THE DRAGON" IS A GO.
EVERYPONY IN POSITION.
MY MOM IS GOING TO GET REALLY MAD IF I GET GRASS STAINS ON HER NEW TURTLENECK...
SUCK IT UP, POINDEXTER.
WAIT...
DRAGONS
BLAAAAA!
ACME AIR HORN
NO!
WOW A BEAUTIFUL DEFENSE FROM BUCK
YOU FEEDBAG!

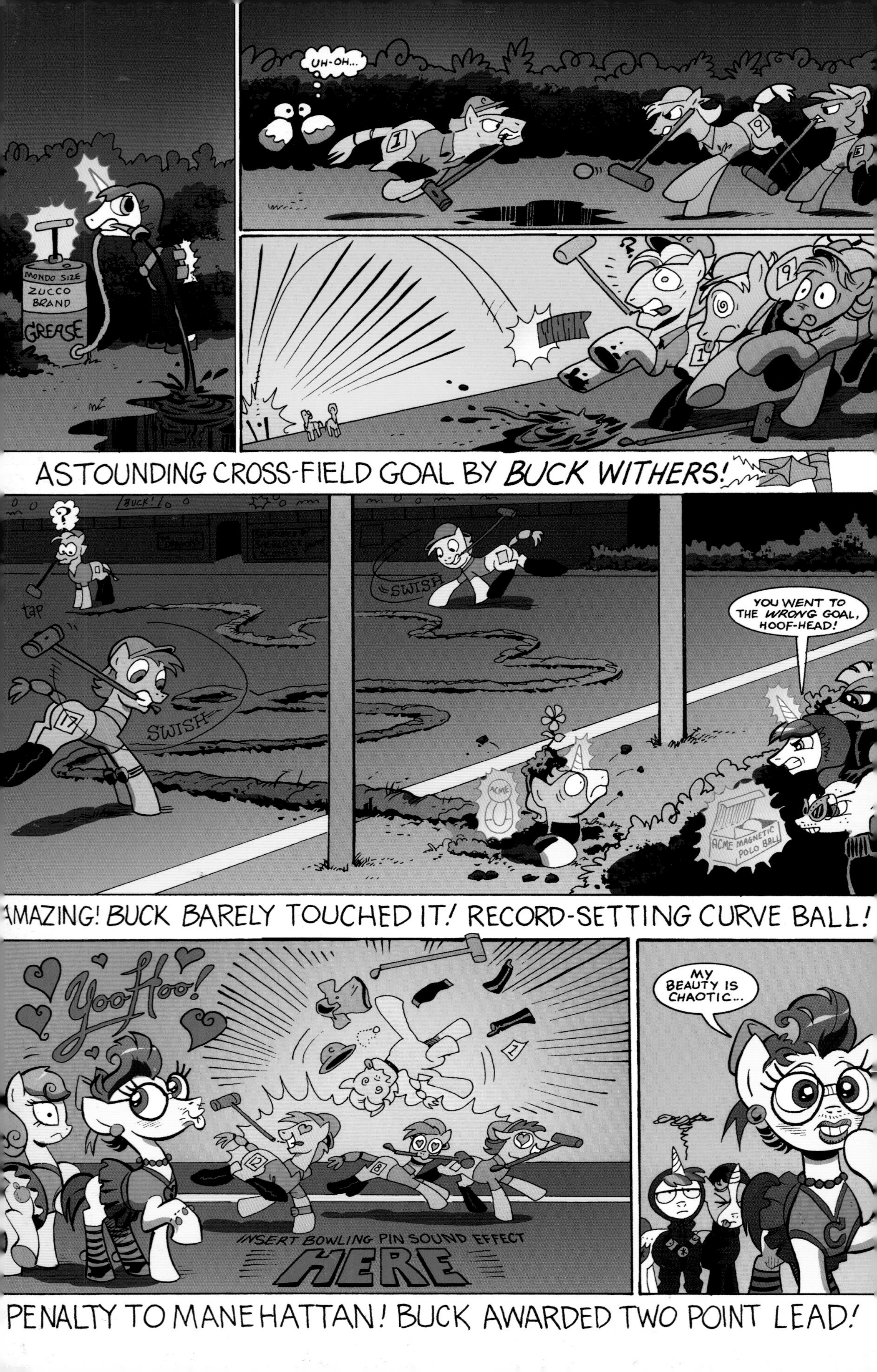
MONDO SIZE
ZUCCO BRAND
GREASE
UH-OH...
WHAK
ASTOUNDING CROSS-FIELD GOAL BY BUCK WITHERS!
tap
SWISH
SWISH
YOU WENT TO THE WRONG GOAL, HOOF-HEAD!
ACME
ACME MAGNETIC POLO BALL
AMAZING! BUCK BARELY TOUCHED IT! RECORD-SETTING CURVE BALL!
Yoo Hoo!
INSERT BOWLING PIN SOUND EFFECT
HERE
MY BEAUTY IS CHAOTIC...
PENALTY TO MANEHATTAN! BUCK AWARDED TWO POINT LEAD!

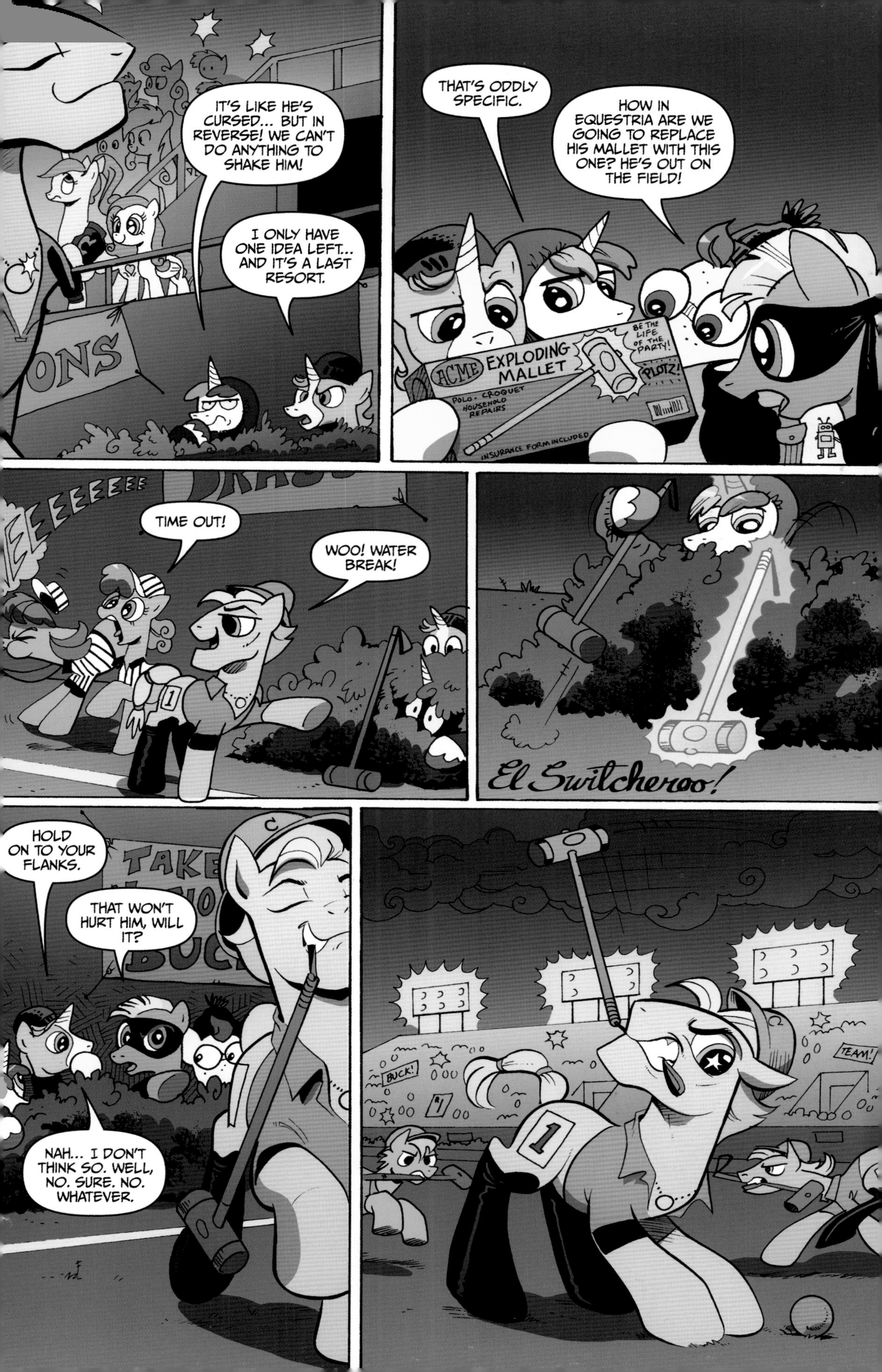
IT'S LIKE HE'S CURSED... BUT IN REVERSE! WE CAN'T DO ANYTHING TO SHAKE HIM!
I ONLY HAVE ONE IDEA LEFT... AND IT'S A LAST RESORT.
ONS
THAT'S ODDLY SPECIFIC.
HOW IN EQUESTRIA ARE WE GOING TO REPLACE HIS MALLET WITH THIS ONE? HE'S OUT ON THE FIELD!
ACME EXPLODING MALLET
BE THE LIFE OF THE PARTY!
PLOTZ!
POLO · CROQUET HOUSEHOLD REPAIRS
INSURANCE FORM INCLUDED
EEEEEEEEEE
TIME OUT!
WOO! WATER BREAK!
El Switcheroo!
HOLD ON TO YOUR FLANKS.
THAT WON'T HURT HIM, WILL IT?
NAH... I DON'T THINK SO. WELL, NO. SURE. NO. WHATEVER.
BUCK!
TEAM!

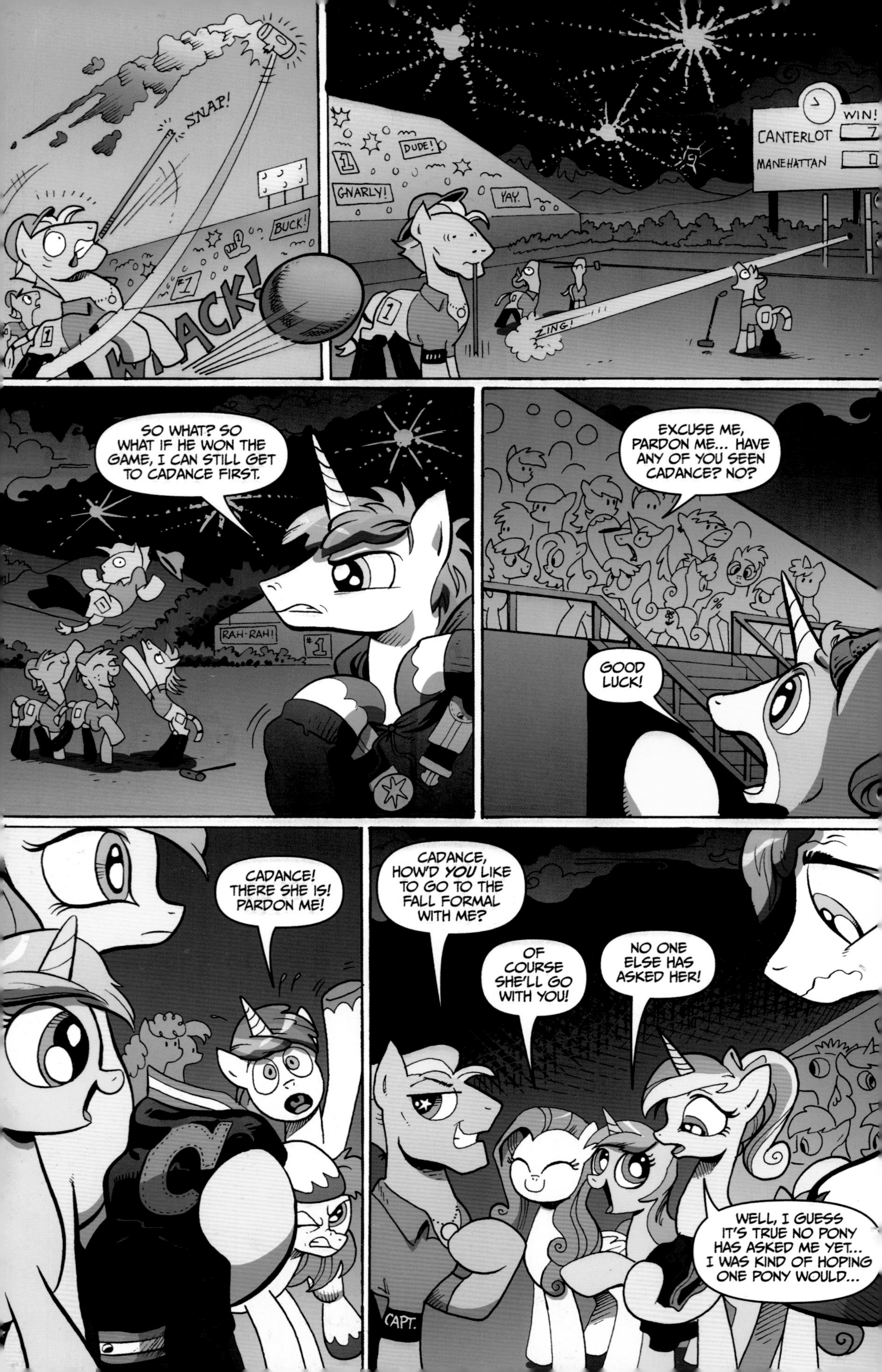
SNAP!
BUCK!
#1
WHACK!
DUDE!
GNARLY!
YAY.
WIN!
CANTERLOT 7
MANEHATTAN 0
ZING!
SO WHAT? SO WHAT IF HE WON THE GAME, I CAN STILL GET TO CADANCE FIRST.
RAH-RAH!
#1
EXCUSE ME, PARDON ME... HAVE ANY OF YOU SEEN CADANCE? NO?
GOOD LUCK!
CADANCE! THERE SHE IS! PARDON ME!
CADANCE, HOW'D *YOU* LIKE TO GO TO THE FALL FORMAL WITH ME?
OF COURSE SHE'LL GO WITH YOU!
NO ONE ELSE HAS ASKED HER!
WELL, I GUESS IT'S TRUE NO PONY HAS ASKED ME YET... I WAS KIND OF HOPING ONE PONY WOULD...
CAPT.

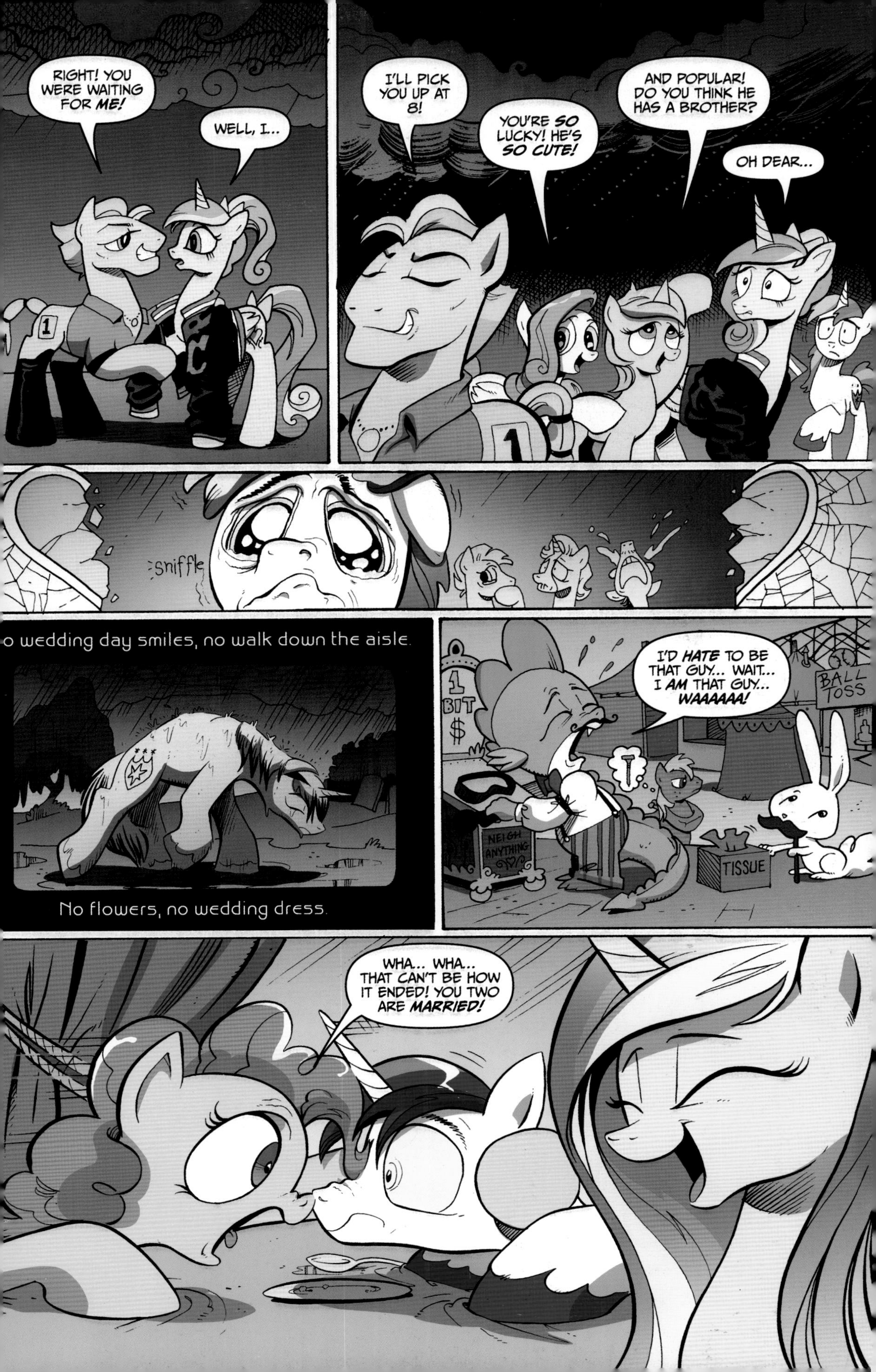
RIGHT! YOU WERE WAITING FOR ME!
WELL, I...
I'LL PICK YOU UP AT 8!
YOU'RE SO LUCKY! HE'S SO CUTE!
AND POPULAR! DO YOU THINK HE HAS A BROTHER?
OH DEAR...
sniffle
o wedding day smiles, no walk down the aisle.
No flowers, no wedding dress.
1 BIT $
NEIGH ANYTHING
I'D HATE TO BE THAT GUY... WAIT... I AM THAT GUY... WAAAAAA!
BALL TOSS
TISSUE
WHA... WHA... THAT CAN'T BE HOW IT ENDED! YOU TWO ARE MARRIED!

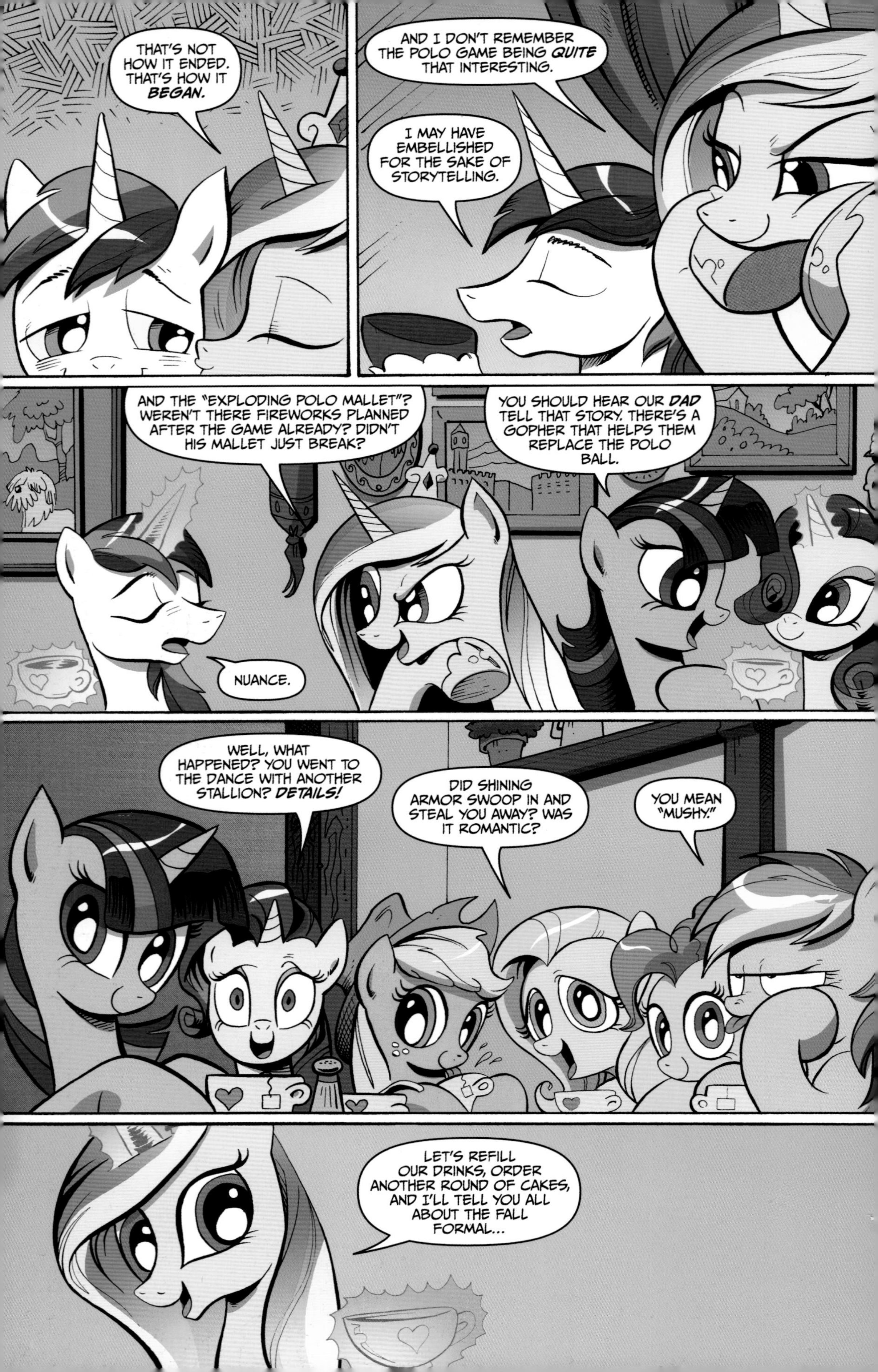
THAT'S NOT HOW IT ENDED. THAT'S HOW IT *BEGAN.*
AND I DON'T REMEMBER THE POLO GAME BEING *QUITE* THAT INTERESTING.
I MAY HAVE EMBELLISHED FOR THE SAKE OF STORYTELLING.
AND THE "EXPLODING POLO MALLET"? WEREN'T THERE FIREWORKS PLANNED AFTER THE GAME ALREADY? DIDN'T HIS MALLET JUST BREAK?
NUANCE.
YOU SHOULD HEAR OUR *DAD* TELL THAT STORY. THERE'S A GOPHER THAT HELPS THEM REPLACE THE POLO BALL.
WELL, WHAT HAPPENED? YOU WENT TO THE DANCE WITH ANOTHER STALLION? *DETAILS!*
DID SHINING ARMOR SWOOP IN AND STEAL YOU AWAY? WAS IT ROMANTIC?
YOU MEAN "MUSHY."
LET'S REFILL OUR DRINKS, ORDER ANOTHER ROUND OF CAKES, AND I'LL TELL YOU ALL ABOUT THE FALL FORMAL...

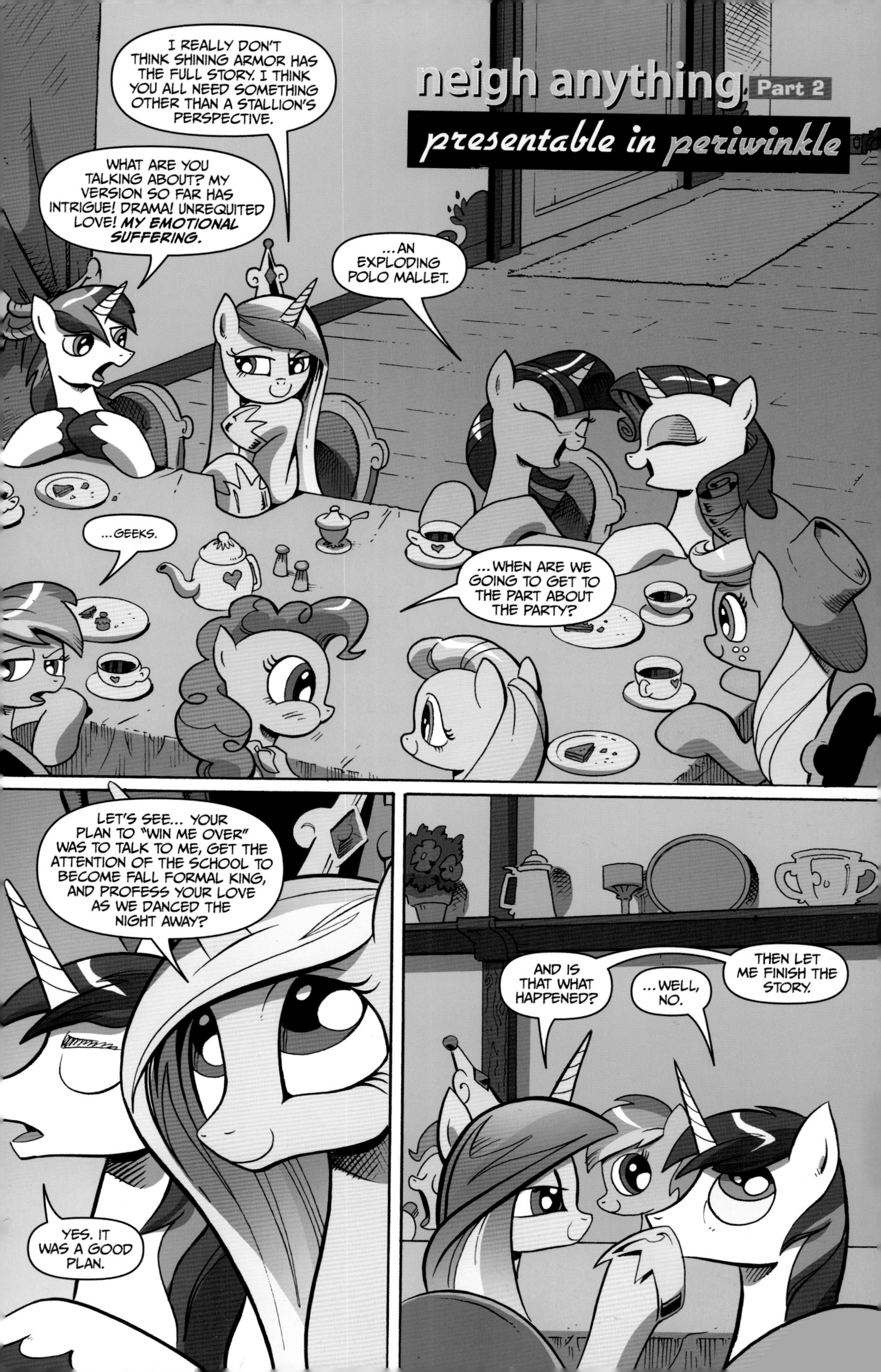

neigh anything Part 2
presentable in periwinkle
I REALLY DON'T THINK SHINING ARMOR HAS THE FULL STORY. I THINK YOU ALL NEED SOMETHING OTHER THAN A STALLION'S PERSPECTIVE.
WHAT ARE YOU TALKING ABOUT? MY VERSION SO FAR HAS INTRIGUE! DRAMA! UNREQUITED LOVE! ***MY EMOTIONAL SUFFERING.***
...AN EXPLODING POLO MALLET.
...GEEKS.
...WHEN ARE WE GOING TO GET TO THE PART ABOUT THE PARTY?
LET'S SEE... YOUR PLAN TO "WIN ME OVER" WAS TO TALK TO ME, GET THE ATTENTION OF THE SCHOOL TO BECOME FALL FORMAL KING, AND PROFESS YOUR LOVE AS WE DANCED THE NIGHT AWAY?
YES. IT WAS A GOOD PLAN.
AND IS THAT WHAT HAPPENED?
...WELL, NO.
THEN LET ME FINISH THE STORY.

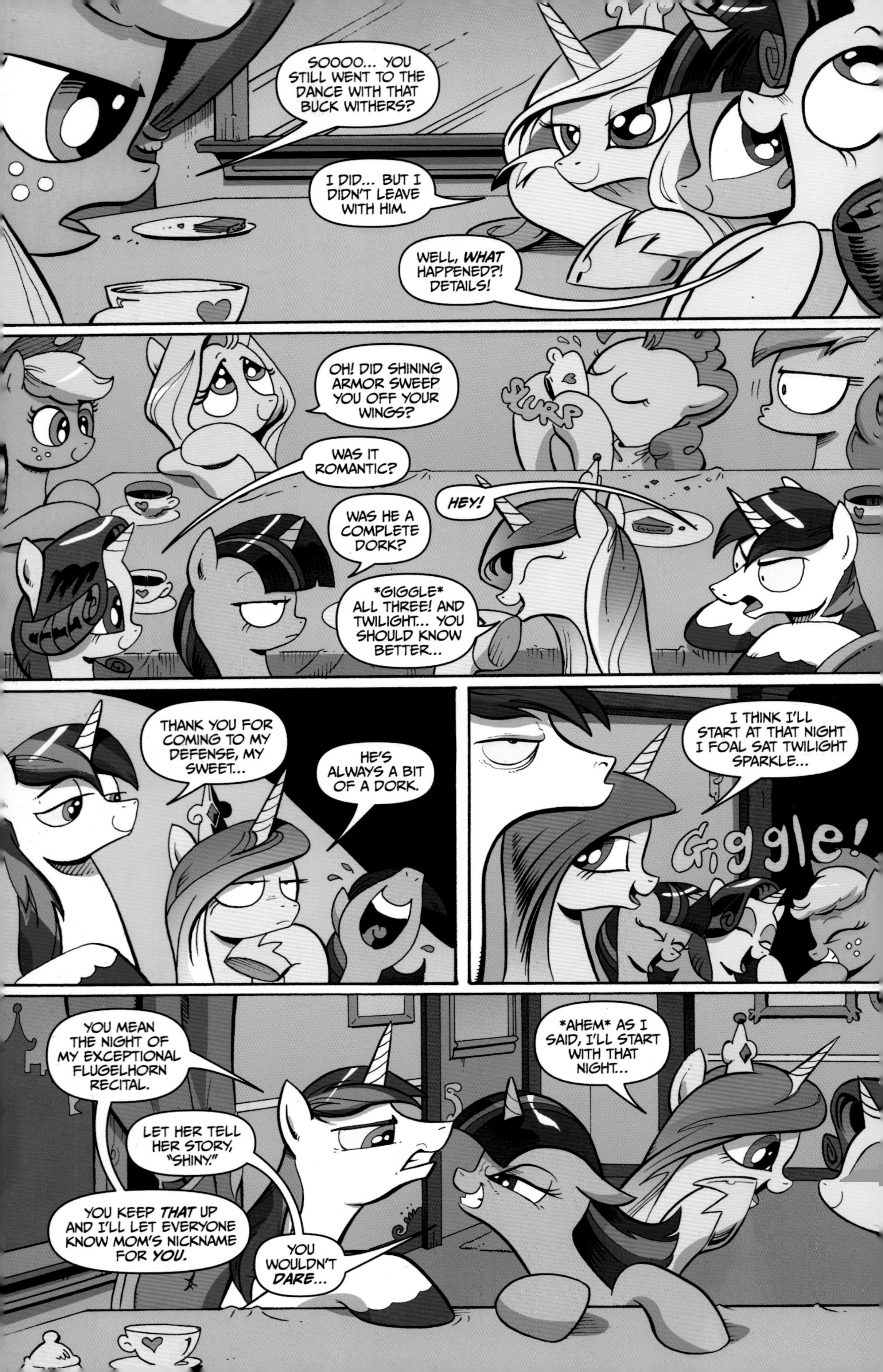
SOOOO... YOU STILL WENT TO THE DANCE WITH THAT BUCK WITHERS?
I DID... BUT I DIDN'T LEAVE WITH HIM.
WELL, *WHAT* HAPPENED?! DETAILS!
OH! DID SHINING ARMOR SWEEP YOU OFF YOUR WINGS?
SLURP
WAS IT ROMANTIC?
WAS HE A COMPLETE DORK?
HEY!
GIGGLE ALL THREE! AND TWILIGHT... YOU SHOULD KNOW BETTER...
THANK YOU FOR COMING TO MY DEFENSE, MY SWEET...
HE'S ALWAYS A BIT OF A DORK.
I THINK I'LL START AT THAT NIGHT I FOAL SAT TWILIGHT SPARKLE...
GIGGLE!
YOU MEAN THE NIGHT OF MY EXCEPTIONAL FLUGELHORN RECITAL.
AHEM AS I SAID, I'LL START WITH THAT NIGHT...
LET HER TELL HER STORY, "SHINY."
YOU KEEP *THAT* UP AND I'LL LET EVERYONE KNOW MOM'S NICKNAME FOR *YOU*.
YOU WOULDN'T *DARE*...

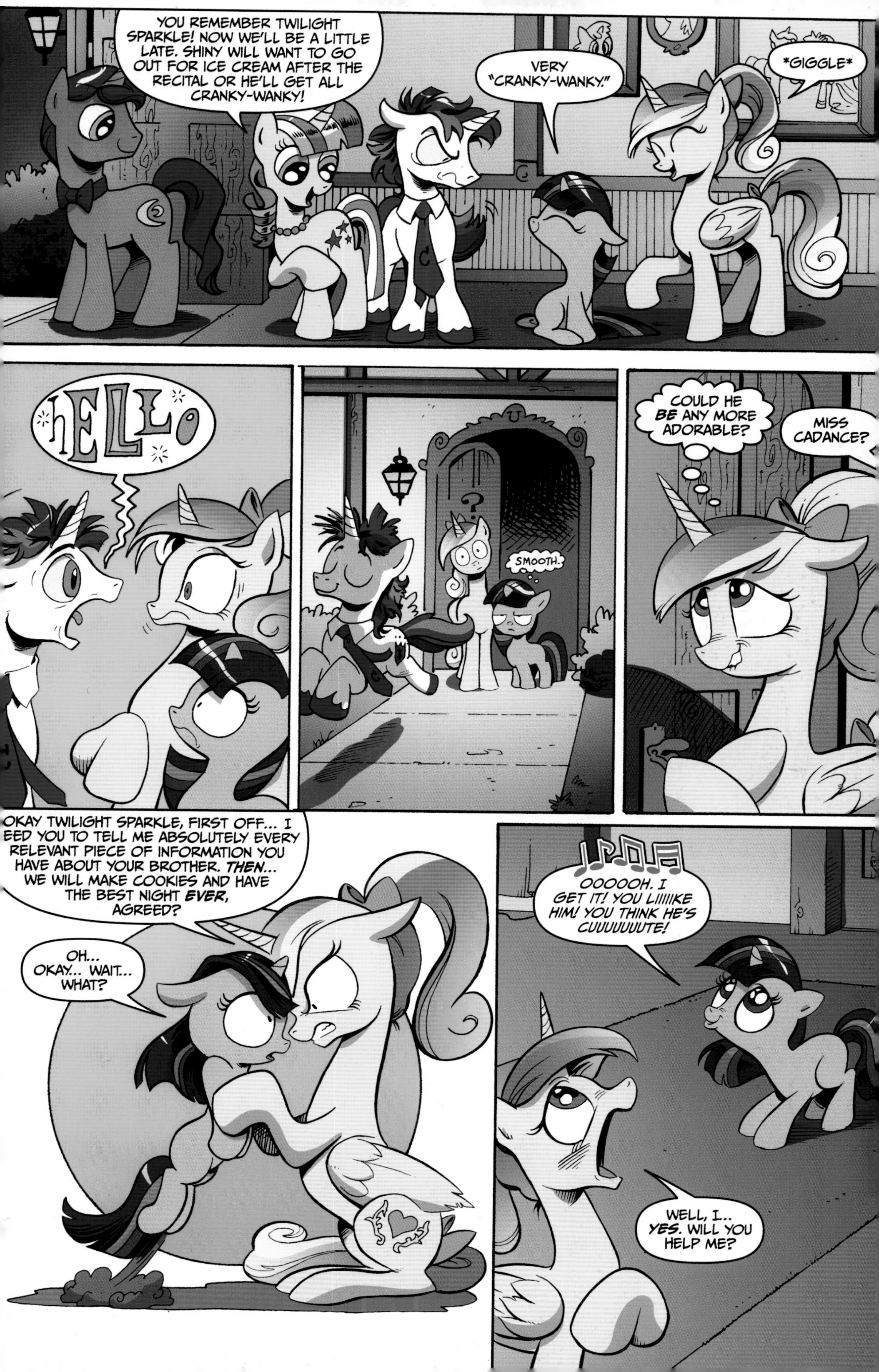

YOU REMEMBER TWILIGHT SPARKLE! NOW WE'LL BE A LITTLE LATE. SHINY WILL WANT TO GO OUT FOR ICE CREAM AFTER THE RECITAL OR HE'LL GET ALL CRANKY-WANKY!
VERY "CRANKY-WANKY."
GIGGLE
hELLO
?
SMOOTH.
COULD HE BE ANY MORE ADORABLE?
MISS CADANCE?
OKAY TWILIGHT SPARKLE, FIRST OFF... I EED YOU TO TELL ME ABSOLUTELY EVERY RELEVANT PIECE OF INFORMATION YOU HAVE ABOUT YOUR BROTHER. THEN... WE WILL MAKE COOKIES AND HAVE THE BEST NIGHT EVER, AGREED?
OH... OKAY... WAIT... WHAT?
OOOOOH. I GET IT! YOU LIIIIIKE HIM! YOU THINK HE'S CUUUUUUUTE!
WELL, I... YES. WILL YOU HELP ME?

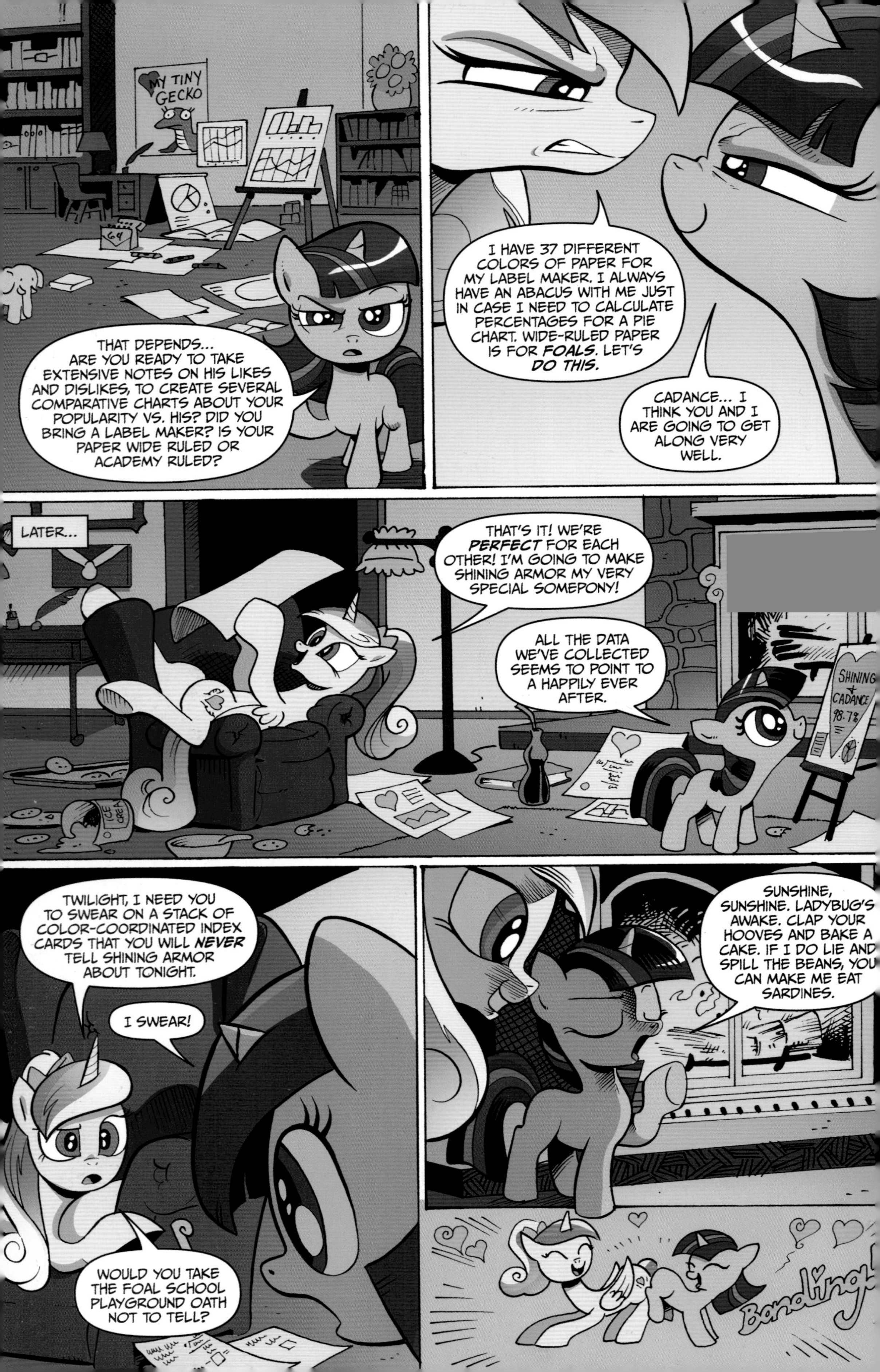
MY TINY GECKO
THAT DEPENDS... ARE YOU READY TO TAKE EXTENSIVE NOTES ON HIS LIKES AND DISLIKES, TO CREATE SEVERAL COMPARATIVE CHARTS ABOUT YOUR POPULARITY VS. HIS? DID YOU BRING A LABEL MAKER? IS YOUR PAPER WIDE RULED OR ACADEMY RULED?
I HAVE 37 DIFFERENT COLORS OF PAPER FOR MY LABEL MAKER. I ALWAYS HAVE AN ABACUS WITH ME JUST IN CASE I NEED TO CALCULATE PERCENTAGES FOR A PIE CHART. WIDE-RULED PAPER IS FOR ***FOALS***. LET'S ***DO THIS.***
CADANCE... I THINK YOU AND I ARE GOING TO GET ALONG VERY WELL.
LATER...
THAT'S IT! WE'RE ***PERFECT*** FOR EACH OTHER! I'M GOING TO MAKE SHINING ARMOR MY VERY SPECIAL SOMEPONY!
ALL THE DATA WE'VE COLLECTED SEEMS TO POINT TO A HAPPILY EVER AFTER.
SHINING + CADANCE 98.7%
TWILIGHT, I NEED YOU TO SWEAR ON A STACK OF COLOR-COORDINATED INDEX CARDS THAT YOU WILL ***NEVER*** TELL SHINING ARMOR ABOUT TONIGHT.
I SWEAR!
WOULD YOU TAKE THE FOAL SCHOOL PLAYGROUND OATH NOT TO TELL?
SUNSHINE, SUNSHINE. LADYBUG'S AWAKE. CLAP YOUR HOOVES AND BAKE A CAKE. IF I DO LIE AND SPILL THE BEANS, YOU CAN MAKE ME EAT SARDINES.
Bonding!

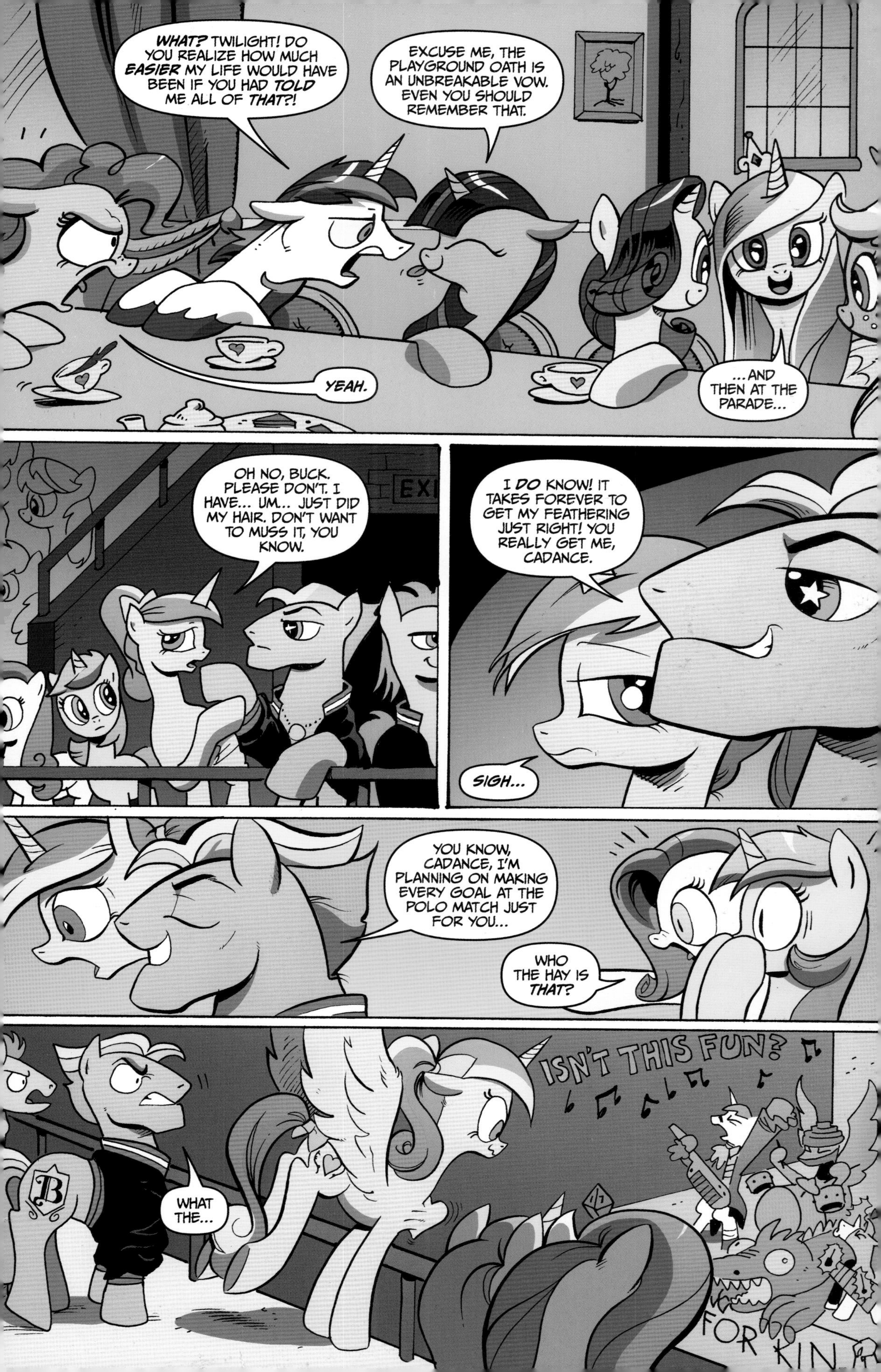
WHAT? TWILIGHT! DO YOU REALIZE HOW MUCH EASIER MY LIFE WOULD HAVE BEEN IF YOU HAD TOLD ME ALL OF THAT?!
EXCUSE ME, THE PLAYGROUND OATH IS AN UNBREAKABLE VOW. EVEN YOU SHOULD REMEMBER THAT.
YEAH.
...AND THEN AT THE PARADE...
EXI
OH NO, BUCK. PLEASE DON'T. I HAVE... UM... JUST DID MY HAIR. DON'T WANT TO MUSS IT, YOU KNOW.
I DO KNOW! IT TAKES FOREVER TO GET MY FEATHERING JUST RIGHT! YOU REALLY GET ME, CADANCE.
SIGH...
YOU KNOW, CADANCE, I'M PLANNING ON MAKING EVERY GOAL AT THE POLO MATCH JUST FOR YOU...
WHO THE HAY IS THAT?
ISN'T THIS FUN?
WHAT THE...
FOR KIN

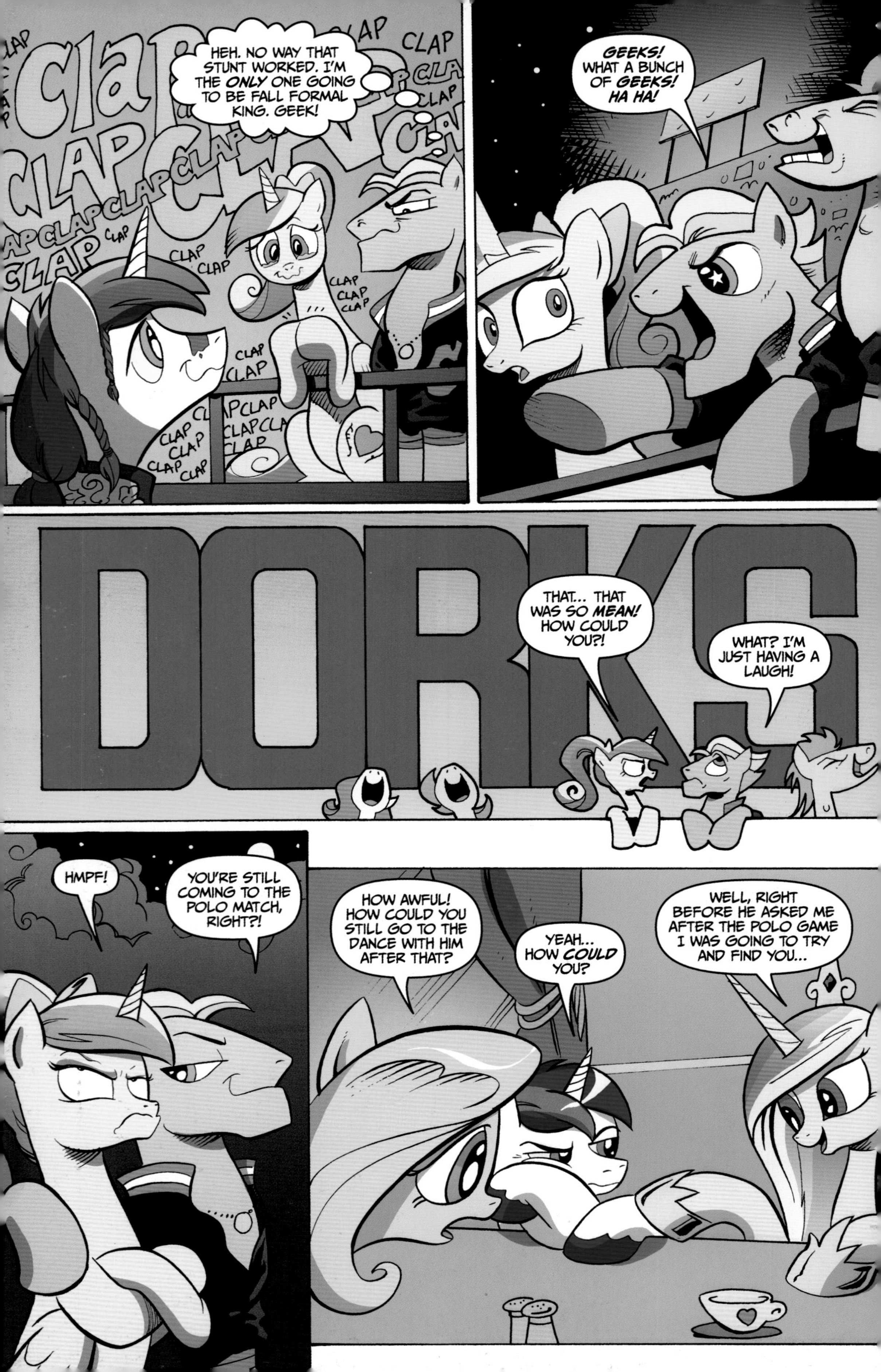
CLAP CLAP CLAP CLAP
HEH. NO WAY THAT STUNT WORKED. I'M THE *ONLY* ONE GOING TO BE FALL FORMAL KING. GEEK!
GEEKS! WHAT A BUNCH OF *GEEKS! HA HA!*
DORKS
THAT... THAT WAS SO *MEAN!* HOW COULD YOU?!
WHAT? I'M JUST HAVING A LAUGH!
HMPF!
YOU'RE STILL COMING TO THE POLO MATCH, RIGHT?!
HOW AWFUL! HOW COULD YOU STILL GO TO THE DANCE WITH HIM AFTER THAT?
YEAH... HOW *COULD* YOU?
WELL, RIGHT BEFORE HE ASKED ME AFTER THE POLO GAME I WAS GOING TO TRY AND FIND YOU...

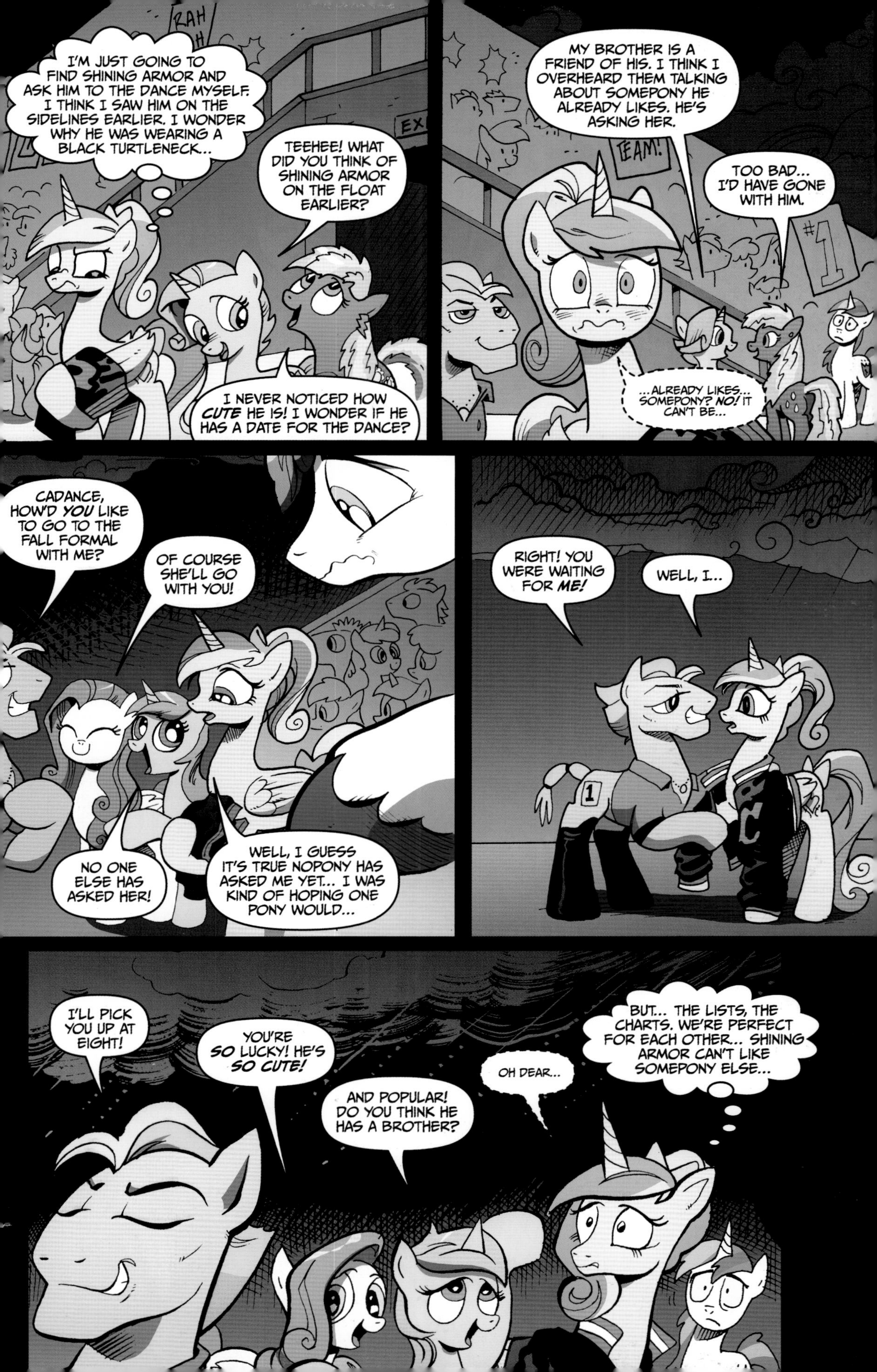

RAH
I'M JUST GOING TO FIND SHINING ARMOR AND ASK HIM TO THE DANCE MYSELF. I THINK I SAW HIM ON THE SIDELINES EARLIER. I WONDER WHY HE WAS WEARING A BLACK TURTLENECK...
TEEHEE! WHAT DID YOU THINK OF SHINING ARMOR ON THE FLOAT EARLIER?
I NEVER NOTICED HOW CUTE HE IS! I WONDER IF HE HAS A DATE FOR THE DANCE?
MY BROTHER IS A FRIEND OF HIS. I THINK I OVERHEARD THEM TALKING ABOUT SOMEPONY HE ALREADY LIKES. HE'S ASKING HER.
TEAM!
TOO BAD... I'D HAVE GONE WITH HIM.
...ALREADY LIKES... SOMEPONY? NO! IT CAN'T BE...
CADANCE, HOW'D YOU LIKE TO GO TO THE FALL FORMAL WITH ME?
OF COURSE SHE'LL GO WITH YOU!
NO ONE ELSE HAS ASKED HER!
WELL, I GUESS IT'S TRUE NOPONY HAS ASKED ME YET... I WAS KIND OF HOPING ONE PONY WOULD...
RIGHT! YOU WERE WAITING FOR ME!
WELL, I...
I'LL PICK YOU UP AT EIGHT!
YOU'RE SO LUCKY! HE'S SO CUTE!
AND POPULAR! DO YOU THINK HE HAS A BROTHER?
OH DEAR...
BUT... THE LISTS, THE CHARTS. WE'RE PERFECT FOR EACH OTHER... SHINING ARMOR CAN'T LIKE SOMEPONY ELSE...

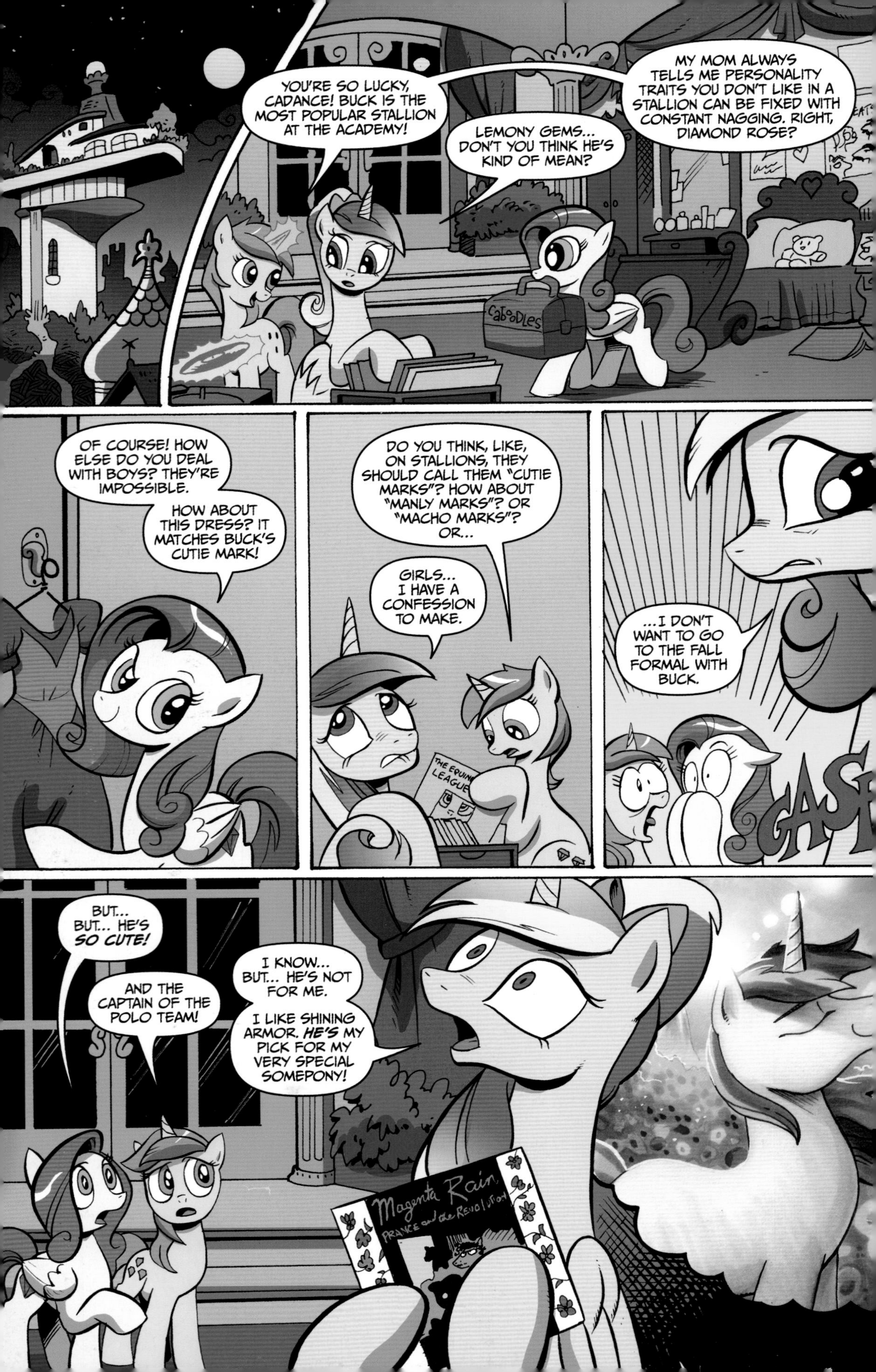
YOU'RE SO LUCKY, CADANCE! BUCK IS THE MOST POPULAR STALLION AT THE ACADEMY!
LEMONY GEMS... DON'T YOU THINK HE'S KIND OF MEAN?
MY MOM ALWAYS TELLS ME PERSONALITY TRAITS YOU DON'T LIKE IN A STALLION CAN BE FIXED WITH CONSTANT NAGGING. RIGHT, DIAMOND ROSE?
CABOODLES
OF COURSE! HOW ELSE DO YOU DEAL WITH BOYS? THEY'RE IMPOSSIBLE.
HOW ABOUT THIS DRESS? IT MATCHES BUCK'S CUTIE MARK!
DO YOU THINK, LIKE, ON STALLIONS, THEY SHOULD CALL THEM "CUTIE MARKS"? HOW ABOUT "MANLY MARKS"? OR "MACHO MARKS"? OR...
GIRLS... I HAVE A CONFESSION TO MAKE.
THE EQUINE LEAGUE
...I DON'T WANT TO GO TO THE FALL FORMAL WITH BUCK.
GASP
BUT... BUT... HE'S SO CUTE!
AND THE CAPTAIN OF THE POLO TEAM!
I KNOW... BUT... HE'S NOT FOR ME.
I LIKE SHINING ARMOR. HE'S MY PICK FOR MY VERY SPECIAL SOMEPONY!
Magenta Rain
PRANCE and the REVOLUTION

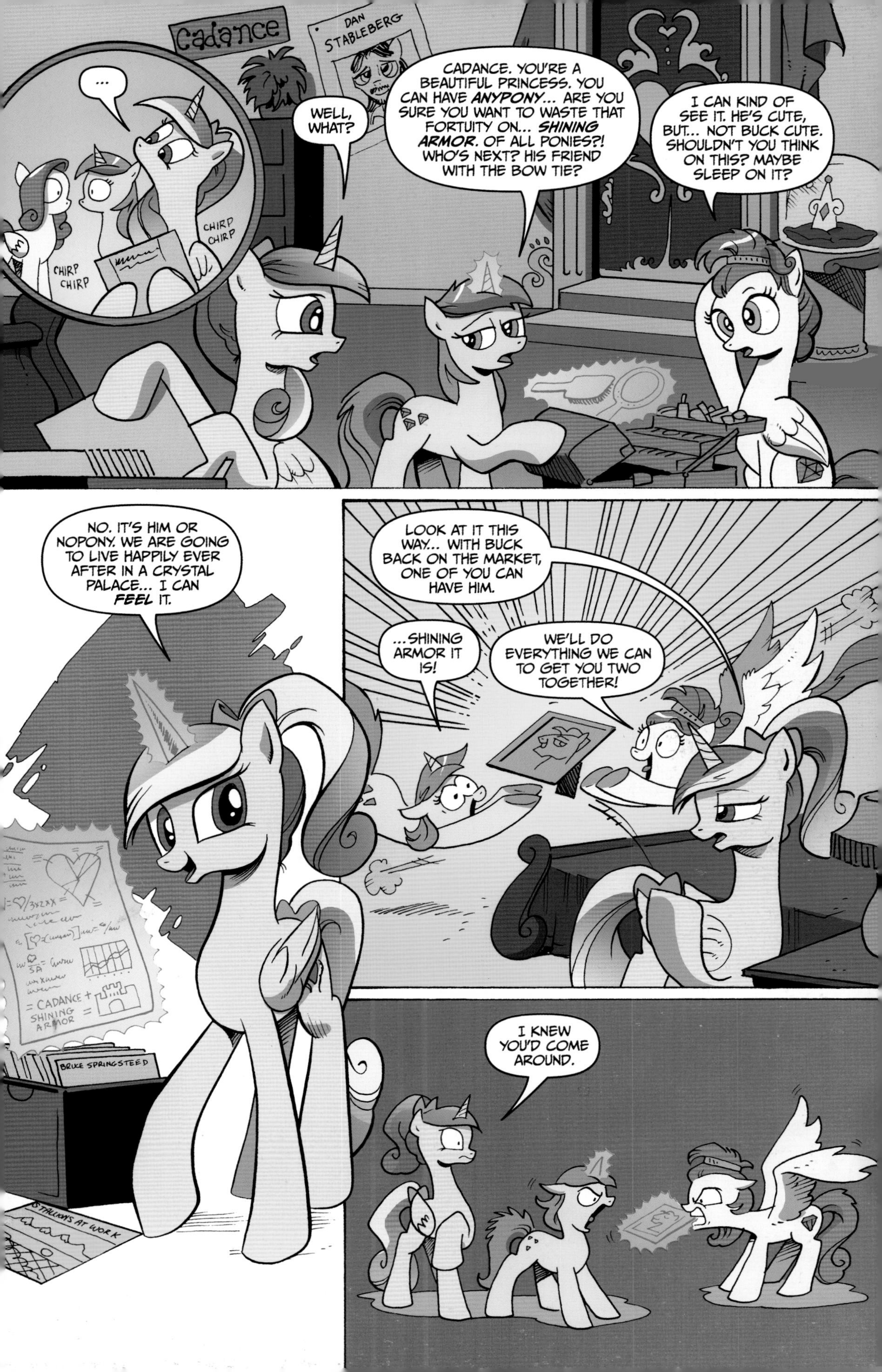
Cadance
DAN STABLEBERG
...
CHIRP CHIRP
CHIRP CHIRP
WELL, WHAT?
CADANCE. YOU'RE A BEAUTIFUL PRINCESS. YOU CAN HAVE ANYPONY... ARE YOU SURE YOU WANT TO WASTE THAT FORTUITY ON... SHINING ARMOR. OF ALL PONIES?! WHO'S NEXT? HIS FRIEND WITH THE BOW TIE?
I CAN KIND OF SEE IT. HE'S CUTE, BUT... NOT BUCK CUTE. SHOULDN'T YOU THINK ON THIS? MAYBE SLEEP ON IT?
NO. IT'S HIM OR NOPONY. WE ARE GOING TO LIVE HAPPILY EVER AFTER IN A CRYSTAL PALACE... I CAN FEEL IT.
= CADANCE + SHINING ARMOR =
BRUCE SPRINGSTEED
STALLIONS AT WORK
LOOK AT IT THIS WAY... WITH BUCK BACK ON THE MARKET, ONE OF YOU CAN HAVE HIM.
...SHINING ARMOR IT IS!
WE'LL DO EVERYTHING WE CAN TO GET YOU TWO TOGETHER!
I KNEW YOU'D COME AROUND.

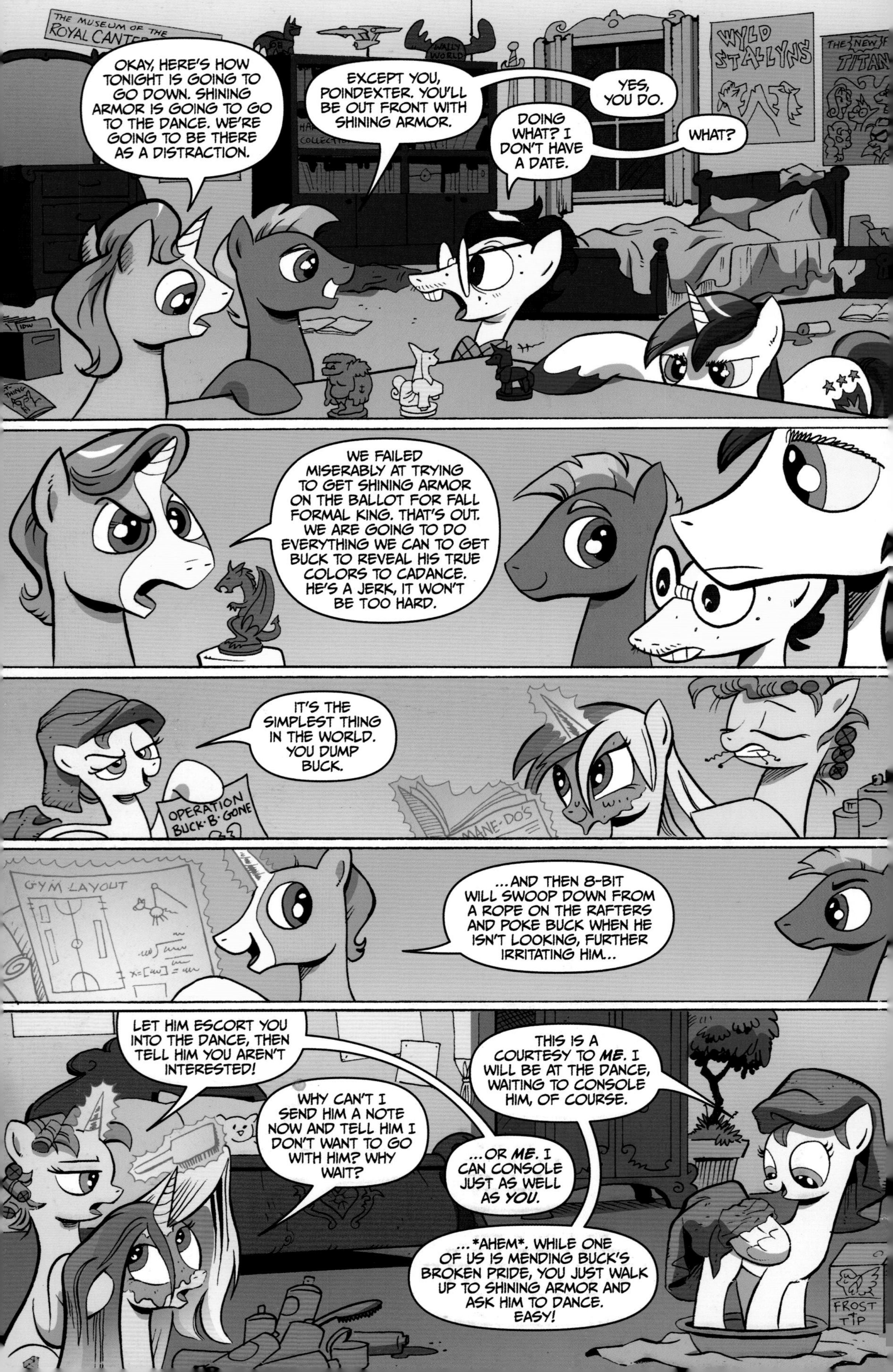
THE MUSEUM OF THE ROYAL CANTER
WYLD STALLYNS
THE NEW TITAN
OKAY, HERE'S HOW TONIGHT IS GOING TO GO DOWN. SHINING ARMOR IS GOING TO GO TO THE DANCE. WE'RE GOING TO BE THERE AS A DISTRACTION.
EXCEPT YOU, POINDEXTER. YOU'LL BE OUT FRONT WITH SHINING ARMOR.
DOING WHAT? I DON'T HAVE A DATE.
YES, YOU DO.
WHAT?
WE FAILED MISERABLY AT TRYING TO GET SHINING ARMOR ON THE BALLOT FOR FALL FORMAL KING. THAT'S OUT. WE ARE GOING TO DO EVERYTHING WE CAN TO GET BUCK TO REVEAL HIS TRUE COLORS TO CADANCE. HE'S A JERK, IT WON'T BE TOO HARD.
IT'S THE SIMPLEST THING IN THE WORLD. YOU DUMP BUCK.
OPERATION BUCK-B-GONE
MANE-DO'S
GYM LAYOUT
...AND THEN 8-BIT WILL SWOOP DOWN FROM A ROPE ON THE RAFTERS AND POKE BUCK WHEN HE ISN'T LOOKING, FURTHER IRRITATING HIM...
LET HIM ESCORT YOU INTO THE DANCE, THEN TELL HIM YOU AREN'T INTERESTED!
WHY CAN'T I SEND HIM A NOTE NOW AND TELL HIM I DON'T WANT TO GO WITH HIM? WHY WAIT?
THIS IS A COURTESY TO *ME*. I WILL BE AT THE DANCE, WAITING TO CONSOLE HIM, OF COURSE.
...OR *ME*. I CAN CONSOLE JUST AS WELL AS *YOU*.
...*AHEM*. WHILE ONE OF US IS MENDING BUCK'S BROKEN PRIDE, YOU JUST WALK UP TO SHINING ARMOR AND ASK HIM TO DANCE. EASY!
FROST TIP

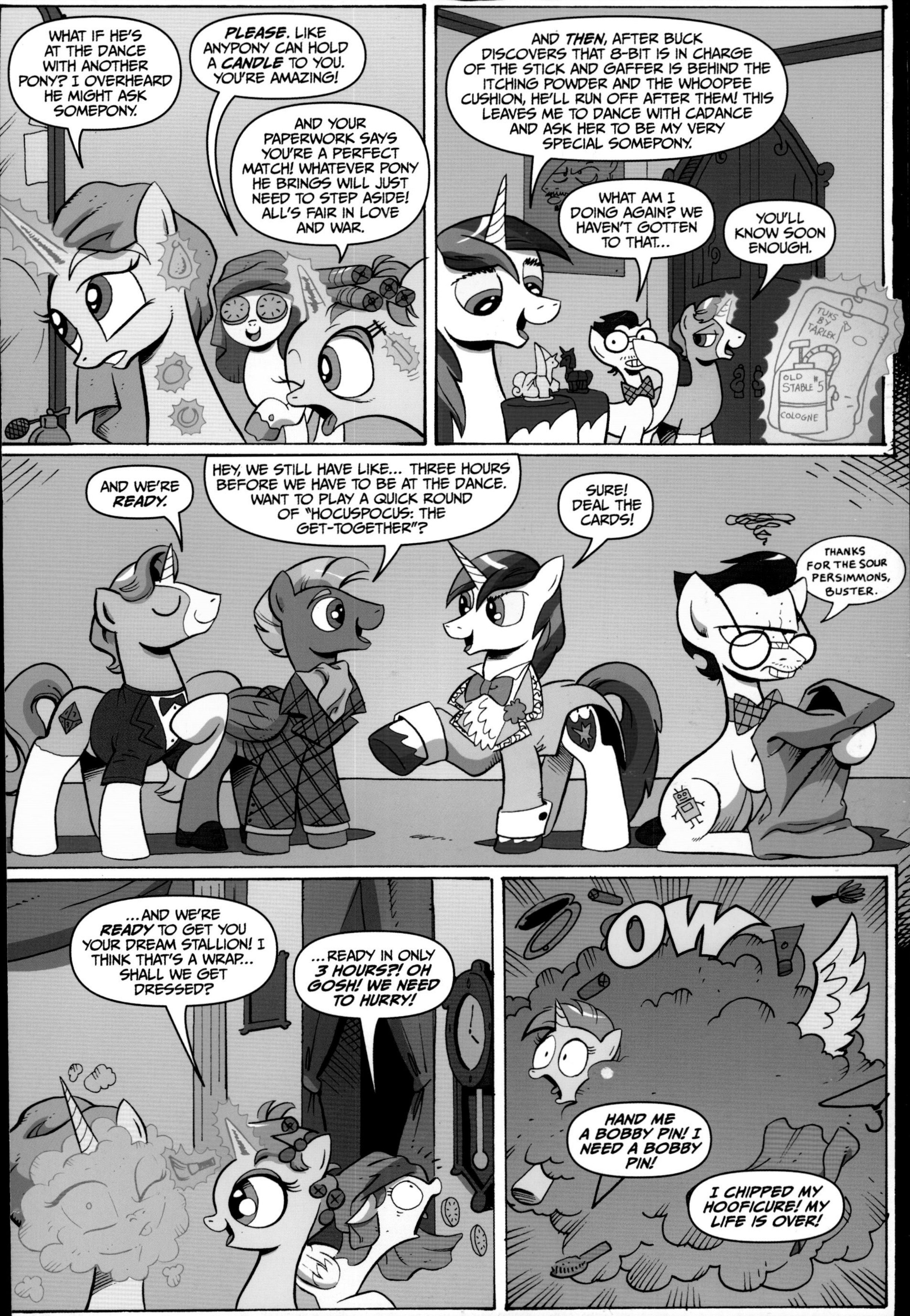

WHAT IF HE'S AT THE DANCE WITH ANOTHER PONY? I OVERHEARD HE MIGHT ASK SOMEPONY.
PLEASE. LIKE ANYPONY CAN HOLD A CANDLE TO YOU. YOU'RE AMAZING!
AND YOUR PAPERWORK SAYS YOU'RE A PERFECT MATCH! WHATEVER PONY HE BRINGS WILL JUST NEED TO STEP ASIDE! ALL'S FAIR IN LOVE AND WAR.
AND THEN, AFTER BUCK DISCOVERS THAT 8-BIT IS IN CHARGE OF THE STICK AND GAFFER IS BEHIND THE ITCHING POWDER AND THE WHOOPEE CUSHION, HE'LL RUN OFF AFTER THEM! THIS LEAVES ME TO DANCE WITH CADANCE AND ASK HER TO BE MY VERY SPECIAL SOMEPONY.
WHAT AM I DOING AGAIN? WE HAVEN'T GOTTEN TO THAT...
YOU'LL KNOW SOON ENOUGH.
TUXS BY TARLEK
OLD STABLE #5
COLOGNE
AND WE'RE READY.
HEY, WE STILL HAVE LIKE... THREE HOURS BEFORE WE HAVE TO BE AT THE DANCE. WANT TO PLAY A QUICK ROUND OF "HOCUSPOCUS: THE GET-TOGETHER"?
SURE! DEAL THE CARDS!
THANKS FOR THE SOUR PERSIMMONS, BUSTER.
...AND WE'RE READY TO GET YOU YOUR DREAM STALLION! I THINK THAT'S A WRAP... SHALL WE GET DRESSED?
...READY IN ONLY 3 HOURS?! OH GOSH! WE NEED TO HURRY!
OW!
HAND ME A BOBBY PIN! I NEED A BOBBY PIN!
I CHIPPED MY HOOFICURE! MY LIFE IS OVER!

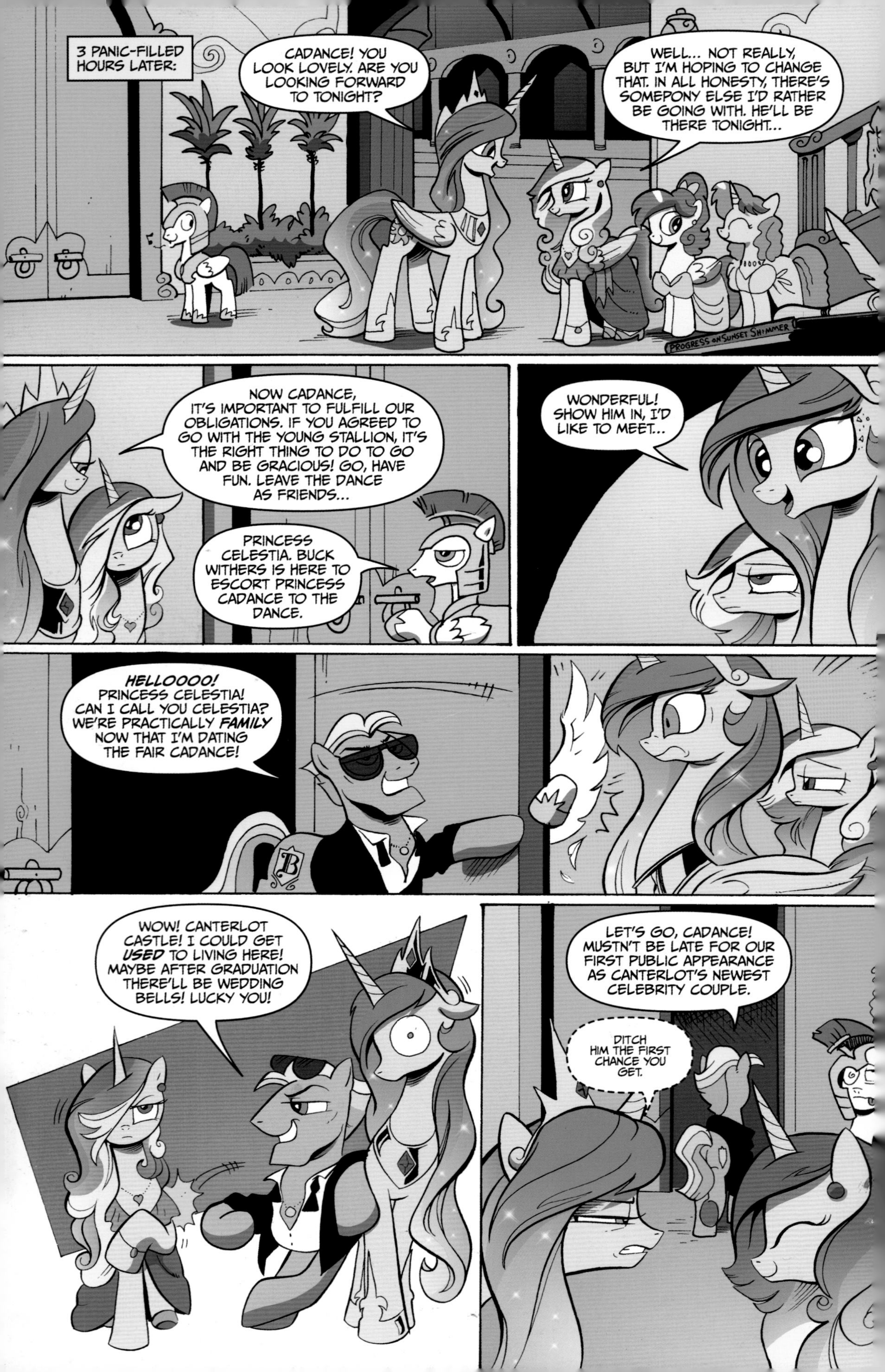
3 PANIC-FILLED HOURS LATER:
CADANCE! YOU LOOK LOVELY. ARE YOU LOOKING FORWARD TO TONIGHT?
WELL... NOT REALLY, BUT I'M HOPING TO CHANGE THAT. IN ALL HONESTY, THERE'S SOMEPONY ELSE I'D RATHER BE GOING WITH. HE'LL BE THERE TONIGHT...
PROGRESS ON SUNSET SHIMMER
NOW CADANCE, IT'S IMPORTANT TO FULFILL OUR OBLIGATIONS. IF YOU AGREED TO GO WITH THE YOUNG STALLION, IT'S THE RIGHT THING TO DO TO GO AND BE GRACIOUS! GO, HAVE FUN. LEAVE THE DANCE AS FRIENDS...
PRINCESS CELESTIA. BUCK WITHERS IS HERE TO ESCORT PRINCESS CADANCE TO THE DANCE.
WONDERFUL! SHOW HIM IN, I'D LIKE TO MEET...
HELLOOOO! PRINCESS CELESTIA! CAN I CALL YOU CELESTIA? WE'RE PRACTICALLY FAMILY NOW THAT I'M DATING THE FAIR CADANCE!
WOW! CANTERLOT CASTLE! I COULD GET USED TO LIVING HERE! MAYBE AFTER GRADUATION THERE'LL BE WEDDING BELLS! LUCKY YOU!
LET'S GO, CADANCE! MUSTN'T BE LATE FOR OUR FIRST PUBLIC APPEARANCE AS CANTERLOT'S NEWEST CELEBRITY COUPLE.
DITCH HIM THE FIRST CHANCE YOU GET.

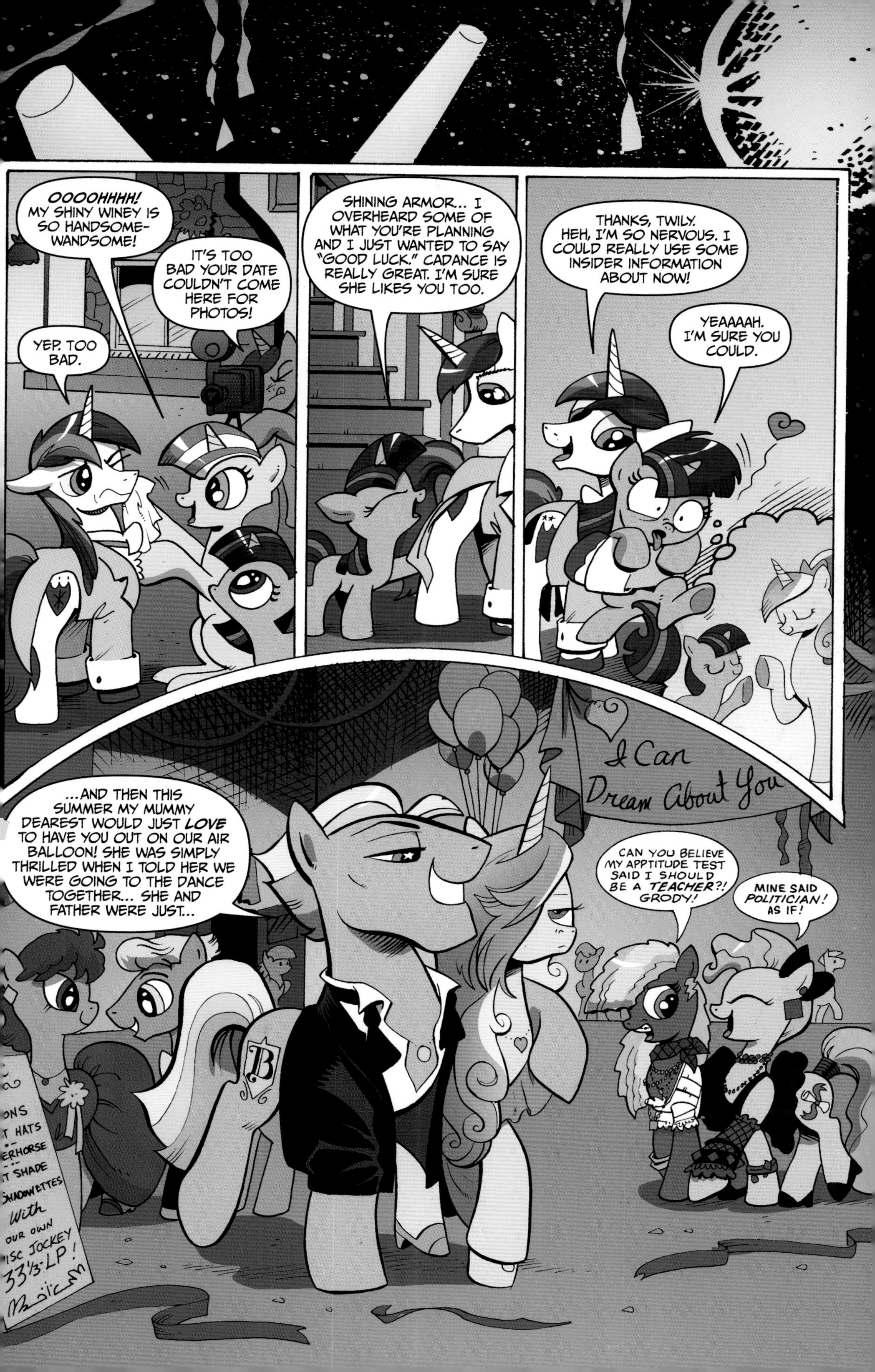

OOOOHHHH! MY SHINY WINEY IS SO HANDSOME-WANDSOME!
IT'S TOO BAD YOUR DATE COULDN'T COME HERE FOR PHOTOS!
YEP. TOO BAD.
SHINING ARMOR... I OVERHEARD SOME OF WHAT YOU'RE PLANNING AND I JUST WANTED TO SAY "GOOD LUCK." CADANCE IS REALLY GREAT. I'M SURE SHE LIKES YOU TOO.
THANKS, TWILY. HEH, I'M SO NERVOUS. I COULD REALLY USE SOME INSIDER INFORMATION ABOUT NOW!
YEAAAAH. I'M SURE YOU COULD.
I Can Dream About You
...AND THEN THIS SUMMER MY MUMMY DEAREST WOULD JUST LOVE TO HAVE YOU OUT ON OUR AIR BALLOON! SHE WAS SIMPLY THRILLED WHEN I TOLD HER WE WERE GOING TO THE DANCE TOGETHER... SHE AND FATHER WERE JUST...
CAN YOU BELIEVE MY APPTITUDE TEST SAID I SHOULD BE A TEACHER?! GRODY!
MINE SAID POLITICIAN! AS IF!

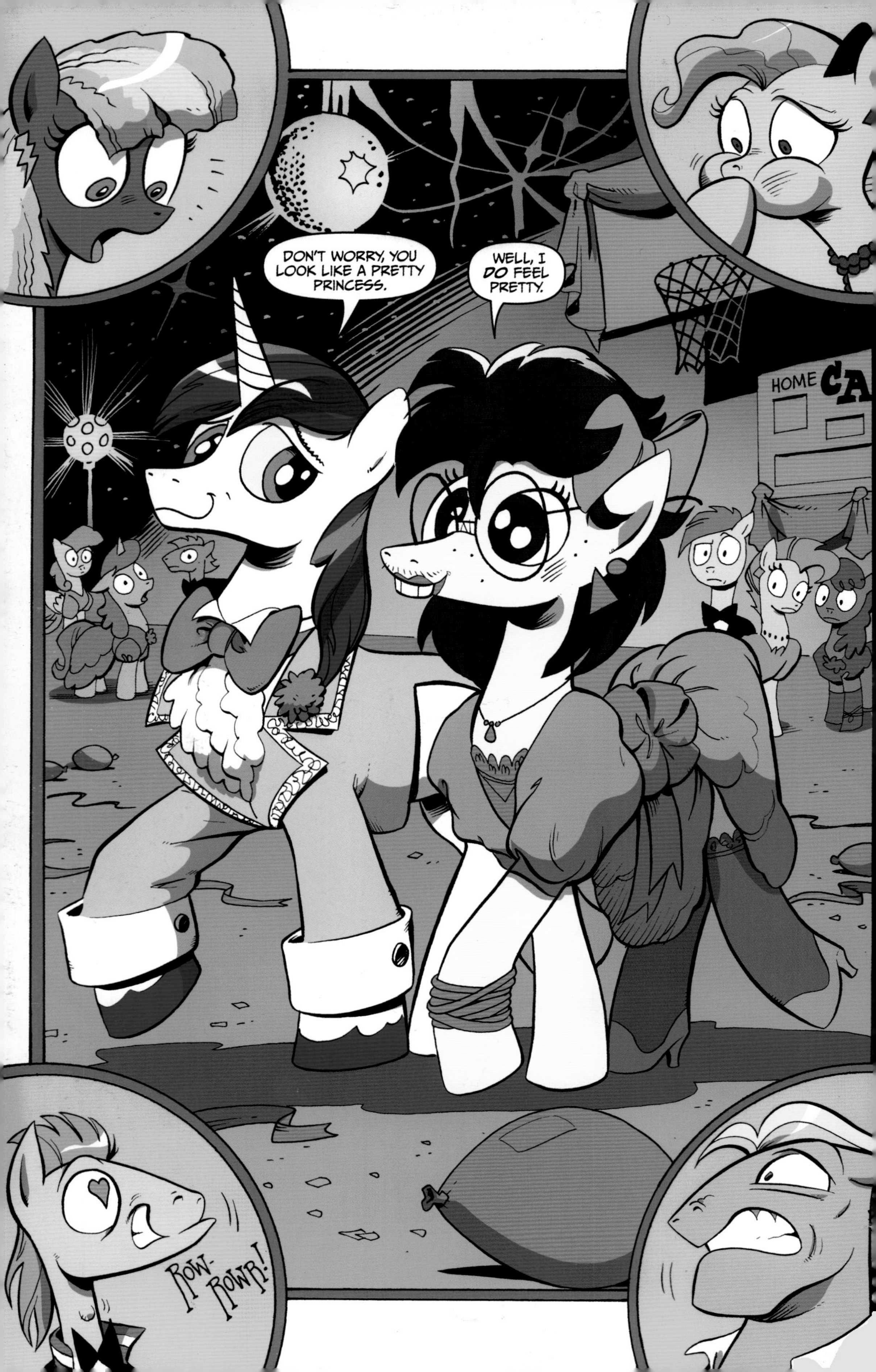
DON'T WORRY, YOU LOOK LIKE A PRETTY PRINCESS.
WELL, I DO FEEL PRETTY.
HOME CA
ROW-ROWR!

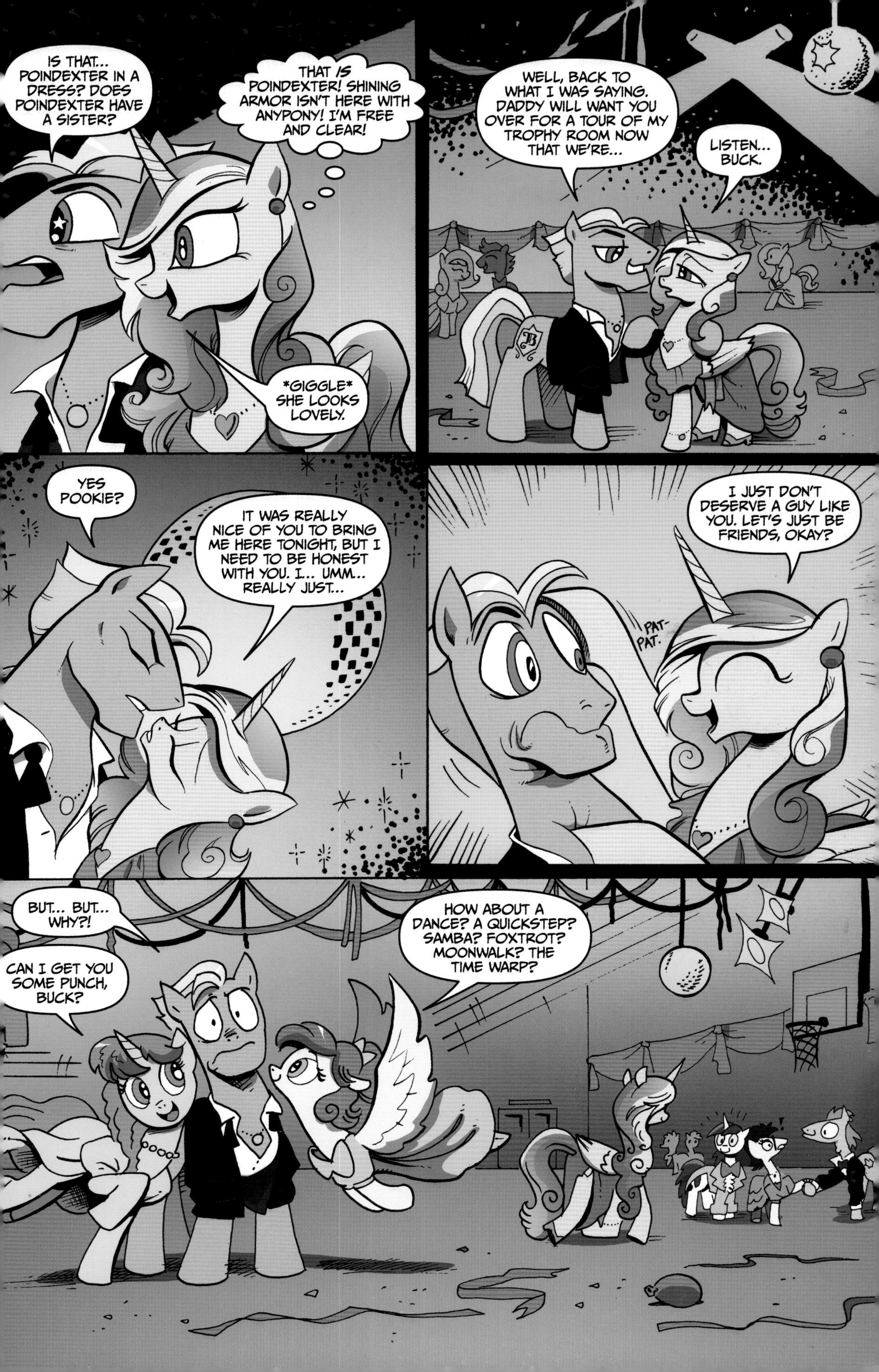
IS THAT... POINDEXTER IN A DRESS? DOES POINDEXTER HAVE A SISTER?
THAT IS POINDEXTER! SHINING ARMOR ISN'T HERE WITH ANYPONY! I'M FREE AND CLEAR!
GIGGLE SHE LOOKS LOVELY.
WELL, BACK TO WHAT I WAS SAYING. DADDY WILL WANT YOU OVER FOR A TOUR OF MY TROPHY ROOM NOW THAT WE'RE...
LISTEN... BUCK.
YES POOKIE?
IT WAS REALLY NICE OF YOU TO BRING ME HERE TONIGHT, BUT I NEED TO BE HONEST WITH YOU. I... UMM... REALLY JUST...
I JUST DON'T DESERVE A GUY LIKE YOU. LET'S JUST BE FRIENDS, OKAY?
PAT-PAT.
BUT... BUT... WHY?!
CAN I GET YOU SOME PUNCH, BUCK?
HOW ABOUT A DANCE? A QUICKSTEP? SAMBA? FOXTROT? MOONWALK? THE TIME WARP?

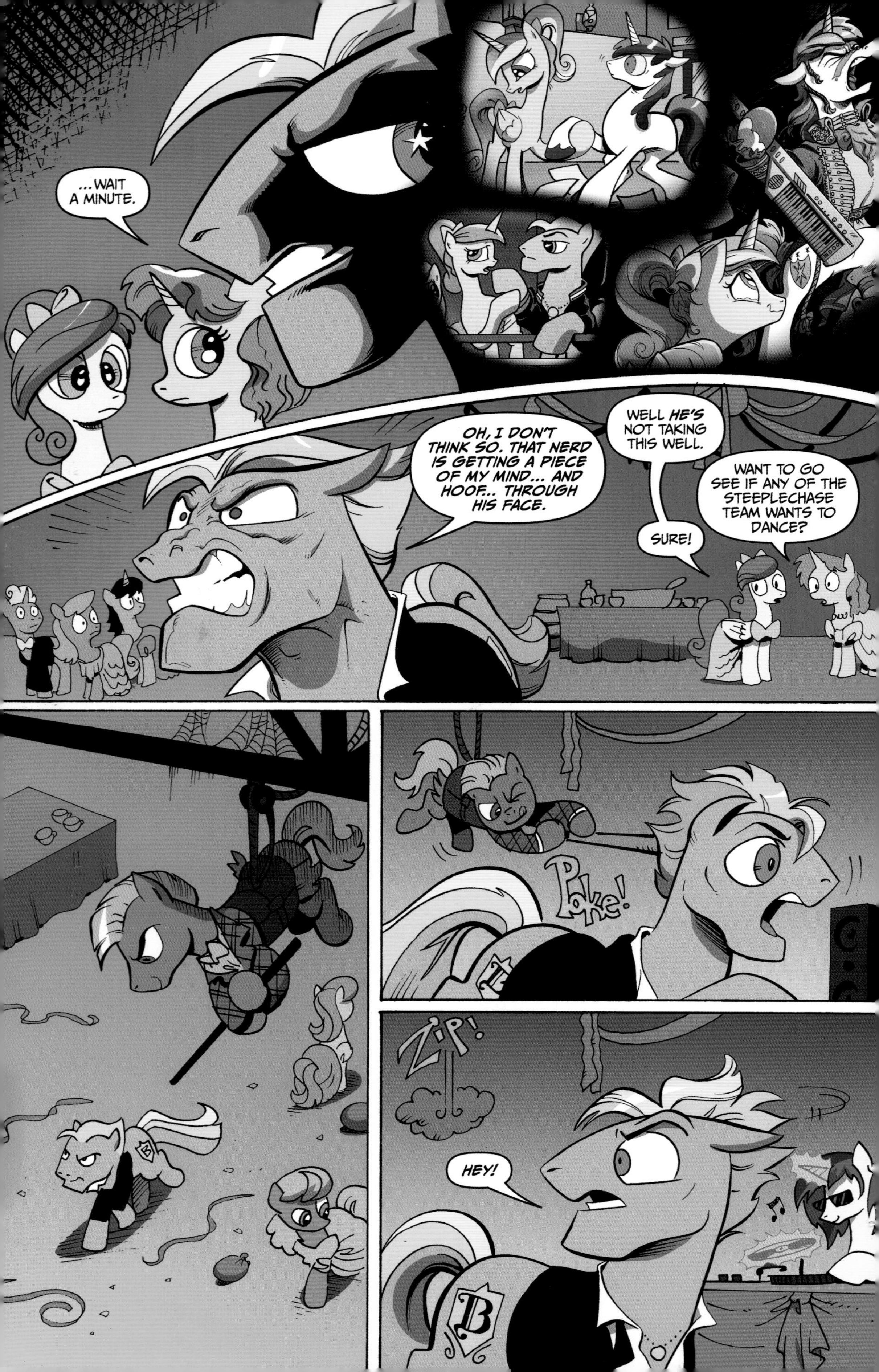

...WAIT A MINUTE.
OH, I DON'T THINK SO. THAT NERD IS GETTING A PIECE OF MY MIND... AND HOOF.. THROUGH HIS FACE.
WELL HE'S NOT TAKING THIS WELL.
WANT TO GO SEE IF ANY OF THE STEEPLECHASE TEAM WANTS TO DANCE?
SURE!
Poke!
ZIP!
HEY!

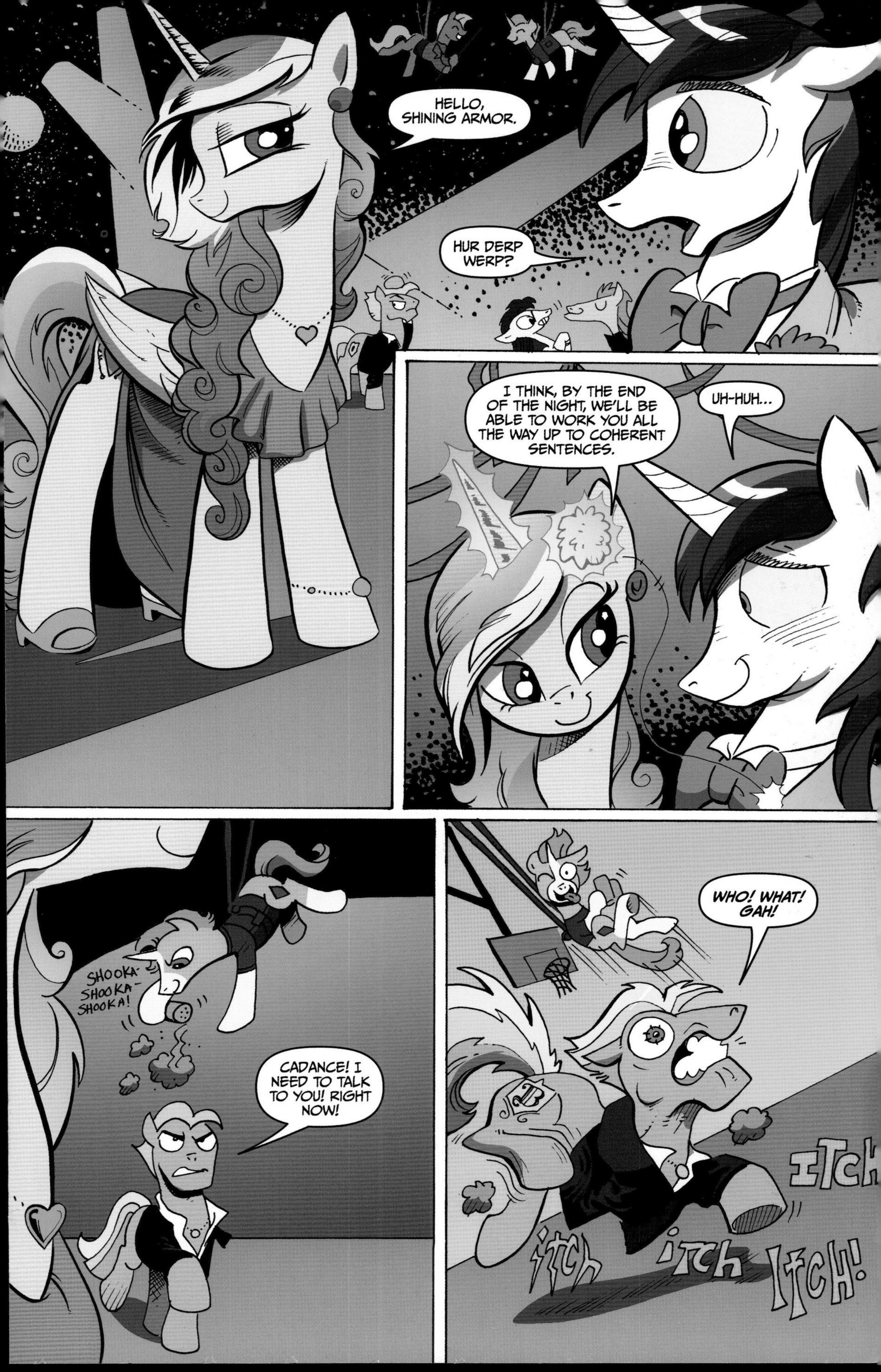
HELLO, SHINING ARMOR.
HUR DERP WERP?
I THINK, BY THE END OF THE NIGHT, WE'LL BE ABLE TO WORK YOU ALL THE WAY UP TO COHERENT SENTENCES.
UH-HUH...
SHOOKA-SHOOKA-SHOOKA!
CADANCE! I NEED TO TALK TO YOU! RIGHT NOW!
WHO! WHAT! GAH!
ITCH
ITCH
ITCH
ITCH!

OH COME ON!

POKE!

HITCHITCH... TCHITCHITCHIT

YOU LOOK VERY NICE, POINDEXTER.

NOPONY HAS TOLD ME WHY I'M IN A DRESS YET.

BECAUSE YOU NEVER GAVE GAFFER BACK HIS REPLICA BAT'LETH SWORD AFTER NIGHTMARE NIGHT LAST YEAR AND THAT STALLION HOLDS A GRUDGE. CONSIDER YOURSELF PUNISHED.

...I STILL FEEL PRETTY. HE CAN'T TAKE THAT FROM ME.

CADANCE! I WANT TO HAVE A FEW WORDS WITH YOU.

BUCK! WHAT HAPPENED TO YOU?

WHAT HAPPENED TO ME?! THAT DWEEB'S FRIENDS HAPPENED TO ME!

WHAT? NEVER!

EVERYPONY! IT'S TIME TO ANNOUNCE THE KING AND QUEEN OF THE FALL FORMAL!

SKIP IT. TOO MESSY

I THINK IT'S NO SURPRISE THAT OUR QUEEN THIS YEAR IS PRINCESS CADANCE!

KING QUEEN

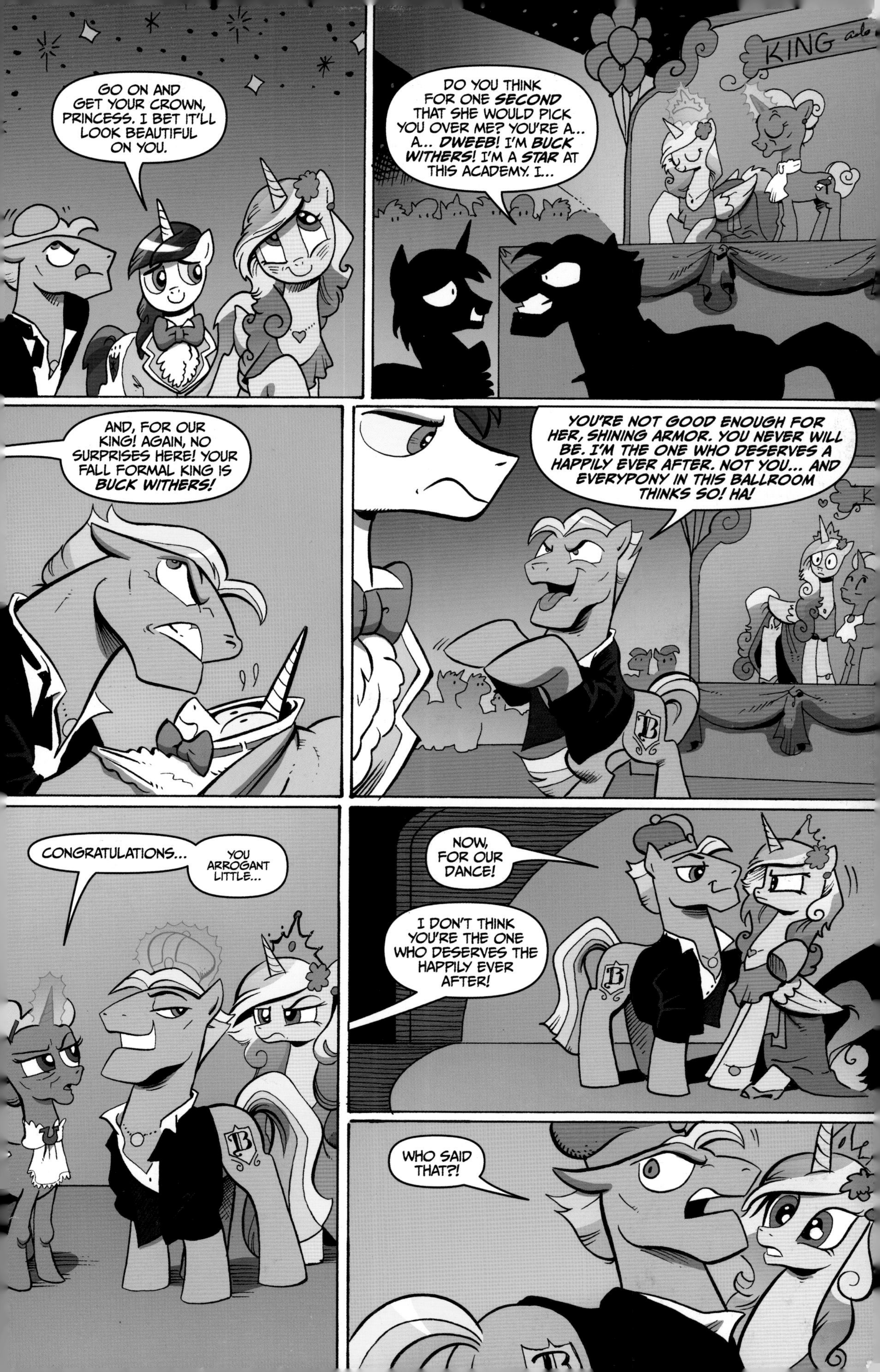
GO ON AND GET YOUR CROWN, PRINCESS. I BET IT'LL LOOK BEAUTIFUL ON YOU.
KING
DO YOU THINK FOR ONE SECOND THAT SHE WOULD PICK YOU OVER ME? YOU'RE A... A... DWEEB! I'M BUCK WITHERS! I'M A STAR AT THIS ACADEMY. I...
AND, FOR OUR KING! AGAIN, NO SURPRISES HERE! YOUR FALL FORMAL KING IS BUCK WITHERS!
YOU'RE NOT GOOD ENOUGH FOR HER, SHINING ARMOR. YOU NEVER WILL BE. I'M THE ONE WHO DESERVES A HAPPILY EVER AFTER. NOT YOU... AND EVERYPONY IN THIS BALLROOM THINKS SO! HA!
CONGRATULATIONS...
YOU ARROGANT LITTLE...
NOW, FOR OUR DANCE!
I DON'T THINK YOU'RE THE ONE WHO DESERVES THE HAPPILY EVER AFTER!
WHO SAID THAT?!

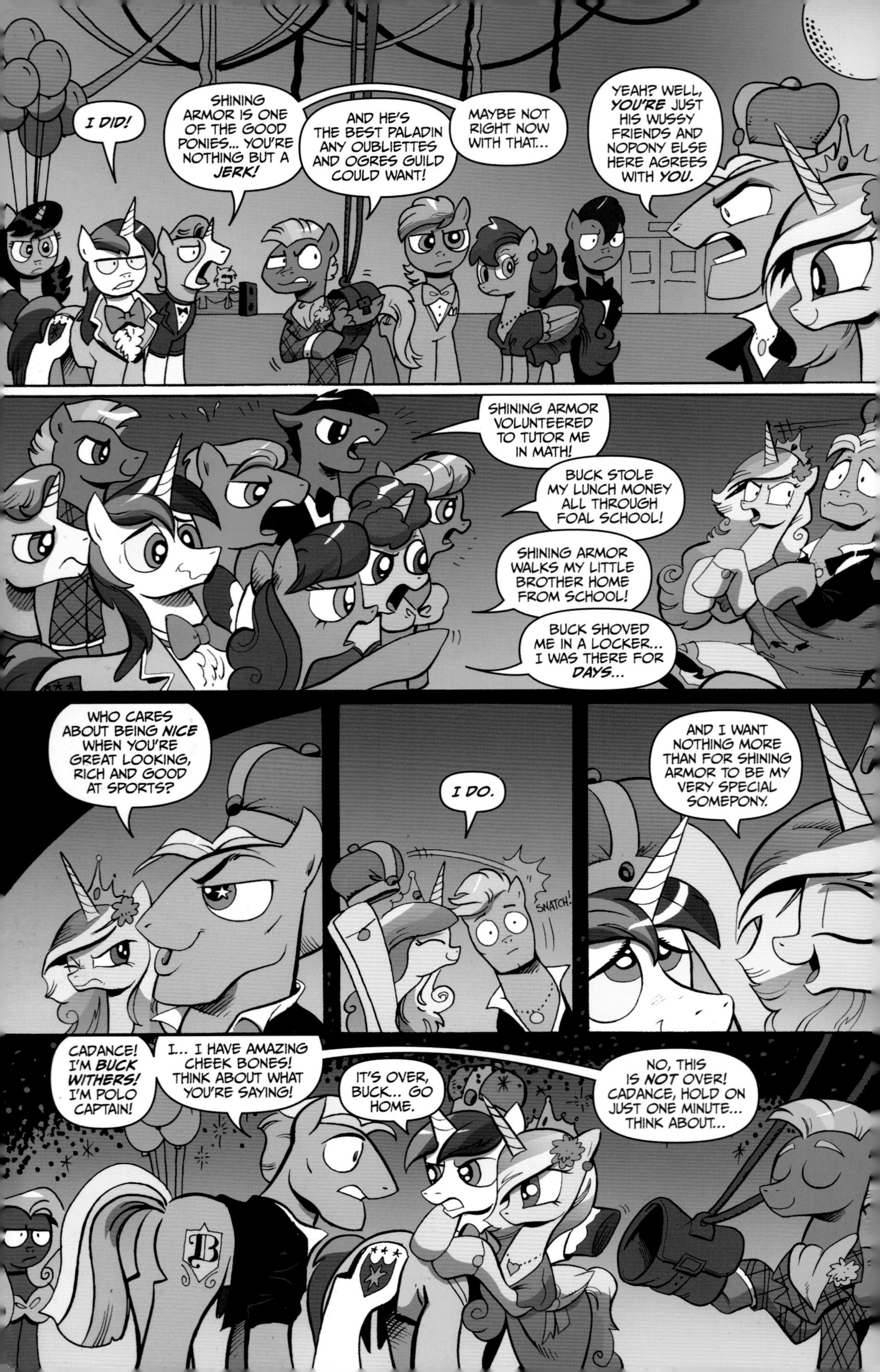
I DID!
SHINING ARMOR IS ONE OF THE GOOD PONIES... YOU'RE NOTHING BUT A JERK!
AND HE'S THE BEST PALADIN ANY OUBLIETTES AND OGRES GUILD COULD WANT!
MAYBE NOT RIGHT NOW WITH THAT...
YEAH? WELL, YOU'RE JUST HIS WUSSY FRIENDS AND NOPONY ELSE HERE AGREES WITH YOU.
SHINING ARMOR VOLUNTEERED TO TUTOR ME IN MATH!
BUCK STOLE MY LUNCH MONEY ALL THROUGH FOAL SCHOOL!
SHINING ARMOR WALKS MY LITTLE BROTHER HOME FROM SCHOOL!
BUCK SHOVED ME IN A LOCKER... I WAS THERE FOR DAYS...
WHO CARES ABOUT BEING NICE WHEN YOU'RE GREAT LOOKING, RICH AND GOOD AT SPORTS?
I DO.
SNATCH!
AND I WANT NOTHING MORE THAN FOR SHINING ARMOR TO BE MY VERY SPECIAL SOMEPONY.
CADANCE! I'M BUCK WITHERS! I'M POLO CAPTAIN!
I... I HAVE AMAZING CHEEK BONES! THINK ABOUT WHAT YOU'RE SAYING!
IT'S OVER, BUCK... GO HOME.
NO, THIS IS NOT OVER! CADANCE, HOLD ON JUST ONE MINUTE... THINK ABOUT...

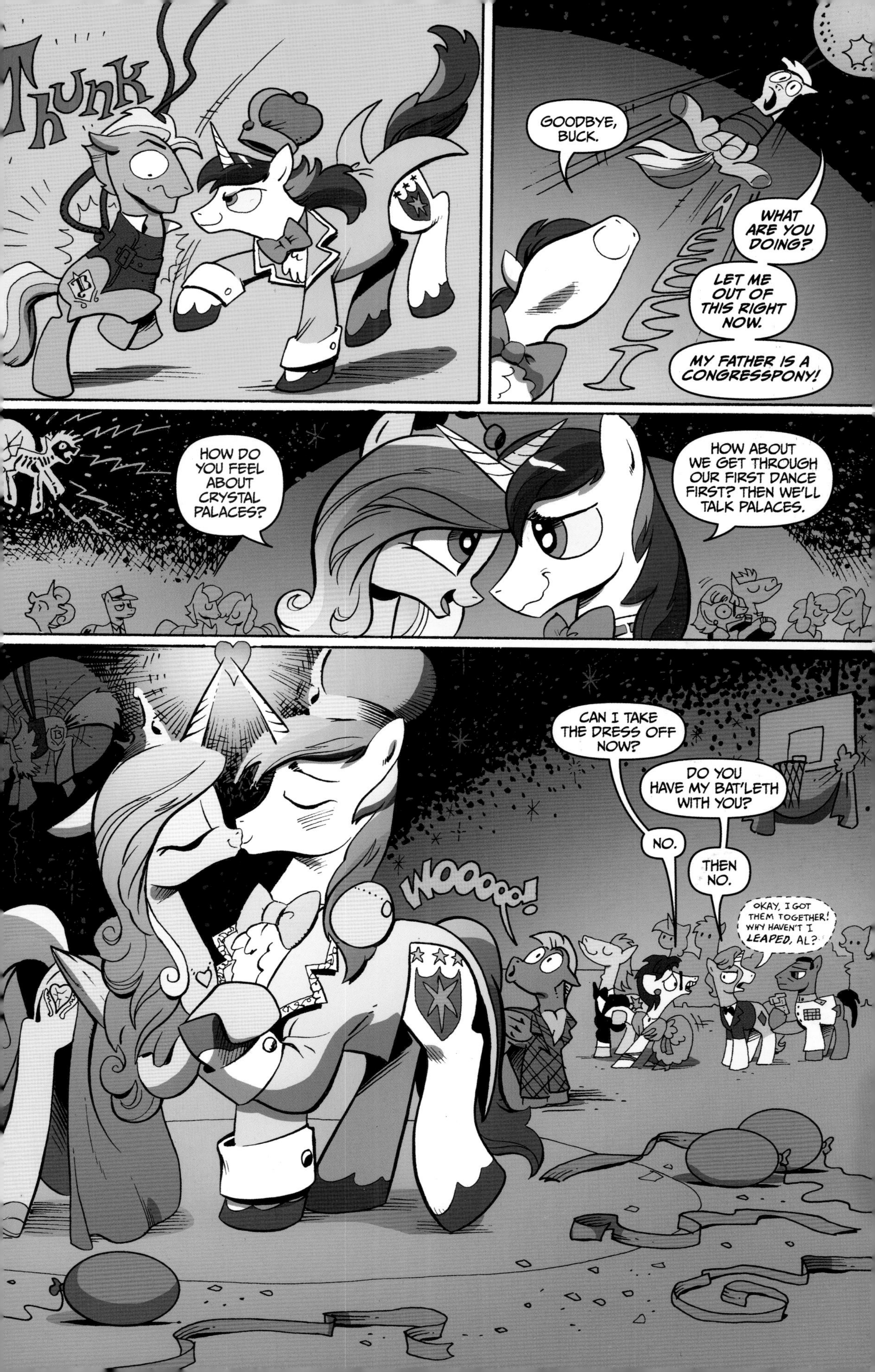
THUNK
GOODBYE, BUCK.
WHAT ARE YOU DOING?
LET ME OUT OF THIS RIGHT NOW.
MY FATHER IS A CONGRESSPONY!
HOW DO YOU FEEL ABOUT CRYSTAL PALACES?
HOW ABOUT WE GET THROUGH OUR FIRST DANCE FIRST? THEN WE'LL TALK PALACES.
CAN I TAKE THE DRESS OFF NOW?
NO.
DO YOU HAVE MY BAT'LETH WITH YOU?
THEN NO.
WOOOoo!
OKAY, I GOT THEM TOGETHER! WHY HAVEN'T I LEAPED, AL?

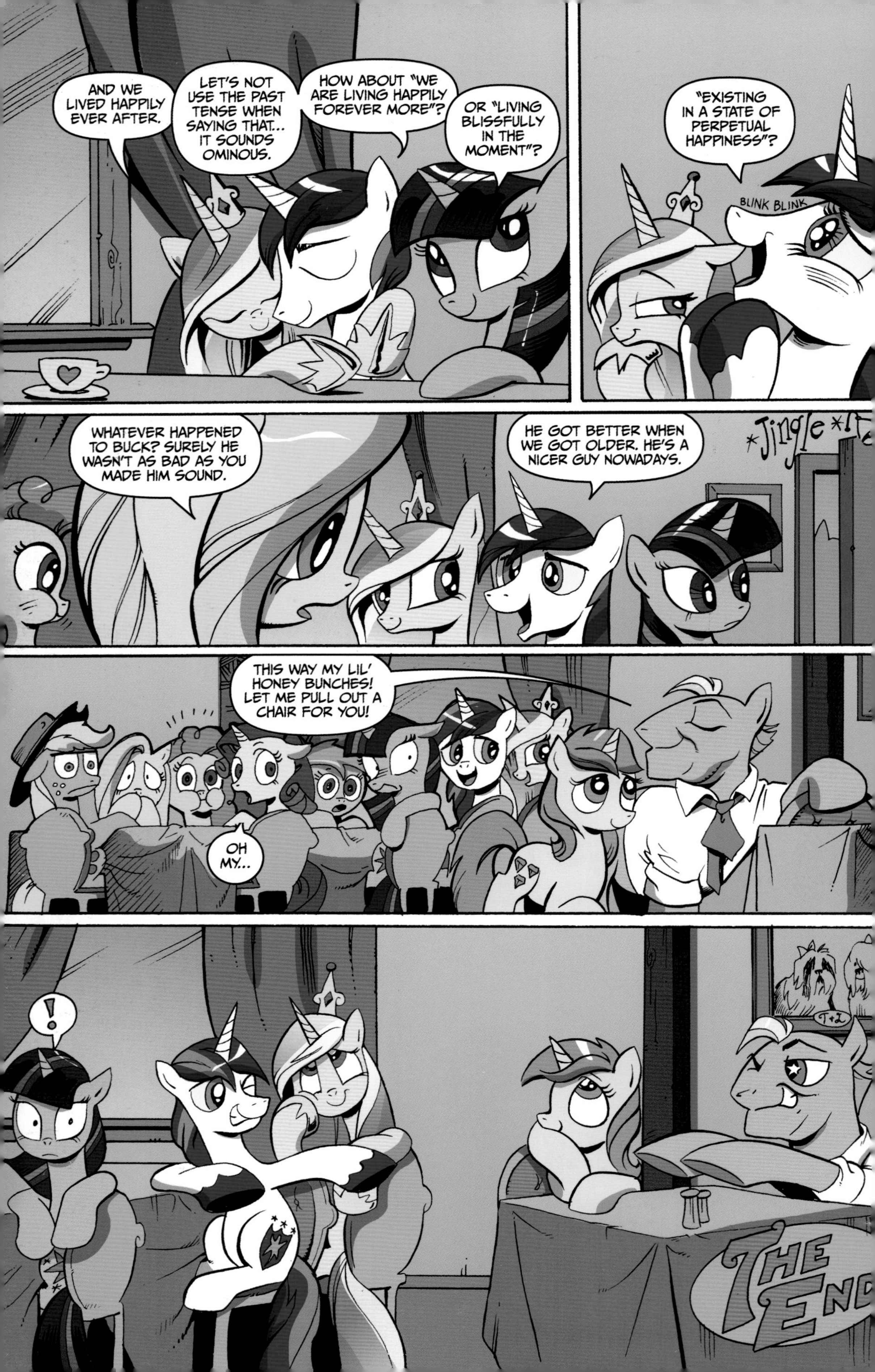
AND WE LIVED HAPPILY EVER AFTER.
LET'S NOT USE THE PAST TENSE WHEN SAYING THAT... IT SOUNDS OMINOUS.
HOW ABOUT "WE ARE LIVING HAPPILY FOREVER MORE"?
OR "LIVING BLISSFULLY IN THE MOMENT"?
"EXISTING IN A STATE OF PERPETUAL HAPPINESS"?
BLINK BLINK
WHATEVER HAPPENED TO BUCK? SURELY HE WASN'T AS BAD AS YOU MADE HIM SOUND.
HE GOT BETTER WHEN WE GOT OLDER. HE'S A NICER GUY NOWADAYS.
Jingle
THIS WAY MY LIL' HONEY BUNCHES! LET ME PULL OUT A CHAIR FOR YOU!
OH MY...
!
T+2
THE END

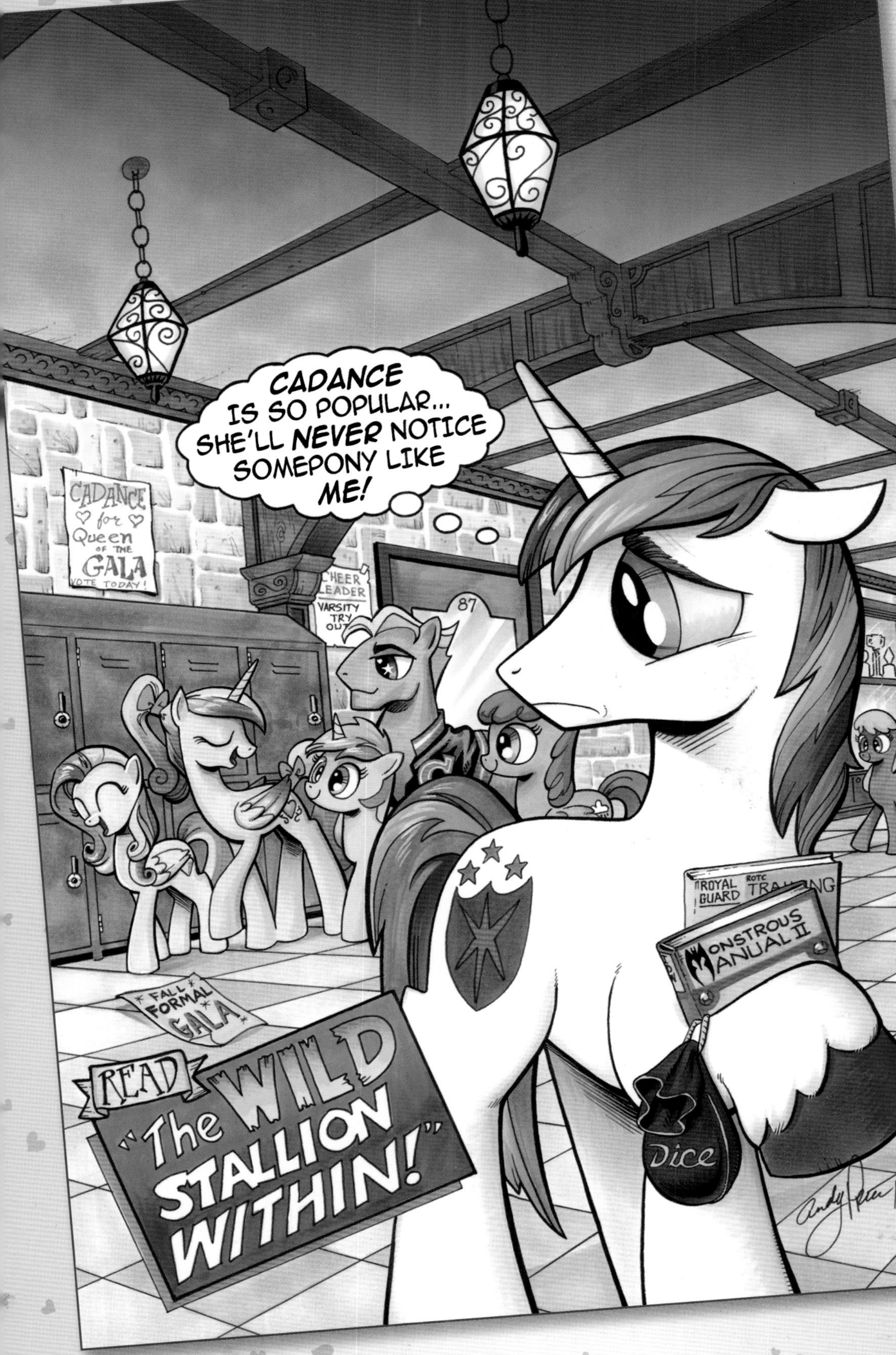
CADANCE IS SO POPULAR... SHE'LL NEVER NOTICE SOMEPONY LIKE ME!
CADANCE for Queen of the GALA VOTE TODAY!
CHEER LEADER VARSITY TRY OUT
87
ROYAL GUARD ROTC TRAINING
MONSTROUS MANUAL II
FALL FORMAL GALA
Dice
READ "The WILD STALLION WITHIN!"

art BY Andy Price

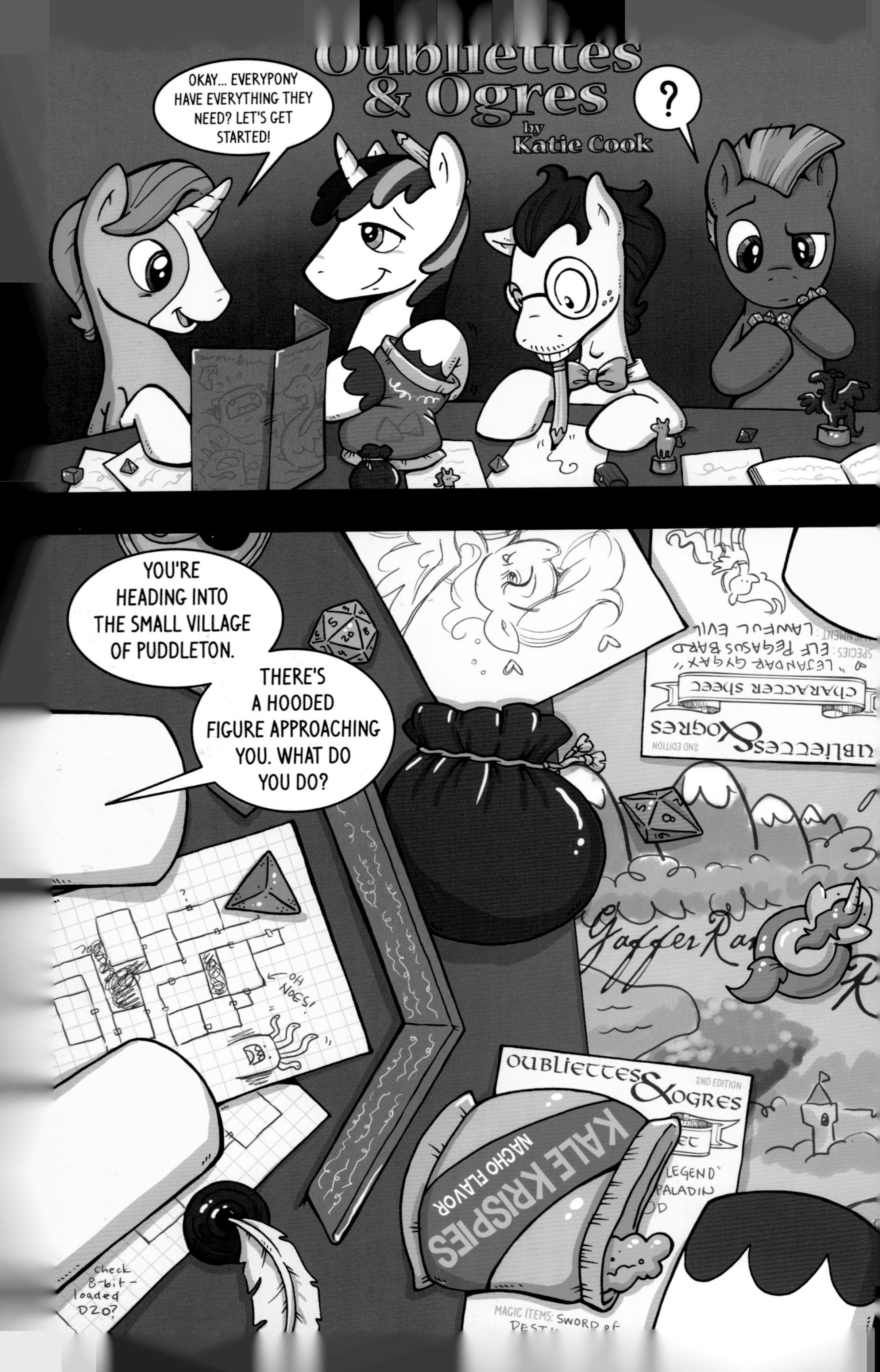
Oubliettes & Ogres
by Katie Cook
OKAY... EVERYPONY HAVE EVERYTHING THEY NEED? LET'S GET STARTED!
?
YOU'RE HEADING INTO THE SMALL VILLAGE OF PUDDLETON.
THERE'S A HOODED FIGURE APPROACHING YOU. WHAT DO YOU DO?
OUBLIETTES & OGRES 2ND EDITION
CHARACTER SHEET
"LEJANDAR GYGAX"
SPECIES: ELF PEGASUS BARD
ALIGNMENT: LAWFUL EVIL
OH NOES!
OUBLIETTES & OGRES 2ND EDITION
KALE KRISPIES
NACHO FLAVOR
"LEGEND"
PALADIN
MAGIC ITEMS: SWORD of
Check 8-bit-loaded D20?

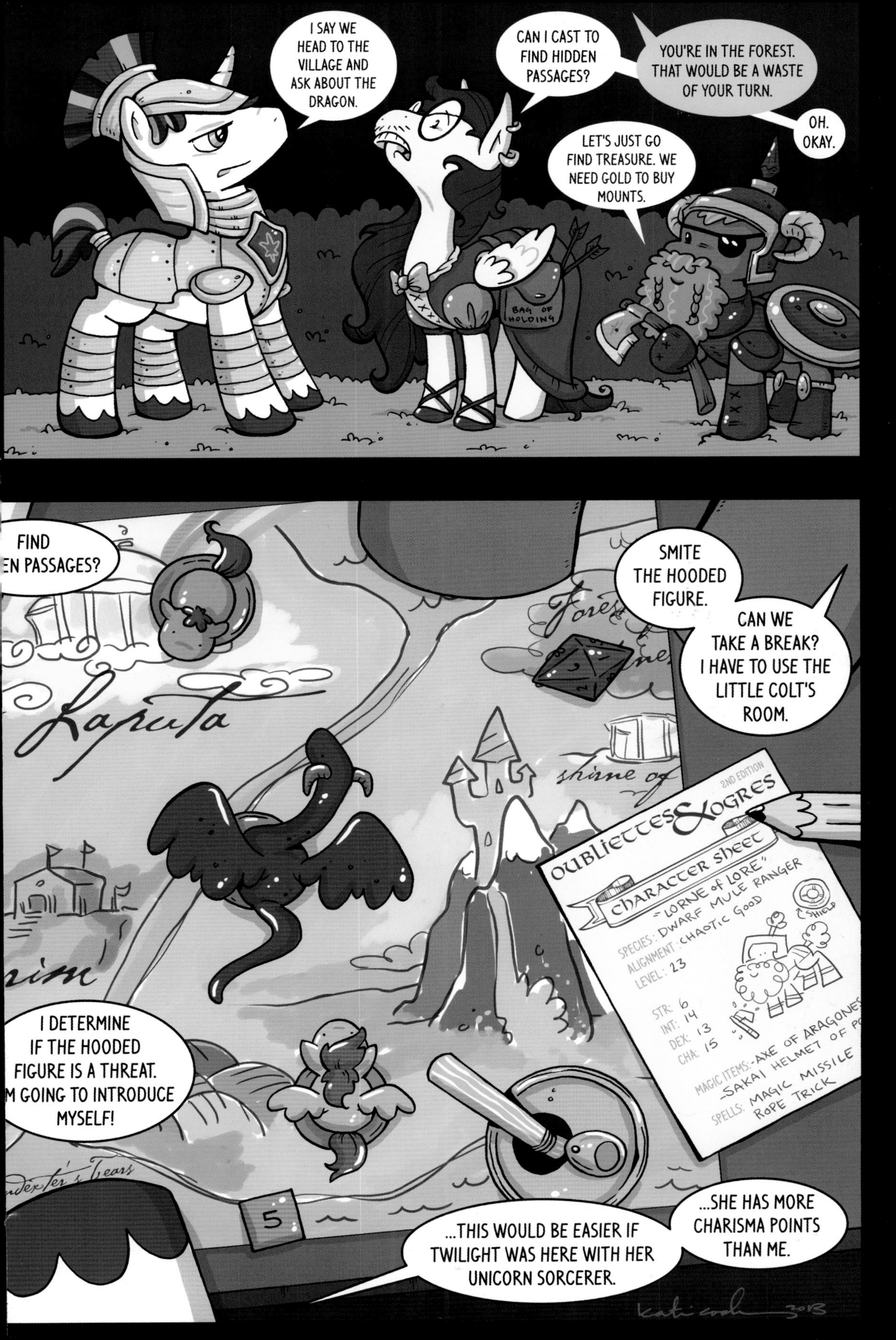
I SAY WE HEAD TO THE VILLAGE AND ASK ABOUT THE DRAGON.
CAN I CAST TO FIND HIDDEN PASSAGES?
YOU'RE IN THE FOREST. THAT WOULD BE A WASTE OF YOUR TURN.
OH. OKAY.
LET'S JUST GO FIND TREASURE. WE NEED GOLD TO BUY MOUNTS.
BAG OF HOLDING
FIND
EN PASSAGES?
SMITE THE HOODED FIGURE.
CAN WE TAKE A BREAK? I HAVE TO USE THE LITTLE COLT'S ROOM.
Laputa
shrine of
2ND EDITION
OUBLIETTES & OGRES
CHARACTER SHEET
"LORNE of LORE"
SPECIES: DWARF MULE RANGER
ALIGNMENT: CHAOTIC GOOD
LEVEL: 23
SHIELD
STR: 6
INT: 14
DEX: 13
CHA: 15
MAGIC ITEMS: -AXE OF ARAGONES
-SAKAI HELMET OF PO
SPELLS: MAGIC MISSILE
ROPE TRICK
I DETERMINE IF THE HOODED FIGURE IS A THREAT.
M GOING TO INTRODUCE MYSELF!
5
...THIS WOULD BE EASIER IF TWILIGHT WAS HERE WITH HER UNICORN SORCERER.
...SHE HAS MORE CHARISMA POINTS THAN ME.

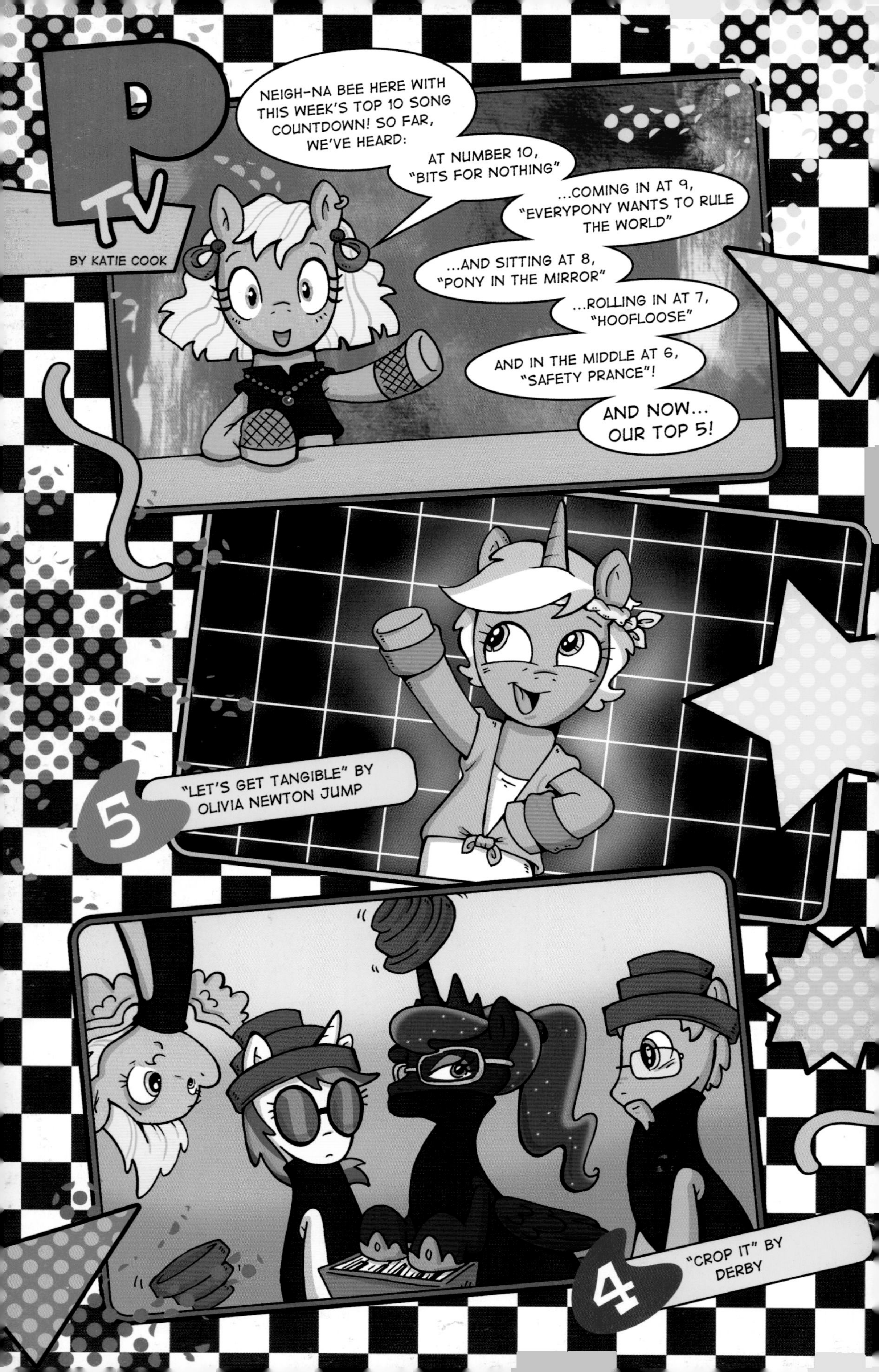
P TV
BY KATIE COOK
NEIGH-NA BEE HERE WITH THIS WEEK'S TOP 10 SONG COUNTDOWN! SO FAR, WE'VE HEARD:
AT NUMBER 10, "BITS FOR NOTHING"
...COMING IN AT 9, "EVERYPONY WANTS TO RULE THE WORLD"
...AND SITTING AT 8, "PONY IN THE MIRROR"
...ROLLING IN AT 7, "HOOFLOOSE"
AND IN THE MIDDLE AT 6, "SAFETY PRANCE"!
AND NOW... OUR TOP 5!
5
"LET'S GET TANGIBLE" BY OLIVIA NEWTON JUMP
4
"CROP IT" BY DERBY

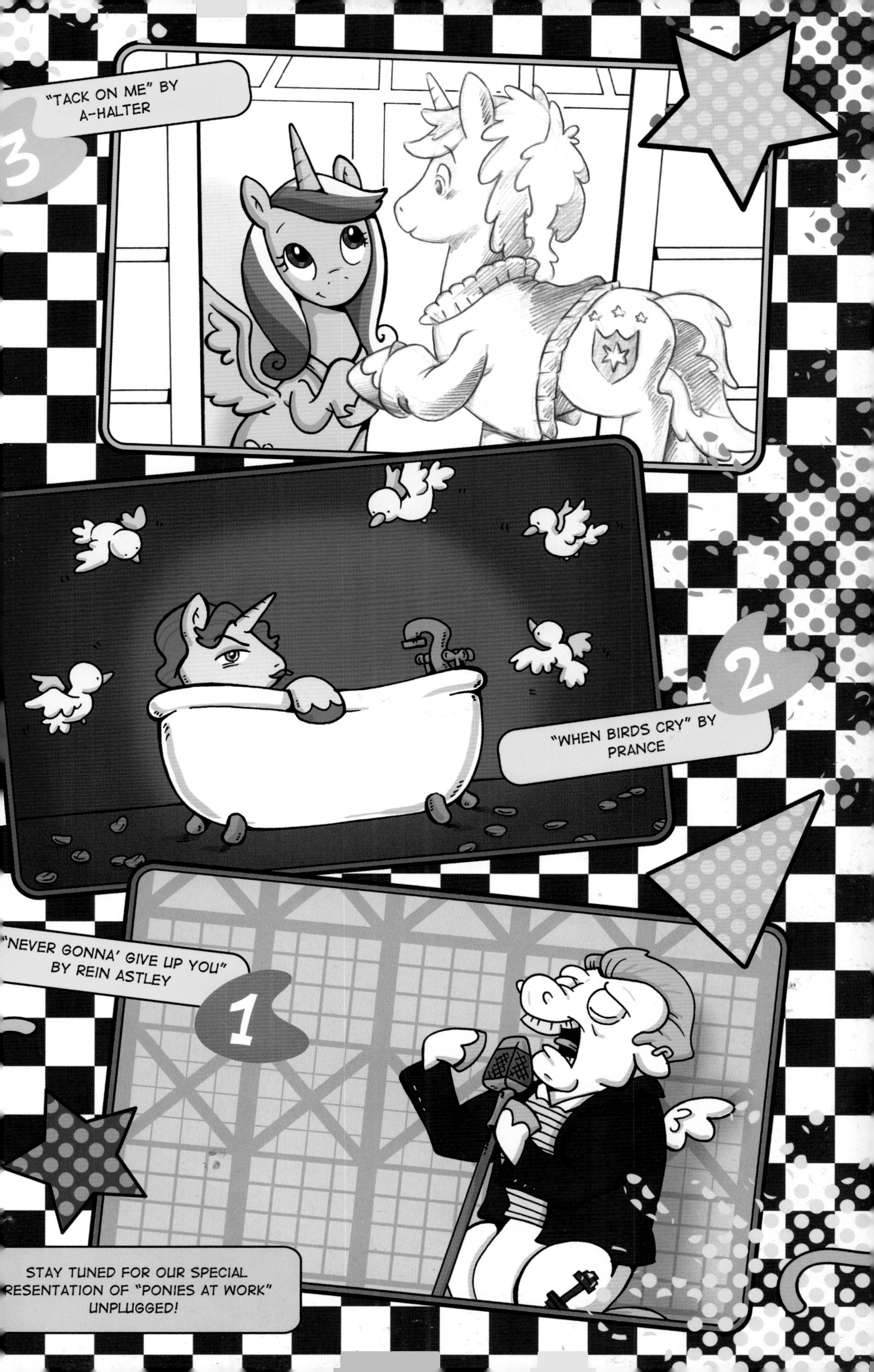
"TACK ON ME" BY
A-HALTER
3
2
"WHEN BIRDS CRY" BY
PRANCE
"NEVER GONNA' GIVE UP YOU"
BY REIN ASTLEY
1
STAY TUNED FOR OUR SPECIAL
RESENTATION OF "PONIES AT WORK"
UNPLUGGED!

Big Mac Paperdoll by Katie Cook

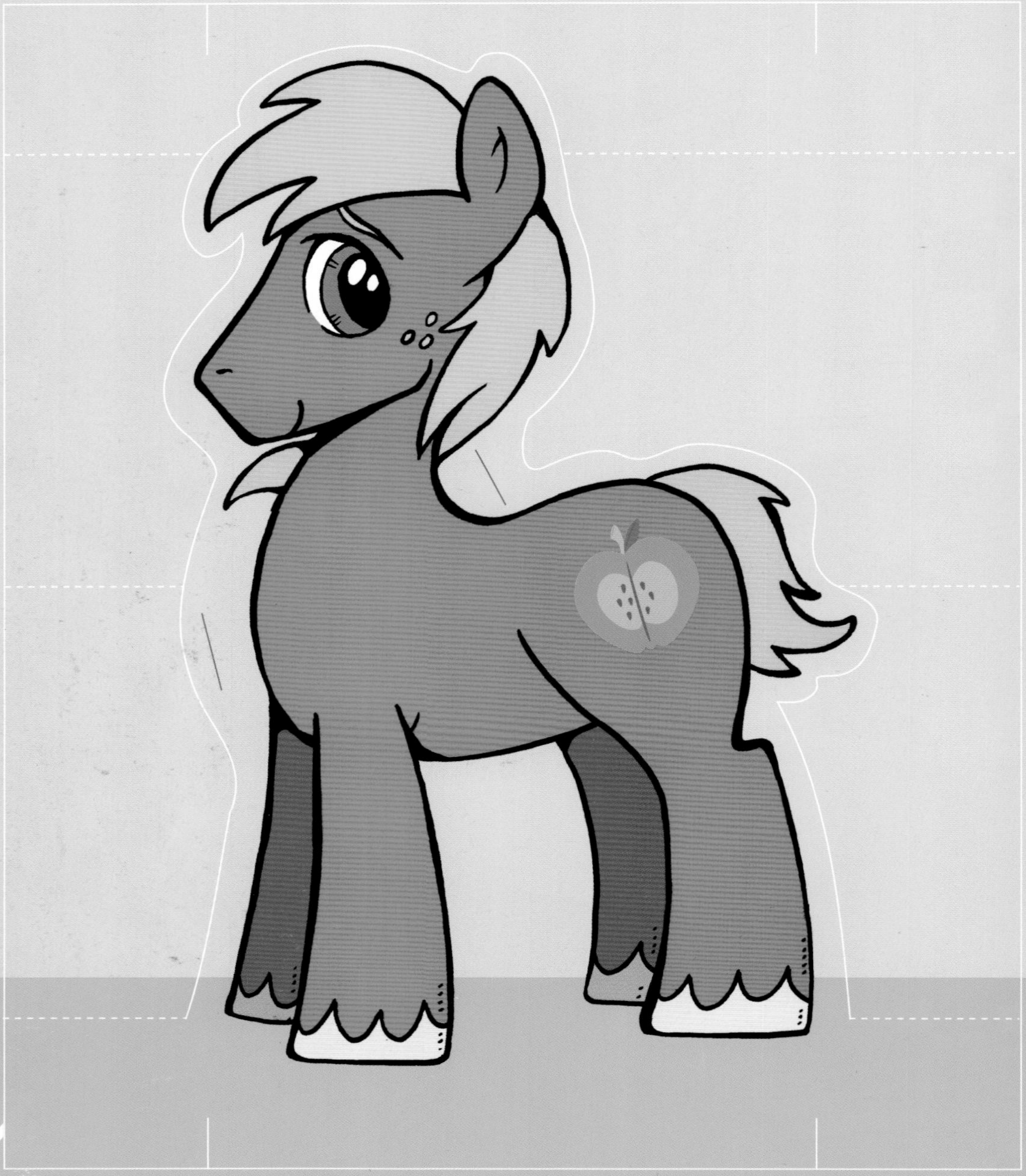

Cut out and fold the Big Mac standee to make him stand on his own! Cut out the different yokes and slide them into the slots by his neck to hold them in place.

Instrutions
cut line:
fold line:

everyday wear

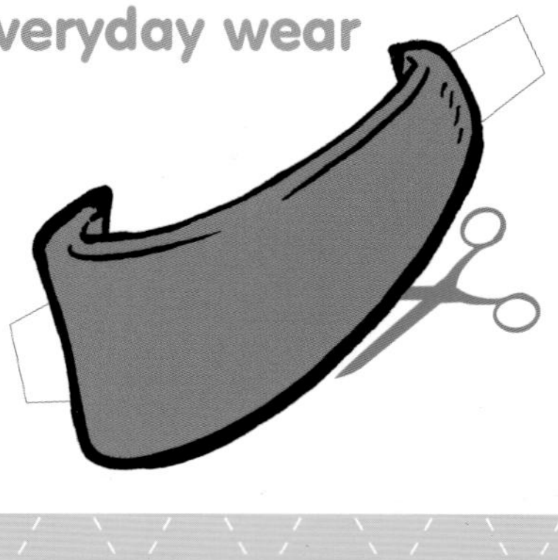

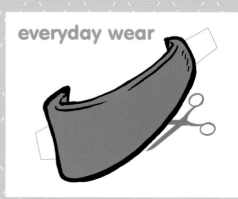

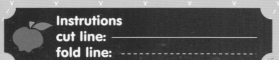

cut out and fold this folder to store all Big Mac's fashions in!

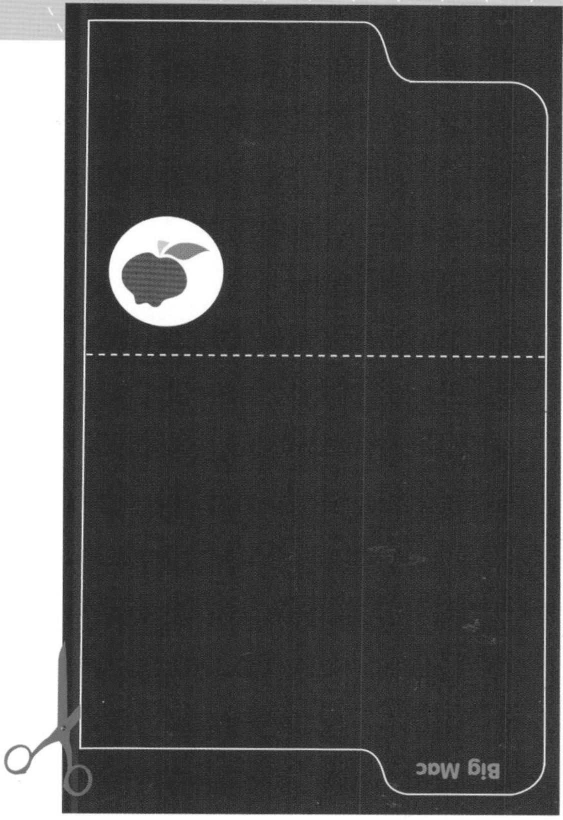
Big Mac

cardigan

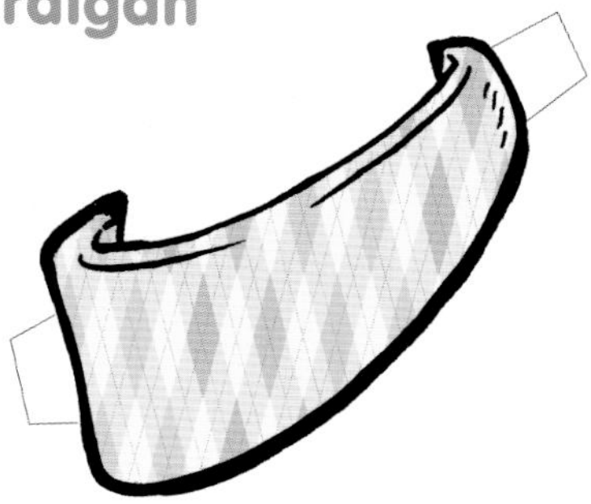

casual friday

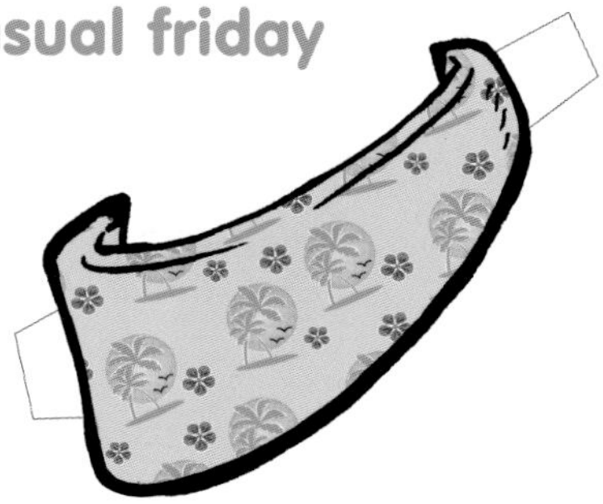

formal

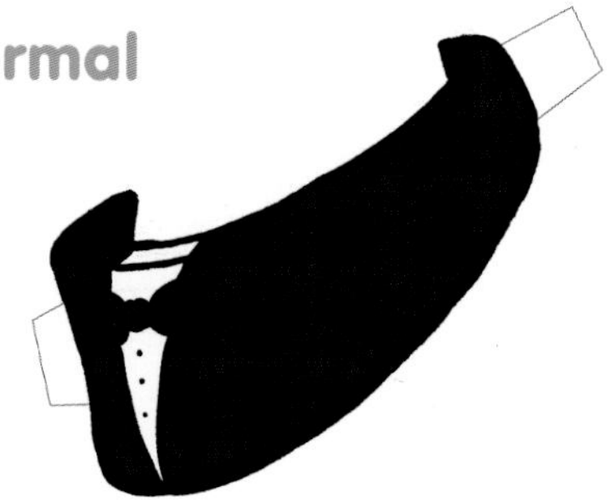

80s

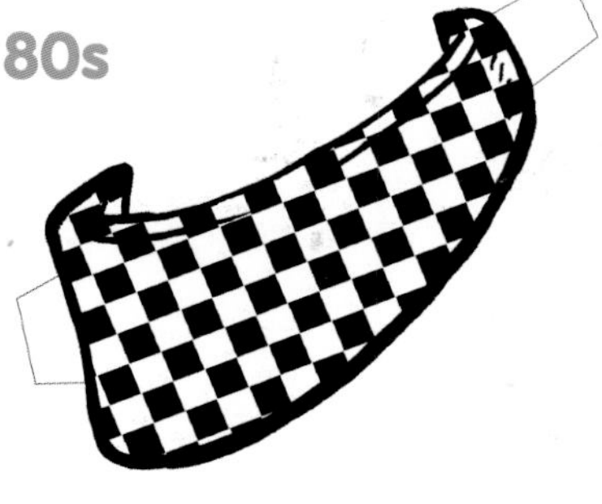

festive

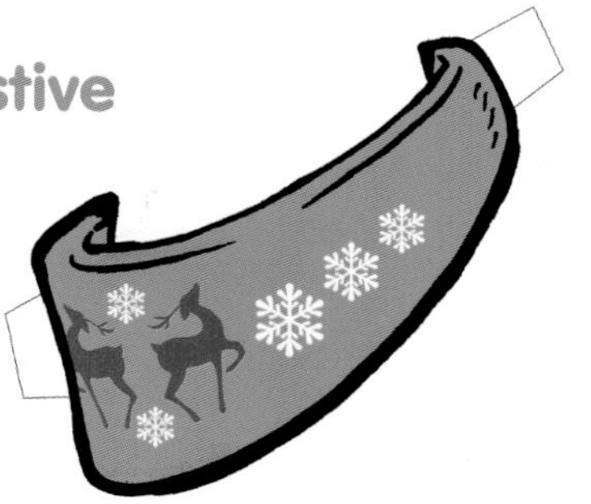

comic con

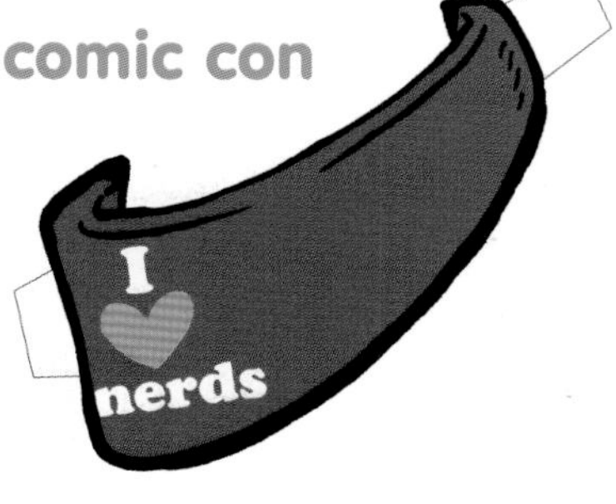
I
nerds

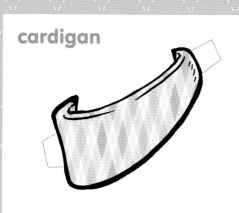

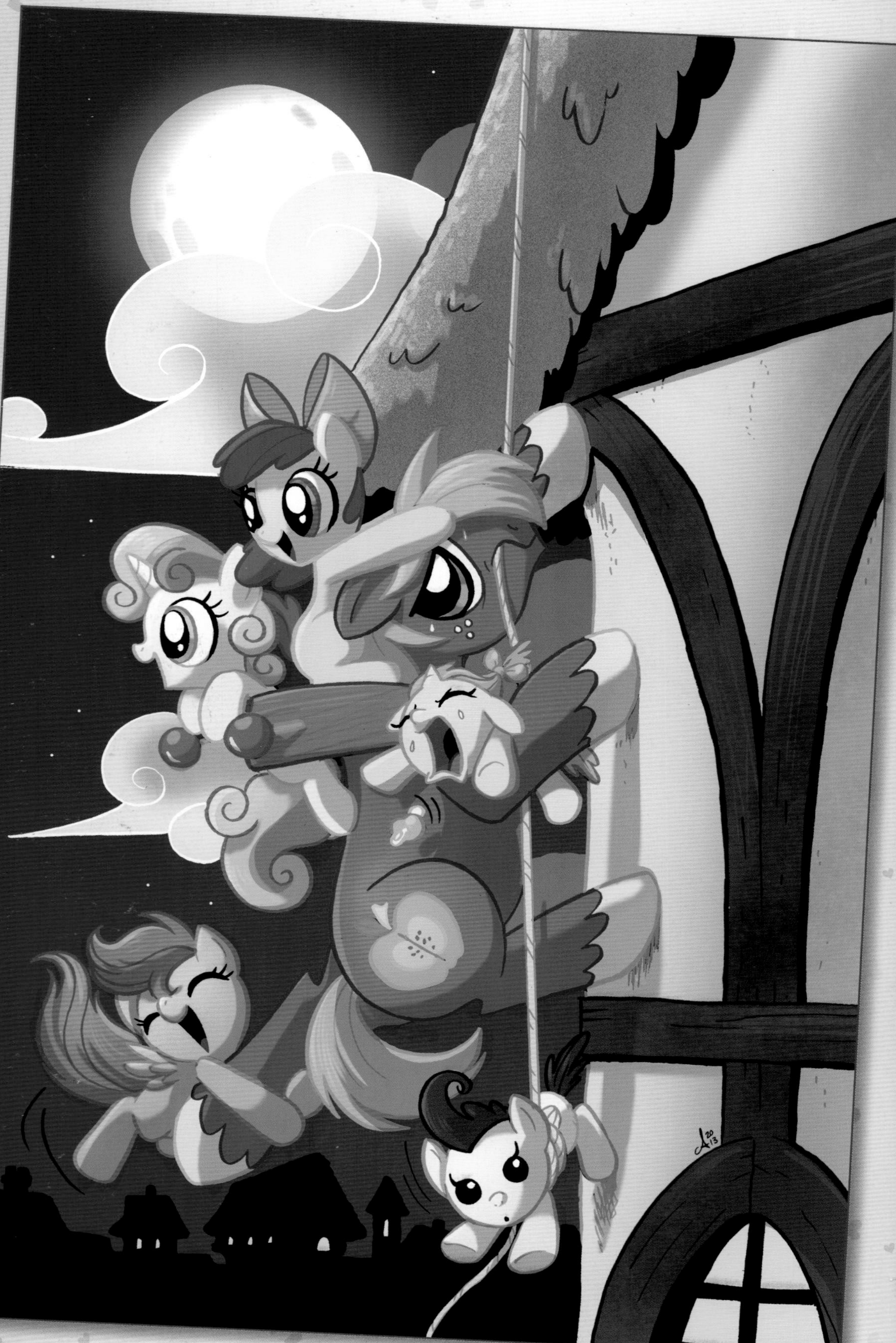

art BY Amy Mebberson

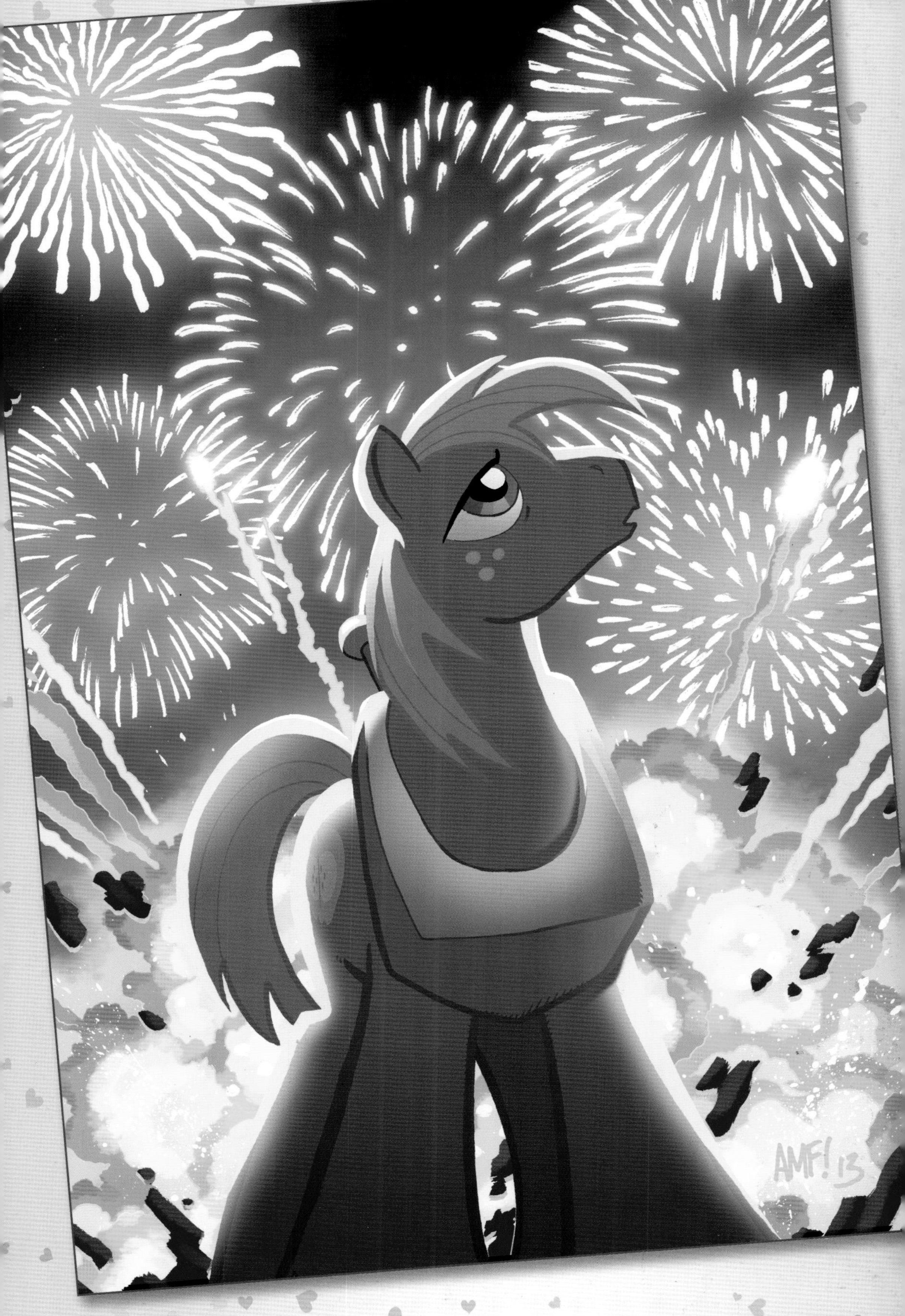
AMF! 13

art BY Tony Fleecs

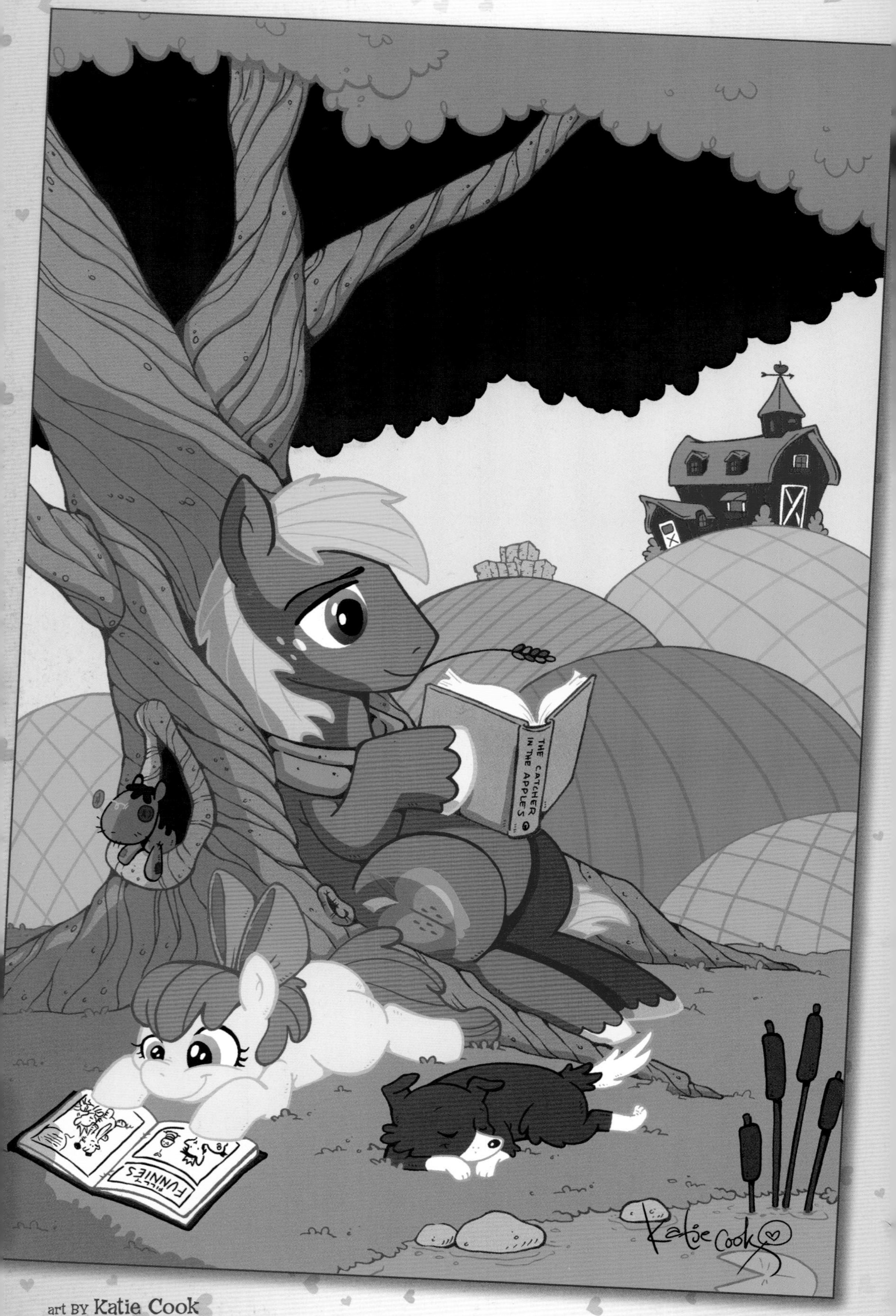
THE CATCHER IN THE APPLES
FUNNIES
Katie Cook

art BY Katie Cook

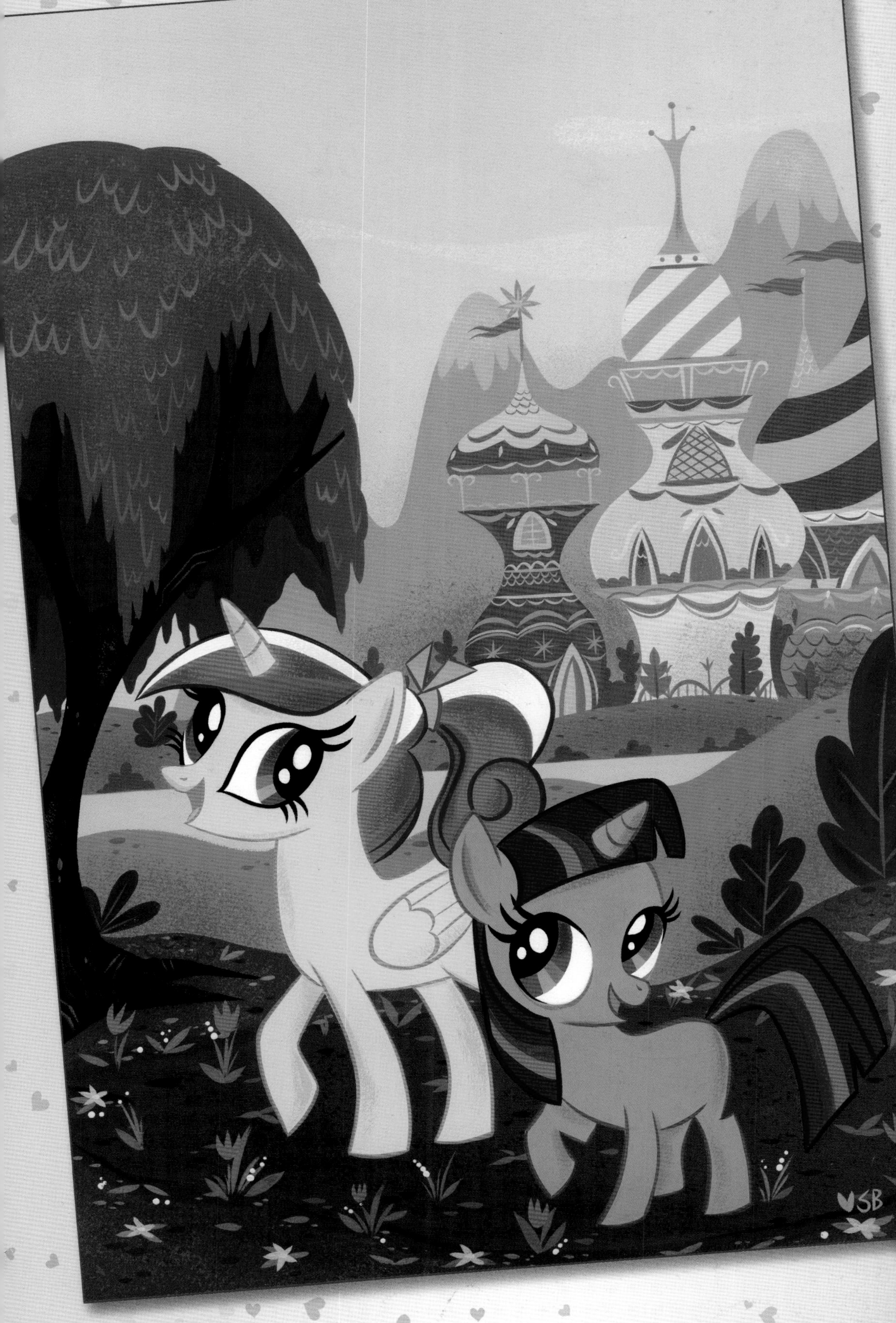
SB

art BY Stephanie Buscema

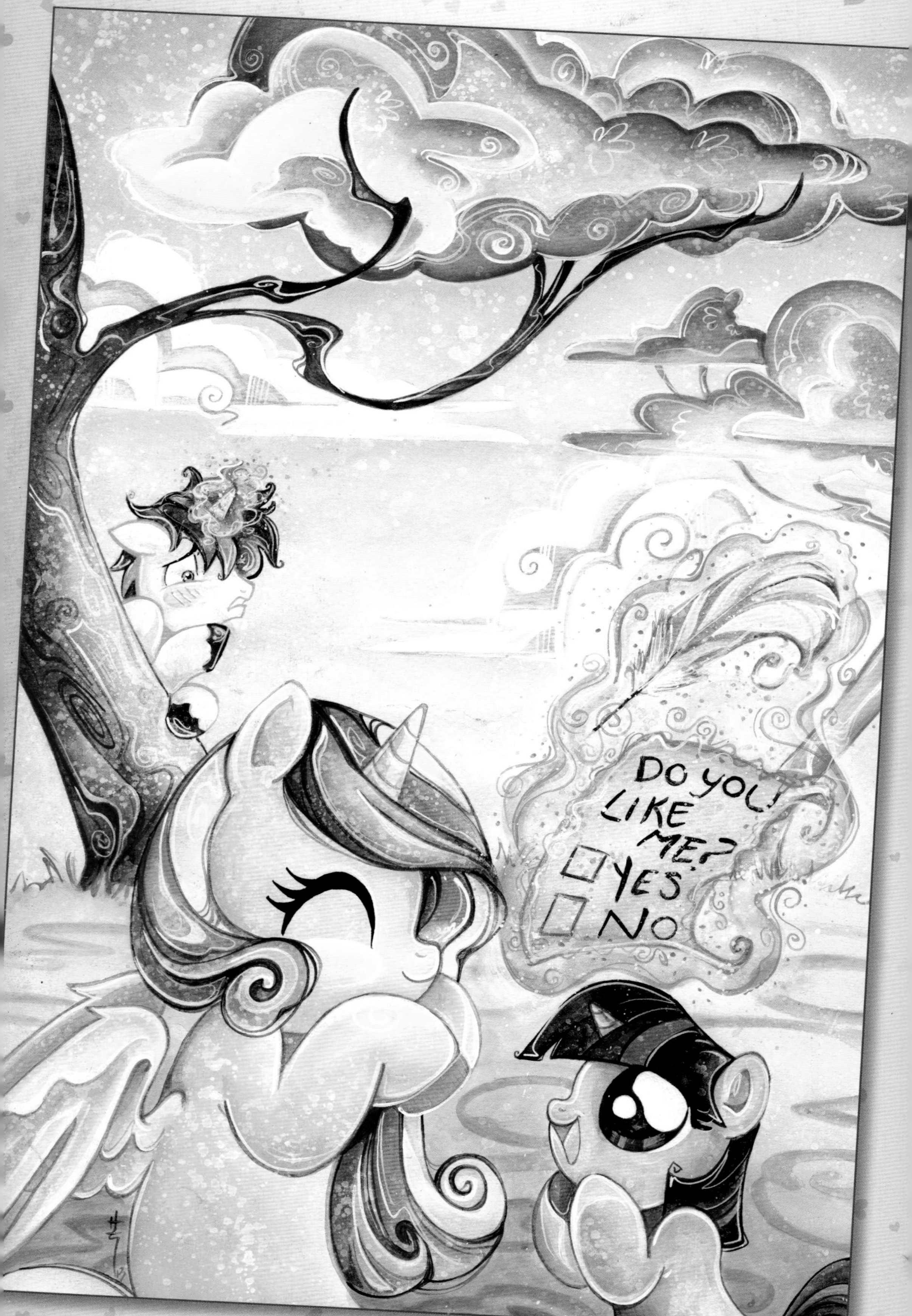
DO YOU LIKE ME?
YES
NO

art BY Sara Richard

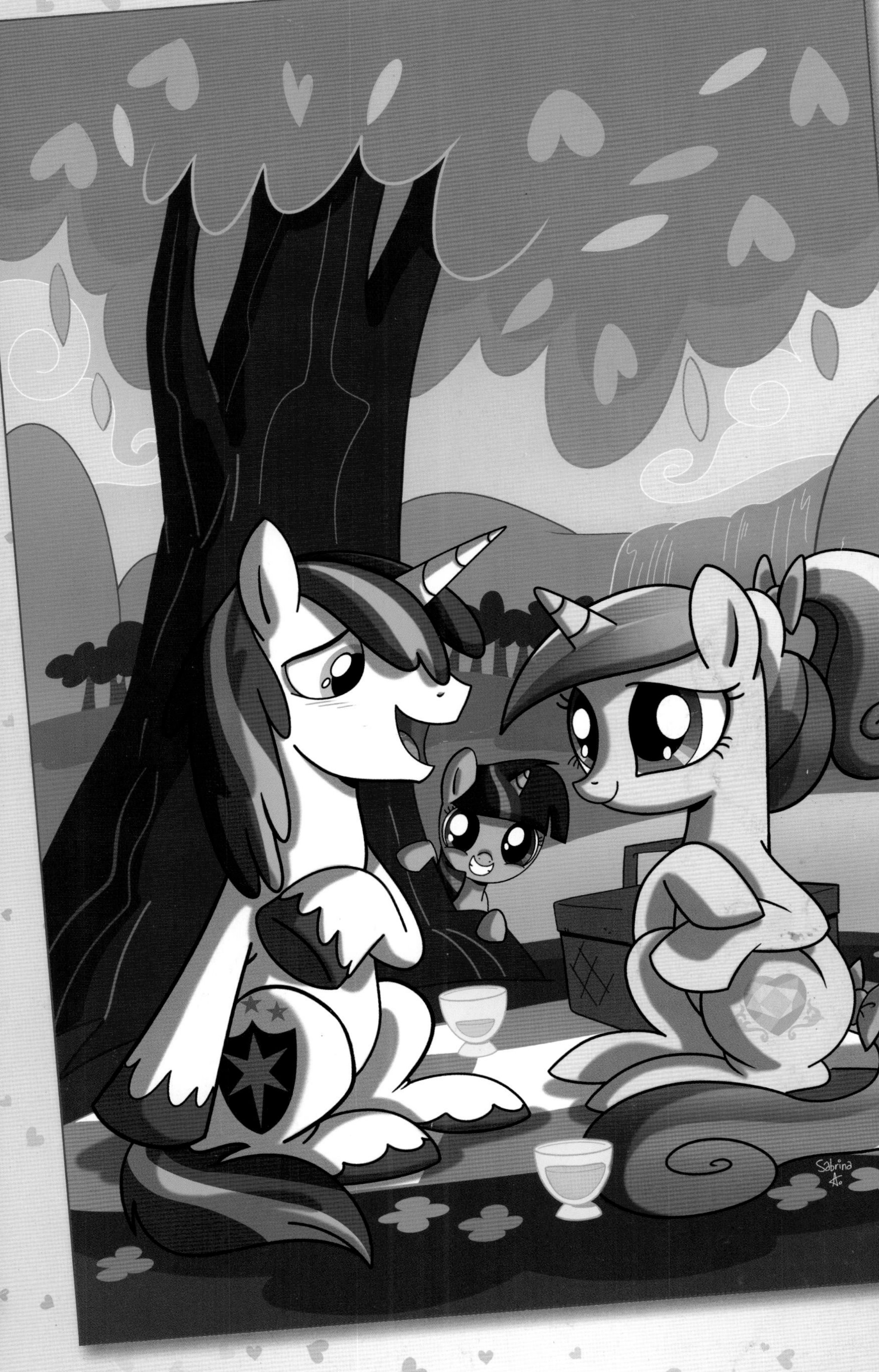
Sabrina A.

art BY Sabrina Alberghetti

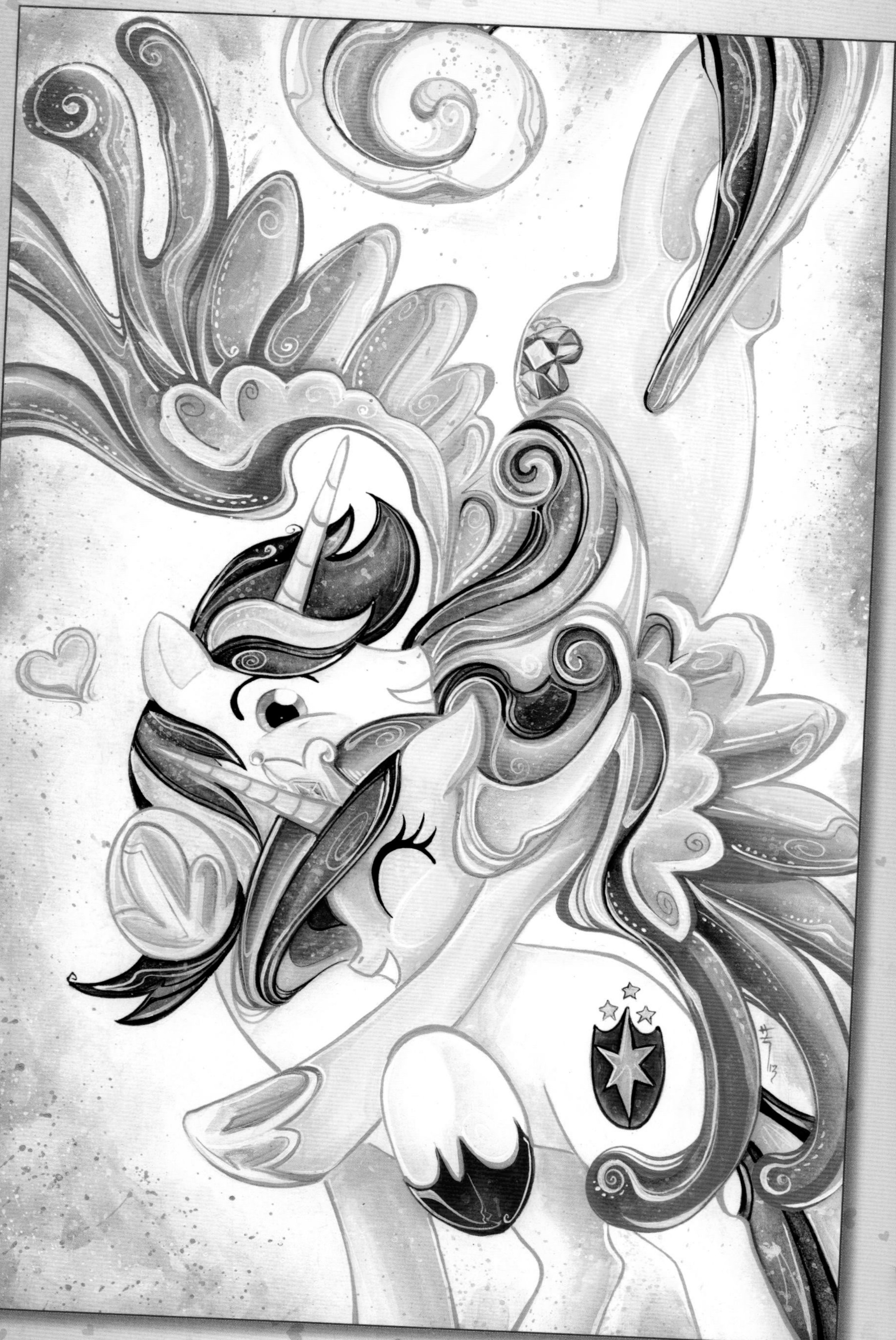

art BY Sara Richard